REBELS DIVIDED

LANCE ERLICK

Finlee Augare Books (Chicago)

This is a work of fiction. All of the characters, organizations, and events portrayed herein are either products of the author's imagination or are used fictitiously, and any similarities to actual persons, organizations, or events is entirely coincidental. Also, though locations used in this work exist, for dramatic effect details have been altered. Accordingly, they should be considered fictitious.

Edited by Leah Carson

Finlee Augare Books, Chicago, IL
ISBN: 978-0-9889968-3-0 (print)
ISBN: 978-0-9889968-4-7 (e-book)
Library of Congress Control Number: 2013941689

Printed in the United States of America

To Sue for believing.

To Dad for introducing me to an interesting life.

To Dave and Jason: may your dreams carry you to interesting places.

ONE

Sticky sweat trickled down Geo's neck as he inched forward. *Tracking Pa is like tracking a rattler,* he thought. He didn't want to sneak up, startle, and risk being attacked.

Shifting his backpack and rifle, Geo applied more of Pa's home-brewed mosquito ointment and cursed the suffocating heat. It was hard to visualize how last winter's snows seemed like they would never end. Pa called it the worst winter in South Appalachia in the two decades since the Second Civil War. Now, being outdoors was like sitting too close to a campfire. *Why can't the weather settle somewhere in between?*

Geo eased forward, careful to keep leaves from crunching beneath his worn leather boots. Across a clearing stood the village of Pumpkin Patch with a dozen log cabins. No sign of Pa. Had he gone inside?

Dense, saturated air carried the stench of rotting food, oils, and other refuse. Civ city-folk from Knoxville dumped their garbage on the Appalachian side of the border to evade their own tight environmental regulations. This close to the barrier, locals scavenged dumpsites for anything they could use. Despite their poverty, they opened their homes to travelers, though with border tensions rising, it was risky to approach unannounced.

A large hand grabbed Geo's shoulder and shoved him down behind a clump of yellow forsythia.

"I told you to wait at home." Pa's whisper thundered in Geo's ears.

1

Geo seethed inside but tempered his voice. "I'm nineteen, Pa. I want to see more of the world than our glen."

"Most of it's not worth seeing. Besides, if Thane Edwards and his Rangers draft you, you'll see a lot you won't like. Look beyond the village in the woods."

Geo raised his binoculars and spotted a dull black mechanical exoskeleton, one of Civ's Mechanized Female Warriors. "A mech?"

"Careful. They work in threes."

Mosquitoes buzzed as Geo picked up the scent of mech hydraulic oils and perfumed sweat. A different hum hovered overhead. He raised his rifle and sighted a Civ drone with thin body and wide wings. It swooped over the borderlands and into the clearing. Before Geo could shoot, Pa lowered the barrel. The pilotless plane dropped its load of incendiaries, climbed, and disappeared above the treetops. Explosions burst in all directions, spewing orange flames and setting cabins ablaze. It was the second attack on villages helping refugees since the last full moon.

With the swiftness of wolves, three black insect-like mechs sprinted into the clearing and encircled the village. Geo wanted to see the faces of the girls inside the mechanical suits, to know his enemy.

He started to rise. "We have to help the villagers."

Pa's tanned arm pushed him down. "Too late. Look in the woods to the left."

The beefy men were almost invisible in camouflage. "Rangers? Why don't they help?" Villagers' land tithes supported the Appalachian Rangers who were supposed to protect against Civ mech attacks.

"Wait, son."

The air filled with smoke and crackled like a campfire. Yet the Rangers didn't plunge in, didn't fire a shot, and Pa's powerful arm held Geo down.

Three bearded men, wearing rags scavenged from dumpsites, emerged from a flaming cabin. They fired rifles into the nearest mech, to no avail. Geo knew from experience with a variety of homegrown weapons that even armor-piercing shells didn't stop mechs. You had to strike a vulnerable spot in their black-coated titanium-polymer shields.

Dozens of men flew out of other burning cabins and fired on all three mechs, stunning them for an instant before the mechs sprayed machine pellets that shredded men's guts. Riddled with shot, men splayed across the clearing. More followed. Still, Rangers didn't intervene.

It was like shooting chickens in a pen. The villagers didn't stand a chance.

"We have to help, Pa."

Pa tugged Geo toward the narrow path away from the village. "We can't."

Three boys not much younger than Geo sprinted from the nearest cabin.

Geo yanked free of Pa and fired his .50 cal into the nearest mech, aiming for where the helmet fastened to the neck-plate. That stunned the mech for a moment, while a slender boy ran and reached the cover of woods. Geo waved him toward Pa, dropped a remote controlled grenade, and kicked leaves over it. He fired a second shot at the mech's faceplate hinge as two bigger boys reached the path.

The mech spun and fired a volley, missed. Geo sprinted down the path, urging the boys along.

When Geo caught up, Pa grabbed him by the collar. "This is why I don't bring you. Think before you act. Now go. I'll provide a diversion."

"I'm not leaving you, Pa." Geo steadied his rifle.

A mech entered the woods, shoving shrubs and tree limbs away from her bloated mechanical shell.

Geo fired into the neck-plate. The mech stopped and raised her weapons. He wondered if this was how David felt when he faced Goliath. After all, Civs were like Sodom and Gomorrah with their godless wicked ways: dishonoring their men, destroying the sanctity of marriage, denying the one true God, at least according to Thane Edwards' broadcasts.

Geo jumped off the path and triggered his two-phase grenade. The first explosion blasted up like a shotgun, spewing shrapnel into the mech's most vulnerable spot, the groin-plate. Even though the titanium-polymer plate could withstand the blast, its clasp and hinges were poor quality, allowing the plate to shift and drop.

The first charge weakened the grenade's phase-two protective coating and ignited a fuse. The second explosion spewed pellets into the mech-plate opening. The mech froze and toppled forward without firing a shot. Geo said a prayer for the mech girl.

Another mech stood behind her downed companion. She had a clear shot at him yet she didn't raise her weapons. With no effective weapon of his own, Geo stared back. Then he shook himself and disappeared into the brush.

* * *

Sweltering in the oppressive heat of another global warming day, nineteen-year-old Lieutenant Annabelle Scott entered the concrete bunker of the mech base east of her Knoxville home. She carried a plastic body bag with the remains of Karen, a sweet new recruit Annabelle had helped train. The explosion had liquefied Karen's torso, spilling her onto the ground like vomit. With the help of Lieutenant Dara Moore, Annabelle had scooped what residue she could off the dirt path. Oh, how she wanted to strangle the boy who did this.

Willing away tears, she tugged off her helmet and shucked her mech gear to escape the sauna within. She would have maintenance check the air conditioner, though she knew the answer: it wasn't designed for oppressive heat.

While Dara rushed off to clean up and change, Annabelle lingered. She and Karen had planned to sneak away to an illicit party to let off steam. Now there would be no party for Karen, because a filthy Outlander had liquidated her. Despite three years in mech service, and countless funerals, Annabelle couldn't help feeling each loss rip away part of her soul. Yet, she couldn't force herself to kill the boy who did this.

Commander Samantha Hernandez approached and gave Annabelle a hug. "Don't blame yourself, Lieutenant. You couldn't have anticipated the rebel ambush."

The hug was comforting, though it seemed odd coming from a husky Hispanic with facial scars from the Second Civil War and a body honed by weightlifting and kung fu. Sam wiped her brow. "The mission was a success. Outlanders will think twice before harboring runaways and poaching wildlife. Get cleaned up for the briefing."

Mission guilt suffocated Annabelle like her water-boarding training. Before the drones swooped in, she had recognized Bret Shaw with someone who might have been his son, George, the one who killed Karen. Three fugitives escaped, Karen was dead, and Annabelle failed to shoot. That wasn't success.

Leaving Karen's mech suit and scooped-up remains on a

concrete slab for autopsy, Annabelle went to wash up. She vowed not to vent with sister warriors. Their warrior ethic didn't permit questioning missions or tactics. Grumbling could land her back in psych reconditioning, and she'd had enough for three lifetimes.

In the locker room, Dara was stripping out of sweat-soaked undergarments. A tall, thickly-muscled amazon the other girls looked up to, this fierce warrior was clearheaded in battle but far too bossy. She hugged Annabelle, intertwining her frizzy brown hair with Annabelle's sagging blonde curls. "I want to put all Outlanders through a meat grinder for what they did to Karen."

Annabelle pulled away; Dara's hugs were unwelcome.

Dara grabbed a towel. "You know I've got your back."

"Thanks." Annabelle yanked off her top, dropped her blue uniform trousers, and shivered.

"Karen would want us to celebrate her life, not drown ourselves in sorrow." With a towel over her shoulders, Dara helped Annabelle with her sweaty bra.

Annabelle ripped her bra off, while being careful not to antagonize a sister warrior. "I'm exhausted." Plus, she couldn't take another mission if it meant watching friends die. She bit that one back.

She grabbed a towel, and followed Dara into the showers. She set the dials to cool, let water cascade over her, and hoped it would wash away the guilt. It didn't.

"You and me against the world," Dara said. "Come to the party tonight."

"I promised a night with Janine."

"Sisters are always welcome." Dara scowled. "Shake out of it. You can't let the others see even a flicker of weakness."

Annabelle forced a smile. Peer pressure was a powerful tool, though lack of private time had her aching to flee into the wilderness, even to the Outland. She turned off the water, toweled dry, and longed to blow off steam.

TWO

Geo followed Pa and the three boys through dense forest. His mind buzzed. Why did that mech pass up a chance to shoot him? Knowing that mechs always pursued, he kept alert for possible traps while balancing his pack and gun.

The three compadres needed his help keeping up. Coming from Civ, they weren't used to running hills in oppressive heat with hyperactive mosquitoes.

Without slowing, Geo took a swig from his canteen and handed it to one of the younger boys, a twin. Dirk stopped to drink.

"Keep moving." Geo grabbed the canteen and handed it to Dirk's brother. The muscular twins looked sixteen, yet they were dragging. "Not much farther."

Mickey, a scrawny older boy, had sweat streaming down his thin face. "Thanks for saving us."

"Save your breath," Geo said. "We're not out of the woods."

"Funny." Mickey panted.

When Pa stopped, Geo motioned for the compadres to get down while he crept forward. Four log cabins stood in a clearing: the Grahams. Using binoculars, Pa scanned all directions. "Clear."

Geo nodded.

"Stay down and keep your eyes sharp." Pa dropped his pack, slipped his rifle over his shoulder, and marched into the clearing toward the nearest cabin with hands in front of him. He called out, "I've come to parley."

Geo trained his .50 cal on the door as it opened. A scruffy, white-bearded man leveled his shotgun at Pa. "Ya come alone?" Geo wished infrared worked in this heat so he could see how many were inside.

"I come with my son and three refugees." Pa's hands reached behind his back for his sawed-off shotgun.

"Just being careful, Mr. Shaw." The bearded man lowered his shotgun and bowed. "Haven't see ya 'round since last full moon. Come on in. Did ya bring any o' your Shaw whiskey?"

"I'll send some along." Pa motioned for Geo and went into the cabin.

The refugees hesitated. After what they had been through, Mickey seemed ready to throw up. The twins looked shell-shocked.

"The Grahams are okay when you get to know them," Geo said. "We need to find you a home." He led them toward the cabin.

"Why can't I come with you?" Mickey asked. "I've never had a brother."

Before Geo could shut him up, Mickey told him he was eighteen, his father left when he was a baby, and he had been on the run three months before crossing the border.

Inside, the log cabin felt like a furnace with a thick odor of grease. The only air came from an electric fan in the window, one of Pa's designs, run off solar panels on the roof. Geo despaired at how few of the innovations written about thirty years ago were here today.

He introduced the boys to the Graham family: the old man, three sons, two grandsons, and six boys they had adopted.

"Mi casa 'n all that." The gray-haired Graham cleared space on a grease-covered table. "Yur welcome to what vittles we got."

Flies swarmed the greasy stove and dirty dishes. If Geo let things go like this at home, Pa would tan his hide. Geo led the compadres to the window fan.

Pa stood by the door. "Can't stay. I know the risk of helping refugees, but these three arrived a couple days ago. They need a place until I find something permanent."

"Don't that beat all?" Old man Graham scratched his gray beard. "Can't feed what we got with Civs gettin' ornery about poaching deer, even though they're on our side of the border."

"I know, but there are few safe havens," Pa said.

Graham poured coffee for Pa. "Rumor has it Thane Edwards don't like ya helping runaways. Says they should come to him. Ya know our allegiance is to you, Earl, but the forest has eyes."

Geo wondered if Earl was Pa's middle name. Geo had heard it now and then, though when he had asked, Pa just shrugged.

"You heard about Pumpkin Patch," Pa said.

Graham winced. "Good people. I don't want no trouble. I can't help ya. Can't hardly keep from starving already."

The price of freedom in the Appalachian Secession was that you reaped what you sowed, less whatever Thane Edwards took.

"I won't prooo," Pa said.

"Bless ya. Ya know we'd do most anything for ya, but it's getting harder."

Pa smiled.

Graham took Pa's hand, raised it to his lips, and kissed. "Bless ya and yur son for all yur days."

Pa backed up toward the door. "Best we go before the all-seeing forest starts rumors you've taken the refugees."

* * *

Annabelle dried and fluffed out her blonde natural curls and tied them back to keep them regulation. She applied lotion to her tanned skin before changing into a clean uniform. Although she loathed makeup, she applied light shading to make sure her blue eyes didn't look puffy from crying all the way to base. Only then did she follow Dara to the briefing room.

In a rectangular hall, vid screens and dense electronics that were linked to satellites monitored drones, warriors, border cams, millions of Union males, and Outlander activities. Ninety-six mech warriors sat ready to do their duty for the Federal Union, for President Tatiana Zell, for America's welfare.

The warriors became an all-female force during the Second Civil War, when many men sympathized with the rebels. It remained all-female after the nation split. The only males in the mech compound were geeks. They worked in isolation on tricky software in exchange for a livelihood they couldn't otherwise expect, or so Annabelle heard. She had never seen them. Mech Command and sister warriors frowned on fraternizing as a breach of their solidarity. Once the geeks trained women to take their places, Annabelle could only guess what would happen to them.

Settling into a stiff wooden seat, Annabelle scanned screens for hints of tonight's missions amid beautiful mountain foliage across the border. After the Patriots hijacked the Tea Party Rebellion, they lost at the polls and seceded. They achieved their paradise with no taxes and no government, yet even that didn't bring peace.

Several cams showed the quarter-mile-wide stretch of land denuded of vegetation that surrounded the forested Appalachian Outland, no man's land.

Commander Sam Hernandez took the podium, commanding their attention despite her compact figure. She had created the Tenn-tucky mech corps during the war. "I want to introduce ten new recruits tasked with protecting the Union and females, while maintaining the peace."

"Hoo-rah!" mech warriors responded.

After introducing the recruits, Sam continued, "For the benefit of new warriors, I'll cover material known to veterans. Bear with me. We are one unit and we will stick together."

"Hoo-rah!"

"For twenty years we've patrolled the anarchy the Outlanders created. Why anyone chooses to live under such brutal conditions is beyond me, yet every day escapees cross the border. Our job is to limit the chaos that threatens our beloved Union."

"Hoo-rah!"

Annabelle mouthed the chant with growing discomfort. If only they had seen what was left of Karen....

"President Zell has pledged to eradicate rebel strongholds," Sam said. "The burden falls to us."

"We stand ready to deliver," warriors said.

Prickly heat swarmed Annabelle. She did not sign up for this gung-ho nonsense. The Union had tracked her from age twelve into the security career path in the name of harmony. Then her tomboyish pranks forced her into a decision: mechs or exile. Her prospects were dismal if Sam booted her out. She bit her tongue until she tasted blood.

Sam used an old wooden pointer to direct the warriors' attention to a screen showing mountain terrain. "Another attack on Union high-speed supply rails through the mountains, the second in a month."

Sam described the situation, assigned a team, and moved to the next screen. "Two boys without papers eluded Knoxville police and may head for the border." Despite active and passive sensors with infrared, boys still managed to cross, which meant more males to track, and ultimately more armed rebels.

Screen three. "I know this sounds trivial, but Outlanders continue to poach deer from state and national parks. Although the deer are on their side of the border, they represent part of our national treasure. President Zell wants this stopped. We identified another village harboring escapees and poaching deer to feed them."

Screen four. "We caught two Outlanders transporting drugs, probably Medallion Cartel. We need to shut this down."

The next screen showed mug photo of a boy and girl. "Police caught her helping this boy over the border. He will be imprisoned. Governor Battani has asked us to deliver her to Biltmoor."

Groans from the floor. Maybe the girl deserved punishment, but three months as a paid companion in the Outland capital was obscenely excessive.

"Okay, warriors." Sam raised her hand to quiet the room. "President Zell wants us to move the barrier two miles east every year until we meet up with North Carolina mech units. We need warriors to guard the barrier for logging crews. It's not glamorous, but the scenery's great."

Everyone looked down while Sam made assignments.

"Final mission," Sam said. "Three more girls kidnapped last night, probably cartel."

Warriors grumbled, mirroring Annabelle's anger and worry for her sisters at home.

"This has to stop," Sam said. "If we can't protect our citizens, then we've failed as a unit."

Volunteers' hands flew up. Sam finished selecting teams and returned to the front of the room. "I don't have to tell you how dangerous it is out there. We lost Karen. Nothing can bring her back or make up for her loss. Our mission is to defuse danger so our citizens can enjoy the bounties of living in the Union."

"We stand ready to deliver."

"The good news: we've not had a rape, assault or other crime by Union males in 18 months within our great state of Tenn-tucky. A cold front will push through tomorrow afternoon. Until then, our infrared is not effective, so stay alert. Remember, we're here to protect and rescue females, capture or terminate escapees before they become armed rebels, enforce borders, and patrol Outland parks.

"Keep your eyes open to threats from our Underground

Railroad helping escapees. Make sure your inoculations and contraceptive implants are current, and remember to work together. Harmony brings success and happiness."

"Hoo-rah!"

Harmony also leads to bland boredom, Annabelle said to herself. The real purpose of rescuing girls was to deprive rebels of the ability to reproduce.

* * *

Once Geo got the three compadres into the forest, thin-faced Mickey pulled him aside. "What was that all about?"

"Folk want to help, but they can't." Geo led the boys along a deer path, keeping his rifle ready and the cabin in view. He tried not to think about the mech girl who didn't shoot, hoping she would return to her big city and leave them alone.

"I mean kissing your father's ring. It was weird."

Geo sighed. He'd had to explain local customs to Civ boys before, but he had his own questions for Pa. "He helps villagers and they give him support. Now, take the twins up the path. I need to talk to Pa."

While the boys shuffled along the trail, the wiry Mickey dwarfed by the twins, Geo waited, expecting another scolding. When Pa kept going, Geo followed. "I don't understand why those Rangers didn't help."

Pa shifted his backpack and kept his rifle ready. "I'm as baffled as you are."

"Unless they're working with Civ." Geo prayed that wasn't so.

"Makes no sense. Our population has dropped since the Secession. Edwards should want all the men he can get." Pa overtook the three boys and headed east.

Geo walked faster to keep up. Seeing the boys reminded him of family he didn't have. "Why did Mom leave?"

Pa sighed. "Must we do this now?" He picked up his pace.

* * *

Pa hurried along the path. He couldn't blame Geo for wanting to know what had happened. They both still felt the hurt, even after 16 years. The right time to explain just never seemed to arrive.

Geo kept up. "You treat me like a kid, but I killed a mech today."

"Never celebrate a kill. Inside every mech is a girl with a family and people who care about her. This isn't male vs. female." *Or at least it wasn't until the Progressive Reunion took power.*

"Then why did Mom leave?"

"She didn't. You had no future in Civ, so we agreed you would join me. Now quiet."

"But I remember Mom at the cabin."

Pa winced and kept moving. Geo was only three at the time. *I removed all pictures of his mom so Geo wouldn't dwell on the past. I guess that isn't working.*

"Before the war, this was our weekend retreat," Pa said. "Our home was in Knoxville. After the war, I brought you here to be free. She had to stay behind. I know it's hard. She does love you. This is just the way the world is."

"Why?" Geo asked.

It's always "why?" Always. Well, the boy is smart. He even reads between the lines in Edwards' online library, too. The party line on "rugged individualism" doesn't mean much when everybody's starving.

Pa reached the ridge overlooking the Grahams' place and headed into the next valley. He sighed. *Neighbors died today and Geo wants to talk philosophy.*

"People get crazy with their ideology," Pa said. "It's a long conversation for later." He shifted direction and walked faster.

"This is about the Progressive Reunion, right?"

The Progressive Reunion had promoted every group except white males, because a few alphas still held power. But the world changed. Men's physical abilities were no longer valued. Boys dropped out of school. Jobs went to women, who had the required social and educational skills. "When the Union limited growth to preserve the environment, men got squeezed, all men, not just alphas."

"Is that why men aren't respected in Civ?" Geo persisted.

Pa nodded. Behind them, the boys huffed along. *Helpless* and *inevitable* were words that stuck in his throat. When the Progressive Reunion seized power, men got suckered into supporting the Patriots; they saw no alternative. After war broke out, they learned that entrepreneur Adrianne Picard secretly provided the Progressive Reunion with mech gear and drones. The war ended quickly. Radical Patriots clung to Appalachia and limited government.

"Both sides carried things too far," Pa said. The Progressive Reunion called for a safety net. More was better, and complete government control was ideal. Patriots decided that lower taxes were better and zero taxes best. Neither side could step back and ask if something in between better served the people without being branded traitors to their side. The Patriots delivered on zero taxes. Ironically, while Edwards preaches no government and no taxes, he holds absolute power.

"Enough chatter for now," Pa said.

Geo gave him a funny look. Pa realized: *The chatter is all in my head.*

"Stay focused," Pa told him. "We're being followed."

THREE

After the briefing, the commander caught up with Annabelle, who was eager to reach the parking garage and freedom for the day. "I want to speak with you privately." Hernandez led the way down a well-lit khaki corridor with low concrete ceilings.

Annabelle felt chilled as she entered the austere office. Had Sam read her rebellious thoughts? Did lack of assignment mean Annabelle faced reprimand for today?

"Have a seat." Sam dropped into a high-back chair behind an ancient metal desk. Scars on her cheeks gave a stern expression even when she smiled. "It's okay to mourn Karen and feel upset. We all miss her."

Annabelle slumped into a stiff wooden seat with rough splinters poking her leg. She stared at a picture of Sam in the Marine Corps before the war. Sam would say, *Never let yourself get soft.*

"I need to know you're 100 percent before I give you another assignment." Sam leaned forward. "Speak your mind."

"They were boys," Annabelle said.

"Who will grow into men, get weapons, and become a threat. We need to crush this transport of escapees over the border."

"Yet we bring females from the Outland."

"You've seen how they're treated. I have yet to find one who wants to return."

That didn't convince Annabelle. Aside from having no choice, she had joined mechs for the opportunity to break out of Union social constraints and see the Outland. Why would she go back to bland civilian life now?

"We need to find who is behind the Underground Railroad."

Annabelle nodded. "Or this war will drag on."

"Without new recruits, the Outlanders will have to surrender and we'll finally have peace."

At what cost?

"Will you be okay?" Sam asked.

"I stand ready to deliver."

"You don't have to say that behind closed doors. What's on your mind?"

A lot Annabelle didn't want to share, but Sam wouldn't let her leave until she gave up something. "We've lived in relative peace for twenty years. Now we're pushing Outlanders into another war."

"They violate the peace when they kidnap girls, run drugs, and attack trains. Patrolling for crime drains resources from our social programs. Now we have a budget crisis."

"What happens if we succeed? No more mechs?"

Sam laughed. "We still have Outlanders in the Northern Rockies and Tex-SoCal. Don't be afraid of peace."

"I'm not."

"Then understand that every train that gets hit, every drug that gets through, and every kidnapping heightens the need to end this stalemate."

Annabelle nodded. She itched to go home and bust loose over losing Karen.

Sam's eyes softened. "You have a promising future and something to prove, yet I sense a dark side. It's hard to see your boss as a friend, but I wish I had more like you."

"But...Karen." This had been Karen's third mission, deemed low-risk, and Annabelle felt responsible. She sucked it up and held her nerve.

"It's okay. It hurts. Let me show you what I saw today." Sam displayed onscreen a replay of the mission from Annabelle's cams.

Annabelle didn't want to relive the horror. She suspected her boss was pushing to see if she was strong. Annabelle closed her eyes when the explosion ended Karen's life, again.

"There." Sam stopped the video.

Annabelle stared at the boy. The image was dark and fuzzy

amidst forest shadows. She wondered if this could really be her adoptive mom's son. She forced back a tear.

"I can't see his face, and the computer can't I.D. him."

"I should have given chase. I should have killed him." Annabelle gritted her teeth. *Make this end.*

"No! You never leave your team. Now why didn't you shoot?"

"I've let you down, Commander. I'm a disgrace to the unit." Despite losing Karen, Annabelle couldn't shoot a boy who might be family. She shoved those thoughts from her mind.

"Stop right there. This isn't an interrogation. I want to I.D. this boy. Did you get a better look?"

Annabelle straightened up and put on her stone face. "He looked like another scruffian."

"And?"

"And—" Annabelle stopped before she betrayed herself. "When Karen was hit, I thought it was Janine. It was her turn. My eyes clouded. By the time I cleared them, he was gone."

"Understood," Sam said.

"I should have run him down. I should have—"

"No, Annabelle, because you didn't see this." Sam showed a different view with Rangers camouflaged in the forest. "If you had left Dara, she would have faced grave danger. Stick with your team. We will catch the boy another day. I have a mission for you."

"You're not putting me on border patrol again." Actually, she would accept that if it meant ending this questioning.

Sam laughed. "You're much too valuable to waste on mundane matters. A prisoner escaped from Oak Ridge Maximum Security. We believe he'll head for the border."

"Must have had help."

Sam nodded. "Could be the Underground Railroad. He'll be armed and dangerous."

"Our own malcontents?" Annabelle thought of friends who had helped escapees, plus her own attempts.

Sam grinned. "No matter how well we care for our people, some of them push for change without understanding the risks. That's what keeps me up at night. Not Outlanders. We can handle them. I worry about citizens who don't appreciate what they have."

Yeah, those like me who find Union regulations too confining, and rounding up boys to be barbaric.

"This is top priority. Go home, rest, be back at oh-five-hundred. You have a good nose for finding people, so I'm putting you in charge."

Annabelle took a cautious breath. "Who's my team?"

"Dara for experience, and Janine, who needs to learn from the best. The fugitive is Cory Philips." Sam handed over an electronic pad with his file.

Annabelle studied the man's image. He looked like a weasel, not an armed and dangerous criminal, though looks could be deceiving.

"If this leads to the Underground Railroad, we could stop the flow of escapees. I'm counting on you."

Itching to shed her uniform and scream to loud music, Annabelle rose to leave. "I won't let you down."

FOUR

Geo watched a deer sprint off to his right. After Pa dropped down, Geo pulled Mickey behind bushes. The twins followed. Looking through binoculars, Geo saw only greenery.

Pa tugged his arm. "When we reach the bend, scoot off the trail and wait, make sure we aren't being tracked. I'll take the boys to the Howells. Once you've cleared the trail, head home and prepare tonight's work."

"I want to go with you, Pa."

"I need you to protect our rear and tend the farm."

"But, Pa, I'm old enough for man's work. Hell—"

"Don't use that language."

"Sorry, Pa."

"Maybe next time." Pa hurried down the path.

Geo ducked behind bushes and scooted to the spot where he had seen the deer. He looked up between trees to see rare contrails of Civ jets and the blue haze of the Great Smokey Mountains. *Damn it, Pa, I'm not a kid anymore.*

The boys' rustling through leaves faded, yet remained like thunder in Geo's trained ears. He lived between two worlds meshed in complex fractal patterns: the written world of Aristotle and Alexander the Great, plus this world where one false move—

Geo's senses picked up the crunch of leaves, and the distinct whiff of hydraulics and perfumed female sweat.

He planted a two-phase grenade on the path, covered it with leaves, and scooted into the forest. Lying still, he braced the .50 cal and held the grenade's remote between his teeth.

A runner approached, making no attempt at stealth. Was this another Civ refugee? Geo waited and prayed the mech didn't crash parallel to the path and stomp on him. With only a spotty view through brush, his first glimpse was a lean olive-skinned figure with backpack and baggy white shirt flapping as he ran. Didn't he know he could move faster without the pack?

The hulking black exoskeleton of a mech clomped through the underbrush like a feral pig, the resistance of vegetation slowing her. Geo fired. The mech stopped to look for targets. Knowing they ran in threes, Geo trained binoculars up the trail for other mechs. Not seeing any, he returned his focus to the one staring his way. *Can you see me?* He prayed the oppressive heat neutralized her infrared, leaving her blind.

Inching forward, the mech scanned the forest. Geo fired again, and recalled Pa saying how there's a girl in each unit with a family who loves her. *What about my mom, my family?*

The mech stepped forward, turned toward Geo, and raised her weapons. He triggered the grenade. The blast thundered in his ears and stunned the mech. Before she could steady herself, the second explosion shot up into the gap. The mech toppled backward. Geo said a prayer, begged forgiveness for taking a life, and asked that her death be swift and her soul delivered.

Geo scanned the woods for other mechs. He didn't see any. The runner returned. It was Carlos Sanchez of the Medallion Cartel. *What are you doing out here?* Geo hadn't seen his friend in weeks, since hunting deer out east.

By the time Geo reached the path, Carlos had removed the mech's helmet. Geo gazed into the tortured face of a redhead panting shallow breaths. He felt ill. He didn't want her to die. It was different when he couldn't see the face. This was a girl, when girls were so rare in these mountains. He wanted to tell her how sorry he was, and wished he could take it back. He forced himself to look at what he had done. He couldn't show weakness in front of Carlos. When her head fell back, he felt an ache in the pit of his stomach like nothing he had experienced before.

"Hey, Amigo." Carlos checked the girl's pulse. "Thanks for saving my weary ass. Not sure how much longer I could have outrun this beast."

Geo stared at the girl's sweat-soaked face. Pa was right; there was no joy in killing. He wondered what it would have been like to get to know her, and how her family would deal with her loss. He thought of his own mom.

"Can I have the gear?" Carlos asked.

Geo nodded. He couldn't bring himself to take her mech suit, though the weaponry would be useful. "We should bury her."

"You want to bury a mech? You gone soft? Leave her for the wolves."

"I humor me in exchange for the gear. Any other mechs?"

Carlos unfastened the shoulder plates. "They split up. I owe you, amigo. Say, you want to come with me into Civ tonight?"

"You've got to be kidding."

"Come on, you a man or a worm?"

"Pa gets steamed if I don't work the farm at night," Geo said.

"Move our way. Then you won't have to worry about mech and Ranger attacks."

"You know Pa."

"Mine, too. It's time to bust loose and do something daring."

It was wrong and dangerous. Pa would be furious. But if Pa wouldn't treat him like a man, then Geo would find other ways. "Okay, but when I say enough, we return."

* * *

The whir of the electric cycle calmed Annabelle as she sped home. It was a warrior perk that saved her from public transport and allowed her to respond quickly when called. Losing Karen hit hard. Over the past few months, they had grown close. Now the ache in Annabelle's heart festered. The urge to strike back left her frustrated. She hoped her adopted sister Janine was enjoying her day off. *I would have killed the boy for you.*

Along the nearly empty highway, Annabelle whizzed past packed buses, crowded restaurants, and shops. Clustered near bus stops, women wore bland pastels intended to diminish perceived disharmony. She craved something sweet and fizzy with a kick, but Union Burgers & Subs only had bitter-tasting sugar-free Dr. Cola, the sole Union-approved brand. *No caffeine.* The only surviving fast food chain also had Union-allowed turkey or veggie burgers that tasted like cardboard. *If you can taste it, it can't be good for you.*

Along with trans fats, the Union banned sugar, salt, and food additives such as garlic, claiming they were bad for the nation's health and a burden on National Healthcare. Worst was beef, which you couldn't even get on the black market. Cattle ranching consumed too much land and cows produced methane, an environmental contaminant.

Annabelle didn't hanker for beef, since she'd never had any, but she hungered to try new things she couldn't get in Knoxville or Tenn-tucky. Travel restrictions kept her from seeing the rest of the Union. She imagined blandness stretching coast to coast.

Annabelle considered starting a club for girls frustrated with blah government-accepted fare. It would be something she could call her own outside the security track. She would call it Expressions. Bring in sassy drinks and tasty food, whatever she could get past prohibitions on alcohol, caffeine, and taste enhancers.

She sighed. It was a pipe dream. Fact was: you couldn't compete against Big Sister.

Annabelle turned on her radio and flipped stations. News was the usual censored community help and harmony blah, nothing about Karen's death or the kidnappings. One station talked up the merits of cluster community living—you never have to be alone.

Annabelle longed for time alone. As for socializing, the Union told her who was okay, and it didn't include boys or rebellious girls.

She switched channels. Lots of Union-authorized feel-good music that hyped social harmony until Annabelle wanted to scream.

An infomercial blared. "Don't take chances with sperm donors. Ensure the sex and genetics of your baby and promote harmony with EggFusion Fertilization, covered by National Healthcare."

Twenty years ago, the procedure of using the DNA from one egg to fertilize another became popular. It heightened a vicious cycle: boys resisted education, society no longer needed their physical labor, so boys gravitated to drugs, violence, and rebel activities. With boys having few economic prospects, women chose girl babies.

Annabelle turned off the radio. Harmony sounded good, yet it left her feeling like a flat tire. The more the Union preached how good she had it, the more she wanted things the Union banned, like caffeine. She would have to wait until morning to get her jolt before her mission.

She reached Battani Estates, where Governor Battani and other members of the Tenn-tucky and Knoxville administrations lived. Its ten-foot steel-reinforced concrete wall and state-of-the-art infrared and motion security systems were covered by ivy and bushes that gave it a false rural flavor. The wall also kept common folk from seeing elite parties. When Annabelle was called in to assist with a disturbance, she found Union-banned alcohol and foods, and pretty boys doing a strip-tease.

We're all equal, except the elite. She tried to remember where she had read that. Some banned book her mom kept hidden? *Animal Farm*, maybe.

She had been to Governor Battani's mansion twice because Mom was a prominent senator before Tennessee merged with Kentucky, and retained a minor role in the new Tenn-tucky legislature. It was another job Annabelle couldn't aspire to after getting career-tracked to security. The highest she could reach was mech warrior. In a society where the government equalized pay, the Union had to resort to career tracking to fill less attractive jobs.

Annabelle dreamed of creating variety in housing, fashion, or food. That was impossible in a culture that saw diversity as creating disharmony. *Universities don't accept security types like me.*

Past the Estates, Annabelle spotted a man in a residential neighborhood not far from a crowded bus stop. He held what looked like giant scissors. She started to call it in, but then spotted his blue day-labor collar. Nearby, a woman sat on her porch, holding a remote, while watching him work.

Like all Union men, he wore a collar with GPS tracking and electro-shock that could be triggered remotely to control aggressive behavior. As a mech, Annabelle had a device that rotated through frequencies in an emergency. Still, despite government security measures, people locked their doors for fear of kidnappings the mechs were charged with stopping.

If the Union's vision of harmony was so great, why did they have to preach it round the clock at church, on radio, in online streams, and at public gatherings? Who could she vent to? Social-media police plastered every expressed thought for all to see. Peer pressure was intended to mold her into harmony, and if that didn't work, they had more extreme measures.

After pulling into the family's two-car garage, Annabelle parked next to Janine's mech cycle and Mom's car, a political perk. She felt thankful, yet ashamed, that her sister had traded missions with Karen. She couldn't have forgiven herself if Janine got killed. With each mission, that possibility haunted Annabelle, and yet Janine begged to follow Annabelle into the mechs.

How could today's mission be a "success" when 20 males died for harboring boys the Union didn't want? Why not let them go? Why not just exchange them for girls who wanted to leave the Outland?

How had things gotten this bad? In the years before the Civil War, men fell behind economically and grew so violent that prisons overflowed. The government clamped down on guns to stop the cycle of violence. Then states seceded and the war began.

Annabelle lingered in the dark garage, relishing a few moments alone. Then she braced herself and entered the great room of her communal home and its welcoming yet stifling press of family: three moms and eight sisters. When Mom married Mama Grace and Mama Helen, they each brought two biological daughters and adopted an older girl like Annabelle. While she had no biological siblings, Annabelle considered all eight as sisters, and the younger ones didn't know of the adoptions.

With blonde hair and a face softened with creams, Mom hugged Annabelle before locking the door. "You okay?" she whispered.

Annabelle nodded. "Can we talk?" She took Mom's hand and led her toward the stairs.

Standing at the kitchen island, Mama Grace waved a plump arm, blew a kiss, and returned to the challenge of cooking for twelve.

Mama Helen pushed glasses atop her head and caught Annabelle by the stairs. "Don't I get a hug and kiss?" She kissed Annabelle's cheek. "It worries us every day you go out that door. Thanks for coming home safe."

While Annabelle welcomed the embrace, a headache crept in behind her eyes. It was hard maintaining harmony in a complex family. She took a deep breath and waved to three young sisters sitting in a corner studying, or pretending to. Then she smiled at two sisters helping Mama Grace in the kitchen. Reassured that she hadn't left anyone out, Annabelle led Mom upstairs.

"What's this all about?" Mom asked as they climbed.

They went down the long hallway, papered in pastel flowers, and passed the moms' master suite and two sisters' bedrooms. The room at the end was the one Annabelle shared with two sisters. It held three modest chests of drawers and three double beds pushed together, neatly made. *Bless you, Sarah.* It helps to have one tidy person per room. Thankfully, Sarah and Janine were out.

Annabelle turned her stereo loud with harmony music and whispered, "I saw Bret at the village we hit. A moment later and he might have been inside."

Mom closed her eyes. "Is he okay?"

"He had a boy with him." Annabelle grabbed a canvas overnight bag for tomorrow's mission.

"George?" Mom held up a photo of him at age three. "Was it him?"

Annabelle grabbed a change of clothes and items she would need if she got stuck in the Outland. "Mom, I could stare at that picture all day and couldn't swear in court. He did look like Bret."

"Oh, my." Mom dropped onto the bed.

Annabelle sat next to her. "Are you okay?"

Mom's dark eyes softened. "He's alive."

"I have to go back tomorrow."

The warmth in Mom's eyes turned to sadness. "Find George, Belle. Tell him I'm sorry for everything."

"I will, Mom." Yet Annabelle had no idea where to find the boy unless he came with his father. When Mom remained silent, Annabelle asked, "Are you ill?" She felt her mom's forehead. "You're warm."

"It's hard to keep so many secrets."

Annabelle knew that well, surrounded by family or sister warriors with little time to herself. And who could she trust? "Mom, please see a doctor."

"I'm on the list, six weeks."

"Mom, listen to me. You're a senator, you have options."

"I must set an example," Mom said. "Why tell people the health plan works if I don't use it?"

Annabelle held Mom's hands and looked into her gray eyes. "Because you're one of the few sane voices and I don't want to lose you. Promise you'll see a doctor tomorrow."

"Tomorrow's Saturday."

"Then Monday."

Lights blinked out, a common occurrence since the Governor shut down the last coal and nuclear plants.

Annabelle felt around for her flashlight. "Damned useless grid."

"It's the price we pay for green energy."

"Yeah, no sun, no wind, no lights. Would it be so bad to have backup power?"

"It's tough getting things through this legislature," Mom said.

Annabelle turned on her flashlight. "I know you're trying, Mom."

"No flashlights. Batteries are only for emergencies." Mom took the light and turned it off.

Annabelle sighed. Mom was right; everywhere were cameras, spies, and lurking environmental police.

"Whatever you do," Mom said, "don't get caught in the Outland. Do you have water pills, your GPS—"

"Yes, Mom. This is my job, remember?"

"If you see—"

"George. Yes, I know, Mom." Annabelle took a deep breath. "Any news on my birth mom?"

"Nothing new, Belle. The Department of Corrections offers any excuse to get us to stop asking."

"I'm not surprised. By the way, George isn't ten feet tall."

Mom gave a nervous laugh. "Protect him, won't you?"

"I will, Mom. But what if he's a bully?" Annabelle couldn't tell Mom she had almost killed him over Karen.

"I refuse to believe that. Look, I have another package if it's not too dangerous. I do wish you and Janine could find other work."

Annabelle grinned. "Then I couldn't deliver packages." She had seen enough in her three years in the corps that she didn't want to return to the Outland as a warrior.

After pulling Mom into the walk-in closet, Annabelle closed the door and turned on the flashlight so she could see Mom's face. "What's really wrong? What aren't you telling me?"

Mom sighed. "We're having company."

"Who?"

"Governor Battani."

"Here?" Annabelle said. "No wonder Mama Grace looked frantic. I hope the power outage won't ruin dinner."

"Gas, remember, and candles if necessary. Why don't you wear your maroon outfit?"

"It looks like a uniform. You mean she wants to see me?" Annabelle hoped this wouldn't delay getting to the party.

"Remember you're surrounded by family," Mom said.

The lights came on.

FIVE

Governor Battani swept into Annabelle's home wearing an elegant red dress no private citizen could buy, since the Union didn't permit any show of wealth that might upset the ideal of harmony. Evidently, that didn't apply to governors. Battani gave each of the women and girls a hug, as if kissing babies for her campaign.

Tall and big-boned, Battani seemed to fill the room. "I just met with *New Harmony Magazine*," she announced in her husky voice. "They're honoring the new CEO at Unitel. We're retiring the last male CEO. Removing gender conflict will increase harmony and happiness."

Annabelle wanted to gag. Why the devil was the governor campaigning in her living room in a power dress? As for the retiring CEO, age 52, they would move him to Catalina like the others, never to be seen again.

With few boys born in Tenn-tucky over the past five years, it wouldn't be long before there were no males left. Annabelle felt a void left by her father, reported dead when she was three. Now that she had glimpsed George in the Outland, she hungered to meet him. He represented everything the Union denied her: masculinity, wilderness, and freedom from the straitjacket of her society.

During dinner, Governor Battani droned on about politics and the Outland problem. Then she asked for a private conference with Annabelle and Mom, as private as thin walls would permit. Mom led them into her first-floor office and closed the door. After the great room, being in such tight quarters with Battani made Annabelle claustrophobic, particularly when Mom sat behind her pine desk, leaving Annabelle and the governor seated next to each other.

Battani grinned. "We're indebted to you for your bravery, Annabelle."

"Thanks." *Where is this going?* She crossed her arms.

"Your mom has been a valuable supporter in making our state a garden of social welfare and security, but the strains of supporting troops and tracking illegals, drug traffickers and kidnappers have reached a critical point. Our economy has slowed. We can't support the burden."

Annabelle's eyebrows furrowed. "You're downsizing mech forces?"

Battani nodded. "After we deal with the Outlander problem."

"You mean get them to honor the peace treaty?" Annabelle glanced at Mom, who looked away. *Not a good sign.* Annabelle felt chilled. "Yet so far, talks have failed."

Eyes narrowing, Battani grinned. "Because…?"

"They aren't motivated to cooperate."

"That's why we've developed a new plan."

Annabelle's gut tightened.

"Can't you guess?" Battani smiled; her eyes twinkled. "Nations have done this for centuries. Alliances reduce the risk of war."

Mom's face took on a sunken look. Annabelle grew suspicious. "What's going on?"

Battani sat back with a triumphant smile. "A marriage between a prominent Union family and Thane Edwards."

"Who?" Annabelle saw the answer in Mom's face. "You've got to be kidding! I'm not marrying a man, a stranger, an Outlander Thane at that." Her breath caught.

"You'll live in Biltmoor with all its accommodations. You can visit your family."

Annabelle stood on wobbly legs. "We fought the Second Civil War to keep from being dominated by men. Now you want me to agree to an arranged marriage? I won't do it."

Mom raised her hand. "Sit down, Belle."

"I know you've made sacrifices for your country," Battani said, "and this goes well beyond, but it's the only path to end this festering wound."

"Find someone else." Annabelle turned away. It took every bit of her mech training to keep from exploding.

"We need peace so we can devote resources at home," Battani said in a cool tone. "Otherwise, we have to cut vital social services. No one wants that. Thane Edwards is pleased with your picture."

"My picture!" Annabelle's legs felt ready to buckle. "What am I, a cow being sold at auction? Seriously, Mom, did you arrange this?"

"Your mom was against it," Battani said. "As Thane of the southern Outlanders, Edwards can offer a comfortable life."

"How dare you tell me how to live!" A lifetime of limitations cascaded onto Annabelle at the horrid prospect of marrying the brute. "I won't do it. Mom, help me out here."

"Enough talk of arranged marriages," Mom said.

"The wedding is in six days," Battani said. "Please reconsider for all your sisters at home and across the state. How many more like Karen must die? Do this for your country, and your family will be well rewarded."

"No!" Reliving the mech-linked pain of Karen's death made Annabelle collapse against a bookshelf. She struggled for breath.

Battani started to speak, but Annabelle's mom opened the door. "Let me talk to my daughter alone."

Battani nodded and left. Mom closed the door behind her.

Annabelle turned to her mom. "How could you?"

Mom sank into a vinyl chair. "Our position is weak, Belle. Our allotment for children is two each, six total. Battani hinted that three girls might have to leave."

Annabelle turned on the wall television to mask their voices. "The adoptees?"

"If I oppose Battani, she'll use this against us."

"What if we three adoptees leave and form our own household? We're all of age."

"They'll take the youngest," Mom said.

"No, not Sarah."

"This whole wretched business stinks, Belle. I worry what will happen if I lose my office. I'm so sorry, hon. While I didn't commit you, I can't openly defy Battani. She assumes you'll do this for family and expects me to attend the wedding in Biltmoor."

Annabelle clenched her fists and turned toward the door.

Mom stopped her. "Please don't go."

"I'm not doing this, Mom. That's final." Annabelle had fought brutes during mech training. Now she had to marry one? He would put his filthy hands on her, pollute her, and make her carry his sons. Her heart was ready to explode.

Annabelle took a deep breath and steeled herself as she did for battle. Her mind weighed in: Battani chose her not only to hurt Mom but for Annabelle's mech training. Battani expected her to spy, living a perpetual hell without Mom or Janine to console her.

"I won't make you do this, Belle. Just know that defying the governor will have consequences for you as well."

"Mom! I thought you were on my side."

"I am. That's why I'm begging you not to party tonight. You're like a caged animal. What if you get caught? There are spies everywhere waiting to tear our family apart."

Seeing Mom hunched over, diminished by the exchange, Annabelle gave her a hug. As unbearable as marrying Edwards would be, she had to consider family, the only family she knew.

Placards on TV caught her eye: *We demand answers, Battani.* Annabelle turned up the volume.

"A group of reactionary agitators took to the streets," a plainly dressed brunette said. "As you see, they are few in number. They dispersed when police asked for their permits."

The usual censored nonsense. A placard held by a gray-haired woman read: *Where are our brothers, sons, and husbands?* Now that Annabelle had seen George, she could identify with the gray-hair, for the Union forbade Annabelle from seeing him as anything but the enemy.

The TV announcer continued, "Do you really want to return to the days when you feared assault every moment of every day, and your lives were controlled by men?" This was a typical Union exaggeration, though violence had escalated prior to the war as men grew increasingly frustrated. That violence kept women from protesting until the end of the war, when it was clear the Patriots had lost. When they refused to surrender, Union protesters had pressured the government to end the slaughter.

Police rounded up the women protesters. They would be interrogated as traitors to the New Harmony.

Annabelle turned off the screen. "I'm going out."

"Please be careful."

"I will, Mom."

"You packed for overnight. Does that mean you won't attend church on Sunday?"

"I will if I'm home." For Annabelle, church meant quiet time alone. She found no spiritual guidance in the Union-approved United American Church of Christ, which split off from the Catholics over the role of women and the handling of sex and financial scandals. Then it united with Lutheran, Baptist, and other denominations to form an American church supporting the New Harmony. Annabelle didn't feel harmonious.

* * *

Geo and Carlos stood on the crest of a ridge beneath cover of trees, scanning the border. Beyond lay the sprawling metropolis of Knoxville beneath the setting sun. Geo imagined his mom living there and wondered if she remembered him.

Carlos' plan worried him. What's more, Pa would be angry that Geo wasn't tending the patchwork fields of crops. To avoid discovery by Ranger patrols or Civ satellites, he worked at night.

The odor of decomposing food and oils wafted in from Civ dumpsites on a westerly breeze. Aside from the stone wall on the Appalachian side, there was nothing to see of the barrier separating them from Civ except a quarter-mile wide stretch cleared of trees. It bristled with thousands of Civ cams and infrared sensors.

"Don't worry," Carlos said. "It's too hot for infrared, and I've blinded the nearest cams. By the time they respond to satellite tracking, we'll be gone."

Dense heat drew sweat so thick Geo bathed in it. While the backpack didn't help, he couldn't leave it. He wiped his face, applied mosquito ointment, and vowed to remember to feel grateful for the cold next winter while shivering in a bearskin. Though the Lord could keep the damned mosquitoes.

Geo helped Carlos lay out his bundle of parts for two hang-gliders. "What happened earlier with the mechs?"

Carlos extended and tightened an aluminum frame that looked like wings on a drone. "Ruiz and Rodriguez were making a delivery. I came to learn the ropes."

"Cocaine?" Geo didn't like that part of this adventure.

"Yeah. And other sweets for Civ girls." Carlos stretched nylon fabric over his frame to make eagle-like wings. "Don't lecture me like your pa."

"I'm not, but—"

"They send mechs to kill us, and you're worried about Civs?" Carlos tested his glider, then turned to help Geo.

"Not when you put it that way, but I'm not taking coke."

"Not offering. Papa has strict rules about family and friends."

Geo locked his frame and pulled the nylon over it. Carlos tugged the material and nodded approval. "Mechs caught us at the border. We split up. Ruiz and Rodriguez didn't make it."

"I'm sorry."

"So don't ask me to weep for Civ girls." Carlos stood with his glider.

Geo examined the strange contraptions in the twilight. "You sure they're safe?"

"Stop worrying. What better way to prove you're a man than to jump the barrier? I doubt even your pa's done that in years." Carlos hung his backpack on his chest and strapped the glider to his back. "Papa needs the sale and doesn't believe I can handle it, even though I've crossed dozens of times. Let's go."

Geo mirrored Carlos with the pack and glider. He felt like a flightless ostrich.

"Bank into the wind until you're over the border cams," Carlos said. "Then swoop in over the treetops."

"Si, señor."

"Don't wiseass me." Carlos ran toward the edge, dropped out of sight, and lifted up over the treetops.

Geo followed, feeling a glorious sensation of weightlessness for a moment. Then the weight of the pack tugged him down toward the ravine. Watching Carlos rise into the darkening sky, Geo swung into the wind and picked up altitude. He wondered if this was how birds felt in flight.

He banked and glided over the cams and the barrier, which looked like a riverbed in the darkening twilight. He felt free as an eagle, able to fly as far as Tex-SoCal. Except crossing five hundred miles of Civ territory would be suicide.

As the line of concrete posts with mini-cams slipped beneath him, Geo wondered if cams pointed up. Maybe not; they had satellites for that. So what was the point of evading the cams? He swooped down over bushy trees, following Carlos. When he came in, too fast, the glider's nose hit the ground and flipped him onto his back with a thud.

Carlos ran to his side and removed the backpack. "I told you not to flip it."

Geo struggled for breath. They were in Civ. This was freedom, after years cooped up in a small glen. Then reality set in: They were in Civ with mech patrols.

Carlos removed the straps from Geo's hang-glider. "Hurry. Satellite trackers will send patrols any minute."

They sprinted across the field toward woods, carrying their backpacks and partially collapsed hang-gliders. Suddenly, Geo realized something. "How do we get back?" They wouldn't have altitude to lift off.

"There's a tunnel that gets us close to the border." Carlos reached the woods first and began dismantling his glider. "If I don't get these home, Papa will kill me."

Once collapsed, they ditched the gliders under bushes and ran through the woods until they reached a creek. The crescent moon provided barely enough light to glimpse outlines ahead. There were no houses or lights in no-man's land this close to the border.

They reached a clearing. Carlos stopped and crouched down near the creek's edge. Geo strained to listen but heard only the wind, cicadas and buzzing mosquitoes.

Carlos emerged with a cycle.

"Won't they hear us?"

"Not on this baby." Carlos mounted and started it. "Civ electric, quiet as the wind. Hop on. We're late."

Balancing both backpacks, Geo climbed behind. Carlos sped off, kicking up dirt on the quietest cycle Geo had ever heard. Moonlight provided barely enough light to see they were on a path. The breeze through his hair was too warm and sticky to cool him. Wasn't there anything between these extremes?

Eventually they stopped. Carlos ditched the cycle behind bushes. They headed on foot toward lit sky and the heavy beat of angry girl music. Illuminated before them was a huge estate, like the spread Carlos' papa had on the east side of the mountains.

They crept to the edge of the woods. Across the stubble of grass and rock stood an enormous white stone building. Here in no-man's land, it should have been vacant, yet dozens of cycles stood out front. Figures—mostly girls, it seemed—headed for the door.

"I thought they didn't have boys." Gathered here were more

girls than Geo had seen in all his life. The few in the mountains were dull and mousy, too fearful to explore the wonders of the world. These girls were frightening in their boisterous talk and swagger.

Carlos took a small bag from his backpack. "Look closer. They're all girls."

"Why dress like guys?"

"Bored girls like to role-play."

"Hell, back home, a guy dressed like a girl—"

Carlos laughed. "Stay here. Whatever you do, don't get caught."

SIX

For once, Annabelle welcomed company. Her need to let off steam was high after watching what happened to Karen. Learning about the arranged marriage had skyrocketed her angst. It was time to party.

She sped her electric cycle east of town, past the base, with her sister Janine holding tight behind her. The breeze brought little relief from the sweltering heat, even after nightfall.

Getting to the party was tricky, even for mechs with travel fobs. Public transit didn't reach the outskirts for fear of Outlander raids. Annabelle took the back roads to avoid hitting roadblocks intended to intercept escapees and raiders. She didn't want to go on report again for being outside the protected zone without good cause. She was supposed to be resting for the morning mission.

"Sorry about Karen," Janine said. While holding on, she used Annabelle's stomach as a virtual keyboard to text her friends. "That should have been me."

"Spin of the wheel." Annabelle hoped to keep her younger sister from dwelling on this; it would only get her to doubt herself. There was no way Janine would quit mechs unless Annabelle did. "Come on, stop texting unless you want the obedience police tracking us."

Janine complied. "Thanks for letting me come."

"Sisters stick together."

Annabelle sped along a dry gully until they approached the edge of the protected zone. Enormous wind turbines glistened in the moonlight, rotating to power the grid. She stopped the cycle, and they dismounted.

Annabelle walked the cycle along the gully to avoid alerting border police guarding a nearby road. After they passed the checkpoint and a chain-link fence, they rode southeast until lights appeared. She parked the cycle behind bushes. While the cycle had biometric locks, there was no point tempting scavengers. Annabelle led Janine the long way to the sprawling two-story concrete structure, the former estate of a wealthy corporate man.

"When I say leave, we leave." Annabelle adjusted her breast minimizer, waist padding, masculine shirt, and suit jacket. "No fuss, no matter who you're with or how much fun you're having. Is that clear?"

In the moonlight, Janine nodded with wide-eyed exuberance.

Despite the heat, Annabelle donned a short brown wig and pasted on a mustache to play the masculine role at the party. She did a quick check of Janine's maroon dress and headed for the mansion's ornate oak entry.

* * *

While Geo hunkered down behind bushes and rocks, Carlos scooted around the woods to the back of the mansion. Geo aimed his binoculars at a group of four approaching the massive iron grill at the broad entry. Seeing female outlines beneath two male-dressers was bizarre. If they wanted guys, there were plenty in Appalachia who would willingly oblige.

Turning his eyepiece, he saw Carlos meet a girl dressed like Al Capone with round face, hat, and cigar. While they exchanged packages, all Geo could think was how these Civ girls came to escape their paradise. It made no sense. They had everything, as best he could tell.

Geo scanned the crumbling drive as a couple strolled into view. He hadn't heard them drive up and prayed the heat hadn't dulled his senses. Dialing up magnification, he studied the taller one, dressed like a wealthy business tycoon with brown hair that didn't fit right. It looked like a hat with a tail of blonde. The mustache was thick and coarse over soft lips. Her figure, with subtle curves, looked neither male nor female, as if she couldn't decide. He glanced at her companion, a sweet brunette dressed in red, and returned his attention to the gender-confused creature. She moved with confidence and athletic agility, unlike girls in the mountains.

Before she reached the door, she turned his way. Light reflected off her eyes was the deep turquoise of the sea before a storm, as he had seen in pictures.

Carlos returned from his exchange. "You want that one?" he whispered.

Geo dropped the binoculars. "Don't do that."

"What you say we grab those two and have some fun?"

Geo clutched the binoculars. "I'm not kidnapping girls."

"It would be a real coup. Delivery plus girls. We'd be legends."

"No." Yet Geo couldn't take his eyes off the strange girl.

"A thousand greenbacks each."

"I said no."

"You can have your pick."

Geo watched the pair enter the mansion. "How would you do it?"

"You in?"

"No."

"Then don't ask." Carlos grabbed his pack. "Help me get a cycle. Even at scrap they'll bring five hundred."

"Let's go before Pa skins me for skipping my farm chores."

Carlos headed toward the cycles. "You should move east."

"Pa wants nothing to do with drugs and stuff."

"Don't have to. You do food and—"

Two mechs swept floodlights over the area. Geo pulled Carlos into the bushes. He wiped sweat from his neck and praised the Lord that the night's warmth blinded infrared, he hoped.

"Let's go," Geo whispered.

Carlos waited until the mechs turned away before heading for the nearest cycle.

Geo pulled him back. A third mech appeared from the right. Though exposed, Geo held his breath and flattened himself against the dirt. The mechs made another sweep. After one of them nearly stepped on Geo's hand, he slid back into the bushes.

"He's here somewhere," a female voice said.

"Damned useless infrared," another voice said.

They split up and continued around the mansion.

"Forget the cycle," Geo said.

Leaving his backpack, Carlos sprinted to the nearest cycle and dragged it into the woods.

Geo grabbed the packs and crab-walked to join him. "You nuts?"

"Something to tell your grandkids."

"I'd have to find a girlfriend first."

"We could hang around until that pair comes back," Carlos said. "They left their cycle in the woods."

Geo was tempted by the thought of seeing those turquoise eyes up close. Turning his attention west, he glanced at the glow of Knoxville. If his mom was alive, she might be there. It was only twenty miles, but it would be suicide getting past checkpoints, even on a hot night, but even so...

SEVEN

Annabelle stood at the doorway, gazing wistfully toward the border, wishing she could see the mountains in the thin moonlight. She adjusted Janine's wig and delicious maroon dress, which left her sister as uncomfortable in the stifling heat as Annabelle's suit, wig and tie. The mustache itched like crazy. Inside would be cooler, thanks to pirated links to the grid. If that didn't work, generators using illegal gas would kick in.

The one who answered the door looked like a muscle-man from mech training. Annabelle recognized Dara. "Fab disguise."

Dara grinned, gave Annabelle a once-over, and pulled her inside. "Yours is tip-top. I have a surprise: live entertainment. Who's your scrumptious date?" She led them into a dimly lit room that extended the length of the house. Rainbow lighting danced off shards of dangling glass.

Annabelle shouted over dense angry music, definitely not New Harmony. "It's Janine's first time, so please look out for her." At least 50 other warriors mingled in the air-chilled room.

Dara took Janine's hands. "Almost didn't recognize you all dolled up. If you're free, I do know how to party."

Janine pulled away, stuck out her chin, and took her sister's arm. "I'm with Annabelle."

Dara patted her shoulder. "Welcome to the Escape, where anything's possible. Party like there's no tomorrow. Drink yourself silly. I hear we got fresh Outlander product if you're brave enough. No limits with tonight's entertainer, but you might have to stand in line. He is a hunk. We caught him this evening running for the border. One rule: Mech curfew for those with missions is midnight. We don't want to disappoint Sam." Dara winked.

Janine headed across the floor, where sister warriors, some dressed like guys, were dancing. Dara held Annabelle back. "We lost Wendy."

"How?"

"She intercepted a cartel run. Her team split up, and so did the Outlander scum. We got two. The third had help."

Annabelle felt nauseated. "Did we recover her?"

Dara shook her head. "Team found blood, but someone moved her and inactivated her tracking chip."

"Damn them."

"Thanks for not giving chase today. That could have been you or me. Outlanders are getting desperate."

"And creative," Annabelle added.

"Sorry about making a pass at your sister. She looks luscious."

"Sweating like a hog."

"Adds luster," Dara said. "Don't worry. You're still my main squeeze."

Annabelle didn't share the feeling, yet she didn't want to offend Dara; they would be working together in the morning. She inched toward the dance floor.

"Want to go upstairs?" Dara asked.

Annabelle kept moving. "I'm too wound up over Karen."

"I can help you unwind."

"Not tonight." Annabelle grabbed a blue drink from a passing tray and swigged alcohol so sharp she closed her eyes until the sting died down.

Dara followed her to the dance floor. "Outland moonshine. Come on, loosen up."

Annabelle dropped the drink on a table. As much as she wanted to wash away thoughts of the raid and the arranged marriage, she didn't want to get drunk. It wasn't just because she had to drive her sister home and couldn't show up in the morning hung over. She didn't like how gloomy it made her, and she didn't want to pass out and wake up next to Dara again.

Two daughters of Knoxville's elite lay slumped on the wood floor. Many of the dancers wobbled, not the graceful revelers they supposed themselves to be. That had been Annabelle on too many nights, trying to escape a stifling life of limited choices. She wanted to scream and did, getting a chorus in reply, the rebellious anger of a generation of girls who had everything except a reason not to silence their minds.

Dara grabbed her hand. Annabelle led them to the dance floor; it was best to keep moving. While dancing, she thought of Mom's stories of George. The boy she saw didn't look so tough.

Music swelled like a balloon inside her, pushing away thought. Or was it the alcohol or whatever they mixed in? All around, mech warriors let off steam, along with privileged daughters, including Battani's spawn, passed out in the corner. *Why not marry* her *to Edwards?*

Leaving the dance floor, Annabelle grabbed a fistful of greasy, illicit fries to soak up the illegal alcohol. Then she popped a forbidden chocolate-covered cherry with a banned caffeine kick. It was a night to let loose, yet this all felt lame.

"What's eating you?" Dara joined Annabelle at the bar. "You're wound tighter than a virgin mech. Let it out." She placed her arm around Annabelle's shoulders.

Annabelle pulled away. "I want to be alone."

"We're planning another Outland Safari. Why don't you come Monday and lose this tension?"

"I don't need pressure tonight, Dara. My skin's crawling and until it stops, I need to be alone." One thing that got her skin crawling was thoughts of riding into an Outland village like cowgirls in mech gear. The Union complained of Outlanders breaking the peace but never mentioned safaris by warriors and Tenn-tucky elite. Rope yourself a live Outlander.

What's the appeal? To try what's forbidden at home. Annabelle wondered if this was better than the other dirty secret: young girls committing suicide.

Seeing commotion in the back of the huge hall, Annabelle weaved her way through the crowd for a peek. A muscular boy stood on a makeshift stage, wearing a maroon collar. He spun his shirt like an exotic dancer. His biceps were as thick as those of men she fought in the arena. She got goose bumps thinking of touching his rippling muscles. *It's a guilty pleasure to want what you can't have,* she told herself. Her heart thumped to a heavy beat of music to which he was gyrating.

Janine joined her. "What's the big deal? I thought the whole point was that we didn't need guys anymore. They're big and brutish and smelly."

"Not when you clean them up." Annabelle could only imagine.

Janine frowned. "You're not turning hetero, are you? Think how tough that would make your life."

Annabelle put her arm around her sister. "No, precious. I'll always love you, but don't you get even a twinge of guilty pleasure watching him?"

"No! I don't mind you dressing like a guy 'cause you're sweet underneath, but look at him. He's like a side of beef."

"Wouldn't you like to sample a juicy steak?"

"Yuck." Janine sauntered off toward the bar.

Cameras flashed as several girls tugged at the boy's jeans. He swatted them away and received a jolt from his collar. In the corner stood the girl with the remote, dressed like a gangster from the 1920s, a popular rebellious theme. The padded costume disguised a lean mech warrior who planted the remote in her mouth like a cigar.

Emasculated, the captive danced with twitchy, hesitant movements. Girls tugged, punched, and shouted at him.

Annabelle considered trying to stop this until she spotted Dara up front leading the chants. The amazon was the one warrior she couldn't afford to alienate. Given the dearth of men, Annabelle decided guys were an acquired taste she didn't need.

Dara grabbed the remote and jolted the muscle-guy. He collapsed to the wooden platform like a puppet. In mech training, Annabelle had seen the collar set on "high" turn an angry beast into a compliant puppy.

Prodded to dance, the boy got to his feet. Girls chanted, "More. More."

Annabelle turned away. There was nothing attractive about a naked guy. She joined Janine at the bar. "You're right. Not worth it. Besides, you're my sweetie, tonight and always."

Janine beamed. "I love the music. It helps drown the ugliness of what we do. I didn't drink much. I promise."

"Thanks. I need you alert and clear-headed in the morning."

"When President Zell takes over the Outland and removes the rebels, we won't have to worry about men anymore."

"Then you and I will be out of jobs." Annabelle squeezed her sister's hand, thankful she wasn't going wild. "Which might not be so bad." At least Janine wouldn't be at risk anymore.

"I don't hate guys," Janine said. "I've never met any except that one gardener."

"He's not typical."

Dara grabbed Annabelle's arm. "I bumped us to the top of the list?"

"List?" Janine asked.

"To play with our captive," Dara said. "Let's show him the penalty for running. Warrior officers get priority."

"Not me," Janine said. "Yuck."

"Suit yourself. Annabelle, if you want to lead, you can't be afraid of guys. He'll be wearing the collar."

Dara propelled her toward the stairs. Annabelle didn't want to go, but if she challenged Dara tonight, Dara wouldn't follow in the morning, which would put Janine's life in danger.

Upstairs, down a long hallway, they reached a room with the door open and several warriors standing around. Inside, the muscle-guy was roped to bedposts. A drunken brunette warrior slapped him. *Disgusting.*

Annabelle's stomach twisted into knots. How could they treat the boy like this? All he tried to do was escape a world that didn't want him. "I'm not doing this."

Dara glared. "It's safer with a spotter. This isn't the arena. He could hurt you before you could stop him."

The implication was clear. Annabelle either joined the group or faced the stranger alone. Leadership demanded a show of strength. "Give me the remote."

Dara grinned. "Take him, and I'll follow you into Hades. Come on, girls. Let's go."

The brunette scowled, slapped the boy again, and joined the other warriors following Dara.

"I'll be outside if you need me," Dara said.

Annabelle shut the door and approached the muscle-bound guy. He curled up awkwardly on his side, since his arms were still strung to the bedposts. He didn't look like a beast, more a wounded puppy. Yet injured animals were dangerous. "You got a name?" she whispered.

"Jim." Even his voice sounded meek.

She saw rope burns on his wrists and ankles. "You shouldn't have run."

He had a sweet, boyish face and looked to be 16 or 17. In fact, he was rather like a redhead she had rescued once. Well, actually several times.

"Do what you came for," he said.

Something primal stirred inside Annabelle. She was alone with a guy. But this was wrong.

She had to do something, or Dara would barge in. "Oh, baby, give it to me," she yelled above the music. Then she whispered. "If I help you escape, where will you go?"

The boy looked up with sad gray eyes. "Too late for me. Please help my little brother over the border. They sent him to the Oak Ridge Geek Institute. It was killing him."

"Come on, do it," she screamed. "You know I'm a mech warrior."

"You're not like the others. Please. Tommy's a good kid, fifteen. He can't make it on his own."

"Yes, yes." Annabelle squeaked the bed. She whispered, "Too risky."

"He's in the woods east of here. Please. You're his only hope. He'll starve."

Annabelle dropped onto the bed, then got to her feet. She held the remote and inched toward the door.

"Please!" he said.

She triggered the collar, sending him into mild convulsions before he lay still. She loathed hurting him, yet she couldn't allow him to utter another pleading word.

EIGHT

Geo expected Pa to be waiting when he got home, upset that Geo hadn't harvested tomatoes, weeded potatoes, or fed the chickens. Pa might skin him alive or worse. *No more books until you learn.*

Pa wasn't home. Instead, Geo's three-year-old Lab, Ralph, bounded up to welcome him. He was a good guard dog. Geo scratched behind Ralph's ears and set out a meat stew.

But I have learned, Geo said to himself, *from books, about another world I want to explore.* He imagined a world full of families living together with a mom as well as a pa and siblings. He shrugged. That was another era.

Geo donned deep-infrared goggles and turned on an infrared beam. He fed chickens in the barn around the rock-face from the cabin, and thought about the girl with a poor-fitted brown wig, dangling blonde hair, mean mustache on soft lips, and turquoise eyes. He tried to imagine gazing into those eyes or touching her face, which sounded weird yet comforting. Then he thought of his mom, and wondered what she looked like. "Why don't we have pictures, Pa?"

Pa wasn't there to answer.

Whiffs of cooking smoke from hundreds of neighbors' fires filled the dense air. Fighting weariness, Geo used the pale green glow of the goggles to locate patchworks of plantings between clusters of trees. He needed to harvest tomatoes and weed the corn before Pa got home.

Pa had gone to great lengths so Civ satellites wouldn't notice the farm and Civ mechs would leave them alone. Plots were less than ten-by-ten, spread over the south face of the mountain, which also improved pest resistance. Two summers ago, when a vicious mold attacked one field, he and Pa saved the others.

To Civ drones, this land looked like dense forest. Pa had laced the treetops with a lattice of solar "leaves" that generated electricity while allowing sunlight through to the garden plots below. He was clever, and Geo wanted to learn more. Yet there was another world beyond this patch of forest, filled with girls and other wonders.

Ignoring the heat, Geo resumed his work, wondering if this night would bring any more surprises.

* * *

Sweat trickled down Annabelle's neck as she held her helmet and stood at attention in the garage of the base complex, surrounded by sister warriors and armored vehicles.

Commander Samantha Hernandez greeted her pre-dawn warriors, her throaty voice filling the cavernous space. "Be careful. I don't want another day like yesterday with Karen and Wendy. Watch for this new explosive. And ladies, it was 101 yesterday, dropping to 50 tonight." She sounded angry. "Infrared won't help until it cools. Be vigilant, work together, and make us proud."

"Hoo-rah."

As other warriors left, Sam pulled Annabelle and her team aside. "I should have you court-martialed for disobeying a direct order."

"I have no excuse, Commander," Annabelle said. At least none she wanted to share. *Did you find out I'm helping Tommy?* Masking her anxiety, she kept her face still as stone.

Sam scowled, stretching the scar on her face. "No, you don't. Catching Cory is top priority and I have no option but to send you out. Don't screw it up. Dismissed."

Sweltering in her mech suit, Annabelle led Janine and Dara out of the garage to an armored four-seater by the chain link fence. Beyond were the woods that led to no-man's land.

Dara stared at the turtle-like vehicle. "You've got to be kidding. What's with this junk when we could airlift?"

Cranking her air on full, Annabelle opened the door and nodded for Janine to get in back. "Mobility." *And we've got a passenger you don't know about.*

"I should be running this mission," Dara said.

45

Annabelle climbed into the modified driver's seat and felt the crush of humidity. "Stop fussing," she said.

"It's hot enough without this sweat trap."

"You want off this mission?"

Dara sighed and slumped into the passenger seat. "Someone has to watch your back."

Annabelle made sure Janine was tucked in. Then she pulled the turtle out of the compound and sped toward the border.

"How do you plan on bypassing Outland checkpoints?" Dara asked.

"You crave adventure. Let me surprise you."

Dara's face twisted up as if she was ready to hit something. She sat and fumed. The pout wasn't as cute on her as on Janine.

When they reached the Union border, Annabelle flashed her orders. The young guard waved them through. Annabelle took the armored ATV to top speed, turbines thundering in her ears. She relished the power. Janine glared in the rearview mirror. *Sorry, Sis, hold on.*

Annabelle directed the turtle into the barrier clearing and sped uphill. The Outlanders' concrete wall, built to prevent mech intrusions, loomed to the right at the tree line. She sprung the turtle's wings and directed them down to hold traction. Approaching the hilltop, she shifted to lift, activated a jet blast, and veered toward an Outland clearing on the other side. The turtle leapt into the air, skimmed over the wall, and thumped onto a grassy field.

"What a rush," Annabelle yelled, hoping Janine wasn't throwing up in back.

"You're crazy," Dara said.

"I thought you liked crazy." Annabelle hoped Janine would keep her mouth shut and hold on. *The worst is over, Sis.* Annabelle couldn't use the com-link to comfort her sister without also sharing with Dara and the base.

Annabelle retracted the wings. She sprinted the turtle up a path into the woods, away from the border and the town of Biltmoor. *That should catch Outlanders and Cory by surprise.*

Dara checked her wrist-com. "Cory crossed a mile up."

Annabelle pulled off the path.

"I said a mile." Dara held out her wrist-com.

"We go on foot from here."

Annabelle put on her helmet, detached her mech suit from the seat, and rotated out of the vehicle. It took a moment for the helmet's link to connect Annabelle with sister warriors and the base twenty-five miles away. It was like talking to yourself and getting a reply, since it bypassed the eardrum and went straight to an auditory implant behind her ear. The first few times she had used the linking device she found it disorienting, like someone rooting around in her brain. Then the sense of connection and belonging overwhelmed the urge to remove the link. You weren't alone anymore. She felt Dara and Janine in her head, her sister a comfort and Dara always a concern.

When she had used private links with Janine during training, it drew them closer, enough that Annabelle hoped her sister would stay calm. Besides the link, the helmet provided sharper vision, infrared when it worked, and acute hearing: wind, crickets, sister warriors getting gear from the turtle, and mosquitoes outside the suit. She inhaled clean fragrance of woodlands, fresher than anything Knoxville had.

The suits were too hot even with air conditioning on full blast.

Annabelle led the others in the direction Dara demanded, even though she was convinced Dara's intel was wrong. Cory was too clever to fall into this trap, but fighting Dara now would kill their cooperation later, when lives were at stake.

As she moved away from the turtle, Annabelle prayed that Tommy had survived the jump. The night before, when she attached him to the turtle's underbelly, she told him, "As soon as we move out, give a hundred-count and make your way uphill to a cave. Then wait for a man called Bret Shaw."

Tommy acted scared and withdrawn, as if in another world. It irked her; she was putting her career, life, and family's welfare on the line for a kid she didn't know. "Are you listening?"

Tommy broke into tears. "You don't have to yell."

"Then pay attention."

"You girls are all alike."

"Explain," Annabelle said, fastening the shield beneath him.

"You think guys don't have brains because we're quiet."

Annabelle shook her head; she didn't know any boys to make such judgments. "I'm trying to help. Do you want to stay in the Union?"

"No."

"Then work with me."

Now it was essential that he got out of the harness before Dara returned. How stupid to take such risks. Yet the boy's hopeless situation had tugged at her until she left Janine at the party to rescue the boy, returning well past midnight for her sister.

When they reached the border from the Outland side, Annabelle scanned the forest with binoculars and infrared. *Useless.* "I don't like this. Cory wouldn't—"

"Cover me." Dara headed left, passing through scrubby bushes around a clearing. She disappeared behind a clump of trees.

Annabelle scanned in infrared and saw nothing but fuzz. "J, stay put. I'll scout the other side."

As she skirted the clearing, Annabelle saw the Outland wall, with no sign of Cory or Dara. From Janine's perspective she saw only green as her sister stayed low. *Good girl.* From Dara's view, Annabelle saw a door through the border wall, which seemed odd. *Who created that, and when?*

Dara acted confused, never a good sign. Then she moved to sever her link.

"D? Don't do it," Annabelle said.

"Couldn't go this morning. Give me some privacy."

"I'll be right there to stand guard." Annabelle started back.

"Stay put. I've got cramps and diarrhea." Violating protocol, Dara severed her link.

Annabelle ran back toward Janine, scanning trees and the border wall as she went.

Sam got on the com-link. "Get your butts over there. What the F is going on?"

"I'm on it," Annabelle said. "J, scan and wait for me."

Halfway to her sister, Annabelle was rocked by a blast. The explosion came from across the clearing.

Annabelle yelled over speaker, "D, link up. You okay?" She reached Janine, confirmed that her sister was fine, and together they ran. *Not again. Not Dara.*

Reaching the twisted remains of bushes, Annabelle halted. "J, scan for me." Steeling her nerve, Annabelle approached shredded bushes covered in blood. Her heart sank. "Sam."

"I see," Sam responded over com-link static. "Where's the body? Where's the suit?"

Annabelle followed a trail of trampled bushes and blood

through the opened door in the wall to cleared borderland. The trail stopped by a set of oversized tire tracks. "Outland motor-carts. They took her."

"Rangers heading your way along the barrier," Sam said. "Fall back. We'll send a team for Dara."

Unable to see the Rangers, Annabelle nudged Janine into the forest toward the turtle. As she did, she severed her link and removed her helmet.

Janine did the same. "I thought we weren't supposed to sever the link."

"Outlanders might have hacked our com," Annabelle said. "How else could they jump Dara? Put your helmet on, return to the turtle, and leave. Don't wait for me. I'll provide a diversion. Meet me at the rendezvous."

"I can't leave you." Janine placed her mech hand on Annabelle's shoulder.

"That's an order." Annabelle wanted to give her sister a reassuring hug, but mech suits were too bulky. She pointed her sister toward the turtle and crouched down to wait.

NINE

Distant gunshots interrupted Geo's dreams of crossing the barrier and seeing that strange girl with turquoise eyes in male clothing, and then visiting his mom. *Would she even want me after all these years?*

He eased onto his stomach and looked down from the hammock he had strung high up in a great maple overlooking Sunset Ridge and the border. Ralph was unusually quiet. Unlike other dogs, he only barked when he was happy, not when danger lurked, which Geo guessed was good since his four-legged friend didn't give them away. Instead, Ralph circled the tree as if desperately hunting for a place to pee.

Ralph looked up and saw Geo's nod. He faced north, tail straight as an arrow. With binoculars, Geo scanned the border and saw mechs, four, five, six, always in threes. They were chasing a man in Civ clothes. *Why aren't the Rangers keeping the mechs out?*

Geo dialed up magnification and saw a slight man in torn city clothes darting from tree to tree like a Civ city-dweller with no sense of how to evade. The man was quick, heading south, directly toward Geo's home. *Pa, should I help?* A refugee deserved refuge, but not a murdering rogue. In the back of his mind, he could hear Pa clearing his throat, but no advice followed.

Moaning, Ralph circled the tree, rustling damp leaves beneath his paws. He must have picked up mech scent.

"Okay, boy."

The mechs must not have seen the man, or they would have split up and whipped along parallel paths. The runner was heading toward Pa's place, which concerned Geo. If mechs captured the man, would he betray Pa?

Climbing down from the ancient maple, Geo considered his options. Many had escaped from Civ; some came from nearby prisons. Yet the runner looked like a wisp of a man, not the hardened, angry type Geo saw last spring, who nearly killed Pa 'cause he wouldn't hand over his rifle.

"Ralph, go home and guard the house."

The Lab gave a muted woof and bounded off.

With a rush of adrenalin, Geo sprinted ahead of the runner, sticking to a deer path to minimize noise. He saw the man to his left, barreling through thick brush. Geo needed to protect Pa's farm, yet he also had to help strangers. *Appalachian Code,* Pa had said. *Mountain hospitality.*

Geo ran beside the slender man, who looked larger up close. The man's desperate eyes flashed at him.

"You want to live, follow me." Mopping sweat from his eyes, Geo darted to the right, back toward the ridge. "Can you climb rope?"

"Not sure."

Bad sign, but Geo was committed. When he reached the ridge, he unfurled a coil of rope from his backpack, looped it around a maple, and fastened it with a hook. "Do as I do and be quiet."

Geo slid down the rope to a ledge and motioned for the man to follow. Then Geo squeezed behind a bush clinging to the ledge and disappeared into a tunnel. Leaving his pack and flashlight, he returned to help the man steady himself onto the ledge.

With graying hair, the man looked Pa's age, with soft Civ skin. "Now what?"

Geo gave the rope some slack and whipped it up toward the tree. He whipped the rope a second and third time before the hook came loose and the rope tumbled into the ravine. Reeling it in, he dragged the coils of rope into the tunnel. "Follow me." Grabbing his pack and flash, Geo crawled along a narrow underground path.

When he reached the tunnel's end, he emerged into sticky sunlight and squinted until his eyes adjusted. With binoculars, he scanned and saw three mechs approach the cliff's edge.

The man emerged from the tunnel and sat, catching his breath. *A Civ softy.* "Thanks. Saved my life."

Sniffing, Geo got no whiff except dumpsites from the west,

though he couldn't be sure mechs hadn't circled around downwind. "What's your story?"

The scrawny man held out his hand. "Cory Philips."

Geo shook, moved up the hill to scan farther, and spotted a drone diving into the ravine.

"Shouldn't we keep going?"

"Where you heading?"

"I was told a man named Craw or McGraw could find me refuge," Cory said.

That got Geo's attention. "You mean Shaw?"

"Yeah."

"You know him?"

Cory shook his head. "No, but I was told he helps people. The Union sent me to prison for being in the wrong neighborhood."

"You travel much?" Geo got up, hefted his backpack and rifle, and glanced at the ridge and the mechs. "Let's go."

Cory followed. "Before the war I saw Europe and Asia. Now, here at home, men can't leave their neighborhood. What a crock. Can you help me find Shaw?"

Geo led the way downhill away from the mechs. "What do you know about him?"

"Just that he helps escapees. They said head south from the border, but those mechs caught me. Hadn't been for you...You're quite a runner."

"Thanks. No more talking." Geo set a quick pace, heading home at an oblique angle in case the mechs followed.

* * *

While her sister ran to the vehicle, Annabelle set off explosives and sprinted up the mountainside, thanks to enhanced mech-suit performance. With helmet reattached, she had five minutes before the com-link reconnected. Sam would be furious, but Annabelle needed time to think. Rangers should not have known they were coming. They must have been monitoring the transmissions.

Halfway up the mountain, she stopped, crouched, and scanned. Below, ten Rangers on horseback appeared with dogs. There were several more on gas-powered mountain cycles.

When her com-link reconnected, Annabelle removed her helmet to sever the link, took a steaming breath, and attracted the mosquito air force. Despite how wrong this morning had gone, she imagined how romantic it might be to sit on this beautiful mountainside surrounded by nature. This was one reason she had joined mechs, not shooting people. Here she was free of social restraints that infuriated her: people telling her what to do, who to see, and that she had to marry some fat ex-wrestler for political purposes.

She wouldn't stay free for long if she didn't get moving. The dogs picked up her scent. Men on horseback and gas-cycles split up. Some headed her way, others toward the turtle and Janine.

Stay away from my sister.

Annabelle attached her helmet without the com-link, took aim, and fired measured bursts into those pursuing Janine. She dropped three and shot at two gas-cycles, silencing them. She tried to steady her breathing. She hated killing. It never got any easier, but she had to be sure they didn't grab Janine.

The dogs raced toward Annabelle, barking in chorus. Maybe she hadn't thought this through. Now they were all after her.

As much as she loathed harming animals, she was not about to let these men take her prisoner. She fired, heard howling from the dogs, and then quiet. She scanned farther down. Rangers broke off their pursuit of Janine to scale the mountain to her left while the remnant climbed her right flank. A rocket grenade exploded nearby, rattling her nerves.

Training took over; Annabelle sprinted up the slope. Sweat streamed down her neck despite the mech-suit's air conditioning on full. She stretched her arms back, used the gun-cams to aim and fired bursts. Focusing on three cams at once was confusing, but her life depended on it.

A rocket blasted a tree nearby and knocked Annabelle on her side. The mech suit cushioned the blow, though it felt like she had taken a pounding. She rolled away from the blast, fired at targets closing in, and slid downhill. Bracing herself on a boulder, she fired both guns at three men on gas-cycles charging her way.

An explosion hit her from behind, blasting her nerves and propelling her forward. She dove over the boulder and located four men on horseback above her. Careful to avoid the horses, she sprayed the riders with machine pellets, slicing one in half. Fighting the nausea of killing up close, she steeled her nerve. Riderless horses galloped past her.

Getting to her feet, she charged up the mountain and sprayed more pellets at targets on her flanks. An explosion crashed nearby, sending Annabelle spread-eagle onto rocky terrain. She was thankful for the suit. While she caught her breath, she rolled and spotted a tree to hide behind. It disintegrated before she reached it. These guys were relentless. *Okay.*

Annabelle launched three grenades. Rangers scattered. She cut them down, got to her feet and ran uphill, putting trees between her and where the RPGs had come from. Farther up, she stopped and scanned. Rangers no longer pursued, no longer fired. She checked her flanks and ahead before proceeding.

Her five minutes up, the com-link reset. Sam was on the line. "What the hell's going on?"

"Local hospitality." Annabelle hunkered down, seeing only trees.

"Why did you sever links?"

"We have a com leak. They were waiting for us."

"Is J okay?" Sam asked.

"Yes."

"Let me see her."

"She's tucked away." Annabelle hoped.

"Never fight solo or leave a rookie alone."

"I have company."

Annabelle severed the com-link and ran up the rocky shrub-covered terrain, savoring the suit's power to help her reach the summit.

After scanning in all directions with and without her useless infrared, she headed down the rocky crest toward the cave. She had to know if Tommy had survived and made it to the cave with all these Rangers.

The cave entrance was hidden in a crevice of rock. Annabelle removed her helmet so she wouldn't frighten the boy. She crawled into the cave, scanning with her flash until she spotted Tommy's face. The little boy crouched in the corner like a frightened mouse. She sighed. The boy's helplessness tugged at her.

"That's far enough," a male voice said.

Cold steel pressed her temple. *Oh, shit.*

"She's the one who helped me," Tommy said.

An intense beam flashed, like the mech-link penetrating her brain. "I'm Annabelle Scott," she said quietly.

The beam softened and lit up the cave. The husky man's face was tanned and leathery, his eyes intense black.

"You're Bret Shaw," she said.

"You shouldn't have risked coming here."

"I had to make sure Tommy was okay. It's been an eventful morning."

"I heard," he said. "Are Rangers still hunting you?"

"I don't think I left any."

Shaw laughed. "It's good to finally meet you. Tell your mom hi. Now get going."

"You really love her, don't you?"

When he nodded, his eyes drooped with weariness.

"She talks about you and George all the time. Is he here? I'd like to meet him." She wanted to add that she had seen George at the village, but she wasn't sure how Bret would react.

"He's home, doing fine. Mom would be proud of him. Now go and be careful. You've taken too many risks. As much as I'd love to talk, I don't want anything to happen to you."

Annabelle turned to Tommy. "This man will help you. I wish I could have saved your brother." She fished out Mom's package and handed it to Mr. Shaw. "This is for George. Oh, and there's a man I'm supposed to catch by the name of Cory Philips. He's been in Knoxville Maximum Security for selling stolen weapons. My boss suspects he's been spying for the Underground Railroad."

TEN

Geo and Cory reached the clearing to the glen. Ralph greeted them, barking rapidly as if telling all that had happened.

"You drink coffee?" Geo asked his guest.

"Sure," Cory said. "It's illegal in the Union, but yeah, sure."

Geo took Cory into the log cabin he called home and heated up coffee and a pot of stew. "What's it like over there?"

Cory sat in a wooden chair by a rough-hewn maple table that Pa crafted out of a tree stump and fallen limbs. "All my life I've lived in cities like Knoxville with lots of lights. Hardly see cars anymore except government folk. What we've got is lots of people."

"You mean girls."

Cory laughed. "I feel like an endangered species."

"What do you do there?" Pleased to be offering hospitality, Geo dished stew into one of Pa's hand-crafted ceramic bowls and handed one to Cory.

"Thanks. Used to be in sales, but no one buys from men now, so I do what I can: gardening, construction, cleaning crews."

Geo poured two mugs of coffee and peppered his visitor with questions about Civ and history while they ate.

"When the war broke out, the Union got mech soldiers," Cory said between bites. "They took the ports, cities, all but Appalachia, northern Rockies, and the Southwest. We didn't stand a chance."

"Why did you stay?"

"I had family in Knoxville. I couldn't imagine that things were as bad as the Patriots said. When the Union put up the barrier, it was hard to leave."

And to get back, Geo could attest, recalling how he and Carlos jumped the barrier. He wondered about that confused girl with turquoise eyes.

* * *

Annabelle reached the rendezvous, an alcove surrounded by boulders. The turtle was nowhere in sight. Janine sat on the ground without her mech gear, head tilted sideways, sobbing. Her brown hair draped across her sweat-soaked face.

Annabelle sensed a trap, but her scans revealed no one except her sister. She climbed nearby rocks and looked more closely. Infrared was useless in this heat. Regular light didn't reveal any sign of horses, cycles or men.

Her body on full alert, Annabelle jumped down and sprinted to her sister. "Where is your suit?"

"I left the sweaty thing in the ATV." Janine spoke as if she had a thick tongue. *Dehydration?* "Air-conditioning quit."

Annabelle had to get her sister to water. When she tried to lift Janine, she found ropes binding Janine's wrists and legs beneath her, and something that froze her blood—synthetic explosives.

Annabelle flipped out a knife from her mech-suit utility belt and began cutting rope. It was too tight to Janine's body for the clumsy mech gloves, but she dared not take them off.

Tears streamed down Annabelle's sweat-drenched cheeks as she looked for a trigger that would set off the explosives and turn poor Janine into what happened to Karen.

She sliced through one rope, didn't find a trigger, and started on another. With ropes loosened, Janine slumped to her side like dead weight.

"One false move and I'll release the dead-man switch." The gruff voice came from behind. A huge man with a scarred face wore a Ranger's uniform with general stars. Annabelle recognized him from mission videos: General Hanrahan. "Try anything and my men will finish the job."

Annabelle cursed herself for letting her guard down. Six Rangers crouched in a perimeter above them with rocket grenades trained on her and Janine. Alone, she would have chanced it, but she couldn't risk her sister.

"Remove your helmet and gear," Hanrahan said. "No tricks. Count of three."

"Sorry I failed you." Janine's brown eyes looked dull. Drool hung on her lower lip.

Annabelle hungered for the mech-link connection to her sister that was almost like reading each other's thoughts. Fantasizing wouldn't set them free, though. "You hurt her, you're all dead."

"Maybe not. Look down. One...two..."

She scooted back and realized the ground had been disturbed. *More explosives.* She released the latches to her helmet and pulled it off, pocketing the biochip in a collar sleeve. Only for Janine would she do this. Yet as soon as she did, she realized her mistake.

Something stung the back of Annabelle's neck like a huge bee.

Reaching back, she removed a syringe; found it empty. Its contents now circulated inside her. That realization came slowly, as if in a fog. *Focus.* She moved toward Janine. *I have to save you.*

She wobbled and fell. Mech hydraulics accentuated her clumsy movements. Annabelle cut more ropes binding Janine's feet, and her sister slumped to her side, motionless. *Fight, Janine. Run.* If they had mech com-link, Janine could hear these thoughts, but she looked to be unconscious now.

Annabelle found it harder to focus. One of the Rangers picked Janine up and carried her out of the alcove. Annabelle couldn't coordinate her movements to stop him. She tried to stand. The suit attempted to respond, but her muscles didn't give clear signals. "Don't hurt her."

"We won't hurt your sister if you cooperate," Hanrahan said.

What the—? Few people outside family and sister mechs knew Janine was her sister. What was going on? Annabelle pushed herself to her feet. "Let her go and I'll come without a fight."

A husky dark-complexioned man came into view. He was dressed as a Ranger with no rank insignia, yet the other Rangers bowed. "Maybe I like girls with fight." With his broad muscular chest, Thane Edwards looked the same as on mission videos she had reviewed; a tough professional wrestler who had used the war to seize political power.

Annabelle stiffened. "I'm not—"

She tried to move, saw double, staggered. It was standard kidnap procedure to drug the girl before carting her off. How did they—

ELEVEN

When she came to, Annabelle lay on a plush royal bed in a large, high-ceilinged room. It had to be Edwards' Biltmoor Towers. Her hands and feet were bound to solid bedposts. *Nice predicament. Sorry, Janine, Mom. Sam, what do I do now?*

She looked around, didn't see her sister. "Janine?"

No reply. She studied tight leather straps on her wrists. Her captor had stripped and re-clothed her in some ungainly fluff of material, like a medieval petticoat. *This isn't happening.*

The round face of a balding older man hovered over her. His thick chest sagged without the uniform, yet still hinted at professional wrestler experience. "Thane Edwards."

"Call me Husband."

"Not unless I agree. Now let me go."

Edwards dropped onto the bed. "Maybe we got off to a bad start. It must have been a shock—"

"Shock doesn't cover it."

He reached for her. "Sorry for the theatrics and scaring you and your sister. I wanted this to be a joyous occasion."

"This might be how you do things here, but not in my world."

"I was taken by your picture and how Governor Battani described you. I can offer much in the way of comforts and protection. I hope in time you'll come to love me."

"Where's Janine?" Annabelle tugged on her restraints to no avail.

Edwards brushed hair from her face. "You're far prettier than your pictures. I can be quite generous, given a chance."

Was this what it was like for Tommy's brother? "You've got me. Let Janine go."

"Would you consider being my wife? Let me woo you properly. I can be charming."

"You want to *date* me? After kidnapping me and my sister and chaining me to this bed?"

"I need a legitimate heir." Edwards ran his fingers along the underside of her arm, giving her goose bumps.

Annabelle willed herself to hold a stern expression. "I can't marry without trust—"

"Ah, you want money."

"Not a trust, you baboon. Trust. Honor. Fidelity. And there can't be trust as long as you hold Janine and me captive."

Edwards took her hand. "Please reconsider. Governor Battani and I want this deal. Reflect on all the lives to be saved if we had peace."

"I'm not property to do with as you please."

"Wedding's in five days. After that, your sister is free to go. And in case you're wondering, she's not in the Towers."

* * *

Geo glanced at the laundry and sewing he hadn't gotten to as he washed dishes in the sink tub. He had heard that long ago, daughters, wives, and mothers did this work. Since it was just Pa and him, Geo had to keep the place up. Mom abandoned him and Pa like worn-out shoes he needed to mend, when all he wanted was to be a man and see the world.

"You make these?" Cory's bony fingers held a fox Geo had carved from a fallen oak branch.

Hairs on Geo's neck bristled at a stranger touching his things. *I need to be hospitable.* He moved Pa's violin before that became a temptation. "Something to do on frigid winter days."

"It would bring a fortune in Knoxville."

"Not for sale." Geo dried a pot, glanced at the flickering oil lamp, and realized what had his nerves on edge. Where was Ralph? Geo slipped his Shaw .45 from the shoulder harness beneath his shirt and released the safety. "What are girls like in Civ?"

Cory picked up a carved eagle and brushed the wooden wings. "What you'd expect. Some cute. Most a pain in the—"

Pa banged the door open and pointed a short-barreled shotgun at Cory, who looked ready to pee himself. "No more talk of Civ girls," Pa growled.

Geo holstered his Shaw .45. "Cory's a refugee, Pa. Mechs would have—"

"That's enough." Pa didn't lower his gun. "Let the man speak for himself." Pa's puffy eyes made him look like he hadn't slept in days.

Cory repeated his tale. When he finished, Pa opened the door. "You can spend the night, but I need to talk to my son. Stand by that oak tree where I can see you."

Like a spooked mouse, Cory scurried out of the cabin into the moonlit night. Pa stood in the doorway, aimed Geo's .50 cal at the man, and whispered, "You haven't finished your chores."

"He was running for his life, Pa. I offered Appalachian hos—"

"There's a reason I don't invite strangers." Pa's dark eyes bore into Geo like knives.

Geo extinguished the oil lamp. "He didn't look dangerous."

"You weren't here last night."

"No, Pa."

"That Medallion boy?"

"You checking up on me?"

"What nonsense you get into this time?"

Geo continued washing dishes in the dark. "I didn't do drugs, Pa, I—"

"This farm won't run itself."

"I want to do what you do," Geo said.

"The Medallion cartel is bad news, boy."

"I'm not a boy."

"Then use your head like a man," Pa said. "If there's a showdown, the Medallion will look out for their own. Remember that. Carlos and Medallion lands are off limits."

"Carlos is different."

"We'd like to believe that, but when he enters the family business you won't be able to trust him. Drugs and kidnappings aren't good for anyone. His family is making too much to stop, believe me. I've tried talking to them."

"They don't sell drugs around here," Geo said. "Only in Civ."

"It's wrong, and the kidnappings have to stop."

Geo thought of Carlos wanting to kidnap those girls and was glad he hadn't. "I don't understand. If Civ is evil, why not let drugs weaken them?"

"They have families, too. We have a truce with Medallion. We don't bother them and they don't interfere. Let's not upset that."

"You're worried about Mom, aren't you?"

"Yes." Pa kept his eyes on Cory.

"Why don't you ever talk about her? Is it because she abandoned you, too?"

"She didn't abandon us. We agreed it would be best if you lived here. She hated guns and refused to carry. She would have been in constant danger. You want to be a man? Stand guard tonight and make sure our guest doesn't try anything. Pray you weren't followed."

"Yes, Pa."

"I need to check the factory and see what they need."

If Cory hadn't been there, Geo would have pushed to go see the factory and what marvelous new gadgets Pa was working on. All Geo had wanted to do was prove himself by showing hospitality. Now he prayed nothing bad happened.

Pa handed Geo the .50 cal, invited Cory in, and sat him at the table. "I hope you understand my caution. These are difficult times."

Geo relit the oil lamp.

"You're very kind to help," Cory said. "Were you with the militia?"

"Until it got cut to pieces," Pa said. "Spies sold us out, but that's ancient history. I can offer you a bed for tonight. It's too dangerous to stay longer. After church I'll find you a place."

"Can I come?" Geo asked. By the stern glare, he saw Pa didn't appreciate Geo asking in front of strangers.

Extinguishing the lamp, Pa headed outside. "Let me show you a bed and the outhouse."

Geo followed them into the moonlit night with Ralph trotting alongside. Was it possible Geo might get to see Biltmoor from closer than a mountaintop?

Next to a rocky outcrop that cast long, dark shadows was a small cabin that in daylight looked like logs splattered against the mountainside. It contained a bed, table, and washbasin. Pa unlocked the door and lit a small candle that barely took the edge off darkness.

While Geo brought fresh water to the basin, Pa showed Cory the outhouse across the clearing. "Don't wander off. There's more to fear at night than mechs and Rangers."

Leaving Cory, Pa led Geo toward the main cabin. "You know what to do."

Geo nodded. "If I watch him, can I come tomorrow?"

"Remember what I said about keeping your mouth shut around strangers?"

"Yes, Pa." Geo entered the cabin with his .50 cal and slipped out his bedroom window. Circling around out of sight of Cory's cabin, Geo reached the oak tree with a good view. He climbed up without making a sound. In the dark, he set up his hammock so he could watch Cory. Then he put on his goggles and activated his infrared G-Reader. Once again, the Biltmoor Corporation blocked the signal.

TWELVE

Senator Coriander Scott was in her study, preparing for another tough legislative session, when the front alarm rang. Reaching the foyer behind Helen, Cora's first image was the husky Commander, Sam Hernandez, in uniform. Cora mustered all her strength not to drop to her knees.

Helen steadied her as dread sank in. "Annabelle? Janine?"

"May I come in?" Sam asked.

Helen led the commander into the great room, where Grace joined them.

Cora braced herself against the wall. "Just say it, Sam. What happened to my girls?"

Sam led Cora to the sofa and sat next to her. "We lost Dara. Your girls were kidnapped."

"How?"

"We don't know yet," Sam said. "But they're alive."

"How can I help?" Cora focused on Helen and Grace, seated across from her. Both looked terrified.

"Is it true Annabelle is to marry Thane Edwards?" Sam asked.

Cora cringed at how she had failed to put a stop to that nonsense. "Battani pushed—"

"And Annabelle said no?"

Cora nodded. "She shouldn't be forced."

"Why would she disobey explicit orders and remove her com-link?" Sam asked.

Cora resented being interrogated when all she wanted was her girls back. "I don't know. She's usually careful." *When she doesn't feel caged.*

"Was she planning to run away?"

"She would never endanger Janine." Cora thought of Annabelle's overnight bag.

"We teach them not to cut the com-link. Is there anything you can tell me?

Cora shook her head. *Annabelle, did you try to meet George?* "Please bring them home."

Sam sighed. "You wouldn't happen to know why the governor called me to track an escaped con, would you?"

"No, why?"

"She asked for our best team and named Dara, Annabelle and Janine."

A stab in the heart for challenging Battani's budget games? "Why would she care about such details?"

"Not sure. I wanted to see your reaction."

"And?"

"This whole business stinks," Sam said. "Especially since they failed to catch the man."

"That's not like her."

"Can I speak to you in private?"

Cora dragged herself off the sofa and led Sam to the study. "What's this all about?" she asked when they were alone.

"I love my job and I'm proud of my warriors, but no soldier wants war. I've lost too many great young women, and not just in battle."

Cora leaned against the desk to steady herself. "Why tell me?"

Sam sat in a vinyl chair and studied shelves of paper books. "Battani's up to something with secret negotiations and your daughter's arrangement. It might end the longest war in our history or set off another round of fighting. She would like nothing better than to upstage President Zell. They're welcome to fight it out, but if the governor plays with the lives of my warriors, that's a different story."

"You don't trust the governor?"

"Do you?"

Cora refrained from smiling. "I don't believe a world without men would be more compassionate, based on our current leadership."

"Yet you remain in the government."

"Healthy societies need alternatives, even a small voice like mine. Unfortunately, diversity threatens harmony and thus the push for a male-free society."

"Women stopped having boys when they failed to adapt," Sam said.

"We failed to give them a future in our New Harmony."

"They've had better opportunities than girls over the years."

"You're baiting me," Cora said. "After 100 years of promoting our girls, we can't give 10 seconds to understand why boys failed and what that meant for our society. It ended in civil war, for God's sake. What's next? Hispanics? Blacks? The disabled? We're a nation of diversity and yet every day the Union squashes choice. It strikes me that George Orwell warned us against a society where everyone was equal except the commissars."

Sam laughed. "I miss our lively discussions, Cora. I'm glad you haven't lost your edge."

"I will if I don't get my girls back."

"I won't sleep until I find my young ladies," Sam said. "But your husband and son—"

"If they're still alive."

"They won't fare well. Battani and Zell want to end our Outland as the first step in taking Tex-SoCal and Northern Rockies. Zell would do it mile by mile. Battani has a bolder plan, I'm afraid."

"Without women," Cora said, "Outlanders are a generation away from extinction. Why not leave them be?"

Sam stood. "Love chatting with you, but I have two young ladies to find. As always, we didn't have this conversation."

Cora hugged the commander. "I wish we could go back to how things were."

"With all the challenges?"

"Maybe we wouldn't have so many girls into drugs, risky behavior, and suicide."

Sam nodded. "Amen."

THIRTEEN

Geo welcomed the first hints of dawn. Birds took flight. The smell of smoke told him neighbors were stoking fires for breakfast or to take the chill off the night. It was a relief after days of sticky heat. He flipped off the G-Reader's infrared screen and rubbed his eyes.

Cory had extinguished his candle at ten and hadn't left the cabin, even to use the outhouse. Geo saw the man's infrared image on the straw bed. When Pa stirred, Geo dropped down from the hammock and went inside to get ready for church. Though no one dressed up due to the rigors of getting there, he would wear clean camouflage jeans and a fresh linen shirt.

"You shouldn't have brought him," was Pa's greeting. "We can't take the risk."

Geo repacked his backpack. "If you'd let me see the world, that learning might stick, Pa."

"You think you're ready?"

"Yes, Pa." Geo checked his .50 cal, Shaw .45, and crossbow.

"Very well. Maybe it's time you got acquainted with girls down in Biltmoor."

"You'd do that on a Sunday?"

"Or not. Get Cory ready. We leave in 15 to pick up Peterson."

Old man Peterson belonged to these mountains long before the War. Arthritic, he depended on his son and the kindness of neighbors like Pa. Every week they stopped on the way to church, approaching with caution because Peterson's first response to visitors was the shotgun, and at seventy, his cataracts were cloudy.

Leaving the mares tied up, they approached the clearing on foot. Pa crouched down, pulling Cory with him. Six Rangers sat on horseback in a semicircle around the front door. Peterson stood in the doorway holding his double-barrel.

Sliding behind some holly, Geo aimed his .50 cal at a Ranger.

Pa motioned caution. "Hanrahan."

The name gave Geo chills. The General had a reputation as a man not to be crossed. He had skinned one recruit alive for going AWOL to visit his dying pa.

Hanrahan sat perched on the finest black stallion Geo had ever seen. "You haven't paid your land tithes, old man. Drop your weapon and bring your son. He's old enough to ride. We'll take him for your debts. No one gets hurt."

Geo wondered why the old man just stood there.

"You take my son, might as well kill me," Peterson said. "He's needed on the farm."

Hanrahan cackled like a crow. "This pathetic scrap of land? He's more use to us. Don't make us come after him."

"I'm not budging."

What was he thinking? He only had two shots.

"Move, old man," Hanrahan said.

"You've left me nothing." Peterson leveled his shotgun at Hanrahan.

When Geo took aim, Pa pushed the barrel down.

Rangers drew. Everyone fired at once. Peterson's body jerked forward and dropped onto his wooden porch. A Ranger fell from his saddle. Another held his chest. Hanrahan and the others dismounted and rushed the door, stepping over Peterson's body. Moments later, Hanrahan dragged Stu Peterson out to the horses. After having his men bandage two soldiers and place another over his mount, Hanrahan led his troop off.

As the clomp of hooves died away, Pa ran to the porch. "You okay, Pete?"

Peterson sat up, raised his shotgun, and shakily reloaded. "Bret, that you? I'm not as agile as I was." He held up arthritic hands. "Damned mechanism jammed. I had them."

Geo helped Pa bandage Peterson's arm, a flesh wound. "I don't understand. They shot you."

Peterson winced. "Vest I picked up during the war."

"Lucky they went for the chest," Pa said. "Let's go."

Geo heard gas-cycles roar up the hill. Hanrahan would leave nothing for Stu to return to, including his old man.

"Give us a hand," Pa said to Cory. "Grab food and supplies."

"Let me, Pa." Geo rushed into the cabin.

There wasn't much besides two mattresses, a Franklin burner, and a backpack. Maybe Peterson had planned to flee. Geo grabbed the backpack, filled with canned garden vegetables and turkey jerky. He grabbed a rifle from the wall and rushed out the back as gas-cycles approached the clearing out front.

He grabbed Peterson's mare and rode bareback to catch up with Pa and the others. Looking back, he saw Rangers set the cabin on fire. On horseback, Geo and the others circled around the burning cabin, bypassed the road, and took the long way along deer trails through the forest.

"What am I to do now?" Peterson asked as they followed the dirt trail to the local parish of the First Appalachian Assembly of God. "Stu's all I got. He's a good boy, but he ain't no soldier. And these hands." He held up gnarled fingers. "Can't start over. I couldn't work the farm if I did."

"We'll find something," Pa assured him.

Geo wanted to offer to bring the old man home but decided to wait until he was alone with Pa. He had read that Civ had medical and social security for folk like Peterson. The Patriots had abolished those when Appalachia seceded and eliminated taxes. Here you were free to make anything of yourself as long as you tithed to the church and Thane Edwards. His Biltmoor Corporation shops charged outrageous prices, which Pa refused to pay.

"I want no charity," Peterson said, wincing in pain.

"I know," Pa said. "But you're among friends. Let's pray for guidance."

"And pay Edwards for the privilege," Peterson said. As head of the church, Edwards received proceeds from the collection plate, leaving the local parish poor like the people it served.

Unlike the huge crystalline Cathedral in Biltmoor, the local parish was a larger version of neighboring log cabins with a sharp angled roof and a wooden cross that Geo and Pa helped replace last year when the old one rotted. They approached a nearby hitching post with dozens of mares. Geo was thankful to see no Ranger stallions or gas cycles.

They crossed a grassy knoll and stone steps, and entered through the oak doorway. The pews, enough to seat eighty, were almost full.

Pa motioned for Cory and Peterson to sit in back. Then Pa talked to a wisp of a boy Geo didn't recognize, another refugee, maybe. Up front stood a simple pine cross Christ might have appreciated over the ornate images Geo saw in art books. Burning incense failed to mask the odor of rotting wood and the ammonia used to clean the stone floors.

Pa came weekly to check on his extended family: refugees he helped and farmers left destitute like Peterson. Work hard, provide for yourself, and prosper, Edwards said in his nightly broadcasts, though it was hard to thrive when he took your only son.

With limited government, only the strong survive, Pa would say.

Geo saw the same faces: boys and fathers with stories of escape, resettlement, and hiding from Rangers. Geo waved to the compadres he had rescued. Mickey looked like he wanted to talk, but the man he was with grabbed his arm and made him sit. It's best to be obedient in church. Up front sat Zak, a big lug of a boy with a bushy beard and long, unkempt hair. He winked and returned his gaze to the altar before his pa "beat some sense" into him. Next to him sat his brother from a different mother and father, a boy like Zak, whom Pa had relocated.

Pa sat. Reverend Horace began the sermon, and Geo tuned it out. He had heard it before: rants against Civ and sin and the need for salvation from a grizzly young preacher with a thick black beard, sent to minister the heathen mountaineers not accustomed to church. Patriot Reverend Buffett started The First Appalachian Assembly before the war, but most of the millions crowding the Appalachian Secession were refugees, not Patriots.

Geo wondered how many of these men had wives or daughters, since females never ventured out for fear of rogues and Rangers, though Geo couldn't see much difference.

"Beware your lust for the female," Reverend Horace said. *Reverend Horse,* Geo thought, since the preacher's rants sounded like braying.

"Lust turns you away from our Lord and makes your mind soft so you fall prey to their wiles. They're a godless people, those Civ girls. They don't believe in Our Lord." He wiped drool from his chin and continued like a gas-cycle gaining momentum. "They know your lust. They exploit your yearning and twist you into destroying your family and betraying your friends. Best put them out of mind. Get about your business of leading the righteous life."

Is that Lord God or Lord Edwards? Geo wanted to raise his hand like when Pa gave lessons and ask where the next generation of Patriots would come from. Pa said it wasn't proper to interrupt a sermon, and it didn't matter because certain people don't let facts change their deeply-held beliefs. It was simpler having one leader for civic and religious matters; Edwards said so when he took over. *Simpler for him.*

"Praise Our Lord for your freedoms." Horace motioned, and collection plates started their rounds for praise to be amply expressed by these poor parishioners. "Stand strong against the evils of D.C. with their oppressive government and hands in every part of your lives." Yet it had been decades since D.C. had any influence over their lives, except for mech intrusions.

Pa paid double to cover Cory and Peterson and passed the tray. It was hard to tithe when Biltmoor Corporation paid little for the tools and food that locals produced.

As soon as the service ended, Geo ran outside to purge the braying with the scent of forest flowers. Home-fire smoke from the north meant cooler weather was coming.

Pa introduced Cory and passed out home-brewed whiskey. *It always helps to bring gifts,* Pa would say. Then the men exchanged stories and gossip. They complained about tithes, drafting sons, Edwards, and where to place refugees. Once a week, folk who otherwise rarely saw each other gathered here. Afterwards, some snuck into Biltmoor to visit bars and cathouses, on Sunday no less. It was a day of rest, after all.

Geo found the new boy by the horses and introduced himself. "You just get here?"

The stick-thin boy nodded but didn't look up. He swatted a mosquito and shooed others.

Zak barreled over with a broad grin and slapped Geo on the back. "This a boy or a Civ girl?"

"Hey, guys." Mickey joined with the twins. "My foster dad said there'd be vittles."

"Have to cook them," Geo said. He introduced everyone to the new boy, Tommy, who kept swatting mosquitoes. Geo dabbed ointment behind his ear. "That should help."

Tommy looked up. "Thanks. Your Pa brought me." He explained how his brother helped him escape. "But they caught him and now he's gone." He started crying.

Zak slapped his own forehead. "We got ourselves a girl."

"Enough," Geo said. "He lost his brother, probably his only family, and got dumped here. Give him a break."

"Aye-aye, sir." Zak saluted. "I mean no harm, Tommy."

"What do you like to do?" Mickey asked.

"Quantum computers and info-net." Tommy smiled, then shrugged as the other boys stared.

"What's that?" Zak asked.

"He's a geek," Mickey said. "Civs put them in institutions to pick their brains."

Tommy nodded.

"Could be useful," Geo said, trying to make the kid feel better.

"How?" Zak pushed his long hair back. "Only Thane Edwards has computers."

"Who's Thane Edwards?" Tommy asked.

"You kidding?" Zak said.

"They're isolated," Mickey said. "A friend's brother got sent. They don't tell you squat."

"Like here." Zak wrapped his arm around Tommy's shoulders. "Ten years ago Edwards was bishop. He challenged Thane Burke to a Patriot's duel, killed him, and became thane."

"How do you know?" Geo asked.

"My pa told me. Edwards took over Biltmoor Corporation and now he runs everything."

"I mean the Patriot's duel. What is it?"

"Damned if I know. Edwards said Burke was illegal and killed him." Zak puffed up his chest. "Maybe I should try."

"I don't think it's that easy."

Zak deflated.

Geo turned to Tommy. "Thane Edwards is over our region, but President Hardcastle is over all of Appalachia."

"He disappeared when Edwards took over," Zak said. "Rumor has it he's in Civ with a gorgeous wife."

"Don't believe everything you hear," Geo said. "Anyway, Edwards thinks he's the successor to Hardcastle."

Pa motioned that it was time to go into Biltmoor.

FOURTEEN

When she awoke from a restless sleep, Annabelle found herself alone, still on the bed, the restraints tight around her wrists and ankles. She wondered where Edwards would hold her sister. She had to rescue Janine, but she needed mech gear to have a fighting chance of getting them both to safety. Where could she find that? At least her mech clothes were on the antique dresser, along with the biochip she had palmed before Edwards drugged her. She hoped.

Long drapes hung over a rectangle of light, a window she could escape from, if she got free. She twisted and turned but couldn't get two limbs close enough to use her training. "Anyone there? I need to use the bathroom."

She tugged her restraints; the posts held solid and the leather tightened. *Janine, I'm sorry, I've let you down.* Annabelle tried to roll over, hoping a different perspective would help. The door squeaked open.

"Excuse me," a woman's voice said. "I didn't know this room was occupied."

"Ms. Cappeli?" It was Annabelle's tenth-grade English teacher, looking older and more wrinkled, and dressed in a white maid's uniform.

The woman closed the door and approached the bed. "Child, what are you doing here? I heard about the wedding, but that's not until Thursday."

"I know I wasn't your best student, but please help me. I don't want to be here."

The woman grabbed Annabelle's right wrist and examined the leather bindings. "You were a handful, quite spirited, destined for more than—well, before all this you might have become an astronaut or something." She released the binding and moved to the right ankle.

Annabelle pulled the binding off her left wrist. "Thanks, Ms. Cappeli. You have no idea—"

"You were a talker. Except when you were keeping secrets, that is." Ms. Cappeli released the right ankle. "Hurry. If anyone comes, it won't go well for either of us."

Annabelle untied her left ankle and climbed off the bed. She rushed to the dresser, checked a secret sleeve in her collar, and found the biochip. "Can I borrow your clothes?"

After stripping out of the petticoat, she pulled on her mech uniform and looked for anything she could use to escape. The huge bedroom held only the ornate bed and empty dresser.

The woman tugged off her maid's outfit. "You should tie me to the bed."

"I can't do that, Ms. Cappeli. Come with me?"

Down to her street clothes, the woman handed Annabelle the white uniform. "I'd slow you down. Besides, only two weeks left on my sentence."

"You weren't kidnapped?"

Cappeli shook her head. "I took a liking to our gardener and tried to help him. They had him wired. They gave me three months for showing kindness. I'll get worse for this, but you deserve a chance."

Annabelle pulled on the loose-fitting maid's outfit over her mech uniform. She gave her former teacher a hug. "I owe you. Please come with me."

The woman climbed onto the bed and fastened her own ankles. "Come on. The sooner you go the better."

With reluctance, Annabelle bound Cappeli's wrists. "You wouldn't happen to know where they're holding Janine?"

"Sorry. Now there was one of my best students. She—"

"Or my mech gear?"

Cappeli shook her head. "Good luck, Annabelle. Make these sacrifices count for something."

Annabelle put on the white cap and glanced out the window. She saw a huge plaza surrounded by shops. It looked a lot like downtown Knoxville, except for the names: Biltmoor Patriot Bank, Edwards Fine Clothing, and Thane's Emporium. She was in Edwards' Biltmoor Towers, a long way from freedom, and too high to jump.

Taking one last look around, Annabelle thanked her former teacher and slipped into the hallway, which was lined with tapestries and paintings like some French palace. *Didn't Marie Antoinette donate her head for such extravagance?*

She hurried down the huge hallway, wondering where to look for Janine. At the end was a stairwell leading down.

Annabelle stopped, listened, and realized she was wasting time. There had to be cams. She made it down to the first floor before running out of stairs. She exited into a carpeted hallway and headed right. The bass discordance of male voices thundered in her ears. She slipped into an empty conference room with tall windows overlooking a side street and another building that obscured the sky.

Opening the door a crack, Annabelle watched uniformed guards hurry down the carpeted hallway to a wide marble lobby. Maybe they had discovered Ms. Cappeli.

Annabelle knew there was a dungeon beneath the Towers, though the stairway to it wasn't on the floor plan she had studied for a mission. Was Janine there, or was Edwards telling the truth and was holding her elsewhere?

More guards appeared by the stairs outside her door. She eased the door closed and looked around. There was nowhere to hide. If she didn't escape, all was lost; Edwards wouldn't give her another chance. *The windows.*

Forsythia hid the bottom part of the glass. She tried the latch; it was stuck. *No time for this.* She hit the window frame; it rattled. *Damn.* She forced the latch, pulled the window open to a blast of warm air, and knocked out the screen.

Annabelle climbed over the window ledge and eased out behind the forsythia. She inhaled freedom. *Sorry, Janine, the place is swarming. I don't even know where you are. Besides, I have my own problems.* Neither the white maid's outfit nor the mech uniform she wore underneath would blend into this commercial neighborhood. Women here were clad head to toe in full-length dresses that gave Annabelle the creeps, harking back to a time when women were chattel.

What to do? Why, when in Rome—Thane's Emporium.

* * *

Geo trailed after Pa and Cory on horseback down the mountain to Biltmoor. Geo didn't want to miss his first chance to visit the capital of South Appalachia.

"These are simple folk," Pa had told Cory when they set out, "with little to offer those who can't farm. We'll do better for you in town."

"Thanks," Cory said. "It's good to be free from Civ."

"Amen."

The most prominent features in the distance were the glass-encased Biltmoor Towers on a hill in the middle of town and the stone and crystalline Biltmoor Cathedral nearby. Here at the south edge of town stood Biltmoor Corporation factories, spewing industrial gases from tall stacks. Factory worker shanties nestled into the shadows of the belching behemoths. Beyond them, subsistence farmers tended small fields. Odors from meatpacking and food processing hung in the air like an oily cloak.

To the west, Edwards had cleared forest to provide lumber for Biltmoor construction. He then turned the land into small farm plots that provided marginal livelihoods for those unable to find jobs within the Biltmoor conglomerate. Between the fields and town were Biltmoor trading houses that bought raw goods from mountaineers at low prices and sold tools and equipment at prices that kept them indebted to Biltmoor and Thane Edwards.

A few miles to the east stood the border, a series of walls and checkpoints to prevent free flow of people between Biltmoor and Grieveport, a ghost town except on trading days. Surrounded by border walls, this slice of no-man's land was a wide field dotted with colorful tents that glistened in the sunlight. This being Sunday, the day of peace, the trade zone was open for business.

Geo scanned the field for hints of what might be for sale. "Can we visit the market?"

"Too risky, and I have business in town." Pa gave him a stern look to drop it, and guided his stallion down toward one of the roads leading into Biltmoor. "Stay close and don't talk."

The moment they reached the paved road, young boys with bloated bellies in ragged clothes ran up to him. Hands out, they begged for anything he could spare. Geo ached to help, though he had heard of travelers mauled over a loaf of bread.

On both sides, makeshift dwellings burrowed into rock. Roofs made of aluminum panels sheltered old women sewing and weaving. It had been so long since he had seen so many women that Geo couldn't help staring. One of the ragged boys grabbed his backpack. Geo brushed him away and tossed a piece of jerky. Two bigger boys wrestled it away. *Is this really freedom?*

Pa cradled his rifle and galloped his brown stallion past shanties onto the main road, which was lined with open-air shops that looked ready to blow over.

A man in tattered rags ran alongside yelling, "Good boots, leather boots, and saddles. Low prices."

Pa grabbed the reigns to Cory's horse and trotted on. A few blocks further, as if they had passed an invisible barrier, the begging ceased. Enclosed storefronts in sturdier buildings offered clothes, food and other items mountaineers made themselves or did without. Geo wanted to see the wonders up close, like factory-canned food, gas cycles, and electronic gizmos.

A battered pickup truck roared past, spooking the horses, and parked in front of the Biltmoor Patriot Bank. Geo steadied his horse.

Pa pulled into a corral that held a half-dozen mares. "Best we walk from here."

He paid the corral master, a scrawny man not much older than Geo, who stared at them with dark, wary eyes. When they reached the street, several gas and electric cycles whizzed past, the kind Geo wanted for his birthday and Pa said they didn't need. Geo needed his own money so he could make his own decisions.

Behind Thane's Emporium stood huge aluminum buildings Pa said were Biltmoor Corporation warehouses and, behind them, prefab homes for those who worked there. Geo was like a blind man gaining first sight. He stared into Edwards' Clothing and Biltmoor Tool & Equipment, imagining what he could buy if he had money.

The few females he saw along the street, covered neck to toe in flowery dresses, were escorted by men. He stared into each woman's face for a glimpse of what his mom might look like.

* * *

Annabelle straightened the maid's uniform and strode onto the wide sidewalk down one side of the plaza. It was cleaner than downtown Knoxville; Edwards could afford the best. She darted across the truck-and-cycle lined street to Thane's Emporium and hoped that when she got out she could find at least one of the cycles that wasn't bio-locked.

A plump saleswoman in full-length floral dress pounced the moment Annabelle entered. "Can I help you?"

The maid's outfit was a dead giveaway that Annabelle didn't belong, but at least it was better than her mech uniform, which would get her arrested or killed. She took a risk. Removing the maid's cap, she let down her blonde hair. "I need something more befitting a thane's wife."

The middle-aged woman gasped. "Annabelle Scott?"

Annabelle nodded. "Excuse the deception. I want to surprise my fiancée. Will you help?"

The saleswoman showed off pricy fashions that were too puffy for Annabelle's tastes. She took several 19th-century outfits to the dressing room, where she put one on over her mech uniform. Feeling like some fluffy doll, she strode out to the saleswoman and asked her to deliver the rest to the Towers. She glanced across the street at the grand twelve-story building, connected by a three-story extension to an eleven-story high-rise, headquarters for Biltmoor Corporation and Thane Edward's palace wrapped into one.

The woman took the clothes.

"Thanks," Annabelle said and gave the saleswoman a hug. "It's a surprise. Please don't say anything until tonight."

The woman nodded. Annabelle counted on her greed to overcome her qualms. This sale ought to earn her a big commission, if Edwards pays.

Tucking her blonde hair under a pretentious pink hat, Annabelle glanced at the palace. *Where is he holding you, Janine? And when I find you, how do I get you home?*

From prior raids, Annabelle knew her way to the edge of town, but come nightfall, without GPS, she risked getting lost on the twisting roads through the forest. If Edwards caught her, this would become a life sentence.

She headed toward the Towers until she was out of the saleswoman's sight. *No point raising suspicion.* She scanned the cycles parked in a rack. A thin boy sat on a ledge, eyeing her. *So much for riding out.*

Guards and Rangers swarmed the towers, so Annabelle headed southeast. *I'll be back, Janine, when I have a plan and a way to find you. Hold on.*

Adopting the affected stride of the few women she saw, Annabelle walked five blocks. So far so good. When she stopped at a crossing, she realized she was the only unescorted woman, and she would be more conspicuous when she reached the poorer outskirts, where well-dressed women didn't go and crimes were common.

She headed back toward the Towers. *If I'm risking it, might as well be for both of us, Babe.* Ahead, Rangers filled the plaza and surrounding streets while cops checked the stores. Spinning on her heels and wishing she had flats, Annabelle entered Biltmoor Clothing and Attire, which was not as upscale as the Emporium. She glanced around at colorful displays of dresses and skirts she couldn't find in Knoxville, and wouldn't buy because they all came down to her ankles. She didn't have time for shopping.

Annabelle tried an ankle-length skirt, blouse, hat, and walking shoes, a poor match, though the skirt dragged and might conceal her shoes. Her problem: no money. She kept the new outfit on and bundled her finer clothing into a neat pile.

"I'd like this outfit," Annabelle told the gray-haired saleswoman, indicating the clothes she wore. "My husband will pay. I'll give you these fine clothes as collateral."

"I'm afraid we can't—" the saleswoman began.

Annabelle ran out of the store. Rangers drew nearer. They would interrogate the saleswoman, which couldn't be helped. Annabelle hurried down a side street and into a residential neighborhood with no women. At the next street, she spotted Rangers moving house to house.

Taking side streets, Annabelle worked her way southeast, wishing she had the masculine outfit from the party. Every few blocks, neighborhoods grew poorer and stores plainer in what they offered. Soon she would be overdressed again.

It was Sunday afternoon. Once the town closed up, she would have to consider where to spend the night. Edwards expected Annabelle to come for her sister, and if she didn't do something unexpected, she would get caught and spend the rest of her life here. *Bear with me, Janine. I know you're suffering.* She kept moving.

By the time she reached poorer warehouses and working class

cottages, she was the only woman out on the street. Shopkeepers were closing their stores. She ducked into a clothing outlet that wasn't labeled *Biltmoor* or *Edwards*. Passing a young saleswoman, she grabbed boy's jeans, a drab blue pullover, tee shirts and a puffy cap. She slipped into a changing room. She tied a tee shirt tight around her breasts and tucked another around her waist so she could fit into the jeans. Finally, she stuffed her blonde hair into the cap. Problem: she couldn't pay.

Annabelle ran out the back door into a filthy alley, littered with beer cans. Several guys stood nearby drinking or something. She suspected something.

Behind her, the saleswoman yelled, "Stop, thief. Stop!"

Annabelle sprinted, crisscrossing side streets toward the east end of town. Whenever she spotted Rangers or cops, she jumped into shadows, praying she didn't meet ruffians who would hold her until Rangers arrived. With each breath, guilt grew over leaving Janine. *I can't help you if I'm strapped to a bed.* At least the air was cooling down, as Sam had predicted.

At twilight, she reached the shanties that encircled Biltmoor. Annabelle stopped. Beyond the shanties were fields, woods, and meandering roads. Without mech GPS, she could get lost. And where could she go? Back home to an arranged marriage?

Something pinged around Annabelle's thoughts. Janine had said her lost mech gear was in the *ATV*, a term she would never use. Had she stashed it in the cave instead? *Were you giving me a coded message?*

Rangers moved among the shanties, no doubt offering rewards for Annabelle's capture. She headed back toward town. If she couldn't reach the suit, why not try for Janine? Then she realized: even if she reached the Towers, and if Janine was there, and if Annabelle freed her, then what? Without help, she didn't have a prayer of getting them both out. She knew of only one place to crash while she figured this out: an establishment called Undercover. The place gave her the willies, creeps, and a thousand other discomforts.

That's when she spotted Bret Shaw. Annabelle took a deep breath and slid into shadows behind a Dumpster in the alley. With him was that little weasel-man Cory, whom Sam wanted her to capture or kill. She hesitated. Orders were orders. This man was a criminal. Yet she didn't want to harm Bret, and he was acting friendly toward the escapee.

With them was the bastard who killed Karen. Annabelle wished she had binoculars so she could better see his face. She hesitated. Could Bret help her and Janine? She didn't trust Cory. What if they were friends? No, her best bet was the boy, despite what he had done. She had to get him away from the others.

The three of them crossed the street and entered a doorway beneath the neon sign: Undercover. Annabelle sighed. *Men.*

She had raided the place several times to recover kidnapped girls. There were also girls working there instead of going to prison for crimes against the Union. With all its talk of protecting females, the Union supplied many of these girls. *Disgusting.*

Annabelle crossed the street and approached Undercover from the alley. She trembled at the thought of entering without her mech team. Being Edwards' bride-to-be was bad enough. Getting stuck here could be worse, and she was entering like one of the local girls. Hadn't the Union fought against this?

She suspected curious eyes and cams everywhere, but saw none. She would have to rely on instinct. Rummaging through the Dumpster, she found hairpins. She used them to pick the back door's lock. Once inside, she hurried down a dark corridor to a room where local girls changed into sexy attire to get bigger tips.

"You don't belong here," a husky female voice said.

Turning, Annabelle faced Haley, a sister warrior she used to party with. "What are you doing here?"

"Three months for helping a guy over the border. You?"

"I need to talk to someone who just walked in."

"You have any idea what you risk by coming here?" Haley asked.

"I'm not on a raid, Haley. I need help. Please don't betray me."

"You know I won't."

"After I talk to him," Annabelle said, "why don't you come with me?"

Haley shook her head. "One week and I'm free. If I run." She closed her eyes. "I can't return home and I can't imagine staying here."

Annabelle nodded. "Help me get changed and I'll be gone before you know it."

FIFTEEN

Geo stared at the three-story brick building. A buzzing neon sign read *Undercover*. First-floor windows were boarded up; those on the second and third floors were shaded. He wanted to turn back.

"I need to see some people," Pa announced. He led them into a closet-sized foyer immersed in hot light.

Behind a thick pane of glass sat an elderly redhead who perused them with dark narrow eyes. Geo preferred open forest to buildings. He would have stepped outside but for Pa's grip on his shoulder. The closet plunged into darkness. A panel opened to their right, leading into a dimly lit room bathed in maroon.

Soothing music and floral fragrances drew Geo inside, or was it Pa nudging him along? Cory strutted to the far end of the large room. He passed small, round tables around which stood men in business or mountain attire and half-clad girls sporting long legs, flat bellies, soft shoulders, and—

Geo wished Pa had better prepared him, as Pa led him past girls in clusters by the bar. Some blend of saucy music and incense had him feeling more intoxicated than Pa's wine. He had read about mechanics and romance, but standing among so many pretty girls with dancing curls and breathtaking curves was unnerving.

"Don't worry," Pa said over the music. "Madam Chrissie will find you an easy partner."

That was the least of Geo's problems. His legs felt rubbery and his neck blistery hot despite air-conditioning blowing full blast. The room closed in around him—so many gorgeous girls.

82

"Can't I go with you, Pa?"

A husky woman walked up. Pa whispered in her ear and handed over a gold coin. The woman's face lit up. "We'd be delighted to introduce your son." She looked Geo over before striding off.

"I have to go," Pa said. "Learn all you can and enjoy." He left.

Geo wanted to follow, yet he didn't want Pa to think him a coward. Hadn't he said he wanted to be a man? *What's wrong with me?*

Madam Chrissie tapped his shoulder. He turned to face nine curvaceous girls lined up for display: blondes, brunettes and a redhead. They posed with expressions that ranged from silly to enticing. He couldn't choose, couldn't think. *I'm a deer in a flash-beam.* Cory was heading upstairs with a redhead and a brunette.

"Go ahead," Chrissie said. "Any of these girls will treat you special."

Geo took a deep breath and told himself this was what he wanted, what he hungered for. Yet it felt wrong. He wished he hadn't just heard Father Horace rant about lust and temptation, because he wanted each of these girls. He couldn't decide.

"Why not the brunette on the end with the pretty smile?" Chrissie whispered. "Choose, and I'll be back."

He tried not to stare at the girls, but their scent filled him.

A stunning blonde with turquoise eyes strolled toward him with an air of confidence. She took his arm and whispered in his ear, "You don't want those diseased ones. Pick me."

Geo hesitated before such a confident beauty.

"Men don't resist," she whispered. "They submit. You want to, don't you? You're not defective." She slipped her arm into his and tugged him toward the stairs.

Geo watched her from the corner of his eye. Something was familiar in the shape of her lips and nose and the color of her eyes.

"Shhh. You want me. I'm fresh. I'll make this easy."

Needing easy, Geo followed. Then it hit him. She was the girl who had dressed like a guy at the mansion with the mechs. Or maybe he wanted to see that because he needed something familiar to hold on to. *Is this what lust does to you?* He saw nothing masculine about her except perhaps her confident stride, and yet her hand was clammy.

She led him into a dimly lit, maroon-bathed room with a queen-sized bed and a stand for clothes. She closed the door. Geo dropped his backpack in the corner and pushed aside heavy drapes to look out onto a dark alley with garbage Dumpsters. This wasn't how he imagined his first time.

The girl did some bizarre dance, jumped on the clothes stand and bounced on the bed. Then she approached Geo. She studied him, her face soft yet determined, her turquoise eyes piercing. "I won't hurt you."

Taking a deep breath, Geo stared at the blood-colored drapes. He wanted her, but not like this. How could he explain this to Pa?

"You've never been with a girl before, have you?" she whispered. "Sorry, that sounded mean. It's not as frightening as it seems."

Geo stared out the window.

"Don't do that." Placing her hand on his shoulder, she pulled the drapes closed. "No telling who's watching. I'm Annabelle."

"Geo." He felt like wet spaghetti.

She cast a soft smile. "I haven't done this either. They kidnapped me and brought me against my will. Please don't turn me in. I need your help."

Was this the turquoise-eyed man-dresser he had seen in Civ? Had Carlos kidnapped her? Or was she manipulating him like Father Horace warned? "You know the penalty for helping escapees?"

"I do, and if we don't make noise, we'll have company. Do you want me?"

Geo closed his eyes. "Yes and no. It feels wrong."

She patted his arm. "Okay, then, let's fake it." She pulled him onto the bed with her.

Encouraging him to join in, she rocked back and forth. The bed made the most ungodly screeching. He started to laugh. Annabelle covered his mouth and dug her fingers into his shoulder.

He cried out. She rocked harder, he rocked harder, and it all felt ungainly and ridiculous. She punched him in the stomach.

"Holy Hell." Geo fell back holding his gut.

Covering his mouth, Annabelle leaned against him, and whispered, "Sorry. Had to be convincing. We haven't got much time. Soon they'll realize I covered the cameras and microphones."

Cams and microphones? Geo stared at her. "Who are you?"

"A girl in a lot of trouble. Please don't turn me in."

Holding his stomach, Geo lay on the bed and studied her

mesmerizing turquoise eyes, inviting lips, and the angles and curves of her face, quite striking in the shallow light.

Annabelle whispered, "Will you help me? I have no right to ask, but I'm desperate." She placed her hand on his hip.

Geo savored the delight of her touch. In his head, he heard the preacher warning that she was leading him into temptation. "How will you escape this house?"

"I have that covered." Annabelle brushed his hair back and stroked his face.

"Don't." Though Geo liked her soft touch, he felt her toying with him. "Even if you do, there's no way to leave town. If we get caught, they'll return you and kill me."

She leaned closer. "If I don't escape, my life is ruined. I can reach the woods, but I don't want to get lost in the dark."

"Catching you would bring a reward. Helping would destroy me and Pa."

Annabelle whispered her warm breath into his ear. "When I reach the circle southeast of town, which road should I take?"

Geo stared at her. His mind replayed Horace's warnings. "If you take any road, Rangers will catch you. They'll demand to know who helped."

"I'll never tell." She stroked his face.

He removed her hand and scooted away. "They'll know I was with you."

"Which road?" She inched closer.

"First road on the left circles town. The second leads to Pumpkin Patch and border checkpoints. You won't make it through town. There are ruffians in the woods."

"There's a cliff overhang that looks like a buffalo head. Where do I leave the road to reach it?"

"You've got to be kidding," Geo said.

"There's a cave, shelter for the night."

"You're nuts."

"I'm desperate." Annabelle stroked his cheek. "I'd do most anything if you'll help me."

Geo pushed her away. "Don't." Her desperation to flee tugged at his heart; a damsel in distress. It would be chivalrous and noble to help her. "You won't get far looking so beautiful."

Annabelle patted his shoulder. "Thanks for the compliment. Will you help?"

Geo stood up, sighing. "You'll reach a spot where two trees fell across the road. They were pulled aside and set up to stand like railings. Turn right and head up the mountain a few hundred feet. I wouldn't suggest this."

"I can't stay here." She stood next to him, too close.

Geo moved away. "Stay off the road. Stop often to listen for movement. These woods have ears. No lights. You'll have to travel by starlight."

She squeezed his hand. "Thanks. Two more things."

"What?"

"A ten-minute head start. Then yell for help. Tell them I escaped."

"I'm coming with you."

"I must go alone," Annabelle said. "Let me tie you up so they won't think you helped." She kissed him on the lips. "If they ask, tell them I suggested this. After I tied you up, I hit you. When you woke up, I was gone."

Geo removed his camouflage jeans and linen shirt, incredulous that he was going along with this. Yet Annabelle caught his fancy. She was special, an angel, or the lustful devil Father Horace warned about. It was too late. She bound his wrists and ankles to the bedposts. He tried not to think what Pa would say: *You fool.*

Annabelle checked the bindings, kissed him again, and smacked the side of his head, hard enough to draw blood. "Sorry," she whispered. "For effect."

She grabbed a small bag she had brought and glanced out the window. "Count ten minutes and call for help. Thanks for everything." She opened the window and slid out.

Geo couldn't move. He felt ridiculous, helpless, and used. Counting seconds, he wondered what he had gotten himself into. *What would it have been like to get to know you? Dang, what will Pa do when he finds me like this?*

SIXTEEN

Margarite fastened her bra, grabbed the rest of her clothes and slipped out of the ornate purple Louis XIV bed, a crypt within the tomb of Bishop Kolinski's royal bedroom. It was over, thankfully interrupted when the bishop was called next door to the rectory of the grand Biltmoor Cathedral. She tiptoed from the room using her designated back entry.

Her windowless cell was barely large enough for her small bed, a tiny dresser, and a chamber pot she had to empty herself because he locked her in when he was away. She pulled on her pink floral dress, feeling dirty from enduring the bishop's smarmy touch. It wasn't just that he was unattractive for a man; he acted effeminate like the girly-girls who washed out of mech training.

Margarite removed a stone from the outside wall of her room and pulled out a link-pad with earbuds that let her monitor conversations in the rectory. She couldn't take credit for the surveillance; that was Kolinski's work. Mech training had enabled her to hack into the system and keep her link-pad concealed.

Clarity was crisp on three images of the rectory, so she could keep the bishop in view. She knew the risk if he caught her, having seen justice firsthand from the man of God. It wasn't swift.

The bishop owed his position and his life to the two men who had come to the rectory for their monthly accounting. He measured his success by how full he kept the Cathedral, surrounding parishes, and his coffers on behalf of Thane Edwards.

Head of State, Cardinal of First Appalachian Church of God,

and Chairman of Biltmoor Corporation, Thane Edwards in royal cravat perused the ledger at a Revolutionary War era desk. General Hanrahan scanned video of today's service. Both seemed unaware the bishop was recording them.

Churches had done well under Kolinski for 20 years. He hoped to hang on for a healthy retirement, which required that he remain useful to Edwards. Built seven years ago, the stone and crystalline Cathedral was the bishop's crowning achievement and a shrine for Edwards. It packed more parishioners with rising collections despite the declining population in surrounding areas. The Cathedral was the second most prominent feature in Biltmoor, exceeded only by Edwards' Biltmoor Towers.

Hanrahan was missing part of his left ear, though he seemed to regard this as a badge of honor. He was dressed, as usual, in a gray Ranger uniform with five stars on his shoulders.

Bishop Kolinski tottered over to an oak wet bar. Beneath his plain gray robe, he wore baggy purple trousers on his chicken legs. It made Margarite want to gag.

The bishop poured three glasses of fine Biltmoor whiskey. "I've seen no sign of Montgomery or McCarthy for weeks." The fourth and fifth Biltmoor Corporation board members.

Edwards rose from the desk. The burly man had been a professional wrestler, hustler, church deacon, and hit man for some right-wing group before the war. "I want them gone." He downed his whiskey like water.

Kolinski stood uneasily. "Are the books to your liking, sir?"

Margarite had thought the man of cloth would be easy to handle given his weak legs, but when she had tried to stop his groping, she discovered his upper body strength. Escape would be impossible since he had her tagged with implants that let him know where she was at all times. *Well, two can play that game.*

Edwards patted the priest on the back. "It's not that I don't trust you, but it pays to check. You're doing well."

"Then can we close the bars and the cathouses?"

"My dear bishop," Edwards said. "They're a thorn in your side, but as head of the church, I see the bigger picture. Diversions provide outlets for our malcontents and allow us to monitor their activities."

"We preach the evils of drink and—"

"Isn't it better to have something to rant against than to drive the rabble underground? We're doing well. Enemies serve to rally the faithful to pay up.

"Focus on the Civ problem. Their crackdown brings more refugees who don't swear allegiance and don't pledge tithes to us. Our finances are strained by mech intrusions and shakedown payments. We need to ease the threat in the west so we can move east and north."

Hanrahan rose and straightened his gray uniform. "I don't trust Governor Battani." He drank his whisky in one gulp, his neck muscles tightening. Scars on his cheek turned purple.

"Neither do I, but we need this deal. If she reneges, we have enough to blast her from office and she knows it. We only have a few days to pull this together."

Annabelle is a nice bonus, Margarite thought. *Like me. Pawns in a bigger game.*

Kolinski refilled the whiskey glasses. "We have a quorum."

"That may not be enough this time." Edwards downed his whiskey. "Our charter requires all board members for major deals, and we can't afford leaks. Remind me why after ten years we don't control all the shares of Biltmoor and why we still have competition." His eyes bore into the general's.

"President Hardcastle vanished with the stock certificates," Hanrahan said.

"Yet McCarthy shows up at board meetings with official instructions. Have you checked the Civ side of the border? The last thing we need is Battani getting her hands on him and his shares."

"If they have him, it's deep underground," Hanrahan said, which Margarite knew was true.

"Find him before they do," Edwards said. "Persuade him or seize his shares." He turned to the bishop. "What about Montgomery?"

"Aside from his small holdings, we haven't been able to dig through the nest of holding companies and foundations to see who owns the rest of the shares he votes."

"Can we disqualify him?" Edwards asked. "Default or forge those shares?"

"He brings fresh proxies when required. If his shares belong to Hardcastle, a forgery could backfire."

"I want control," Edwards said. "Buy them if necessary."

"We haven't the money, sir." Kolinski poured another round.

"Between payments to Civ and past stock purchases, we can't swing it. Every time we buy, the seller takes the proceeds to create something new we have to deal with."

"Then seize properties. Use eminent domain."

"And risk rebellion?" the bishop asked.

Edwards turned to Hanrahan. "Make sure Montgomery and McCarthy can't vote. That'll bring their sponsors out of hiding."

Hanrahan bowed. "It shall be done."

Edwards downed his third glass of whiskey. Margarite had seen him do five without effect, though his partners weren't so lucky. "We may have caught a break," he said. "I got a message from Cory."

"We can't trust the man." Hanrahan left his whisky and returned to the screen.

"You'll like this. He claims Bret Shaw is behind transporting people over the border. Cory tested it himself, even got invited to Shaw's home."

Hanrahan stood. "He knows where the bastard lives?"

Margarite held her breath. Shaw might be a thorn in Edwards' side, but the Underground Railroad was top priority for mechs. Until now, they hadn't been able to identify Shaw. This made her degradation at the bishop's hands worthwhile—almost.

"Shaw's been undermining us for years," Edwards said. "He helps squatters who refuse allegiance to us. They won't tithe or buy from our stores, all in breach of contract. Now he's smuggling refugees to build his empire? I'll give you the coordinates. I want him and his son dead."

"If the boy's old enough, I could use more men," Hanrahan said. "Don't worry. I'll break him first."

"Your call," Edwards said. "Cory asked for a handsome reward, so I offered some of the shares Hardcastle granted Shaw as long as he votes our way."

"He's a weasel," Hanrahan said.

"Let him be our weasel, then. Make him a board member instead of Montgomery. It can't be any worse. Find Shaw's certificates and do your magic so they revert to us."

"Yes, sir." Hanrahan sent texts to his lieutenants, which Margarite scanned.

Edwards checked his com. His face turned red. "Shaw and his son are at Undercover with my bride. I don't like coincidences.

Find them. Kill the Shaws. Bring the girl, alive."

Hanrahan jumped to his feet and rushed out of the rectory.

Well, Annabelle, let's see how clever you are this time.

Edwards poured another drink, downed it and headed for the exit. Margarite took that as her cue to close up shop before Kolinski came looking for tension release. She transmitted a coded message via shortwave, then pushed her link-pad into the wall and replaced the stone.

SEVENTEEN

Annabelle dropped into the dark alley from Undercover's second-story window and recovered the bag of clothes she had tossed behind the Dumpster. In the shadows behind the reeking container, she tugged on her mech clothes and on top of that, the Biltmoor jeans, top, and cap, making sure her blonde curls were covered.

Glancing up at the open window, she took a deep breath. Maybe she had hit Geo too hard. Part of that was anger at his killing Karen. Most was to stop her confused feelings for this striking man-legend. He had hesitated instead of acting like a brute. If only they'd had more time, what a tale she could tell him about his mom and other family, who took Annabelle in. She couldn't. She didn't want to replay her angst over her own dead father and imprisoned birth mother, while Janine remained a prisoner.

Worse, it worried her that she had considered letting Geo escape with her. She hadn't cringed at his touch. She wasn't sure she could have resisted him. Something new stirred deep within, something she didn't understand. She was glad she hadn't let him tag along to complicate things.

She jogged down the alley, heading east. *It's best to trust no one.*

She made her way to the edge of town, dodging more cops and Rangers than she had ever seen before. She needed to get her hands on Janine's suit and hoped it was in the cave near where Edwards had captured them. Then she would contact Sam for help, and return to rescue Janine.

Annabelle wiped a tear from her cheek and kept moving. *Hang tight, Babe.*

Beyond the shacks that made up the poor fringe of Biltmoor, Annabelle hit postage-stamp fields lit by shifting shadows from flickering oil lamps. She stumbled between tomato plants and cucumber patches until she reached where roads intersected southeast of town. She spotted dozens of Rangers blocking the intersection, and was thankful she had taken the long way.

She crossed the first road, which Geo said curved around town. She hoped he hadn't misled her. She didn't think so; he acted too sweet and smitten.

Annabelle guided herself by crescent moon, glimpsing the road below. She hurried through the brush, stopping now and then as Geo had suggested. At least the cold front had gone through. The heat of the mech suit would help with that.

* * *

Geo, Pa and Cory evaded the Rangers by traveling on foot, since Pa didn't want to risk it on horseback. The moment they reached the dark forest, Geo cradled his rifle and headed northeast toward Annabelle's buffalo head. He didn't need another lecture on how he wasn't yet a man.

Pa had found him roped to the bedposts. Cory sneered at Geo's stupidity. Madam Chrissie looked annoyed until Pa gave her another gold coin.

"My son's naïve in these matters," Pa explained as they left by the back door.

Pa told Cory there was no refuge for him in Biltmoor and led them in silence through town. Avoiding major roads, they had scooted past the shanties east of town and into crop fields. All the while, thoughts of Annabelle and those piercing turquoise eyes plagued Geo. With each footfall, he felt energized by the prospect of catching up, though she had a half-hour head start.

Pa caught up with Geo, grabbed his arm, and whispered roughly, "Where the heck are you going?"

Geo pulled free and glanced back to see Cory's infrared image falling behind. "I need to make sure she didn't get lost, Pa." He kept going.

"You helped her? My God, son. How rash." He sighed. "I paid good money for you to have one of Chrissie's girls, not this intruder. Have you lost your senses?"

Geo scanned left and right. "How was I to know she wasn't one of the girls?"

Pa blocked Geo. "We're going home. You don't even know this girl. You met her in a cathouse."

"Where else would I meet girls, Pa? Besides, they kidnapped her. She's not like the others." Geo brushed past Pa and kept walking.

"I'm not upset that you helped her, but you did your deed. Why risk everything now?"

"She's special."

"It's noble of you," Pa said, "but nobility gets you killed. You're taking risks for a stranger you'll never see again. Oh, you're hoping to catch up with her, aren't you? You're in over your head. She wants to go home, not shack up. You said it yourself. She's not like local girls. This is a fool's errand."

"My mind's made up, Pa. I have to see Annabelle safe."

"Annabelle Scott?"

"She didn't give me her last name."

"Let's go." Pa hurried ahead.

"You know her?"

"No more talking."

Geo had to hurry to keep up with Pa as they crested the next ridge. He was dying to ask about the girl, but with Rangers patrolling the road below, they couldn't break silence. When he looked back, he barely saw Cory. He stopped to listen, heard rustling, but saw no heat signatures. At least he wasn't sweating like a hog, or needing to plaster on mosquito repellent every ten paces.

* * *

In the dark, Annabelle circled the buffalo rock formation several times before satisfying herself that this was where Edwards had captured her.

When clouds stole the moonlight, she searched the rocky enclosure foot by foot in the dark. Clouds drifted away; she spotted the opening. She heard what sounded like heavy breathing and halted.

If she ran, she might head into a trap. If she stayed, they might spot her infrared image in the cool night air. She crouched behind rocks, making herself small in the hope she would be mistaken for an animal. She held her breath and waited.

Clouds obscured the moon once again. Recalling the layout and hearing nothing more, she crept around the edge of the enclosure until she reached the cave opening. She got down on all fours and crawled inside, hoping no one else had the same idea.

Eyes closed, Annabelle inched her way around the cave, reaching up and down for a spot where the bulky mech suit might be hidden. She was certain she had made her way back to the entrance when her fingers touched one of the titanium-polymer plates. Heart thumping, she tugged. The suit fell on top of her and clanked onto the rocky floor.

She waited, listened. Could she still hear breathing? No, it was her heartbeat in her ears. Slowly, Annabelle slipped into the leg frame and strapped on the chest and back panels. She was thankful for the quick release system. Then she felt around the ledge above for the helmet. Without it, she would have no connection or GPS. She banged her head on the rocky ceiling and reached further into the ledge. Her fingers touched the smooth faceplate; she pulled out the helmet. *Thank you, Janine.*

After removing her sister's biochip, Annabelle inserted her own. As soon as she pulled on the helmet, the com-link connected. For the first time in days she savored the cozy warmth of connection with sister warriors.

"Where the heck have you been?" Sam asked.

"Good to hear your voice, Commander." Annabelle smiled. "Edwards kidnapped me and J. It's a long story, but he's holding J in Biltmoor. I sense other mechs in the area. We need to rescue her tonight."

"That's negative," Sam said. "Get your sorry ass back to base. Do you need assist?"

"We can't leave J another night."

"Stand down until we can negotiate."

"You mean until I trade myself for her," Annabelle said. "Now that I've met the bastard, there's no way I'll marry him. He's a disgusting slob with no regard for women."

"You should not have gone off grid. My hands are tied until after the wedding. Do not return to Biltmoor. Is that understood?"

Suspecting the line was compromised, Annabelle severed the link. *I guess I'm on my own, Janine.* Yet too many mechs had died alone.

EIGHTEEN

With clouds playing hide-and-seek with the moon, Geo was glad the cooler night let him use his infrared goggles. He sensed a disturbance below that he couldn't see. He felt it, or rather, his hearing picked it up without definition. Cresting a hill, he spotted Rangers on the road heading toward Biltmoor. Crickets chirped, an owl hooted, and mosquitoes still buzzed. Geo glimpsed moonlit shadows and a recently trodden path. *Annabelle?*

Ahead was a clearing and path they had to cross to reach the buffalo head. Geo crossed first, then Pa, followed by Cory, making noise like a Civ crashing through bushes.

"Halt!" a low guttural voice said.

The command came like a stabbing headache. Geo slid to the ground behind bushes. From his backpack, he pulled a poncho that doubled as a sleeping bag and infrared shield by reflecting heat like a mirror. Pa slid into the underbrush without making a sound. Cory froze in the clearing like a deer.

Pa gave up his hiding place to tug Cory into the woods.

"Stop and show yourselves," the harsh voice said.

Shots blasted from several directions with tracers lighting up like fireflies. Geo moved down to help Pa and drew the poncho around them.

Pa covered Cory with branches. "Stay and don't move," Pa whispered.

He headed uphill without making a sound. Geo followed. The buffalo head was up the path to the left. When Pa headed east,

Geo hesitated. He had to help Annabelle. It wouldn't do for the Rangers to catch her.

Shots rang out. "Got him."

Bushes rustled as Rangers thrashed about. Draped in his poncho, Geo hid in the bushes and stayed low. *I should be with Pa instead of fussing over a girl I'll never see again.*

The rustling drew nearer. At first, Geo couldn't make out who it was. Then he realized it was Pa, stumbling down the hill. Geo rushed to his father's side and pulled him into the bushes, covering them both with the poncho. Pa held his stomach.

"You're hit." Geo pulled a handkerchief from his pocket. "I'm sorry, Pa. Sorry."

"Too late. Ambush. No time."

"Let me bandage you," Geo whispered. He placed the cloth over Pa's wound and wished he could see more than his infrared allowed.

Pa held the handkerchief. "Can't help me. Stomach and chest."

"No, Pa." *You can't die.*

"Shut up. Listen. Stay free." Pa pushed a ring onto Geo's finger. "Find Willis. Get certificates."

"What certificates?"

"Help neighbors."

"I'm not leaving you."

Pa punched Geo in the chest. "Go. Be stubborn to stay alive."

Pa pulled himself to his feet and scrambled down the path toward the clearing. More shots rang out. Each bit into Geo's heart. *No, Pa. It's my fault. I killed you with my selfishness. Don't leave.*

Pa rolled over and fired at a mech ambling toward him. *What's a mech doing with Rangers?* The mech stood near Geo's head, pouring machine pellets into Pa. Geo fumbled in his pack for a grenade. His hands trembled. He dropped the remote. It was too late.

The mech moved toward Pa, joined by a single Ranger, a big man with stars on his shoulders: Hanrahan. Gripping the ring, Geo took that moment to move uphill toward the buffalo head.

Pa couldn't be dead. Yet no one survived a mech's machine gun. Pa's last order was to stay alive, escape.

NINETEEN

Annabelle emerged from the cave in full mech body-armor and heard shots nearby. Seeing no images on her infrared screen, she moved along the rock enclosure until she reached the trail. Below, her infrared picked up dozens of horses and riders waiting, while scores of men scoured the area. *Looking for me? How thoughtful.*

Turning on her com-link, Annabelle sensed a connection with three sister warriors nearby, including her friend Julianne. "What's the situation? I heard shots."

It took a moment to orient herself to four infrared views at once, hers and those of the other mechs. She tried to locate them, and distinguish them from Rangers swarming the area.

"I told you to return to base," Sam said.

"Team's surrounded, Commander. Rangers have RPG's. I saw Cory in Biltmoor. I think he's headed this way."

Sam sighed.

"Is Cory the mission?"

"Yes. Other units are on the way. Stay until they arrive."

Annabelle jumped at a heat flash; an RPG fired into the mech circle. "Incoming," she said, opening fire on the elevated heat signatures of horsemen. She cut down three before others rode off.

The blow to the chest felt personal, though it happened to another mech a hundred yards away. Julianne's com-link severed. *Damn them.*

Annabelle turned her guns on another RPG aimed at her. Her fire ripped men to shreds. Below her, the other mechs fired on

Rangers who had the high ground. With boosts from the mech suit, Annabelle jumped up, grabbed hold of the rock above the cave and climbed until she located no heat signatures above her. She opened fire, knowing mech suits would protect her friends. Like dogs barking amidst geese, Rangers scurried.

"I told you to wait," Sam said.

"They hit J with an RPG," Annabelle said, referring to Julianne.

"Thanks. I'm okay," Julianne said, back on the com-link. "Hurts like hell. Next one would have been up my rear. Sam, you've got to get the air and exhaust fixed."

"We're working on it. Any sign of the target?"

"Lost him," Julianne said. "Thanks, stranger. Glad you're back."

"Return to base. All of you."

Clicking off her link, Annabelle scanned the mountainside. Two mechs below gave off unique heat signatures. A third mech, Julianne, stood up.

Annabelle scanned the rest of the hill to make sure Rangers were gone. Maybe she could ask Julianne to help free Janine. It was a long shot. Julianne was by the book, which almost got her killed. On the other hand, Sam thought Annabelle a hothead for jumping in with guns blazing. Well, except for Karen and Dara, she didn't lose friends.

Annabelle spotted a lone figure moving up the mountain. Her first thought was a Ranger trying to get behind her, but they worked in pairs and the signal was too slight for a Ranger. It had to be that weasel Cory.

Engaging full mech power, Annabelle sprinted uphill, pushing bushes out of her way. She considered shooting, but she wanted this bastard alive. The mech gear should have given her advantages, yet she had trouble focusing on the ghostly heat signature that expanded before fading to nothing. It was the wrong shape for a deer. It couldn't be Cory—too fast. *Maybe Geo followed me and got caught in the crossfire. Silly boy. I told you to stay away.*

Annabelle pushed herself harder, crashing against bushes. If Sam wouldn't help, maybe Geo could. Her com-link returned. Before Sam could yell, Annabelle severed the connection. She tripped, tumbled back to her feet, and kept running. The runner was quick. Maybe legends were true; he was reputed to be a marathon runner. He must have spotted her, for he took evasive maneuvers.

Annabelle crested a ridge and was startled by hundreds of heat signatures scattered across the slope. She dropped to the ground and prepared to fire. The signatures faded like phantoms. *Must be a flash decoy.* This boy was good. That encouraged her to think that he could help. Her com-link reestablished itself, a failsafe against going off grid. She severed it.

After locating the strongest image, she scrambled to her feet and ran downhill. She jumped over tree branches when she saw them, or tripped and recovered when she didn't. She pulled up her stun gun and aimed, missed and kept going.

* * *

Geo ran more on memory than night vision. He hoped the mech, despite infrared and periodic searchlight, had to be cautious. Overwhelmed by guilt at getting Pa killed over some girl, he tried to reconstruct what had happened. Cory made noise like city folk out in the woods. Rangers appeared as if waiting—for Cory? For Annabelle? A mech was there with Hanrahan, more mechs. Then something went terribly wrong: blazes and explosions.

It had taken every bit of skill, stealth with the poncho, and strength Geo possessed to sneak up the slope surrounded by Rangers and mechs. Then machine pellets milled trees and Rangers, each pellet capable of shattering bone, severing nerve, or slicing arteries. *Live to fight another day,* Pa would say.

The presence of all those mechs convinced Geo they would rescue Annabelle, which made him feel even more stupid for chasing after her. He should have listened when Pa said to forget the girl and go home. Now he was all alone.

No time to feel sorry for yourself, Pa would say. *Get your ass moving.* He should collect Pa's body to give him a proper burial. What about Cory? Was he waiting for Pa, or had they killed him as well?

While fumbling in his pack for another of Pa's flash-flares, Geo stumbled and rolled down the mountainside. He couldn't keep running from this mech, he realized. He needed to find a cave that should be nearby, about a half-mile uphill. He would have to time this right. He set off scatter-flares and continued running.

Stumbling over a fallen tree, Geo tumbled head first down the hill. The mech scanned with its search beam, over his head. Geo was still at least 100 yards from the cave. He couldn't see the two companion mechs, and besides, he couldn't outrun all three.

When he reached a clearing, Geo squinted through the darkness for the cave's opening. He dropped a grenade along the path, kicked leaves over it, and pulled the poncho around himself. Pa's invention consisted of nano-aramid fabric coated with a gold-impregnated aluminum polymer. It reflected heat like an infrared mirror, rendering the occupant ghostlike.

With the grenade's remote in his mouth, Geo felt around the rocky hillside for the cave opening. The area lit up, blinding him for an instant. When he could see, Geo flipped out his rifle and aimed for the mech's eye-visor hinge.

"Put your weapon down," a female voice said. "I'm not here to hurt you."

Activating the remote, Geo backed up. He hoped to lure the mech over the grenade. *Stay alive and free,* Pa had said.

She advanced, guns aimed at his chest and head. "Please put your gun down and let's talk."

"You first." Geo moved back. He could trigger the blast and make a run for it, yet this mech was strange. She wanted to talk. In his experience with mechs, it was kill or be killed. "Okay, what's your game?"

She moved closer and looked down at the two-phase grenade. "Geo, please don't scramble my guts." Her voice sounded shaky. She lowered her weapons. "If you promise not to attack me, I'd like to talk to you about your mom."

What? "You killed my pa, and now you bring up my mom?" He moved closer and took aim, then stopped himself. He was too close to the grenade. Stepping back, he prepared to release the remote.

The mech moved forward and unfastened the latches of her helmet. "I'm sorry about your pa. I pray I didn't hit him. I couldn't live with myself if I had."

"Why would you care? You're a mech."

"I was captured after delivering a young boy to your pa. I've had my fill of killing. I just want to talk." She removed her helmet and shined a light on her mane of blonde curls and sweet face.

"Annabelle? You're a mech?"

"Guilty." She tucked the helmet under her arm and dimmed the light. "I couldn't tell you before or you might not have helped. I'm thankful you did, and now I've returned the favor."

"How do you figure?" Geo asked.

"If I hadn't pursued you, others might have." Annabelle

loosened her collar and fanned herself. "By the way, thanks for not shredding my guts like you did Karen's. Are you planning on shooting me?"

"That was you?" Geo lowered his rifle. "Your friend had no problems killing villagers. She was about to kill me. You had me in your sights and didn't shoot."

"I'm tired of the killing." Annabelle sighed. "Please, this is hard. Karen was a dear friend, but I couldn't shoot you then and I can't now. Can we talk?"

"Turn off your light or we'll have company."

She flipped off the light, plunging the alcove into darkness.

"Pa was killed looking for you." Geo deactivated and pocketed the remote. "He didn't deserve to die."

"I'm sorrier than you can imagine."

"How do you know him?"

"He and your mom worked together to help people resettle," Annabelle said.

"They did?" A gnawing pain resurfaced in Geo's gut. Why hadn't Pa mentioned this?

"We can't stay here. Other mechs will look for me."

"What do you mean 'we'?" Geo asked

"Come with me and I'll explain everything."

"I'm not going anywhere with you and that stupid gear." Geo hefted his backpack and rifle, and pushed past Annabelle in the dark. Night vision helped him spot the disarmed grenade, which he stuffed into his pack.

"Geo? I can't see." Annabelle turned in circles, waving her arms, making far too much noise.

"Stop that." Geo scanned for mechs and Rangers. "Put your helmet on and go home. You don't belong here."

"I'm not leaving without you. If I put the helmet on, other mechs will know where I am and they will see what I see. The plan is—"

"I'm leaving. You can hole up here until morning." Geo started down the path.

Annabelle grabbed his arm in her mechanical grip. "Please come with me. Your mom sent me. She wants to see you."

"Are you arresting me?" Geo tried to pull free, but her grip was solid. "Because if you are, you'd best shoot me now."

She released her grip. "I can't see, Geo. Please don't run off. I need you to come with me. There's no time to argue."

"Why? After all these years?" Geo continued down the trail.

Annabelle followed. "Because as a mech, I can cross the border. Please come with me."

"I lost Pa and I can't even bury him." Besides, Geo couldn't trust a mech.

"Geo, wait."

"I need to settle family business."

"You mean vengeance," Annabelle said.

"Maybe. You know, you'd fetch quite a sum if I brought you in. If I don't, you'll bring me nothing but trouble."

"Which will it be? I'm not leaving without you."

"I'm not going with you." Geo focused on the path ahead.

"Geo!"

"Quiet. You're attracting attention."

Annabelle crashed through underbrush like a feral pig, pushing everything out of her way with the mechanical suit. When Geo stopped, she crashed into him. "Sorry. I can't see without night vision."

"Are you trying to get us killed?" Geo whispered. "Go home."

"If you won't come with me, then I'm going with you."

"Then take the suit off. You're making too much noise."

TWENTY

Annabelle removed the mech suit and hefted the weight over her shoulder. With it on, she was a bull charging through underbrush. Now she felt vulnerable. She missed the bond to sister warriors, as well as her com-link. She was cold in the light sweaty mech uniform she had worn under the gear.

This wasn't going according to plan. She had hoped to get Geo's help by mentioning his mom. Instead, they were wasting time while poor Janine suffered; Annabelle didn't want to think of the details. Geo wasn't coming around. She had to gain his trust.

When he stopped again, she bumped into him. "You haven't asked how I know your mom."

Geo sighed. "Must you talk?"

"Your mom is my mom. That's why I couldn't hurt you."

"What?" He glared at her. Annabelle wished she could better read his reaction in the dim moonlight. "How disgusting. You offered yourself to me at the cathouse. And to think I wanted you. God, what do they teach you in Civ? I chased across the mountains to make sure you didn't get lost. I got Pa killed. How could you?"

"I didn't think you'd accept, and you didn't. I wanted to tell you, but—won't you please help your sister?" Hearing him move away, she trudged after him. Bulky and cumbersome without the benefit of its hydraulic lifts, the mech suit on her shoulder weighed a ton. Yet she couldn't leave it. *This isn't going well, Janine. Be patient. I'll get to you as soon as possible, but I need help.*

"Geo, Mom talks about you every night." She waited for his

reply to sense how far ahead he was. When he didn't respond, she continued, "She loves you very much." No reply. Annabelle felt alone, shivering in the cool breeze. "Geo, please don't be angry with me." She couldn't see him.

"You misled me." The voice came from beside her. "I thought you were available, different from the others. You're just like the preacher said, lustful temptations, misleading. And my sister? Damn you for making me feel anything toward you. Go home."

"Geo, I've really messed up. You have every right to hate me, but I'm desperate. What I told you about being kidnapped was true. Your sister Janine was with me. She's still a hostage." Annabelle bit back tears. "I needed your help to find the cave and the mech suit so I could call for help. My people abandoned me. Janine needs us."

"More stories. More temptations?"

She moved toward his voice. "No, Geo. I only want to free her. I don't know where the Rangers are holding her." When he didn't say anything, she added, "Geo, please. I beg you. If I wanted to kill you, I could have. If I wanted to capture you, I could have used a tranquilizer. She needs us. I have nowhere else to turn."

"We'll see."

"Will you help me find her?"

"I'm going home," Geo said. "If you insist on following, either put on the suit or ditch it. You won't be able to keep up."

"If I put it on they'll track us."

"Give it here." Geo grabbed the suit.

"You can't wear it. It's biometrically adapted to me."

"I'm not wearing it," Geo said. "I'm getting rid of it."

"You can't. It's government property."

"Don't worry. I'll hide it." He returned the way they came.

Unable to see much, Annabelle followed the sound of the suit banging into bushes. She had to hurry to keep up. When they reached the opening where she had met him, clouds parted. She stood over where the grenade had been and shuddered at how close she came to Karen's fate.

By moonlight, she moved to the cover of rocks while Geo pulled the gear into the cave. When he emerged, he rummaged through his pack.

Annabelle tried another approach. "Won't you help a girl lost in the wilds?"

"You like to pile it on, don't you? You're not defenseless; you're a mech killing my friends, and you deceived me."

"I didn't kill anyone at the village. I swear. If my boss studies the video I'm—"

"Enough," Geo said.

"I need your help."

Geo drank from his canteen and handed it to her. She held up her hand to pass despite her thirst. Poor Janine had emptied the mech suit's water supply.

"What's the matter?" Geo asked. "Don't you share with other mechs?"

"That's different."

"Why? Oh, I get it. What do they teach you girls? You can't get pregnant sharing water."

"You know a lot for an Outlander," Annabelle said.

"Just practical things."

"Give me that." She reached for the canteen.

He held it back. "Say please."

"Please offer your sister a drink." She took the canteen, sipped, and found the water refreshing with a slight mineral taste. She took a long drink.

When she finished, Geo took the canteen and attached it to his pack. "You might know your way around Civ, but this is my world. Stay close and quiet. No more talking."

He took her hand and led her along the path. She found his grip firm and reassuring, particularly when he stopped from time to time to listen. It was rather like having her mech-link connection with sister warriors. Annabelle heard cicadas and an occasional owl. The wind was cool with a whiff of smoke.

Geo stopped, pointed toward a bright star behind them, and ran his arm in the opposite direction. He headed southeast. She smiled, comforted that he could navigate at night without all her electronic aids.

* * *

Geo wasn't sure what to make of this mech girl who claimed to be his sister. She looked nothing like him, and he could always spot family resemblances. Yet she had passed up several chances to kill him. That counted for something.

He held her hand so she didn't crash about. *Oh, Lord, please purge all impure thoughts of this girl.*

He stopped, listened, and heard nothing unusual. He smelled fires from the north and odor from that Civ dump, which got worse every year. He didn't smell mechs other than Annabelle. *Good.* A couple of deer grazed nearby. Maybe he would bag one later, when he didn't have to drag it so far.

"Why 'Geo'?" Annabelle asked in a whisper. "Man of the Earth?"

"Short for George. Now quiet. Your voice carries." Geo moved to the top of a ridge. In the valley below, he spotted images of three riders on horseback. He aimed his rifle and sighted one.

"Why did you kill Karen in such a cruel way?" Annabelle whispered.

"Quiet." He pointed to horsemen moving along the valley floor.

When the riders rode away, Geo scanned for other human signatures and didn't see any. "It was the only way I could stop that mech and save those boys. Let's go."

"She was a sweet girl, only seventeen."

"Sorry, Annabelle. It was either her or me, and she was killing civilians."

"They were helping escapees and poaching."

"Just trying to survive," Geo said. "So I have two sisters?"

"Three. Sarah was born nine months after you left."

Geo covered Annabelle's mouth and pulled her to the ground. He spread the poncho/sleeping bag over them and drew her close, too close. Though the nano-polymer fabric reflected heat, reducing their infrared signature, it was only sized for one person.

When she cleared her throat to talk, he clasped her mouth, gave her his night-vision goggles, and pointed at six horsemen heading their way. He pulled her into the fetal position so the poncho would cover them both and felt her tension. He prayed she would shut up for once.

Night glasses were useless inside the shielded poncho, so he slowed his breathing and listened. He heard her breathe and couldn't decide if she was scared, angry or both. Outside he heard voices. With the clomp of hooves not ten yards from his head, Geo was tempted to look, but that would release heat and expose his position.

Instead, he fumbled into his pocket and pulled out a fiber-optic scope. He bent it, slid it through the dirt, and curved it up into the night sky. On his wrist-com, he took in a 360-degree view. Two riders spotted deer and shot, scaring them away. They scanned for signatures in flight.

What troubled Geo was that Rangers rarely ventured this far at night, since they were easy targets for mechs. Yet he had seen two units, maybe a larger unit splitting up.

By feel, he assembled his crossbow with its crank-spring to add tension. He tried not to grunt with the strain of pulling it taut. He notched an arrow and slid over his .50 cal. Then he found a grenade and held the remote in his mouth, without activating it.

Adrenalin surged, spurring alertness. He wanted to strike the Rangers for killing Pa and yet Pa said don't fight unless you have to. *Sorry, Pa. I should have listened. Is it possible I have three sisters you never mentioned? How could you keep that from me?*

The horses galloped away. Geo waited, suspecting a trap. Heat signatures retreated. When they were gone, Geo removed the poncho. He would have to take the long way home to avoid patrols.

"That was close," Annabelle said, stating the obvious. "But you don't have to act so familiar. Couldn't you have a signal or something?"

"Are you incapable of shutting up?" Geo whispered.

"I'm used to being connected with my team and my family."

"Don't. The woods are full of ears. Let's go." Geo hung the rifle and crossbow on his shoulder, pocketed the grenade and remote, and tossed a flash-flare out into the valley. He didn't detonate it.

"What—"

"Hush." Geo led them along the ridge where Rangers had been. Not trusting night-goggles, he stopped and sniffed the air for human or mech scent. Annabelle carried some from her suit, which made him jumpy at how she dulled his senses.

The moon shone again. He welcomed not having to hold her hand and kept repeating: *She's off limits.*

TWENTY-ONE

They moved up the forested valley. A moonlit clearing loomed ahead, revealing the stone walls of the Kurdises' cabin, where Geo hoped they would find a friendly face on a dangerous night. Then he smelled the toxic odor of gunpowder on flesh. His heart sank.

"What's wrong?" Annabelle asked.

Geo scanned the woods and clearing in infrared, finding nothing larger than a raccoon. He inched forward and came upon the body of old man Kurdis, sprawled in the dirt with his son. "He was only sixteen. Is this your work?"

"We don't kill civilians. We hunt escapees. My last mission was the dangerous guy I saw you with in Biltmoor."

"Cory?" Geo touched the father's neck. Warm. No pulse.

"He's a gun runner, murderer, and spy."

"As a mech, you would say that." Geo checked the son and bit back tears. Even by moonlight, they looked like they had been tortured. He could only imagine where the attackers took fourteen-year-old Vivian. Poor girl rarely left their cabin. This world was hell for girls, hell for anyone except Edwards and his cronies.

This has to change.

"Did those Rangers do this?" Annabelle asked.

Geo considered her question. "They rarely bother us up here."

"We should bury them."

"Sure, let's announce we were here. Not another word." Geo moved to the clearing, saw no heat signatures in the stone cabin or the surrounding area, and sprinted to the front door. It was open.

He scanned the interior with his night-goggles. Someone had trashed the place. There was no sign of Vivian.

Annabelle closed the door, plunging them into total darkness. She turned on her flashlight. Geo saw she no longer wore her skimpy outfit, but rather a tight, dark blue mech uniform.

"You won't make it out here looking like that," Geo said. Nothing about her resembled him: intense turquoise eyes, gentle nose, blonde curly hair, angles of her face, light skin.

"Where I come from, this outfit is practical and fashionable."

"Here it draws attention." Geo entered a bedroom. The bed lay gutted like an animal, with straw spilled over the rough wood floor.

"Doesn't look like they had much. Why would Rangers do this?"

Geo held up a shredded dress. "They had something Edwards wanted."

"His wife?"

"Daughter, fourteen." Geo left the bedroom. "After his wife died, Kurdis kept Vivian hidden." Geo entered another ransacked bedroom and shook his head. Pa would have a fit.

"If you don't like my appearance, what do you suggest?"

Geo scavenged through the closet. "We need to cut those blonde curls, for one thing. It's a dead giveaway."

"You're not touching my hair."

Geo handed her a pair of jeans and a beige linen shirt. "Try these. You won't look so conspicuous."

"Big word for an Outlander." She held up the jeans to see if they would fit. "You carry a dictionary in your backpack?"

"I can offer more if that impresses you."

"It doesn't," Annabelle said. "Can you leave while I change?"

Glancing at her in the flashlight beam, Geo tried to see any resemblance. "Is that eye color natural?"

She held up the jeans and shirt, and glared at him. "Genetic quirk. Now can you leave?"

Geo rummaged through the closet, finding mostly worn-out clothes. "I probably won't see anything you haven't already shown me. Hurry up."

"You won't let me forget, will you?"

"You weren't modest then."

Annabelle tugged off her boots. "Are you always mean to girls?"

"Only know-it-all Civ girls."

"How many Civ girls do you know?" She got one boot off.

"Including you, one."

She sighed. "I guess I'm not giving a good impression then. I'm not used to boys. There weren't any at school, and our neighborhood is zoned to exclude them. Plus, I'm used to being in control of my surroundings." She pulled the pants, shirt and boots next to the bed and sat on the wood floor.

"Apology accepted." Geo found rifle shells in the back of the closet and pocketed them.

"I wasn't apologizing." Annabelle glared at him while pulling off her blue mech trousers.

"I know. Hurry, we need to go."

"Why can't we stay? Or is there a hotel nearby?"

Geo shook his head. "Nearest hotel is the woods."

"Look away!" She tugged on the jeans. "The cabin would give us shelter."

"Not really." A simple pine chest had been knocked over and bashed. He checked its drawers. "Infrared penetrates the walls and I can't hear what's coming. There's only one exit and no toilet." He pointed at her boots. "We'll have to get rid of those."

Annabelle slid behind the bed so he couldn't see. "What's wrong with my boots? They're top of the line."

"Nothing out here looks that new." He pulled a pair of well-worn boots from the closet and handed them to her. He averted his eyes. "You'll probably need extra socks."

"Is all this necessary?"

Geo sat on the bed, facing away. "You'll draw less attention as a boy. As a girl, you would have to pass as my wife. Even so, it'll involve fighting."

"You wouldn't fight for your sister?"

"I can't believe Pa kept that from me."

"I'm sure he didn't want you wandering into the Union and getting caught," Annabelle said. "And what about Vivian? I thought there weren't any girls in the mountains."

"Mrs. Kurdis died when Vivian was young. The old man didn't want to send her away. Instead, he struggled to feed another mouth. She couldn't work the fields for fear of Rangers or ruffians."

"You don't like girls much, do you?"

"I'd probably like them plenty if I got to know any." Geo turned to see her clothed in baggy jeans and top. "Around here, you get by as long as you can work or have family to care for you. Kurdis was ill, and he couldn't afford heart medicine."

"That's why you need National Healthcare, like we have."

"Let's cut your hair." He fetched his knife.

She backed away. "Don't touch."

"You want to look pretty or stay alive?"

"Both." Annabelle grabbed her clothes and boots and headed for the bedroom door.

Geo blocked her way. "Where are you going with those?"

"Government issue. I'm not leaving them."

"First your mech gear, now this. The whole point is to blend in. Let me do your hair." He reached.

"No!" She shoved his hand away. "I don't suppose they have soap and water so I could wash up."

"I'm sure you'll find soap powder in the kitchen. You'll have to fetch the water."

"How sanitary."

"Listen to you. I bet you've had shots for cholera, typhus, salmonella, and malaria."

Annabelle nodded. "So?"

"Ninety percent of the cells in the body are bacteria."

"More in your case. I can't believe I ever thought you could help."

"Climb off your pedestal," Geo said. "People out here are poor and make do. Why don't you return to your great life in Civ and stop bothering us simple folk? You're too soft for this world."

* * *

Annabelle clenched her fists. "Too soft, because I'm a girl? I'm a mech warrior." *I can whip you any day.*

"You hide behind mechanical gear. Without it, you're lost."

"I can take care of myself. Come on." Annabelle dropped her clothes against the wall and put up her fists. "Right here, right now. You and me." She was surprised at how much venom coursed through her.

"I'm not fighting you."

"Because I'm a girl?"

"Maybe."

"Then you'll get your butt whipped. Show me how simple folk fight."

Geo sheathed his knife into his jeans and headed into the living room. Annabelle followed, shoving a smashed wooden table and chair out of the way. She jabbed him, and savored first contact. "A mech can do anything a man can."

He moved away. "You can't ride a horse in your gear or you'd kill the poor animal, and those mech scooters scare the pigs and chickens."

"Okay, but you get the point." She faked a blow, testing him, willing him to respond. "President Zell says we have to adapt to males becoming extinct since no one's having boys anymore." She punched his shoulder and bounded back, enjoying the rush of adrenalin. "A group of us don't want that. Some are in prison." She tapped his jaw and moved aside, judging his reaction. She was disappointed he wouldn't engage. "I believe there's a better way." She jabbed with her right and tapped his jaw with her left.

"I won't fight you," he said.

Grinning, Annabelle tapped his chest and moved to the side. She was no longer sure if she wanted to fight or just wanted a reaction. Geo turned and took a defensive stance.

"Any action men take is counterproductive," Annabelle said, "so the movement has to be led by women. Too many are scared of bringing strong men back."

"Why tell me?"

"I'm not like the other mechs." Annabelle spun and planted her foot on his chest, sending him reeling backward against the wall. *Sorry.*

Geo scrambled to his feet and started to attack, but caught himself. "I'm not fighting you, so stop it."

She attempted several blows that he blocked. She spun behind and tapped the back of his head. "That could have been fatal. I'm just saying I can handle myself."

Geo faced her. "What do you want?"

She liked him standing boldly before her, not scared like he was when they first met. He was different here in the mountains, more confident. She faked a blow. "To show you I'm not one of your wimpy girls or a damsel in distress."

Dodging, Geo kept his distance. "What?"

"A helpless woman." Annabelle advanced.

"I know what a damsel is." Geo backed away. "Why do you keep poking me?"

"I deserve your respect." Annabelle attacked with mech swiftness.

Geo tripped over a battered chair, got to his feet, and retreated around the small room. He stopped and threw a punch, which she blocked. He threw another and another. Each time she anticipated and blocked him. She watched his warm brown eyes darken with irritation at a girl beating him, something she had seen in mech training. With annoyance turning to anger, he punched harder. She blocked, provoked. He attacked. She swept his leg and dropped him to the wood floor with a thud and groan. *Sorry.*

She jumped on top and pinned his arms beneath an old Franklin stove. She felt a rush of unexpected warmth like the way she felt at night sharing a bed with her adopted sister Janine. *I don't want these feelings for the one who killed Karen. I don't want to think of anything but rescuing you, Janine.* She steeled her nerves. "They train us to fight men so we'll overcome our fear of your superior muscle mass. To become a mech you have to face a guy in a fair fight."

He struggled to free his arms; she forced them further under a corner of the stove.

"They kidnap boys from Appalachia for your training," Geo said.

"We only use criminals." That was the party line, anyhow. Annabelle balanced her weight over him in a way that sent flashes of heat to her cheeks. She didn't want to fight him after all.

Geo jerked his body to throw her. He couldn't. "I guess they don't tell you everything. I know two locals who were taken, beaten, and dumped like garbage over the border."

Stunned, Annabelle sat up. "I'm sorry. I didn't know." All the men she had heard of had escaped Union prisons.

He tried to throw her.

She came down hard, applying her weight to pressure points below his knees and in his shoulders. "Say auntie."

He rocked to get her off. Frustration clouded his sweet eyes. He twisted and turned to no avail.

"I like your determination, Geo, but you suffer from Male Competitive Syndrome, and I can do this all night." Except now she was looking for a graceful way out.

"Male what?"

"I've read that boys have an innate need to compete. That makes cooperation difficult, and it led to their defeat before and during the war."

Geo twisted and rotated, but he couldn't free his arms.

"Your problem, Geo, is that while you're stronger, you waste energy. Focus your mind on defeating your opponent."

"I'll try to remember that."

"If you have to remember, you lose. Train yourself to anticipate your opponent's next move, and confound him. I'm getting up." Annabelle let go and scooted away, willing the heat in her cheeks to chill. "I told you I wouldn't hurt you. I just don't like being told I'm not good enough."

Geo stood and dusted himself off. "Like Pa not treating me like a man. When he did, I got him killed." He held his defensive pose.

Annabelle backed away. "Don't blame yourself for what others did."

"He was there because of me."

"Because you were following me."

Blushing, Geo turned away.

"Did you give him my name?"

He nodded.

"Then he was coming for me. It wasn't your fault. Mine maybe, but that won't bring him back."

Geo took a deep breath. "Will you teach me those moves?"

Annabelle grinned. "I'd be delighted to after you direct me to a bathroom."

"There's one behind every bush." Geo grabbed his backpack and rifle. "Let's go before Rangers or mechs return. We'll stop when we reach the woods."

She grabbed her clothes. "I'm—"

"From here on, no lights, and no talking." Geo took her light, turned it off, and handed it back.

She didn't know whether to be angry or thankful that he knew what he was doing.

TWENTY-TWO

Humiliated yet impressed at Annabelle's fight performance, Geo suspected she wasn't being truthful. She had looked at him so oddly while pinning him to the floor: part playful puppy, part hungry mountain lion.

Trees shielded the quarter moon. He waited, listened, watched for heat signatures. Two deer passed by. Geo took Annabelle's hand, and they ran across the clearing to the tree line. He moved ten paces in, stopped, and let go. "This is as good a place as any."

"For what? Oh." Annabelle moved away.

"Here." Geo took her clothes and began digging a hole with her boots.

"Not while you're watching."

"Like I'd want to. Stay where I can look out for you."

"Turn away," she said.

"I'm scanning for company. Come morning you'll have to pee standing."

"You've got to be kidding. I'm a girl."

"I hadn't considered that."

Geo widened the hole, dropped her clothes and boots in, and covered them. Then he moved into the clearing and scanned the area. "If you squat, you won't pass for a guy."

"Any other complaints?"

Geo spotted the heat signatures of five horsemen heading up the valley. "We have company."

Annabelle stood next to him. "I'm done. Now how do I wash my hands?"

"Hold them out." Geo squeezed Pa's homebrewed hand sanitizer. "Rub it in good."

"What, pray tell, is this?"

He put the bottle away and waited until she was done. "Skunk oil and rabbit brain."

Annabelle glared at him, her face hot in infrared.

Deciding he didn't want to hold her hand, Geo gave her a looped end of rope. "Hold this and follow." He held the other end and headed south, straining to see the trail through his goggles.

Geo crept along a deer path, watching the horsemen move straight up the valley. He triggered the remote, activating the flash-flare he had left earlier to create dozens of heat signatures down the valley. Horsemen trotted off toward the flashes.

"Is that—?"

"Hush." Tugging the rope, he hurried uphill along the path. When they reached the crest of the ridge, he stopped and looked back. Though flash-flare images had vanished, horsemen scoured the valley, chasing phantoms.

Geo faced Annabelle and wished he could see more than her green glow. "They're not after me, are they? I'm a nobody. They're after you. If you're one of Edwards' girls, he'll stop at nothing to reclaim you."

"How could you say that about your sister?"

"So you say. You found me in a cathouse and again out here. How do I know you're not saying that to get my sympathy?"

"Geo! I'm not one of his girls. At least not yet."

"There's a surefire way to find out. He brands his girls."

"Disgusting. Where?"

"You don't want to know."

"That's barbaric." Annabelle touched his shoulder. "I wasn't lying about Mom. She mentions you every night. I grew up on legends of you killing a bear when you were twelve."

"Bear is code for mech. It was attacking Pa."

"Geo? She's a girl, not an it."

Geo moved along the ridge. "I protected Pa. He didn't even thank me. He was angry that I'd put myself at risk."

"How many girls have you killed?"

Too many, Geo thought. "I don't count, and I don't look for trouble."

Annabelle touched his arm. "I'm proud of how you take care of yourself. You could have killed me and didn't."

"For a mech, you do a lot of talking." Geo no longer saw Rangers, only green haze from his night vision goggles.

Annabelle followed close. "I'm used to feeling connected. Unity brings victory and all that bull. Besides, after being surrounded by people, silence feels lonely."

"Try it, you might like to it." Geo checked both sides of the ridge and kept moving.

"Mom's quite proud of the man you've become."

"How would she know?"

"Messages I carry back and forth," Annabelle said. "She wants to see you if I can arrange it."

"Why, after all these years?"

"She's in the opposition. There's no way she could get past border guards. As a mech I can."

Geo spotted Rangers down the next valley but kept moving. "What's she like?"

"Strong, beautiful, smart. By day, she's a state senator. At night, she runs FGS Boots, like the ones you're wearing. She named the brand for you: For George Shaw."

"You're funning with me."

"I'm not," Annabelle said. "She stayed in Knoxville because of the girls, but I get jealous at how much she loves you. She has me bring you things like boots and books."

"How do you know mine are FGS?" Geo made sure the poncho covered him to minimize their heat signature, and continued along the ridge.

"There's an emblem on the heel. I need you to trust me because I need your help."

Geo stopped. "What now?"

"I feel sick at what they're doing to Janine. We have to rescue her."

Geo stared as best he could with night-vision, wishing he could read her face. "I don't like being conned. You're not telling me everything."

Annabelle touched his arm. "I wanted to when I met you in Biltmoor, but my best bet was to contact my commander. Instead of helping, she ordered me home. There's some deal between our governor and your thane."

"What kind of a deal?"

"I don't know details," Annabelle said, "but it would end the fighting, no more border crossings, increased trade."

"And?"

"Me having to marry Thane Edwards."

Geo stepped away. "Jeeze, Annabelle. You've got to be kidding. You used me to escape—"

"Geo, don't leave. I can't see. Mom can't help because Battani threatened her. My boss won't help. I've been betrayed, Geo. They're forcing to marry the gross bastard."

"You've met him?"

Inching along the ridge, Annabelle reached for him. "He kidnapped me to hold captive until the wedding. I escaped. When I saw you, I was afraid you'd react like you are now."

"Why didn't you ask Pa?"

"He was with Cory. Janine is your sister, Geo. She needs us. I can't do this alone." Annabelle lost her balance and flapped her arms.

Geo caught her and led her to a ledge to sit. "You're asking a lot. Until yesterday, I didn't even know I had any sisters."

"I know. Please don't abandon us."

"You mean like Mom abandoned me?" He sat next to her and stared down into the valley.

"She didn't." Annabelle clutched his hand. "The Union is no place for boys. She had girls to worry about. They made a decision to split up for our benefit. She thought she was doing right by you because of what would have happened if you'd stayed."

"I don't care what she thinks. She left us." But he did care. A burning ache still rumbled in his gut.

"Geo, don't let Janine suffer because Mom and I aren't perfect. This would break Mom's heart."

"Don't start with the guilt trip."

"Sorry," Annabelle said. "I get that a lot at home. If you can't do it for Mom or for me, do it for Janine. She deserves a life. You showed me kindness once."

"I didn't know you were a mech."

"A mech in trouble. Will you help?"

More temptations. What would Father Horace say?

TWENTY-THREE

From the ridge, Geo infrared-scanned the next valley through a thick crop of trees. Now that cooler weather had settled in, he could spot Rangers, but it also made hiding tougher. Horsemen scoured the valley. He would have to detour the long way or wait them out. He returned to Annabelle, shivering below the ridge. "Your husband must be mighty ticked off to send all these Rangers out."

"He's not my husband."

"We'll see." Geo grabbed his pack and moved to a level spot nestled between rocks. "We should cut and dye your hair. Blondes fetch a high price in Biltmoor."

"Are you trying to show how worldly you are for a virgin?"

"Only girls can be virgins."

"Anyone who hasn't done it is a virgin."

Geo scraped leaves into a pile toward the most sheltered part of their U-shaped enclave. "I suppose you're a virgin?"

Annabelle hesitated. "That's impertinent."

"It's quite pertinent, since you're acting like some goddess."

"I am not."

He transformed his poncho into a sleeping bag. "With guilt trips and all."

She crouched in the corner across from him and pulled the shirt collar up around her neck. "What were you doing in a cathouse?"

"When I insisted Pa treat me like a man, he said it was time."

"Yuck."

Geo laid the poncho/sleeping bag across the leaves. "There aren't many girls up here and they like experienced guys."

"What about saving yourself for your wife?"

"Like that'll happen." Geo shoved his backpack to the side and rested his crossbow and rifle next to the makeshift bed. "Girls with spirit go to Civ. Those who stay are frightened mice."

"Like Vivian."

Geo arranged the sleeping bag over the leaves for cushioning, with his feet and best infrared protection toward the path. "Why were you in a cathouse? Oh, yeah. Bored Civ girls come for a taste of something wild."

Annabelle shrugged. "I went to meet you. Don't tell me you're planning on sleeping out here."

"It's too risky to keep moving."

"We should have stayed at the cabin."

Geo crawled into his sleeping bag. "Look between the clouds at that beautiful starry sky. Bet you can't see that in Knoxville with all your grid lights. So spill: When did you lose your virginity?"

"I'm not discussing that with you."

"Suit yourself, but it'll be a cold night."

Annabelle curled up by the rock with her back to him. Geo marveled at her stubbornness. He felt guilty making her shiver.

She rolled over. "You wouldn't happen to have a blanket?"

"Just the sleeping bag," Geo said.

"I don't suppose you'd be a gentleman and let me have it."

Geo watched her outline, shivering. *Damn it, Pa, why didn't you tell me about my family?*

"Men!" Annabelle rolled over. She turned and tossed, moving closer inch by inch until she was on his sleeping bag. She turned toward him. "You're no gentleman, and I wish I could see your miserable face. Making me freeze!"

When he didn't say anything, she continued, "Are you asleep? Don't you dare go to sleep with me shivering."

"Other than being cold, are you okay?" Geo watched her image vibrate.

"Absolutely. I've been kidnapped, told to marry a bloated jerk, dragged through the woods with no toilets, and you want me to freeze out under the stars."

"I'm sorry Appalachia doesn't meet your expectations."

"I'm not used to sleeping alone," Annabelle said. "There, you got me to confess. I'm cold and I'm used to sleeping with Janine, who is being held hostage, and Sarah, who is scared to death in a huge bed by herself. And you have me scared of the dark because I don't have night vision goggles."

"So what's this horrible experience that proved to you how terrible men are?"

"Aside from you making me shiver?" Annabelle snuggled against him on the sleeping bag. She sighed. "I hung out with Dara and Margarite, before Margarite was kidnapped and Dara was killed. Dara captured a guy in no-man's land. It was horrible. I can't help thinking of poor Janine and Margarite."

"What happened?"

"They tied him down, gave him CV and forced him to perform. It was—"

"Disgusting?"

Annabelle sobbed. "I can't believe I had anything to do with that. I wish I could take it back, make it go away. And I never told a soul, you bastard."

"Come here." Geo held her and felt gooseflesh on her arms. "You're freezing. You would have been kinder to give him Midge."

Annabelle pulled away. "Don't even kid. That's what kidnappers use. They probably used it on me, because I can't remember a thing from when I was captured until I woke up in Biltmoor."

"Come here. All I have for tonight is this sleeping bag. Climb in."

"I'm not getting into bed with you."

"Annabelle, if you are my sister, do what is practical."

"Fine, but no touching."

"Got it."

Geo scooted as far to one side as he could. It was tighter than he expected when she wiggled in behind with her back to him. He prayed she didn't rip the bag. He got a whiff of her, a mixture of mech hydraulics, floral shampoo, and warm musk.

Annabelle wiggled her butt downward. "Don't touch me." She wrestled him for space until her rear settled into the small of his back.

"You comfortable?" he asked.

"Quite, thanks, but don't touch."

Like how could he not, with her butt nestled into his back? "I saw a patch on your shoulder. Were you injured?"

"It's an aluminum patch to mask implants they give mechs for tracking. It's what we do to visit certain places."

"Like the party with that guy?"

"Don't mention that again." Annabelle shifted position. "The sky is beautiful out here. Are we safe from Rangers?"

Geo took one last look with his night-goggles and patted his knife, crossbow, and .50 cal. "I'm sure we are." He would have to sleep light.

Dear Lord, please protect Annabelle and keep me from having impure thoughts about her.

TWENTY-FOUR

Geo woke to the dew-filled dawn. Birds chirped in the trees, while squirrels scampered across rocks. It was a peaceful contrast to the guttural snores of his companion. He inhaled her sweet musky odor and felt burning heat along his back and legs where Annabelle was tucked into him.

Geo eased her arm from around his waist and wondered if this was how she slept with her sisters back home. He had to flush that image. He wiggled out of the sleeping bag into the cool damp air. Her snoring assumed a chainsaw quality. In contrast, her face, framed by bouncy curls, looked so peaceful. He couldn't wake her.

He grabbed his pack and weapons, and headed to the top of the ridge to look around and cool off in the unusually cool June morning. Nothing had happened between them, yet he didn't trust how she kept touching him, tugging at him, as if there was something else going on.

He headed downhill to a spring, where he washed his face and filled his canteen. The peace of the morning gave way to disturbing thoughts. With Pa gone, Geo had lost the only family he knew. Then Annabelle showed up, telling him he had another family. She didn't act like a sister, but maybe that was because she hadn't grown up in Appalachia. Annabelle wasn't scared of him. She was independent in an annoying way, and she seemed quite clever, even for a warrior. He needed to send her home before she got him twisted into whatever scheme she was working.

* * *

Annabelle woke to a hard nudge to her rump. Yawning, she clung to a lingering dream of Geo guiding her through the wilds of his world. At first, she'd despised his masculine odor, then found it comforting and arousing. Face chilled and body toasty, she felt around. He was gone, and so were her clothes. She scooted deeper into the sleeping bag. Her bare feet touched something wadded up at the bottom.

Another nudge. "We got ourselves a blonde filly, prized one at that."

Startled fully awake, Annabelle stared up at a huge boyish man, a hairy beast like those she had fought in training. She reached toward her feet. *My jeans, thank goodness.* She pulled the pants up around her hips.

Above her loomed three other faces: the boys she had hunted at the village. The ones Geo helped when he killed Karen.

Where the hell are you, Geo?

"Good morning," Annabelle said in as gruff a voice as she could muster. She should have listened to Geo and cut the hair. *Too late.* She tucked a tee-shirt around her waist and fastened the jeans.

"It is a good morning," the man-child said. "Don't get many fillies up here." He reached down and mussed her hair.

Squirming away, Annabelle scooted down in the sleeping bag. She tugged the linen shirt over her head. Two boys who looked like twins held the bottom of the bag to keep her from standing up.

Geo's pack was gone. The bastard had abandoned her. "I got lost. Could you help me to the border?" She smiled at the brute and sat up.

He pushed her back onto the leaf-covered rock. "You have any idea how long it's been since I saw a filly like you?"

You have never seen a filly like me. Just give me a chance.

"How about a kiss," the brute said.

Annabelle pushed his face away and tried to crawl out of the sleeping bag. He held her arms above her head. She wiggled and squirmed, getting one arm free. She hit him, more like a slap.

"Thou shalt not covet thy neighbor's wife." Geo stood on the rock above them with his rifle in one hand and a strange-looking crossbow in the other. "You need to ask yourselves whether this one's worth the risk. I can take out one of you, maybe two, possibly all four."

The brute dropped Annabelle's arm. The boys backed away.

"Is your fun worth dying for?"

"Now, Geo, don't be like that," the brute said. "I didn't know you got lucky. You know Edwards will want his tithe of her."

Annabelle scampered out of the sleeping bag. "No one is tithing me, whatever that means."

"About what you think it means, sweetie." Geo jumped off the rock and landed beside her. Then he gave the brute a hug.

Annabelle stepped between them. "You know these guys?"

"Zak was born here," Geo said, "His pa's been here since before the war. These three arrived from Civ a few days ago."

"Yeah, you should have seen Geo whack a mech," the wiry boy said.

She cringed at the memory of Karen and started to say something. Geo grabbed her around the waist and pulled her toward where he had dropped his pack.

"Honey, it's time to make breakfast for our guests." Geo winked and fished out a pot and skillet from his pack.

With the brute eyeing her, she grabbed the utensils. "I don't know how," she whispered.

Geo turned to the guys. "Seems I need to learn my new bride how to cook. Make yourselves comfortable and start a fire." He led her away from the enclave, down the hill.

Once they had left the others behind, Annabelle shoved him. "Why did you ditch me? That's what you were doing, wasn't it?"

"I wouldn't leave my valuable sleeping bag." Geo bent over a spring-fed pool and filled the pot with water.

She knelt next to him and splashed water on her face. "Thanks for getting your priorities straight."

"You said you could take care of yourself."

"Next time, make sure I'm awake, dressed, and not tangled in a sleeping bag. Speaking of which, why wasn't I wearing clothes?"

"The bag's a heat mirror. You probably got too hot." Geo set the pot aside. "Sorry they frightened you." He mixed grits with water.

"And what's this wife bit? Why not tell them I'm your sister?"

"Then Zak would want to date you. He's not your type." He handed her some blackberries. "When we get back, mix in coffee and boil. Stir the grits. Pretend to be a homesteader wife."

"You're impossible. No wonder your women left." She wasn't

126

as angry as she pretended to be, though. Not angry at all, in fact, which surprised her.

* * *

Over grits and coffee around a small fire, Geo told Zak and the three compadres about Pa and seeing Rangers all night. The retelling brought back the horror of the night, watching Pa get shot and then peppered with pellets by that mech with Hanrahan. That still made no sense. None of it did. Geo couldn't eat.

Zak finished his second helping of grits. "They went up and down the valleys last night tearing up homesteads, asking about you, your pa, and this blonde girl. There's a huge reward for you and Blondie. Got folks wanting a sit-down."

Annabelle poured another round of coffee. "What's a—"

"Honey, please don't interrupt." Geo saw anger in the tightening of her turquoise eyes. If she wanted an explanation, it would have to wait until they were alone. "Civ girls get so uppity. You'll have to excuse her." He pulled out two biscuits, handed one to Annabelle, and waited until she took it.

Zak burst out laughing. "I can't fathom you snagged a filly before me." He wiped his chin and continued, "Thought we'd best warn you before you stumbled onto Rangers, not that you would."

"Couldn't find you," Mickey said, "until we heard an angry bear cussing a storm." He imitated Annabelle's loud snore.

"Blondie makes such interesting music," Zak said, "we thought it was a mating call."

"I don't snore." Annabelle said.

Geo squeezed her hand. "Actually, honey, you do."

She glared at him while scooping out the last of the grits for Zak.

"Rangers are drafting again," Zak said between mouthfuls of grits, "so I've scattered the young men. Folk won't take kindly to Rangers killing your pa."

Geo's stomach tightened. "Thanks," he said. "Can you get word out that we meet tonight?"

"Your place?"

"Yeah. No! Let's meet at the factory. Since Pa can't be there, I should go. Have folk keep an eye out for his body. He deserves a proper burial."

* * *

127

Annabelle was relieved when Zak led the three boys south. Geo snuffed out the fire and folded his poncho/sleeping bag. "I'm not doing dishes," Annabelle announced.

"Didn't ask you to." He grabbed the utensils, his backpack, and weapons.

"Then what was that nonsense about me cooking and not talking?"

Geo carried everything down to the spring. "Zak needed to see you were off limits so he wouldn't get any ideas."

She grabbed the pot and rinsed it.

"You need to talk less," Geo added, "until people get to know you." He hung the pot and skillet from his pack.

Annabelle grabbed his arm. "Can we rescue Janine now?"

He removed her hand. "I'm sending you home."

"You can't. I need you. Janine needs you." She squeezed his hands.

He yanked free. "This is creepy. No sister gets physical with a brother she just met. I've had enough of you touching, grabbing, and snuggling with your clothes off. You don't look anything like me. And if you're not my sister, you have a lot of explaining to do."

She dropped her hands. "I was scared last night, Geo."

"And so desperate you'd say anything. Why?" He turned to leave. "Never mind."

"Please don't be angry with me," Annabelle said. "If you'll give me a chance I'll explain everything."

Geo picked up his pack. "How refreshing. Why should I believe you?"

"I've never felt this vulnerable, like you see right through me. You've got my blood boiling and I'm scared."

"What are you talking about?"

"My father left the same time as yours," Annabelle said. "He was killed crossing the border. They imprisoned my mother for helping him. Your mom took me in. She's the only mom I know. She raised me, talking about you every night until I felt I knew you."

"Why didn't you tell me this last night?"

Her eyes watered. "I was pledged to Edwards. I was afraid you wouldn't help me unless you thought I was your sister."

"Go on."

"I didn't want you taking advantage of me last night. I have no experience with boys. I need us to focus on saving Janine."

"I don't buy it. You're holding something back. None of this justifies lying." After settling his pack onto his back, Geo picked up his rifle and headed uphill.

"Geo, don't leave me. I've come clean."

"Really? You haven't forgotten to tell me something else? Like why you kept touching me while telling me you're my sister?"

Annabelle grabbed his arm. "Okay, I like you more than I expected, more than I wanted to after you killed Karen. I found it sweet and reassuring at first that you didn't jump me in Biltmoor." She looked down. "I found you cute and sexy." Looking up, she saw him blush. "I'm sorry. You're not used to assertive girls, are you?"

He pulled away and kept climbing. "I can't turn off and on like that. You're sexy, you're my sister, you like me. It doesn't excuse lying."

She followed him. "Please don't send me home to marry that bastard. Janine is your biological sister. She doesn't know I was adopted, and all this will be a huge shock to her. I was the oldest, and the others were too young to understand, so Mom decided not to single me out. Civ betrayed my dad, my birth mother, Janine, me, you, everyone I care about."

"Aren't you just saying this to get me to help you?"

Annabelle stood before him and closed her eyes. "Please give me another chance."

TWENTY-FIVE

Geo didn't know what to think of Annabelle's stories, but he decided not to send her home. She would only follow him anyhow.

He led her through the valley and up to the next ridge, taking the long way to disorient her and avoid Rangers. While she seemed in great shape and didn't complain, he could tell she was tiring. He found a cleft in the rocky terrain where they could rest while he scanned the hillside and valley below.

Home was over the next ridge. Geo longed to talk with Pa, but Pa wouldn't be there. Geo had left him to Rangers, and Lord knows what they had done with him. Geo applied mosquito repellent behind his ears and handed the bottle to Annabelle.

Her face glistened in sweat. "Mom told me how you ran twenty-six miles at Olympic pace."

"Uh-huh."

"She said you ran to a neighbor with medicine and made it back in two hours."

"You believe everything Mom tells you?"

Annabelle looked sad and broken this morning. Last night, she had tempted him, dashed his hopes, and then admitted she lied. It was too much deception for one day.

"I'm sorry for everything," Annabelle said, as if she could read his mind. "I wasn't thinking clearly." She picked up a stick and dug a flower design in the dirt. "I grew up wanting to be like you—well, how Mom described you—not a scared mouse like I was in the dark."

"Sorry I left. I had some thinking to do."

Annabelle scooted next to him, her face suddenly playful. "About what?"

"Pa was all the family I knew and he's gone. It makes me want to hurt someone."

"Not me, I hope."

Geo shook his head. "So you joined mechs to live the legend?"

"I hoped I'd find you and we could be close."

He studied the pensive look on her face, wondering what it meant. Then he returned his attention to the valley. "I know we need to save her, but we're being hunted and we don't know where she is."

"I keep thinking how much worse things are for her."

"I'm sure." Geo handed her his canteen. "Fess up. Why did you really join the mechs?"

Annabelle drank and returned the jug. "I was mostly forced to. But I also felt my life was in a straitjacket. Now I can go off grid, mask the implant, and do reckless things, like approaching you."

"In a cathouse?" He handed her some turkey jerky.

"Not a well-thought-out plan. I saw a window of opportunity to meet you and grabbed it."

"Why would you want to come to Appalachia anyhow? All you've done is complain."

She chewed into the turkey. "The Union was to be the Garden of Eden for women. Health benefits and protections are wonderful."

"But?"

"We're so protected that we glide through life as if we're watching someone else's story. When I was 12, they pushed me toward security work. I could be a guard, a cop, or join the mechs." She stared at the jerky stick. "We can't eat beef, fries, salt or sweets because they're bad for you. We can't wear flashy clothes because that makes others feel inferior. It isn't real. Girls want to rebel, but they don't know what to do."

"So they party, do drugs, and dress like guys," Geo said.

"What are you talking about?"

"First time I saw you."

Annabelle gasped. "You were there? Oh, my God."

"Stupid, eh?"

"I'm impressed you got away."

Geo grinned. "I had help."

"We have no real guys. They send brains to geek institutes. It can't be much of a life. Strong guys become manual laborers in the farm districts. Other guys either run away or go to prison."

"Don't get sucked into our legends. Our life is a daily struggle to survive."

"I'm not disappointed, except maybe for the scare this morning."

He moved away, "Really?"

"Okay, I miss toilets." She smiled. "But you're more intriguing than any legend. You're real. You get to see a beautiful sky every night." Annabelle gripped his arm. "You're richer than our wealthiest politicians in their gated communities."

"Don't." Geo removed her hand. "This isn't a romantic life, especially for a girl."

* * *

Geo was surprised that they encountered no Ranger patrols or mechs on their way down the next valley. They passed postage-stamp farm plots and came upon the Howells' homestead, a hamlet with the burned-out shells of eight log cabins.

He scanned the area. "Stay in the woods," he told Annabelle.

"Any weapons? I do have training." She looked expectantly at him.

"How do I know you won't turn on me?"

"Come on, Geo. I never meant to hurt you."

Geo removed his revolver, checked the rounds, and handed it to her. "Don't waste ammo." He planted her off the path, surrounded by bushes, with a clear view of the charred cabins.

"Shouldn't we go in together?"

"Watch my back." Geo left his backpack.

Closer to one of the charred homes, Geo caught a whiff of mech hydraulics. He had seen burns before. This one looked like the work of a mech flamethrower. At least there was no scent of burned flesh.

The charred remains were still warm. Geo saw nothing of value. These people barely scraped by. Between drafted sons and seized land tithes, the Howells, like their neighbors, already gave Edwards everything they had.

He peered up and down the valley through his binoculars. Other cabins smoked. *The Tuttles and the Hammonds*, he thought, his heart sinking. *And maybe our home, too.*

Geo ran back to where he had left Annabelle. She was gone and so was his pack.

Confound it! I should have known better than to trust a mech! Now what?

He guessed she would return the way they had come. Then he heard movement in the brush behind him. He turned to see her hefting his backpack toward him.

He sighed. "I said stay put."

"I had to go."

"I told you not to squat."

Annabelle handed him the pack. "No one's around. Besides—"

Geo pointed across the clearing at two men perched in trees. "There's always someone." He pointed at the scorched cabins, frowning. "This was mech work. It's a controlled burn."

"Don't look at me. I've been with you. And if mechs were after me, they wouldn't torch people's houses, unless they resisted."

"These folk would resist," Geo said. "This was all they had. Are you people trying to starve us out?"

"Nobody's given me those orders," Annabelle said. "But by the looks of it, you're doing a great job yourselves. You can't support these people on small garden plots."

"Really?" Geo headed up the next hill. "Come on. No talking." He decided to let her keep the revolver. *Just don't point it at me.*

TWENTY-SIX

Geo smelled smoke before he caught a glimpse of his home. Even so, the sight came as a shock: torched garden plots: corn, tomatoes, broccoli and cauliflower. Staples they would need for next winter. *Who did this? Rangers, mechs? Why?*

The little cabin where they had sheltered Cory was now nothing but smoldering charcoal smeared across the rocky mountainside. The main cabin, home, clung to the rock face. It looked intact, but smoke drifted out his bedroom window. To the right were two more garden plots turned to ash.

He glared at Annabelle. "How important are you?"

She stared back. "How do you know they aren't after you? After all, they killed your pa, then came here."

To the left of the clearing, the cap to the water pump rested on the ground. The outhouse was nothing but burned embers. Geo studied the trees with his binoculars. At least the bastards hadn't attacked the canopy or the microwave transmitters. That was something. "This is mech work."

"I haven't heard about mechs working with Rangers."

"Mechs on safari? You know about those, don't you?" They hunted people as well as deer. Geo dropped his pack. "I'm going in to see what's left." He readied his .50 cal and headed for the cabin. *Be cautious,* Pa would say. He choked back the pain in his throat.

Geo ran to the front door of the smoldering cabin, paused, and looked back. Annabelle hovered right behind him, her hot breath on his ear. *How annoying.*

He put on his night goggles, motioned for her to wait, and covered his nose and mouth with a handkerchief. As soon as he entered the cabin, smoke penetrated his eyes and nose. Hot images flared from his bedroom.

Something connected with Geo's jaw, sending him back against the door, slamming it shut. He dropped his rifle and groped for it. He couldn't find it through the smoke. He rolled into the corner where the sink basin had been and reached for Pa's shotgun. *Gone.*

An image charged toward him. Geo yanked free the sink drainpipe and swung it at his attacker. Missed. His lungs demanded oxygen. He jumped up and crashed through the window, gulping fresh air as he tumbled onto the porch.

Across the porch, a muscle-bound Ranger grabbed for Annabelle. She blocked and threw jabs. Wearing fire-protection gear and a shield, another Ranger jumped on top of Geo. His bulging muscles strained the fire outfit. The Ranger removed his helmet and slammed it down.

Geo squirmed aside, narrowly missing the blow. He scrambled to his feet. The Ranger landed a punch to the gut. Geo buckled over, stayed standing, and took another hit to the jaw. He backed up and tried to focus through the stabbing pain. His grisly-faced attacker tapped his head as if to activate a com-link.

Geo tackled the man and got in a couple of blows. His Ranger got to his feet and squared off. "I'm going to enjoy this."

So am I, Geo thought. The man pulled a knife and lunged at Geo. *Miss the blow,* Pa always said, which was easier to watch than to do. Geo dodged and pulled his own knife from his jeans.

Something's wrong. Why don't the Rangers just shoot me? Geo lunged at his opponent, and missed. Searing heat sliced his shoulder, a glancing blow. It felt on fire. A fleeting look at Annabelle told him she wasn't doing any better. She backed up toward the house. His Ranger charged; Geo parried and spun away to see Annabelle drop onto the porch.

"Nooo!" Geo started toward her.

His attacker blocked but didn't swing. Her Ranger straddled her, holding a pair of cuffs.

Annabelle plunged both feet up into her Ranger's groin. He grinned. "Wearing a cup, sweetie." He unlocked the cuffs and prepared to drop down on her.

Annabelle leaned back and used her feet to shove the Ranger

six inches off the ground. His skull connected with the porch overhang, strung with potted plants. Geo could almost feel the nails plunge into the Ranger's skull. Annabelle pulled away, spun to the side, and leapt to her feet.

With a ghastly groan, her Ranger hung for an instant by his skull before he slumped onto the porch, holding his head.

Geo's attacker turned to look. Annabelle lunged at him. Geo plunged his knife into his Ranger's neck and sliced across the throat. The man slumped to the ground. Geo grabbed Annabelle and held her tight. "What were you thinking?"

She smiled up at him. "That two-on-one sounded great. I wasn't about to lose you."

Geo pulled the knife from his attacker's neck, made sure the Ranger was dead, and wiped the knife clean on the Ranger's uniform. *Oh, Lord, forgive me for taking a life.* He turned to Annabelle. "Let's move them." He checked her Ranger's pulse. "How were you able to lift him?"

"They train us to spike and focus adrenalin. Now my back's killing me." She hunched over like old man Peterson.

Taking his grisly-faced attacker by the wrists, Geo dragged him toward the hillside. Annabelle tugged at her Ranger but didn't get him very far before Geo returned to help.

"Thanks," she said. "I feel useless."

"You're anything but. That was the best fighting I've seen." He took her Ranger's wrists and dragged him across the grassy clearing.

Annabelle ambled beside him. "You lost focus because of me. You need to trust me to do my part and concentrate on yours."

Geo dropped the second Ranger in the rear of what had been Cory's cabin, up against the rock wall. He removed the Ranger's fire shield and kicked ash over the bodies.

"We need to go," she said. "The Rangers called this in. The place will be swarming soon." She hunched, holding her back, smiling and trying to act strong. She wasn't like any girl he had met.

"I know you're scared," he said.

She straightened up. "I'm not scared, I'm sore. I'll get over it. Let's go."

Geo examined the water pump: scorched handle broken off, pipe crushed and fused. It looked like mech burn. He kicked the battered pump housing. "They were thorough." He headed for the woods. "I need to check a few things."

Wincing, Annabelle joined him. "Geo, there's nothing left."

"This doesn't add up." He picked up his pack and returned to the smoldering cabin.

Annabelle followed.

"Wait outside—"

"I'm staying with you. Maybe there are other guys in trees. It gives me the creeps."

Geo looked across the clearing at the shed where Pa kept the still. It lay hacked apart and burned to the ground. "They took your whiskey, Pa. Now why'd they go and do that?"

"The monopoly," Annabelle said.

Geo gathered his pack and crossbow and prepared to reenter the smoking cabin that had been his home. *What to do with Annabelle?* She was in pain. She needed rest, but could he trust this mech warrior filled with deceptions and half-truths? "How did they know where to find this place? We've kept it hidden for years. You know, I've had nothing but trouble since I met you."

"I didn't do this, Geo. I don't have mech connections or com-link, and you're family. Well, Mom's family."

"What about your implant?"

"It's masked," Annabelle said, "and if it wasn't, mechs would search for me, not torch your place. Who else knew about this place?"

Geo sighed. "Cory Philips." He touched the cabin doorknob. It was hot, so he covered his hand with his handkerchief.

"I told you he was no good. Don't go in. You'll get yourself killed."

He opened the cabin door and smoke billowed out. He put on his infrared goggles and his attacker's fire mask. He handed her his handkerchief. "Put this over your nose and mouth, keep your eyes closed, and hang onto my waistband."

"What are we looking for?"

"A tunnel." Geo crawled across the blistered-wood floor with Annabelle's fingers tugging at his waist. Flames licked the bedrooms to the left and right, a slow burn because Pa used fire-retardant materials when he built the cabin. A few of Geo's beloved books were going up in smoke by the smell. The great room was empty; bastards took all the furniture, including Pa's hand-carved maple table. All that remained in the middle of the floor was Geo's rifle. He grabbed it and kept moving.

Geo crawled to the wall that hugged the huge boulder at the rear of the cabin. He felt around the base of the Franklin stove, which was still anchored to the floor. Sliding a latch, he pushed the stove aside and pulled up a steel plate. He reached down and felt around—no water. *Good.* "You first."

"Do we have to?"

"Go before the smoke gets worse! It's down four feet, only one way to go. At the other end, push up the steel panel and set it aside. Don't let it fall into the tunnel." He moved her hands to the pit, helped her climb down, and prayed it wasn't burning on the other side.

Coughing and wheezing, she climbed down. Geo took one last glance at the living area and bedrooms, ablaze in infrared. *Pa, you wouldn't have let this happen. It's my fault.*

Geo climbed down after Annabelle, and pulled in his pack and rifle. Then he eased the heavy steel plate over the hole, stopping the flow of smoke. He ratcheted a gear that pulled the heavy Franklin stove over the steel plate and anchored it. Then he set a mech grenade on a ledge beneath the floor, and palmed the remote.

TWENTY-SEVEN

When he reached the other side, Geo removed his mask and inhaled. There was only a hint of smoke, which meant Pa's air purifiers were working. Annabelle turned on her flashlight as Geo replaced the steel plate and sealed it.

He stumbled to the limestone wall. At a panel, he triggered sprinklers for the cabin. *Good thing I forgot to switch the water on after last winter's freezes. Rangers would have dug until they found the source. Plus, it would have flooded the tunnel.*

Annabelle flashed her light in his eyes, blinding him. "Why don't you trust me? You keep bringing up that I'm a mech, like I did this."

"Trust you, after you lied to me?"

She closed her eyes. "I was scared, Geo. Are you going to keep punishing me?"

"Watch this." Geo flipped on a bank of bioluminescent lights, illuminating the large living room, shaped to conform to the cave. There was a kitchen to the left, a meandering hall leading to bedrooms, and to the right a bank of wall screens and electronics.

Annabelle's deep turquoise eyes nearly popped. "Wow."

"Pa never showed this place to anybody but me," Geo said. His throat caught for a moment. He cleared it. "There's a bathroom down the hall with indoor plumbing and soap just for you."

"Is that a joke?" She flipped off her flashlight, twirled, and stopped at shelves of books and artifacts Pa collected from before the war. "Have you read these?" She scanned the bindings. "People don't read paper anymore, do they?"

Geo nodded. He used a remote to project cam shots onto the wall-screens. "Different feel to hold the actual words, though I read more electronic these days. I've read the entire Bible, not just the Thane-approved parts."

"How about these histories?" Annabelle asked.

"Uh-huh." Geo paced through exterior cams. One showed water spraying the shell of his bedroom with the roof and two walls ablaze. He was too late.

"I never heard of a guy who could read," Annabelle said, "except math geeks, of course."

"Pa insisted I keep up my studies," Geo said.

"Quite a collection. I can't believe you hide all this in a cave."

Geo laughed. "Pa says it pays not to advertise."

"A good thing, or Rangers would have taken them."

"Burned. They don't like books."

"They censor us at home as well. You said there's a real bathroom?" She didn't wait for an answer.

While she was gone, Geo replayed video recordings of the Ranger attack. Hazy green images showed Rangers hacking at the shed across the clearing and dismantling the still. They broke into the outer cabin, his home, and carried out Pa's hand-carved maple table, the one he and Pa labored on last winter when they got snowed in. Pa had let Geo help with the carving and sanding. It was like watching them kill Pa all over again.

When the Rangers finished removing furniture and dishes, they tossed the few books Geo kept in the cabin into a pile in the middle of Geo's bedroom floor. They poured fluid over the books, but didn't light it. Finally, they kicked and bashed the Franklin stove in frustration before leaving.

Pa, I know you don't like bringing in strangers, but I'm sure you would want me to protect Annabelle. So why didn't you tell me about Mom and my sisters?

Annabelle shuffled toward him, rubbing her back. "Bless you for the bathroom. Delightful and clean. I could get used to this."

"Lie down and let me massage your back before it freezes up." Geo pointed to the sofa in front of the screens.

With effort, Annabelle tugged off her borrowed beige linen shirt, revealing a pale blue bra. She crept onto the soft leather sofa. "This is heaven after last night." She propped her head on a small cushion. "How can you have electricity with no power grid?"

Geo stared at the red and purple marks along her arms and across her back. He wanted to wring that Ranger's neck, but the bastard was already dead. Geo sank his fingers into the taut muscles of Annabelle's back. "Pa built a solar grid in the tree canopy. It triggers bursts of microwaves into storage cells."

"That's right. Mom said he was an engineer."

"Among other things." Geo was careful not to push on her bruises. "The entire system is wireless and intermittent."

"That explains why our surveillance didn't flag it."

Geo massaged the powerful muscles up and down her back. They didn't ripple like Zak's. They were lean and purposeful for performance, not for show. She had a graceful hourglass figure.

He returned his attention to the video screens. Mechs sprayed fire inhibitors to protect the forest; then they torched the fields.

"Your hands are fantastic, Geo. Just what I need."

"Not too rough, I hope."

"Not at all." Annabelle sighed. "More pressure on my lower back. It feels like something's out of place."

Adjusting his pressure, Geo worked her knotted muscles.

"Oh, yeah. Much better. A little lower."

But lower was her butt. This morning she had nestled it into his back. He pulled away.

"Don't stop. That was perfect."

Geo faced the screens. A mech torched the still.

Annabelle turned, revealing her taut stomach.

Geo covered her with a blanket and stared at the screen. "Mechs working with Rangers? It makes no sense."

* * *

Annabelle pulled on the linen shirt and approached the screen. She wished he would continue the massage, but decided to leave it at that. It was a big step for Geo to bring her into his wonderful cave hideaway and make her feel better. "That's an old model mech suit. See the crude seam between the helmet and suit? We no longer use them."

"Then someone sold them to Edwards."

"My commander wouldn't."

"Tell me you don't dump old suits over the border," Geo said, "in your environmentally pure dump sites."

Annabelle shook her head. "A company picks them up and

crushes them. They're melted down to be recycled."

"Are you sure?"

"This is a dangerous development," Annabelle said. "Battani is so hot for this deal with Edwards, I wouldn't put it past her."

"You think she sold them?"

"If she did, she'd leave tracking devices. Someone in mech command would know. This means Janine and I are in more danger than I thought."

Onscreen, two Rangers took up position in the cabin and waited. It was the two Geo and Annabelle had fought. After a while, they set fire to Geo's books.

Annabelle turned to Geo. "We have to get Janine before they do something terrible to her."

He flipped screens to show current views from the cams. "Pa says acting impulsively gets you killed."

"I'm sorry, Geo. I wish I could change things. He's not coming back."

"You don't get it. He lives in every cubic inch of this place, every design, every gadget, the walls and fixtures. He speaks to me even now."

"Ghosts?"

Geo shook his head. "There were times I didn't pay attention, and yet his words penetrated my thick skull. He would know what to do. He told me to carry on, and I wish he was here to tell me what that meant."

Annabelle placed her hand on his shoulder. "Let's figure it out together. By the way, whatever you did to my back, it hasn't felt this good in a long time."

He shrugged. "We rarely see doctors. When Pa's back troubles him, I work his muscles."

* * *

Geo dimmed the lights and severed the electronic connections to reduce their infrared footprint. After checking that the fuel cell charge was high, he disconnected the microwave receivers.

"We have company." Annabelle pointed to the screens.

Six Rangers on noisy gas-cycles spilled into the grassy clearing in front of the cabin. Behind them, an armadillo pulled up. Twenty Rangers jumped out. *What the hell?* Geo turned down the monitor's volume to spare his ears. "Gather anything of value," he told her. He palmed a memory cube from the cam system.

Annabelle spun around. "These books are priceless."

"Leave them. I have electronic copies. We need survival tools."

Geo opened a drawer below the screen and removed a revolver and ammo to replace the one he had given to Annabelle. He was itching to fight. He could take out a wave of them, but more would come, were coming—another armadillo. "Grab weapons and ammo, we'll get food on the road."

"Road kill?"

He unlocked a closet and removed grenades. "Don't knock it." He was loathe to use grenades on his home, even to stop Rangers. Destroying Pa's handiwork was sacrilege. Still, he had a few surprises he and Pa had scavenged off a dead mech a while back.

Annabelle fingered one of Geo's two-phase grenades. "Do you have a plan?"

Two mechs arrived, removing any doubt they were working with the Rangers. Across the clearing, Ralph circled a tree. *I know, boy. Save yourself.* Geo turned off the water to the sprinklers. It was useless now, as was his plan to take out the Rangers. Mechs would be much tougher.

"Some hospitality you have." Annabelle stared at crates of rifles, ammo and RPGs. "You planning to start another civil war?"

"Just to protect my home," Geo said. "Pa was in the war and kept what he could salvage. He believed in being prepared." Geo placed a grenade beneath a floor panel.

Annabelle went through a cabinet in the kitchen. "How do we get out?"

"I said forget the food. Grab a canteen and fill it." Geo planted another grenade under the floor.

"Geo, talk to me. You're not thinking of making a stand. There must be twenty of them, plus the mechs."

Geo stared at the screen. Two mechs stood before the home cabin, weapons drawn. Rangers fanned out behind them. Between the mechs stood a Ranger with general stars, the one who had stood over Pa.

"Show yourselves," the general said. "We know you're in there. Don't make us blast you out."

"That bastard shot Pa," Geo said. He adjusted the volume on the cam's mike so he could hear better.

"General Hanrahan," Annabelle said.

Geo dimmed the bioluminescence and turned on his flash beam. "You know him?"

"I studied his dossier. He was there when I was captured."

Two mechs flamed what was left of the cabin. *Bastards. Think, Geo. What would Pa do?*

"Last chance," Hanrahan said.

The ground shook as mechs blasted the cabin frame. Fire retardant could only do so much,

"I've counted fifty Rangers and three mechs," Geo said. The outer cabin disintegrated under blistering fire. *All that work, Pa.*

"Grab whatever you can carry," Geo barked. He took a data-cube from his desk and tucked it into his pocket. "Any idea how to take out three mechs?"

"You can't be serious. Mechs can blast us to pieces before we could do any damage."

Mechs plunged into the rubble of Pa's cabin, tossing roof timbers like toothpicks. They kicked aside debris. Geo wondered if Annabelle was still hiding something. He couldn't imagine why General Hanrahan would personally come out here. *Maybe we should go our separate ways.* "You're right. We are sitting ducks."

Geo transferred cam images to his wrist-com and turned out the bioluminescence. He grabbed his pack, a canvas bag of electronics, and a bag with grenades and ammo. "I'll get you out the back way and draw their forces. You escape, save Janine, and go home." He nudged Annabelle toward the rear of the cave.

Annabelle pushed back. "I'm not leaving you to die alone. I've lost too many friends that way."

Pushing past her, he reached the hall's dead end. "Don't be a martyr. One of us has to save Janine."

"You send me out and I'll circle around and hit them out front. I'm not leaving you. I'm a warrior. This is what I do."

"With a suit, maybe." Geo opened the door to a small guest bedroom, with a low tile ceiling to accommodate the cave's shape.

"Without if I have to. I'm sure your pa wouldn't want you dying for this place."

He checked his wrist-com. Mechs ripped up the charred cabin floor. Rangers approached the Franklin stove and pushed. The cables held. A mech blasted it, shredded the metal frame, and kicked until the shriveled hunk of metal sprang free of the cables and rolled onto its side like a dead raccoon.

Geo faced the boulder separating them from the mechs. "Pa said, 'Live to fight another day,'" he muttered.

"He was right, Geo. Let's go."

Rangers in fire gear blundered through the cabin, picking their way across the cindered wood floor. Two came to the spot where the Franklin stove had stood.

"Looks like they're tracking us," Geo said.

"Infrared."

"This place is shielded." Geo grabbed two spare ponchos. No use putting them on, though; Rangers wouldn't believe they had disappeared like that. He tucked the ponchos into a loop on his backpack.

The view on his wrist-com showed Rangers studying the ash-covered steel plate. One mech removed it, sending it skipping across the cabin floor like a pebble. When the mech shone a light into the hole, a Ranger dropped down. He came back up dripping wet, and pointed toward the cave.

"It leads behind the boulder," a masculine voice said.

TWENTY-EIGHT

"Annabelle, I know you're in there." This was a different voice, coming over a loudspeaker: Thane Edwards.

"We've been tracking your heat signature. You can hide, but not for long. We have you surrounded. We will post sensors. There's no chance of escape."

Looking over Geo's shoulder at his wrist-com, Annabelle saw Edwards in Ranger uniform, standing behind a tree across the clearing. He was talking into a microphone. *How daring. Why don't you step out where I could hit you, you bastard?*

"Why is he telling us?" Geo asked.

"So we'll give up."

"Annabelle, we got off on the wrong foot," Edwards said from the cover of woods. Three mechs stepped into the cabin and cleared Rangers out of the smoldering hulk. "I should have been gentler. I wanted to protect you from the brutes that live in these mountains. They aren't like you and me."

So, you are *here for me.*

"That boy is trouble like his father. He'll bring you grief with his lies. Come out and I'll forgive you and take you back."

"You'll forgive me?" Annabelle headed down the hallway.

Geo grabbed her wrist. "He's baiting you."

"Come out now, Annabelle, and I'll let the boy go."

"Don't do it," Geo said. "You can't marry that bastard."

"If I go, you could sneak out the back," Annabelle said. "Once they have me, they won't look so hard for you."

"You'd be stuck with him. Besides, the tunnel is flooded."

"I'll release Janine," Edwards shouted. "I'll send her home."

Geo dropped Annabelle's wrist and sighed. "Maybe you should go, for Janine's sake. If we die, no telling what he'll do to her, maybe even make her stand in your place."

"Don't even think it," Annabelle said. "There's no guarantee he'll release her. Remember, he kidnapped us. He might hold her so I don't run, and he'll track you down and kill you. No deal." She was surprised at how strongly this resonated.

Edwards signaled the general. From opposite sides, two mechs blasted the boulder that separated the cabin from the cave, sending fireworks of chips in all directions. The boulder defied the attack. Annabelle held her breath.

Geo pulled packs and supplies into the small bedroom. He moved the bed, revealing a panel behind the headboard.

An eerie cracking split the air like thunder as blasts pulverized the boulder. It split in two, splashing daylight into the cave.

Geo opened the panel. "Get in."

All Annabelle saw was darkness.

* * *

Geo helped Annabelle into the dark opening and pushed bags and weapons after her. He activated the remote for the grenade he had left near the Franklin stove, and dived in after her. He hit the panel remote to seal the opening and pull the bed back against the wall. Then he switched his wrist-com's speaker to his ear-bud.

Annabelle shone her flashlight on a craggy stone tunnel, barely wide enough for two. "What's this?"

"Turn that beam off. Here, wear this." Geo handed her the spare poncho, and he put on his own infrared-shielded covering. "It'll get hot, but if you can stand it, they might lose our signal."

He triggered the grenade. Distant explosions sounded like fireworks. Tremors rumbled the ground. Geo's wrist-com showed a mech freeze and fall: bulls-eye. The blast tossed a second mech like leaves. The third fell back. *Lord, forgive me for taking another life.*

Rangers scattered, firing their weapons into the shattered boulder. That sent shells and rock chips spewing in all directions.

Annabelle knelt next to Geo. "What was that?"

Geo handed her night-vision goggles and pulled on his own. "Mech grenade to slow them down." He crept to another panel and removed it. He crawled through and pulled the bags and weapons after him. This was a bare cave, squeezed between the rear wall of the living quarters and a huge rock.

Annabelle followed. "What if we can't shake them?"

"We go out fighting." Geo replaced the panel. "Probably won't get far with all the sensors and Rangers, but it's our best shot."

Picking a unique frequency on his remote, he triggered a hydraulic lever system, another of Pa's marvels. "This will be uncomfortable. You can't make a sound. Make sure every part of your body is covered by the poncho."

She touched his arm. "Will this work?"

Geo reached out to feel the rock rising, thanks to hydraulics. "It's a long shot."

His wrist-com showed the two remaining mechs line up on either side of the split boulder between the outer cabin and the cave. They blasted, sending rock fragments in all directions.

When the blasting paused, Annabelle pressed against him. "What are we waiting for? And what's that hum?"

"Quiet. Just wait." *Hydraulics take time.* A musty breeze stirred from beneath the rock. Pumps strained to lift it inch by inch, with a smooth purring that belied the strain. Already, the reflected heat in the poncho was making Geo sweat.

On his wrist-com, he watched a mech clamor over the rubble into the cave. When the mech signaled, a swarm of Rangers rushed in. Geo said another prayer and triggered a weapon remote to a scavenged mech gun he and Pa installed above the cave opening. He didn't watch his mech gun spew pellets, cutting down the first wave of attackers. He was thankful the image was small and fuzzy because he detested what mech guns could do.

Sweat streamed down his neck as Geo stuck his hand beneath the rising rock to check the size of the opening. "Okay. You first."

"What if the rock falls?"

He pushed his gear toward the dark, narrow opening. "Then we're worm food."

"Thanks."

"Push your bags ahead of you until you reach a stone wall. Then turn around and make sure the poncho covers you completely. Now go. No more talking."

Mechs entered the cave and located Geo's mech gun mounted on a ledge. One mech pulled it down and disabled it.

Using his infrared scope, Geo watched Annabelle's ghostly

image scoot under the rock. The wrist-com showed Rangers entering the cave, flooding it with halogen light.

Geo slid under the rock, pushing his pack, bags, and weapons. He reached the other side, sweating from exertion. He could barely see Annabelle's image. *Good.* He turned around, triggered hydraulics to lower the rock, and adjusted his poncho.

Rangers poured into every room and closet of Geo's cave home. His ear-bud picked up their chatter. "They aren't here."

Mechs tore down the outer walls of the cave home. Rangers pulled the view-screens off the wall and grabbed Geo's laptop, furniture, dishes and food.

Pa, what do you say we deprive them of their loot? Geo said a prayer and triggered several grenade remotes. The cave floor erupted like a volcano, tossing one mech on top of several Rangers, while the other mech took a direct hit. *Sorry, Pa. I can't let them have it.*

The last mech stood and blasted what was left of the floor, ceiling, and walls. When the shooting stopped, General Hanrahan entered, stepped over rubble, and poked what remained of walls and floor.

"The place is empty, my lord," the mech said. "And probably booby-trapped."

Geo wished he had another mech gun to take out the bastard who killed Pa.

The general stood in the middle of the debris, seemingly unfazed by the destruction. "Thane Edwards will want every book out front, examined for anything hidden inside. Give any other paper items to me. You're welcome to split the rest."

Hanrahan directed the mech to remove chunks of flooring, wall and ceiling. Rangers swarmed over the cave, pulling everything out. One Ranger found Pa's violin, his comfort late at night. General Hanrahan grabbed the violin like a bat, looked ready to smash Pa's treasure and then seemed to reconsider. He carried it out to his truck and tossed it in the back like firewood.

What had taken Geo and Pa months to build, Rangers cleared out in hours. They picked the place clean, piling items in the grassy clearing. Sweating, Geo downed half the contents of his canteen. Annabelle's body swayed with slow breathing. She was practically lying on top of him, heating him like an oven. He moved away.

TWENTY-NINE

Covered head-to-toe in the oven-like poncho, Annabelle slowed her breathing. She heard those clumsy clods destroying Geo's beautiful home while they searched for her.

She took another sip from her canteen. If she surrendered and married the bastard to save Janine, they would probably kill Geo. Part of her wanted to stay with Geo and hope beyond reason he would surprise her with a way to escape and save Janine.

Annabelle couldn't see him through the ponchos. If only she could see what was going on, but after those final explosions, there couldn't be any working cams.

She sighed. Geo was hurting over the loss of his pa and his home, but they were wasting time while Janine rotted alone in a cell.

She scooted closer to Geo. He moved away. Before, there had always been the comfort of Janine depending on her.

Now, I'm becoming too dependent on Geo, she realized. *Since when did I need a guy's help? Well, now I do. We're lying on a stone floor with rock all around us, and I have no idea how to move.*

She nestled next to Geo, hoping he didn't move again.

* * *

Geo felt increasingly annoyed as Annabelle kept bumping into him. *Like we aren't hot enough already.* He focused on his wrist-com and one remaining view inside the cave, stripped of its walls, ceiling, and floor. He pulled up his mobile cam at the end of a fiber-optic extension that rested on his pack. No light. Good, given all the banging.

Rangers had blasted the cave to bare rock. Now they inspected every inch of wall and floor. *Good luck.* Unlike the outer cabin, nestled against the mountainside, the cave home had no clear back to indicate another trap door.

Rangers pointed scanning equipment in every direction. Apparently, they didn't pick up any heat signatures. *The sweat-bags must be working. Annabelle probably can't handle the heat, though.*

Geo directed his wrist-com to pick up exterior cams. Pope Edwards, no, only Cardinal, of the First Appalachian Church of Do-What-I-Say stood over piles of Pa's possessions. "All this loot and the bastard couldn't pay his tithes."

Yeah, a tithe to the Cardinal, a tithe to the thane, and another to the Chairman of Biltmoor Corporation, along with cuts on everything bought or sold. No wonder Rangers were loyal and he could take what he wanted.

Edwards kicked a kitchen cabinet Pa made, buckling the side. Then he used a stick-light to set a pile of books ablaze. Geo thought of *Fahrenheit 451* and shed a tear for the *King James Bible* and other treasures that may never see print again. *Pa, they don't understand.* Not checking titles, Edwards even burned one of his own Thane's Bibles.

Rangers packed three armadillos and some trucks with Pa's possessions. The last items in the clearing were munitions. Edwards and General Hanrahan instructed Rangers to load them into an oversized truck with the general's stars on its side.

Edwards kicked a crate. "Where the hell did he get this firepower? It stinks of rebellion. The last thing we need is trouble from the mountaineers."

Geo turned up the volume.

Hanrahan lifted an RPG into his truck. "Leftovers from the war."

"He was supposed to turn them over." Edwards picked up a grenade and examined it.

Geo took another drink, the last from his canteen. *Wish I had the remote to that one.*

"My lord." Hanrahan moved another crate. "The Shaws won't be bothering us anymore. The old man will serve as warning to others, and we've covered every possible escape. If they died in the blast, we would need Civ forensics to confirm."

"I want the certificates and the rest of Shaw's documents. Find them."

"We've examined every scrap of paper, every drawer, cupboard, and closet. They must have gone up in the blast."

"You're slipping, general," Edwards said. "First you can't find Shaw. Next, you find him, but no documents. Then you lose his son and the girl."

"She's a mech, sir."

"Tell me something I don't know." Edwards climbed into a loaded armadillo. "Search until you find them. If she's alive, she'll come for her sister. Without mech support, she's on her own. If she's gone, we'll need a stand-in. But we don't need Civs blaming us for losing the girl before the wedding." He drove off.

Hanrahan grabbed the nearest Ranger, gave him the keys to his truck and told him to deliver the weapons to his base.

An excited Ranger approached the general. "We found two skulls, sir."

"Male or female?"

"They're too badly burned to tell. There were bone fragments everywhere, like they were blasted."

Geo felt a pang. It was probably Billy Joe and Henry Lee, two boys who helped Pa on Mondays in exchange for food.

THIRTY

Hanrahan pulled out with his Rangers. Geo replayed the exterior cam footage on his wrist-com and watched them set up cams and infrared sensors targeting the cave. If he and Annabelle ventured out, Rangers would return. She was practically on top of him again, her body swaying to slow breathing.

Making sure he remained beneath his poncho, Geo scooted around until he faced the cave's dead-end, and a fiber-composite panel that was stronger than steel. Using a remote burst-transmitter, he activated a code. The panel slowly rose.

"Almost over," he whispered. "There's a door by your feet. Don't try to turn around. Just crawl backward as far as you can, then wait. Don't stick your feet out from under the poncho."

He heard her poncho scrape across the limestone floor. When the sound stopped, he eased the bags forward, one by one, careful not to make sudden movements that might trigger any potential motion sensors.

Geo crept in next to Annabelle and closed the panel. Still surrounded by darkness, he triggered a second door. "Same thing again. Make sure you're covered."

"In sweat," she said.

When her movements stopped, he followed with bags, weapons and himself before closing the second panel and inhaling stale air that was mercifully smoke-free. He removed the poncho and turned on overhead bioluminescent lights. *Thanks, Pa. Your solar leaves really came through.*

153

"You can come out now."

"What about infrared?" Annabelle removed the poncho and blinked in the bright overhead lights. Her blonde hair lay matted against her face and neck.

"Double-shielded. If they didn't track us coming in, their current equipment shouldn't find us." They both stood up stiffly, working out the kinks in their muscles.

Eyes popping, Annabelle looked around ultramodern living quarters. "You are full of surprises, Geo. We're still in a cave?"

"Pa created all this after the war." Geo dimmed the lights, which glowed across the ceiling. This room was smaller than the middle home, and filled with electronic gear, some of which Pa had salvaged during the war.

Annabelle scanned a small library of printed books in glass-enclosed bookcases. "Why didn't we come here earlier?"

"I didn't want to use this if we didn't have to." Geo went to a sink in the kitchen, poured two glasses of water, and handed one to Annabelle. "This was Pa's private sanctuary." Geo closed his eyes, drank, and savored cool liquid sliding down his parched throat.

She cocked her head, hurried across the room to a desk, and picked up a package. "This is the book I gave him two days ago from Mom." She handed it to Geo. "Open it."

He ripped the brown paper to reveal a leather-bound copy of *A Tale of Two Cities*.

"This proves I'm not lying about Mom." Annabelle opened to the title page. "To George from Mom." She smiled. "See."

"Maybe."

"I told her I'd seen you." She patted his arm. "She had me bring DWM books banned by the Union."

"DWM?"

"Dead white male authors."

Even Geo had to smile at this.

"Mom thought she was saving her collection by sending it here." Annabelle sighed. "Instead, Edwards burned it."

"Not all of it." Pulling away, Geo placed the book on the counter. "At least not yet."

He sat before a virtual keyboard and 3D screen and pulled up images of the outdoors surrounding their hideaway. Thinking of the wonderful library Mom had touched and passed on tightened his throat.

Annabelle rested a hand on his shoulder and pointed at a framed picture on the wall. "That's Niagara Falls. Mom has an identical one in her study."

Geo glanced at it and shrugged. "Lots of people probably do."

She kneaded her fingers into his muscles. "It celebrates hidden mysteries. Did you know there are caves behind the falls? Mom took me before they banned travel."

"So?" The scene outside the cave was strangely placid. Not even a squirrel scurried about.

"That's where he proposed to Mom."

Geo scooted closer to the screen and triggered flash-decoys. "Why give me this book?"

"Have you read it?"

"Electronically. It's about the French Revolution. Is she saying Appalachia is the French reign of terror?"

"I don't think she's being mean." Annabelle continued massaging. "It's about things not turning out as expected. It's a beautiful story."

The massage was great. He liked her touch. But not how she stirred his blood. He got up and moved away. "The hero dies in the end."

"He sacrificed himself for a greater cause."

Geo placed the book behind protective glass. "Unrequited love?"

"You have something against love?"

"One lesson of the French and Russian Revolutions is when you overthrow tyranny, be careful you don't replace it with terror."

"Are you trying to impress me that you've read more than I have?"

Books—histories, novels, philosophy—caught his eye. With everything that had happened, their stories seemed an oasis of calm.

Annabelle squeezed between him and the books and placed her hand on his chest. "I know it's been a horrible day, but I'm worried sick about Janine."

He removed her hand. "Stop doing that." He took a deep breath.

Eyes downcast, Annabelle clasped her hands before her. "We touch at home. I guess it's a girl thing." She gazed up. "I need your help. Janine needs us."

"I don't like being touched." Though he did. Even with her face moist with sweat and hair stringy, she looked beautiful, not in the manner of Undercover girls, but rather like someone DaVinci might paint. "You love her, don't you?"

"She's a terrific sister. You'll love her, too. Smart and enthusiastic."

"I mean you love her."

Annabelle gasped. "Geo!"

He turned and stood before the screen. Rangers in the clearing responded to the flash-decoys. "I don't know what they teach you...."

"It's not what you think. Please, I'm begging you. Janine needs us. No matter what you think of me, can you do this for her?"

He pointed at the screen. "We aren't going anywhere until we can get past their sensors."

Annabelle frowned. "Can't we blast them?"

"And bring a swarm of Rangers?"

"We can't just sit here." She took his hand.

He pushed her away. "Stop grabbing."

She tripped, regained her balance, and came at him, faking a punch. When he blocked, she swept his legs, sending him crashing onto the hardwood floor. She jumped on top. "I'll fight you for it."

Geo scrambled free. "What's gotten into you?"

She spun behind him. "I'm desperate, Geo, I need your help."

He leapt to his feet. "You're crazy. After what we've been through."

Annabelle grabbed his arm and flipped him.

Spinning into a somersault, he landed on his feet in a crouched position and stood up. "You want to fight?" He pulled off his shirt.

She lunged at him; Geo grabbed her arm. She pulled free and swept his legs. He jumped and dropped onto her, pinning one arm. She thrust her fist into his ribs and threw him back. Without letting him catch his breath, she followed through. She landed beside him, and scooted until she had one of his arms pinned under the sofa.

He thrust the butt of his free hand into her hip, throwing her up onto the leather sofa. It gave him a moment to scoot away. When he got to his feet, Annabelle didn't move. Concerned that he'd hurt her, he knelt next to her.

She jumped him, knocked him onto the floor, and straddled

him. "Good, focused move, but you fell for the simplest trick in the book."

"I didn't mean to hurt you. If you're done with fight lessons, can you get up?"

She stood and held out her hand. "It felt good to let off steam. Now can we get Janine?"

Geo stood and wiped sweat from his forehead. "I want to help, but out there we'll need a plan."

"Good fight." She patted his shoulder and lingered. "Mom must be worried sick. I wish there was some way to tell her I'm okay."

Geo removed her hand. "What would you tell her?"

"Don't kid around." She studied him. "Are you serious? I thought Edwards blocked all signals out here."

Geo sat at the virtual keyboard and watched Rangers scurry outside, setting up and moving equipment. "It's slow. I have to send bursts in relays and hack their systems. If I do, you can't name us or our location, and it can only be understood by her."

Annabelle stood behind him. "You really can?"

"That's how I've read books like *Tale of Two Cities*."

She rested her hands on his shoulders, removed them, and sat next to him. "Must be some hack. The Union censored that book."

Geo sent a probe seeking connection. "I've been thinking about Cory. I'm sure he betrayed us, but you said you tracked him two days ago in the morning and I found him around eight in the woods."

"Can't be. He was at the border."

"I was there."

Annabelle closed her eyes. "I knew our com had been hacked."

"Or you were betrayed."

"Who? You can't think the Commander would betray me for Battani's deal?"

Geo sent two Net-probes. "You said she wouldn't let you help Janine. Maybe things aren't so great in Civ."

She sighed. "You're right. The Union is moving toward an all-female society. Lots of us think that's wrong. Women who speak out get punished. Some get sent to your cathouses."

"But how would you have children without men?"

She clasped his hand. "We fuse the DNA of one egg into

another, grow it, then implant it. It bypasses men altogether."

"I feel obsolete." He removed her hand.

"Girls will be, too. Our labs can take a fetus at four weeks and carry it to term in an incubator. Pretty soon, women who want children won't have to get pregnant at all."

Geo stood and pulled away. "What a crock. Civ's so big on all-natural: alfalfa sprouts, wind turbines. Then they make test-tube babies? What's natural about that?"

"I know. But the big shots have us all under their thumb. Mom keeps fighting in the legislature, but—"

"Hey." The screen showed a probe had made a connection. "We're in." He sat at the keyboard. "What do you want to say?"

"Tell her: 'Mom, I'm okay'—"

"No dice." Geo sat as far from Annabelle as he could. "We can't let on that the message is from you."

"I have to tell her something."

Geo got up and returned with Dickens' book. "She sent this. She might be the only one who knows. Why not send a quote?"

" 'Tis a far better thing…" she began.

"No." He handed her the book. "I believe it says, 'It is a far, far better thing that I do…' "

" '…than I have ever done before.' " Annabelle smiled. "She would love that."

Geo sent the message, then scrambled a dozen probes to break links along the way. He severed the connection.

"I hope she'll take it as encouragement," Annabelle said. "Now, how do we find Janine?"

"Let's see what the Biltmoor system says."

"Were you expecting company?" Annabelle pointed to a screen on the left. Three armadillos pulled up.

He nodded. "I gave them some false signals to chase." The Rangers waved sensors in all directions. Geo dimmed the cave's lights.

Soon the armadillos pulled away along with most of the Rangers. A handful retreated on foot up the mountain.

"This'll take time," Geo said. "Why don't you use the shower?"

Annabelle's face lit up. "An honest-to-goodness shower with hot water?"

"Make it short. There's a new toothbrush in the cabinet with paste."

She smiled and patted his shoulder. "You never cease to amaze me. Thanks."

* * *

Geo triggered more flash-flares, left the living quarters, and hurried down a narrow corridor. His head nearly brushed the low ceiling. Toward the rear of the cave, a gray door contained a keypad and retinal scan. He stared into the scanner and entered a code. The heavy metal door released.

Inside was a vault Pa showed him when he turned eighteen. Geo provided another retinal scan, then voice, fingerprint, and keypad code to open the vault. He entered a closet-sized reinforced steel chamber stacked with plastic crates.

Opening the nearest container, Geo searched for anything on Willis or the certificates Pa mentioned. Nothing. He could just make out the splash of Annabelle's shower down the hall. He moved to the second crate: dense legal documents in small print on legal paper. Pa had said he would never convert these to electronic, fearing that data cubes could fall into the wrong hands.

The next crate documented the Shaw Foundation. It had notations on helping neighbors like Peterson, and lists of corporations that made no sense to Geo. If only Pa hadn't kept him in the dark. He had considered breaking into the vault last month, but Pa would have known. He always did.

Geo scanned papers on the Biltmoor Corporation: its rise as an energy company out of Knoxville, how it got into banking, manufacturing, and retail, and how it eliminated competitors, one by one. No certificates.

He found a document listing Biltmoor's board of directors with Edwards, Hanrahan and Bishop Kolinski. *So the church and corporation are entangled.* He didn't recognize Richard McCarthy, but the final name was Willis Montgomery. *Pa, is this your Willis?*

In another crate, he found documents on Biltmoor finances and a letter from President Hardcastle commending Pa for work during the war. So, Pa knew the President. *Wow.* The letterhead held the emblem of an eagle surrounded by the flag, matching Pa's ring. Geo studied the ornate geometric design beneath the eagle.

"Great shower!" Annabelle said.

Startled, Geo closed the crate and spun around.

Annabelle ran her fingers through her newly washed, wavy blonde hair. "Find anything helpful?" She looked amazing.

"Sorry we don't have a hair dryer," Geo managed. "Too much electricity and heat."

"That's okay. Rangers are still hanging around out there."

He hurried back to the screen. Two armadillos parked outside. Rangers milled about. Ralph lingered in the woods, protecting the still. A Ranger took aim and fired but missed. Ralph took off. *Good boy.*

So the Rangers aren't buying that we're dead. Well, can't help that right now. There were six more crates to check in the vault. He wasn't sure he wanted Annabelle in the vault. Yet he hadn't seen anything he wouldn't want her to see. "Come on. Pa told me to find certificates." Geo returned to the open vault.

"What kind?"

"Wish I knew."

"Birth, marriage?"

"I'm guessing Biltmoor Corporation." Geo carried a crate into the hall for Annabelle and grabbed another crate for himself. This one had documents on Shaw Enterprises and the factory Pa ran for the mountaineers' benefit. There was also some paperwork on Pa's designs and inventions. Too bad he could never get patents, since then he would be competing with Edwards' Biltmoor Corporation.

Thoughts of the factory brought a new worry: maybe the Rangers had destroyed it, too. Geo had told Zak to meet him there tonight. Now Geo wasn't sure when they could leave the cave.

Frustrated, he sealed the crate and pushed it into the corner. "Find anything?"

Annabelle looked up. "Only records of his activities during the war. Why don't you take a shower? It'll make you feel better. I'll finish up."

"Well, okay." Geo wasn't used to sharing, but maybe sharing the workload might be okay.

He left the vault and checked the wall-screen. It was quiet. He set off a third round of flash-decoys. *Let's see what you fellows do this time.* Then he took his shower, trying to imagine how they would get past the Rangers.

THIRTY-ONE

Annabelle stepped into the vault, opened crates, and skimmed documents. She might not get another chance. All her mech training kicked into overdrive.

This was the innermost sanctum of the Underground. Pa was a top Union enemy who had thwarted efforts to capture or shut him down for more than a dozen years, a man Sam sent her to find. It was her duty to identify, capture or kill him, and bring intel on his activities and helpers.

Yet, he was Mom's family. Mom would be devastated. Annabelle needed Geo's help to find Janine, and he had trusted her enough to bring her to this safe place and let her into the vault.

Pa had kept copious records of his activities during the war. He was involved in moving troops and civilians, obtaining weapons, and defending the mountains against mech intrusions. That had led to the stalemate and the truce. He had been instrumental in creating the Outland. Yet he kept this so quiet that even Geo didn't know.

The Union would pay dearly for such a treasure trove. It would buck her for promotion. But it would also kill Mom and destroy Geo. *What's more, it won't save you, Janine.*

She filled her mind with facts on Biltmoor and Shaw until her head ached. Her thoughts twisted back on themselves.

It all slammed to a halt when Annabelle stared at a list of names, and one in particular: Willis Montgomery. *Daddy?* Tears streaming down her cheeks. She shoved the paper back into the crate. Hearing Geo padding down the hall, she closed the lid and returned the crate to the vault.

* * *

Refreshed from his shower, Geo checked the screen, noting a single armadillo with fewer Rangers. They replaced sensor equipment and rescanned before leaving.

He joined Annabelle by the vault. "I'm starved, what about you?"

"Famished," she said, and followed him to the living area.

In the kitchenette along one wall of the great room, Geo opened a closet door, revealing a refrigerator. He pulled a pot off the shelf, checked the date, two days ago, and put it on the stove.

Annabelle joined him, her eyes puffy. "What specialties do you make?" she asked lightly.

"What do you like?"

"What I like and what the Union allows are two different things." Annabelle lifted the lid. "I see red meat. Mmmm. Taboo. What kind?"

"Mystery meat. Trust me, you'll like it."

"Just tell me."

"Nope." Geo stirred the stew.

"What's the plan for rescuing Janine?" She patted his shoulder.

He pulled away. She pouted, which he found easy to ignore.

"How much do you know about military history?" Geo asked, stirring the pot.

"Oh, loads." Her tone was sarcastic. "I got top marks in it in mech training."

"Then you know that when you're an underdog, you've got to do something unexpected." Geo scooped out two bowls of stew and set them on the thick oak table.

Annabelle sat down and poked her spoon through the meat. "So what is this?"

Geo sat across from her. "Just eat it." He stuffed a piece of meat into his mouth.

She sipped the broth. "Tasty." She sampled a piece of meat. "Rich, buttery. Kind of sweet. And salty."

Geo studied her.

"So what is it?" she asked.

"It's either possum or skunk. I don't recall."

"Yuck." Annabelle dropped her spoon. "You couldn't serve something decent?"

Geo grabbed his chest. "You're rejecting mountain hospitality? Skunk isn't bad if you remove the glands. Of course, catching the little rodents can be tricky."

Annabelle glared at him. "You tricked me."

"You just said it was tasty." Geo spooned another chunk into his mouth.

"Well...it is, I guess. It's been hard to find tasty food at home, although Mama Grace is a good cook."

"Mama Grace?"

"Too complicated to explain. Is this really skunk?"

"It's Angus beef," Geo said. "Cured and sautéed in onions and mushrooms. Does that make it taste better? Actually, possum isn't bad, though it's not Angus."

"Is there more?"

Geo dished more stew but withheld her bowl. "Tell me about Mama Grace. We're not going anywhere."

"Oh, all right," Annabelle said.

He handed her the bowl.

"I have three moms: your mom, Mama Grace, and Mama Helen. I have eight sisters, and we're crowded into a communal home with no privacy. Satisfied?"

"I guess that explains why you bump into people." She didn't seem to mind this remark. "Are you sure your dad was killed? Lots of refugees made it."

"Don't get my hopes up."

"What was his name?"

Her eyes watered. "I don't know his first name, but my mom's name is Dorothy Montgomery."

"Could he be the Willis Montgomery Pa told me to find?"

"I have no idea. Just drop it."

Annabelle's face looked ashen, like dark clouds were descending over her. He studied her while she ate in silence. *Wow. You really are upset if it stops you from talking.*

They finished eating. Geo checked the screen and set off another round of decoys. He washed the dishes and Annabelle dried. "The vault had so many drawings and formulas I didn't understand," she said.

"Pa's inventions. We can't patent anything. Biltmoor would take the designs. Then we'd have to buy from Edwards."

"They'd be worth a fortune in the Union, though the government would keep most of that."

Geo shrugged and returned to the screen, noting one armadillo with twenty Rangers. When the sun set, they acted confused, replacing sensors they had already changed and testing them on themselves. Maybe they were scared. Severing heads was a popular Ranger penalty for failure.

Annabelle sat next to him. "How can we find Janine? Edwards said she's not in the Towers."

"Let's see what my probes found." Geo displayed several searches that hit dead ends. "Usually, I break into their site for weapon ideas, though most of them don't work against mechs."

"You mean he uses them on his own people?"

In the twilight, the infrared screen showed a dozen more Rangers up the mountain. A probe returned with com-link chatter. Geo downloaded the results onto a data-cube. "Let's listen in."

"You can do that?"

"Edwards records everything. It's impossible to listen to it all, but my programs reduce voice to text and search keywords."

The search brought six mentions of Janine. Geo displayed them.

Annabelle grabbed his hand. "There. He moved her to the towers. When?"

"An hour ago."

"We have to go."

Geo pulled up the other listings and found nothing significant. "We need to figure out how to get in and out of town, and then in and out of the Towers."

"I've done that."

"Edwards won't make the same mistake twice. Grab a backpack with weapons and some food. It's time to see if we can surprise our friends."

"And get Janine? Please?"

"Patience."

THIRTY-TWO

Geo and Annabelle wrapped themselves head to toe in fresh ponchos, fastened around their feet, and with narrow breathing slits on top. Geo led Annabelle out beneath another boulder using hydraulic lifts. Before long, he was sweating. *So much for the shower.* The day had warmed and the night would be muggy even without the suits, but not warm enough to fool infrared.

They climbed a steel-composite ladder up a shaft that opened amidst a clump of maples. Geo adjusted his remote viewer, scanned his surroundings, and fired a hooked harpoon up into the branches of a nearby maple. That would trigger motion sensors, but it couldn't be helped.

He tested the line to make sure the hook had found purchase on an upper branch. Then he hoisted the pulley into place with its electric motor, and attached the harness to Annabelle and her pack. "When you reach the top, remove the harness and get out quickly. Only look through the remote viewer."

Geo sent her up and waited, listened, and scanned with his bumblebee cam on his wrist-com. Rangers approached from all sides. The pulley stopped.

He heard an armadillo approaching the clearing out front. He checked the Rangers' positions, closed his eyes and triggered flash-flares. Geo activated the pulley with his remote and switched his wrist-com to viewing infrared cams in front of the cave. A second armadillo, surrounded by hundreds of floating images, roared up the dirt road and into the clearing. A clump of heat signatures poured out. Nearby, three pairs of Rangers closed in.

As the harness descended, Geo sealed the opening to the shaft and covered it with a planter that blended into mountain vegetation. He strapped the harness around himself and his pack, then activated the motor and gathered the trailing line while ascending into the tree. The whir of the electric motor thundered in his ears, the pulley wasn't moving fast enough, and the poncho had him sweating like a summer downpour. Rangers swooped in beneath him. He stopped the motor twenty feet above them, swinging in the breeze like a snared possum.

Rangers ran handheld sensors and checked stationary ones. Geo triggered another round of flash-flares. Men scattered, chasing these decoys. Geo resumed climbing, blinded by the phantom images. He stopped, listened. Images faded. Solid ones scouted in circles. Geo kept climbing until he reached the top.

Two more armadillos pulled up out front of the cave. Rangers swarmed in from the surrounding mountainside. Crouched in the tree next to Annabelle, Geo gathered the line in loops and fastened them onto a nearby branch. "Time to wait, quietly," he whispered. He drank from his canteen and recalled his bumblebee cam.

One thing he had learned in observing mechs and Rangers was that mechs fought in 3D, while Rangers were 2D fighters because they hadn't faced air attacks since the war.

* * *

Placing the zip line from this tree down to the valley below had been Geo's idea. Pa had called it a waste of time. Now, as he and Annabelle glided down the line in a harness, he imagined Pa being proud instead. Geo fired another round of flash flares. Rangers scurried below in noisy confusion. He prayed they didn't look up.

Drenched in sweat, Geo opened a vent above his head to let in cooler air. It didn't help much. The temperature had to be at least 85, and it was damp. He adjusted his remote cam attached to his backpack, and didn't see any infrared images ahead.

The zip line ride ended. They climbed down from an oak tree, and Annabelle started to remove her poncho.

"I wouldn't," Geo said, "unless you want company."

"I'm dying in here. It feels like I never took that shower. Which way to Biltmoor?"

"I need to see Pa's friends."

"Oh, come on! We need to get Janine before they move her again."

"Biltmoor is that way." Geo pointed northwest; he headed east. "Through bands of Rangers and Ranger mechs."

Grabbing hold of his pack, she caught up. "Can I at least remove the hood?"

"Just your face. Don't give anyone behind us a target."

She grabbed his arm. "What'll it take to get you to help me?"

"In case you haven't noticed, we're being hunted. If we're not careful, Janine will have no one looking out for her. I want to help; I do. But you haven't convinced me of a way to get in and out." Geo adjusted his infrared goggles, slung his .50 cal over his shoulder, and detached from his pack the collapsed crossbow.

"I should have gone for her myself."

Without stopping, Geo extended the crossbow's frame and locked it into place. He cranked the spring to increase tension on the bow. "Even with Edwards' mechs?"

"You don't understand. Janine depended on me. I let her down."

"We'll find a way. Now quiet." Geo crouched down and pulled Annabelle behind bushes. In the dark, he notched a short arrow into his crossbow and aimed across the clearing at a four-legged heat signature.

"What are you doing?" She gripped his arm.

Holding his breath, Geo adjusted his aim and eased the trigger, sending the arrow with high-strung tension across an open, moonlit trail. "Don't you ever shut up?"

"Are you shooting a deer? This is park land. That's poaching."

He watched the infrared image jerk, attempt to trot off, and stagger before dropping. "There are more deer than we could ever harvest, so many that they destroy our crops."

He scanned infrared in all directions, seeing nothing larger than a badger. He crossed the clearing.

"We just ate. Why kill a defenseless animal?"

Geo knelt next to the deer and begged forgiveness for taking a life. "Pa said to bring something when you visit."

"We don't have time for visiting."

"You want to spend another night outdoors?" Geo pulled from his pack a length of rope and cut it. "Find a strong branch to help carry the deer." He tied the front legs and had the rear legs tied by the time Annabelle returned.

"Is this necessary?" she asked.

He placed the branch between the animal's legs and covered the head in plastic to keep from leaving a blood trail. "Grab the back and follow me. For God's sake, let me do the talking. I don't need you giving away that you're a mech. They aren't popular up here."

"Then we go for Janine?"

"Yes. No talking." Geo lifted the front. When Annabelle lifted her end, he moved forward, wondering how he would explain her when they got where they were going.

* * *

Geo had only visited the factory once before. It operated at night when Rangers usually avoided the mountains and Geo had farm chores. All he knew was that Pa watched over the place, so it made sense for them to go there now.

When they got close to the factory, Geo removed his poncho and motioned for Annabelle to do the same. "We don't sneak up on friends," Geo whispered. He attached the ponchos to the packs, sweat side out. He wiped his brow and scanned the area. "Remember, no talking."

They pushed forward, laboring under the deer's weight. Geo looked for the hidden cave entrance. The factory was in a cavern enlarged and reinforced before the war. Supposedly, Union mechs never found it, hidden behind trees, bushes and kudzu.

Via infrared, he spotted scouts on either side of the narrow path. Annabelle must have seen them, too, because she stopped and dropped the branch. Geo put down his end and approached her. "It's okay."

"I don't like this."

"I know." He took her hand and led her to a moonlit wall of kudzu.

Annabelle let go of his hand, backed up to the wall, and grabbed her revolver.

He pushed her hand down. "Don't."

"Who goes?" Light glinted off a shotgun in front of them.

Annabelle raised her gun.

Geo took her revolver. "Zak, we brought a deer if you can help us get it inside."

Zak pointed his shotgun at Annabelle. "She shouldn't be here."

"Home's destroyed. Nowhere else is secure," Geo said. "I'll vouch for her."

Annabelle squeezed his hand. She was probably itching to say or do something.

Zak slipped away, met with other infrared images and returned. "This way, my lord." He grabbed the front of the deer.

Taking the rear, Geo whispered to Annabelle, "Stay close. It'll be tight with the deer. No lights."

She smiled. In the greenish glow, the image reminded him of the Cheshire Cat.

They meandered down a winding corridor blasted and chiseled out of rock. It was only six feet high to make it difficult for mechs, and so narrow Geo scraped his shoulders carrying the deer and his backpack. The passage was booby-trapped. He hoped there were no short fuses. He didn't fancy getting buried under tons of rock.

At the last turn before the first cave, Geo scanned the darkness for two openings: an infrared spotter, and a stolen mech machine gun to deter unwanted guests.

They entered through a steel doorway that was set at a right angle to the path, making it difficult to ram. Around another corner, bioluminescence bathed a long cave, cooled by Pa's air circulation system.

Several farmers Geo knew from church sat along one cave wall making rope from hemp. Next to them, a loom weaved coarse cloth for pants or finer cloth for linen shirts. Both used Pa's nano-fabric for durability.

A burly man with a broad face and thin black hair approached, O'Brien, Geo recalled. "What's she doing here?"

Two muscular men took the deer and headed down a wide corridor that mountaineers had blasted out of rock. Several men in worn linen shirts and camouflage jeans gathered around.

Zak approached O'Brien. "Geo found himself a bride, but Rangers destroyed his home, so he can't leave her."

"I've seen her on posters in Biltmoor," a rope-making farmer said. "She's pledged to marry Thane Edwards."

Geo took Annabelle's hand, glared at her, and prayed she would keep her mouth shut.

"Edwards' bride here?" someone echoed.

"She was pledged against her will," Geo said.

"Edwards is marrying a mech warrior," the farmer said. "She's a mech."

So much for keeping that quiet. Several men approached, guns drawn. Annabelle reached for her revolver, but Geo had it. He pushed her behind him, against the cave wall. "Yeah, she was a mech. Then her own people sold her into slavery to Edwards. She didn't kill my pa, didn't kill me, and didn't destroy my home when she had the chance."

"She'll bring the thane's wrath upon us," the farmer said. "I say we blast her before she destroys us."

Geo held up his hands. "Don't get crazy. In the name of my pa, I beg you. My anger is with Edwards. He killed Pa, destroyed my home, and enslaved Annabelle's sister. Now he wants to do the same to her. He attacked Mr. Peterson in his home and took his son. He killed Kurdis and destroyed homes up the valley: the Howells, Tuttles, and Hammonds. He tried to kill me. As I stand here before you, I vouch for Annabelle."

"How do we know she's not working for them?" the farmer asked.

"Is that any way to speak to the new Earl of Shaw?" Hunched over, Peterson ambled toward Geo, knelt and kissed Pa's ring on Geo's hand. He rose and turned to the men. "When you were hunted, who shielded you? When you were hungry, who fed you? When you needed work, who provided for you?"

The other men bowed or knelt. Some came forward and kissed the ring. That had to be the weirdest thing Geo could recall.

"Geo?" Annabelle whispered.

He motioned for her to be silent.

"The Earl is dead. Long live the Earl," one of the men said, and then they chanted in unison, all bowing, including the farmer who had challenged Geo.

When the chanting died down, the burly O'Brien came over, knelt, and kissed the ring. "I'm sorry for your loss, my lord. I stand ready to give you my pledge."

Geo nodded. The man stood and turned to the others. "Okay, back to work. We have a long production list for tonight."

Peterson took Geo by the arm and led him down a lit corridor blasted out of limestone. "So this is the young lady's got everyone abuzz."

"Which is getting old." Annabelle turned to Geo. "What was that all about?"

"I have no idea," Geo said. "Pa rarely brought me here."

"He thought he was protecting you," Peterson said. "Let me show you around." He led them into a wide cave lined with steel beams and nets to protect against falling rocks. By the walls stood presses and milling machines. No doubt they were powered by fuel cells recharged from a solar array like the one Pa had at home. "I'm so sorry about your pa. He was a saint to these folk, helped them to a better life. This is our steel works."

The twins Dirk and Harold waved and returned to moving gun barrels for hunting rifles. Everyone in Appalachia owned a gun, though using it for other than self-defense was risky. That announced where you were.

"What's this about an earl and kissing the ring?" Annabelle asked.

Peterson chuckled. "Mr. Shaw was loyal to the mountain folk, his extended family he liked to say. He was sick over the way things turned out with Thanes Burke and Edwards. President Hardcastle actually gave him the title of 'earl' during the war. We all owe our lives to your pa. He has done so much. I used the title just now to remind everybody of that."

He turned to Geo. "These are simple folk. They need a clever leader to make sure Edwards doesn't trample them. I hope you will pick up where your pa left off."

Geo pulled on Peterson's frail arm. "Whoa. Pa never prepared me for this."

"He didn't want you becoming pigheaded, believing you were better than the rest of us. I encouraged him to get you involved when you turned eighteen. He thought he had time. He made me promise if anything happened to him that I'd step forward and help you in any way I can."

"Thanks," Geo said. "What does being earl make me responsible for?"

"This factory, for one. Your pa owns it. His Shaw Foundation is set up to keep this from falling into Edwards' hands. Before the war, your pa had his own engineering design company until the Union made it difficult for him to do business. He used to come up here as a part-time park ranger to get away. That's how we met."

Peterson led them down a short corridor to a steaming hot cave where men were blowing glass. The cave was lined with stacks of canning jars. "Before the war, we set up our cave defenses here and stockpiled whatever we could in case we got cut off.

"I remember like yesterday the battle for Knoxville. Our base was across the border, an old mansion converted into a military compound. Mechs swept in from the north. It was all we could do to reach the forest. Your pa saved my life, along with thousands of others. We came here to keep fighting. Then the war ended and we didn't get to use this stuff."

Peterson led them into a low-ceilinged cave with large steel tanks used for growing photosynthetic "leaves" for the solar arrays. "After the war, when Thane Burke took over, President Hardcastle entrusted your pa with keeping this hidden. When Edwards killed Burke and took power, Hardcastle disappeared. Your pa used this equipment to help folk survive and be self-sufficient instead of relying on Edwards and his cronies.

"Your pa changed his name from Scott to Shaw because Burke and Edwards were eliminating rivals," Peterson said.

Geo nodded as they entered another stone corridor in the cave maze. "What's expected of me to fill Pa's shoes?"

Annabelle took Geo's hand. "Don't forget Janine."

"I haven't." He didn't pull away this time. It was best the men saw them together.

"Day to day, not much," Peterson said. "Foreman O'Brien lives here. He's brilliant with tools and treats this equipment like his babies. He doesn't want it taken by Civs or Edwards."

"I won't do that," Annabelle said.

"Good to hear, hon," Peterson said. "Locals buy from the factory on ledger with whatever they can barter. Your pa was generous with credit as long as folk tried. Workers get a modest wage on ledger, since we don't have money, and everyone pitches in. Your pa worked with O'Brien to schedule best we could. He never took tithes, though he did have stuff made for experiments, like solar arrays and microwave relays that run our electricity. He was fair and in return, he could count on their loyalty.

"Now, with Ranger raids, everybody's afraid. The folk need to know things will get better. If you continue your pa's legacy, you can count on their support."

"I want to," Geo said. "But it's overwhelming."

"You can count on me," Peterson said.

"Can you help us rescue my sister?" Annabelle asked.

"Where is she?" Peterson asked.

"Biltmoor Towers."

"Annabelle." Geo squeezed her hand. "We talked about this."

She squeezed back. "I'm worried sick about Janine and you're talking about running a company. How long will that take?"

"What are you asking?" Peterson said. "These are farmers and workers, not fighters. Two boys died trying to protect Shaw's place."

Geo winced. "I was afraid of that. Let's give them a proper burial."

"Many were killed last night by Rangers on the rampage. Don't ask these people to do more than they're capable of."

"I understand." Geo got between Annabelle and Peterson before she could make another pitch. "Since you knew Pa so well, do you know anything about Willis and his certificates?"

"Ahhh, the Biltmoor Corporation," Peterson whispered. "Your pa invested in the original company along with Hardcastle and others. When Edwards took over and Hardcastle disappeared, your pa figured it best not to be seen owning shares. He hid his certificates of ownership, which now become yours."

"Where?"

"No idea. Somewhere Edwards couldn't touch them. Rumor has it the thane is holding Hardcastle in a dungeon until he can control his shares."

"And Willis?" Geo asked.

"A board member who votes your pa's shares."

"Where can I find him?"

"Probably in town," Peterson said. "If you want to hurt Edwards, take Biltmoor Corporation from him. You'll be doing us a huge favor as well, though from what your pa said, Edwards has an iron grip."

Peterson led them into a small cave with partitioned rooms. "Here we do special projects and test new ideas."

"Tommy?" Annabelle hurried into the first partitioned room and approached a frail boy hunched over a mech helmet.

The new boy Geo recognized from church dropped the helmet and cowered in the corner.

"It's me, Annabelle. I helped you cross the border."

The frightened boy looked up with a puzzled look. "Don't take me back."

"I won't. I'm just thrilled you're safe. Mr. Shaw didn't make it."

The boy looked down. "I'm sorry. He was a nice man."

What? A mech girl, sworn to hunt escapees, had helped this boy? Geo shook his head.

"Let me know if there's anything I can do for you," Annabelle said.

"I like it here," Tommy said. "They let me make things." He smiled and returned to the helmet.

"Tommy," Peterson said, "this is Geo Shaw. He's taking over for his pa."

Geo stood next to the boy. "What are you working on?"

Tommy looked up with a thin smile. "I bypassed the bio-chip so we can use captured suits."

"No!" Annabelle said.

Geo pulled her aside. "Annabelle."

"I know. They had—"

"Annabelle?"

"Okay," she said. "Since the bio-chip allows other mechs to know who's talking, what will they see if you override?"

"I can leave the identity that's on the bio-chip or make it anonymous," Tommy said.

"Wow."

Tommy's face lit up. "I could also set up short-range channels so you can have a team not connected to the mech base."

"How about hacking Biltmoor Corporation?" Geo asked. "Or Civ computers?"

"Biltmoor uses Civ technology. Union girls made me hack Biltmoor." He looked at Annabelle.

"I'm not like that anymore," Annabelle said. "I'm sorry I couldn't help your brother."

"You have family here now." Geo patted the boy on the shoulder.

Peterson checked his watch. "We'd best get to the production meeting."

THIRTY-THREE

Geo stood at the rear of a cave room with a steel-reinforced ceiling. Three walls were stone; the fourth was paneled. O'Brien sat at the head of a hewn oak table. He offered his seat to Geo, but Geo preferred to stand and observe. It was best that O'Brien ran this meeting, since Geo did not intend to manage the plant day-to-day. He had matters to settle with Edwards first. For now, he wanted supplies and a plan.

The farmer who questioned Annabelle closed the heavy oak door. Geo scanned the faces around the table. The gruff O'Brien was a tool man who fought in the war twenty years ago. Geo stood behind Annabelle, who he hoped wouldn't complicate what Geo needed to ask. Sitting across from them, Peterson hunched over, bent with arthritis.

Zak sat in for his pa, who couldn't attend. Though he was a big lug of a guy, Zak wasn't a trained fighter. Thin-faced Mickey, the oldest compadre, sat next to Peterson; he had the math smarts to help figure supply issues. He wasn't a fighter, either. Geo's fighting experience was limited to what he had gathered from books, and from dodging mechs and Rangers.

Two big men with Polish names Geo couldn't pronounce sat beside O'Brien. They had been with him during the war. Most of those who had fought back then didn't have much training, and the war ended so quickly that many saw no action.

Geo wanted justice from Edwards. It wouldn't come without a fight, and he didn't have fighters. Still, everyone used a rifle with enough accuracy to feed families and neighbors.

O'Brien launched into problems with an old lathe that was slowing repair work. The foreman followed with the night's production list: tractor repair, farm tools, hunting rifles and ammo, solar leaves, and fuel cell batteries. Satisfied they could handle the night's production without the lathe, O'Brien asked for new requests. Peterson read off what he had received: a mechanical plow, two solar arrays, and a refrigerator to store beef. Geo imagined Pa bringing Geo's ideas and making samples that others might want. He heard Pa's ghost telling him not to bring his troubles to these people, but Pa was gone, probably still lying on the mountainside.

When O'Brien finished the list and looked up, Geo cleared his throat. "I have some requests."

The foreman's eyes narrowed.

"We could use two dozen mech grenades, three compound cross-bows with a dozen short arrows each, a couple RPGs, and hang-gliders. I have designs for the gliders."

"Is that all?" O'Brien didn't take notes.

"It's a start."

"Are you planning to start a war you can't win?"

Geo scanned the faces. He hated making this request. "You knew Bret Shaw as benefactor of this community. I lost my pa because Edwards put himself above the law, killing and terrorizing without consequences."

"With all respect to Bret Shaw, boy," O'Brien said, "you may be the new earl, but you've lived a sheltered, spoiled life. Look around. These folk struggle day to day for survival. You don't understand their needs like your pa did. Using limited resources for weapons deprives folk of tools they need to get by. This was not Bret Shaw's way. You're not your father."

"No, and I'm not fit to fill his shoes, but when he saw tyranny, he took up arms and fought side by side with many of you."

"We lost and suffered for it," O'Brien said. "I share your loss. We all do, not just because he was a benefactor. He was a good friend. He understood the perils of war and helped maintain the peace for 20 years. Now you ride in with no memory of what we've been through, itching for a fight."

"Edwards killed Pa, and we haven't lifted a rifle in his memory."

"You took Edwards' bride. Return her and restore the peace."

"I—" Annabelle began.

Geo squeezed her shoulders and addressed the men next to O'Brien. "Friends and neighbors, Rangers destroyed our homes and killed Kurdis. They took Peterson's son and others."

"Return the girl," O'Brien said. "This is not our fight. There are 50,000 Rangers to 5,000 of us. If you drag these folk into your vendetta, they'll lose everything."

"Some of us already have," Geo said. "Edwards terrorizes by sending his Rangers. He collects tithes from the church and from us for living on our own land in exchange for protection he doesn't give. His monopolies overcharge us, so we have to work at night to make what we need."

"Don't knock self-sufficiency, boy. It's worked for twenty years."

"People in town live like slaves," Geo said. "I'm sure they'll help if we show them we're serious."

Mickey raised his hand like at Sunday school. "I'll join you."

O'Brien sighed. "Just what we need: another youthful crusade. Geo, your pa bought us a hard-won peace. He wouldn't approve of upsetting the balance over this girl. If you succeed, you'll weaken the Rangers. They're all that keeps Civs from taking over."

Geo stared at O'Brien. "Let me talk to the workers. Let them decide."

"Who do you think they'll believe: a nineteen-year-old kid or a man they've known for 20 years? I'm sorry, son. Your pa wouldn't want you misusing this company for personal vendettas. That's not how he led, not what he believed. If you think otherwise, you didn't know him."

Annabelle rose from her seat and moved around the table from Geo.

"Listen to you." She pressed her back to the stone wall. "You've let Edwards squeeze you into tiny plots that wouldn't support a squirrel and still you won't stand up and say 'enough'."

"You're a mech," O'Brien said. "You speak for Civ."

Annabelle moved away as Geo approached her. "Not anymore. They sold me into slavery. Mechs have orders to move the border a couple miles a year until they squeeze you into surrendering. Once Edwards has his new treaty with Civ, why would he let you keep your little plots? Civ is pushing Edwards to disarm civilians. That means you. Will you fight before or after that happens?"

"No one's taking my guns," said the man on O'Brien's right, and the others nodded.

Geo looked at Annabelle with increased respect. He nodded. "All I'm asking for is volunteers."

"You struggle to survive," Annabelle said, "but for what? Your women have left or been taken by Edwards. Without women, your population will collapse. Then Civs will walk in. Is that what you're surviving for?"

"Why would a mech help us?" O'Brien asked.

"I don't like what Civ's doing, either."

"Let me talk to the others," Geo said.

O'Brien stood by the door. "Fancy speeches don't impress me. I sympathize with your loss, but it's folly to drag farmers and workers into this. I'll give you provisions and you're welcome to stay, but no speech-making."

He opened the door. The two Poles and the farmer left. O'Brien motioned for Mickey and Zak to leave, too. Then he closed the door. "Son, I don't mean to be harsh, but these folk shouldn't follow you, because you can't win." He left.

Annabelle approached Geo. "I thought I was helping."

"You did great," Geo said. "But he's right. I have no business asking these people." Even if every able-bodied man joined, they would put up a poor showing against Rangers.

"You gave your best shot," Peterson said. "I'd come, but I'd hold you back with my arthritis and all. For your pa's sake, don't do anything rash. Let me know how I can help."

"You've already been a great help." Geo turned to Annabelle. "I guess it's you and me."

She smiled, though he saw worry in her eyes. "For Janine."

"Absolutely." Geo ran after O'Brien and stopped the foreman in the corridor. "I get what you're doing."

Annabelle joined them.

"Nothing against you, son," O'Brien said, his jaw fixed.

"Appalachian Code requires me to seek justice for Pa."

"You're nuts. No one has gotten close to Edwards in ten years. You know how he took out Thane Burke."

"Exactly," Geo said.

"You want to challenge Edwards for leadership? Even Civ mechs couldn't get to him. You've got more guts than I gave you credit for, or less brains."

"Probably brains."

"It's all or nothing," O'Brien said. "Edwards became Thane by killing Burke. You sure you're up for that?"

"Pa didn't deserve to die, and I can't even bury him. Besides," Geo put his arm around Annabelle's shoulders. "I'm not letting Edwards get his grubby paws on Annabelle."

O'Brien shook his head. "Your pa would kill me if I helped you with this fool's errand."

Annabelle tucked her arm around Geo's waist. "Then do it for Geo's sister. Edwards has her locked in the Tower, and I'm not giving up until I see her safe."

"O'Brien, let me talk to the new boys and Zak," Geo said. "We'll make our own supplies and leave by daybreak."

The foreman took a moment and then nodded. "Don't break anything. I'll give you what we can spare."

"Bless you," Geo said. "If for any reason I can't return, I'd like Mr. Peterson to be in charge, if that's okay."

"As you wish, Earl." O'Brien nodded and left.

Geo hurried through the maze of caves with Annabelle beside him.

"I'm confused," she said. "If you're Earl and this is your company, why does he talk to you that way?"

"Think about it, Annabelle. These people barely scrape by and I come upsetting a delicate balance. Pa wasn't a tyrant, and I don't want to be. O'Brien is right. I want these people to help, but it would be suicide."

Annabelle grabbed his arm. "You don't think we can help Janine?"

"We'll get her if I have to talk to Carlos and the cartel."

"No, Geo. They kidnap girls and push their stupid drugs."

"Edwards fears them," Geo said. "That's worth something."

"You should fear them, too."

"I grew up with Carlos. I trust him."

"Don't, Geo. Promise me."

"We're out of options."

"Then I have an idea." Annabelle picked up her pace.

THIRTY-FOUR

Annabelle barged into the partitioned cave where Tommy bent over the mech helmet. He flinched and backed into the corner until he recognized her.

"I'm sorry for how my people treated you," Annabelle said.

Tommy stared, uncertain.

She backed away. "I'm excited about your short-range channels. Can you secure them so only synchronized mechs could hear?"

Tommy nodded.

"How far can they communicate?"

"Five to ten miles."

"What are you thinking?" Geo said.

"It would take too long to explain," Annabelle said. "Tommy, can you make two tonight along with biochip overrides?"

"If it's okay with Mr. O'Brien."

"He said you can help us," Geo said.

"I'll do it for Annabelle," Tommy said, "for saving my life."

Geo took Annabelle by the arm and led her down the corridor. "Care to explain?"

"Peterson said during the war their headquarters was in a mansion across the border that was turned into a bunker. That bunker is in no-man's land today. It could be where Hardcastle is."

"What makes you think that?"

"I've been there," Annabelle said. "Stupid girl parties with loud music, lots of mechs, and off limits in the middle of nowhere. It's the perfect place to hide someone."

"What does that have to do with mech suits?"

"Hardcastle fled when Edwards took over. He was buddies with your pa. I'm not clear why our people would hold him, except he was charismatic. I think your pa tried to negotiate his release."

"And?" Geo asked.

"If we freed him, he would owe us. He might help bring justice for Pa and free Janine."

"You're crazier than I am. You want to take on the entire Civ mech force and Edwards' Rangers."

Annabelle laughed. "Wasn't it that dead white male Newton who said you could move the moon with enough leverage?"

"I thought you couldn't read that stuff."

"With Mom's help, I do my own hacking."

They reached the cave with metal fabrication equipment. Mickey was stacking boxes of ammunition. He dropped them when he saw Geo. "Did you convince the old man?"

Geo watched a press stamp out 20 shiny shell casings. "No, but he'll release you guys to help me gather supplies."

"I'm still learning my way around. What do you need?"

Geo gave him a list, including grenades, crossbows and arrows.

The Brache twins shut down their rifle-boring equipment and joined them. "When do we leave?" Dirk asked.

"I told them we're getting payback over your pa," Mickey said.

"You don't have to do this," Geo said. "It would involve sneaking past Rangers to get to town and more to reach the Towers."

"You'll need help," Dirk said. "You and your pa saved us."

"I'm in," his brother said.

These boys would put their lives on the line for Pa, while the grown men wouldn't help. Geo felt a twinge of guilt.

"Let's find the grenade equipment," Mickey said, leading them out of the cave.

They moved from cave to cave, through a deep complex, honeycombed through the mountain. *And to think Pa never mentioned his work.*

Down a long narrow corridor that seemed off on its own, they found a cave with components for grenades and other explosives. Peterson and Zak were setting up equipment with, surprise, Peterson's son, Stu. Geo punched Stu's shoulder and received one in return before they clasped arms.

"I thought I'd never see you out of Ranger uniform," Geo said.

"I saw what they did up the valleys," Stu said. "I can't do that to friends. My pa says you're looking for volunteers. Count me in. I only got a day's training, but I learned there are many unhappy Rangers."

"Maybe they'll join us," Geo said, "even though it's a suicide mission."

When Annabelle eyed him, he cautioned her not to speak.

Peterson showed Dirk and his brother the intricacies of forming two-phase grenades. "These are volatile chemicals, so be careful." He picked up two completed grenades and handed them to Geo. "I figured you'd need these."

Annabelle examined the device that had killed Karen and other friends. The nano-mesh blend of titanium polymers allowed for two separate blasts. "This was a great country before we started fighting among ourselves. When will it end?"

"Edwards is a tyrant," Geo said.

"It's more than that, Geo. Tyrants are merely opportunists, selling their brand of nirvana to hold onto power."

"Snake oil," Geo said.

Annabelle squeezed his hand. "What we're struggling for is more real than either of our worlds."

"When did you become the philosopher?"

She laughed.

"I want to show you something," Geo said. "It might prove useful." He found a steel skillet and sprinkled white powder into it. "Sodium is used to ignite the second blast. Stand back." Geo splashed water. A moment later came a flash and explosion. "Chemical lightning."

"What the hell?" Peterson grabbed Geo's arm. "Don't do that in a confined space like this."

"Sorry." Geo turned to Annabelle. "Sodium makes water give up hydrogen and heat. Heat and oxygen then ignites the hydrogen. The problem is to contain the sodium and the explosion." When Peterson turned away, Geo pocketed a vial.

O'Brien entered the cave carrying a box and backpack. "Another of those damned grenades misfire?"

"No," Geo said. "Have we had problems?"

"Only when the sodium and water vials shatter." O'Brien put

the box on the table and set the backpack next to it. "This is all I can spare, plus whatever you make tonight. I have to get back to production. The guys left some food. Zak can take you." O'Brien hurried out.

* * *

After they placed the last of the supplies in backpacks, Zak led them to the kitchen, a low-ceilinged cave with long wooden tables and, along one wall, refrigerators, stoves, and micro-cookers.

"We rotate kitchen chores," Zak said, "but dinner is over. O'Brien thought we shouldn't eat separately, seeing as we've got a girl."

"Excuse me!" Annabelle said.

In a refrigerator, Geo found deer steaks that looked fresh. "Annabelle, see if you can find a grill."

"That's not the deer we brought, is it?" She checked cabinets beneath the counter.

He counted out steaks. "I hope so. You worried about eating Bambi? We could find you some rat."

"Stop it," Annabelle whispered. "I'll try the deer."

"It's gamier than beef, though I think you'll like it."

"Don't laugh," Annabelle whispered. "What's a grill look like?"

He pulled out a medium-sized grill, fired it up, and placed the steaks on it. "I take it you don't cook."

"Mama Grace does our cooking," Annabelle whispered. "Or we eat pre-portioned meals with no red meat."

"You should try fresh." Geo put corn and asparagus into separate pots. "The stew you ate had potatoes, turnips, celery, carrots, mushrooms and zucchini, all local so we don't have to buy from Edwards. It's a feast fit for a king, or at least an earl."

Zak laughed. "I figure we eat healthier than our thane does."

When they sat down to eat, Geo looked from Zak to Peterson, to the three compadres and Annabelle. "Here's what we're up against: 50,000 Rangers, Edwards' cam system and town-dwellers taught to fear us mountain folk. One option is to do nothing, in which case Edwards gets away with murder and Janine suffers."

"Not acceptable," Annabelle said.

"The second is to rescue Janine and get her and Annabelle to Civ. Then we run like hell while Edwards goes on the rampage."

Annabelle cut her steak. "I was betrayed by Battani and my

boss. I have nowhere to go."

"Option three is to free Janine and confront Edwards as best we can."

"Kill him, in other words." Annabelle tasted the deer steak.

"Unless you have a better idea," Geo said. The reality of what he faced finally sank in. "Anyone who wants to back out should do so now. Edwards will pull in Rangers from all around for his big bash and the wedding, meaning we'll face his full force."

"Minus the bride," Annabelle said. She pointed to her steak, "This is good."

Geo smiled. "If I know Edwards, he'll have someone at the altar."

Annabelle frowned.

"Aside from a beefed up Ranger corps, Edwards now has old model mechs," Geo said. "That means Civ is supplying him."

"Which I don't understand," Annabelle said. "We must have traitors giving them to him."

"Edwards has spies everywhere, and infrared cams."

"Any way to blind the cams?" Annabelle asked.

"I don't know how." Geo pushed his asparagus around his plate and considered her suggestion. "Past the roadblocks we'll be dealing with cops and security guards as well as Rangers. We have to get into the Towers, find Janine, find Edwards, and get him alone."

"No one gets Edwards alone," Peterson said. "Hanrahan is always at his side, or he leaves trusted seasoned Rangers."

"What about getting out of the Towers and out of town?" Zak asked.

"If we don't deal with Edwards, it won't matter," Geo said. "Where could we go? Rangers will sweep the region looking for us."

"What are you saying?" Zak asked.

"It's suicide, but I can't live with myself if I don't try."

While they ate, they talked about what to do. Zak wanted to tunnel under Biltmoor and come up by the Towers. That would take months and risk discovery from infrared and motion sensors. Mickey suggested going in from the Civ side and jumping rooftops, which sounded like fun but would be too visible. Annabelle brought up disguises, since that's how she had escaped Biltmoor.

"What about hang-gliders?" Geo asked.

"We'd be exposed," Zak said.

"At night with infrared shielding?"

Annabelle said, "Like—"

"Like the new designs Pa and I worked on," Geo said. "We'd show up on radar like a flock of geese. They wouldn't expect us."

After they ate, Zak took them to the lab, where they experimented with Pa's infrared design. They spent hours trying to get the material to work properly. Geo realized it would take too long to develop something they could use. With dawn only hours away, Geo took Annabelle to a small cave Pa used when he stayed the night. It had a counter and washbasin, and a mattress on a ledge, up off the floor.

"Why do you keep interrupting me?" Annabelle asked when they were alone.

Geo closed the flimsy wood door. "They don't know about the poncho. Pa said a secret doesn't stay that way when more than one person knows."

She nodded and pushed on the fragile door. "How safe are we here?"

"About what you'd expect." Geo lifted the sheet and flashed his light to check for bugs. "A few snakes and a weasel now and then."

As Annabelle shone her light around the cave room, Geo shook his head. She was so intense, brimming with energy despite what they had been through.

Geo turned down the sheets. "You first."

She flashed her beam into the ledge opening. "Why? So you have me cornered?"

"No, so the two-legged snakes and weasels leave you alone."

"You're joking." Annabelle tried to lock the flimsy door. When she couldn't, she climbed onto the ledge. "You will help me find Janine in the morning?"

"Yes, my lady."

"Remember, I'm not your wife."

"Whatever you say, my lady." Geo climbed onto the ledge after her and faced the door. "Right after I see Carlos."

"You mean after I contact my friends to see if they'll help."

"As you wish, my lady. Get some shut-eye. We leave before dawn." Geo set the alarm on his wrist-com and turned out his flashlight, hoping she would keep her distance.

THIRTY-FIVE

Waking to a vibrating alarm in his ear, Geo felt Annabelle snuggled against his back, her arm draped over him. He savored the comfort of her next to him and her sweet, familiar fragrance until that feeling transformed into something more intense.

Turning over, he gazed at her. Was she this physical at home, or was she trying to get him bonded to her so he'd help? She looked so sweet, innocent, and vulnerable, how could he doubt her?

Suddenly she had his head in a scissor lock against the ledge.

Unable to release her grip or pull her from the bed, he croaked out, "Annabelle!"

She released him and clamored out of bed. "Sorry. I'm not used to waking to a male face staring at me."

Placing her hands on his upper arms, she leaned her head on his shoulder and relaxed into him, which gave him a stronger dose of her sweet, musky morning scent. He wanted to stroke her hair, to put his arms around her.

He pulled away. "We need to get moving."

By the time they reached the surface, the sun was poking over the horizon. Geo sent Stu and the three compadres ahead to move supplies closer to Biltmoor while he took Zak and Annabelle to the cave where they had left her mech suit. They had to double back three times to avoid Rangers combing the area. Most of the troops stuck to the roads, watching heavy traffic from the north as guests arrived for Edwards' big celebration.

Leaving his backpack with the horses tethered a mile from the cave, Geo led the group single file. He carried his .50 cal, crossbow and a small canvas bag of mech grenades. He stopped now and then to listen and look for Rangers. When they reached the cave, Geo and Zak waited outside while Annabelle suited up.

Zak edged away from the cave. "It's not too late to skedaddle."

"You can," Geo said.

"Just checking." Zak looked for a good place to hide.

In a few minutes, Annabelle emerged in black mech gear, holding her helmet. Geo's gut twisted. *I'm outta here.*

"If I wanted you dead…" Annabelle removed her mech glove and patted his shoulder. "Don't even think that way. I see it in your eyes. Go. Tommy's feed shows Julianne three miles north."

Geo's wrist-com showed three mechs heading southeast. Tommy had identified the lead as Julianne, thanks to his hack into mech tracking software. "I hope you know what you're doing."

"So do I."

Geo placed five grenades around the clearing and showed Annabelle how to cover them. He handed the remotes to Zak and ran northeast on a collision course with the mechs.

The sun peeked through trees like laser beams as Geo approached the mechs. He spotted one of the mechanical insects. He leveled his rifle, aimed for the helmet seam by instinct and fired, wondering whether Annabelle had turned on her link to give the mechs a distress call.

He didn't wait to find out. Jumping over branches and rocks, Geo sprinted back across the mountainside toward the cave. He prayed there weren't other mech teams in the area. *I never should have let Annabelle call them. She must be getting to me.*

Geo approached the cave. The odor of hydraulics and perfumed sweat grew stronger. Mechs blasted trees around him. He saw no sign of Annabelle when he reached the clearing in front of the cave. Mechs thrashed through the underbrush to his right and left. One mech fired, shattering rock in front of him. Geo darted toward the opening. The third mech was probably flanking him. He didn't see her.

He dove into the cave entrance as mechs blasted rock around the clearing, and then scrambled toward the back where a narrow passage led to an exit. Behind him, explosions blasted the cave entrance, spraying shards of rock. Geo kept crawling.

THIRTY-SIX

Wearing her helmet with com-link severed, Annabelle concealed herself behind rocks. Zak eyed her as if she might zap him. On the wrist-com, attached to her mech glove, Annabelle saw three mechs close in on Geo and shoot. Though mech suits were designed to withstand their own weapons, Annabelle didn't want to risk hurting her friends or exposing her position. She took aim just in case. Two shots blasted too close to Geo. *Damn.* Then he was inside the cave. The closest mech fired at the cave entrance, splattering rock fragments. Annabelle waited. *Patience,* Geo kept telling her.

Two mechs joined the first and blasted the cave entrance with machine pellets and slasher grenades. Annabelle waited until all three mechs stood in an arc around the entry for maximum firepower. *Too predictable.*

"Freeze. Stop shooting," Annabelle said, her voice masked. "You move, we detonate grenades."

All three mechs looked down, probably feeling the terror Karen and others had felt before their deaths. *Careful. They could haul me back to Civ and an arranged marriage.*

"Remove helmets or we detonate. Count of three, two, one."

Two girls released latches on their helmets and popped them off. Annabelle recognized a new recruit and a younger warrior. The recruit shook so badly her suit twitched. *Sorry, girls.*

"Remove your helmet or all three die," Annabelle said.

The third mech removed her helmet. It was Julianne, looking embarrassed and angry.

"Toss your helmets toward the cave."

Julianne looked around. "Others will come."

Annabelle reset and severed her com-link. She turned to Zak. "Don't harm them as long as they stay put." *Please stay put.* She moved behind Julianne and poked her with a stick. "You! Into the cave. Bring the helmets."

Julianne turned toward Annabelle. "You have no idea what trouble you're in. Surrender and we'll go easy on you."

"Or I could blast you and take my chances." Annabelle nudged her friend. "Move. Tell your team to stay and not to try anything. We've got them covered."

Julianne gave the order. She pushed the helmets into the narrow cave opening and crawled in after them. Annabelle followed. When she reached a room-sized cave that allowed sitting up, she saw Geo had introduced Julianne to his revolver. He turned on an LED that lit up the ragged cave. He looked fine.

Sighing with relief, Annabelle removed her helmet. "Sorry for scaring you and your team."

"I figured it was you." Julianne gave Annabelle an awkward hug. "I thought we lost you when you went offline."

"Someone leaked my mission and got me and Janine kidnapped. I don't trust the com-links. Janine is being held in Biltmoor, and Sam won't let me go after her."

Julianne pointed to Geo. "Who's that?"

"He's helping me free Janine, but we need your assistance."

"It's not a leak," Julianne said. "We have a traitor. When you didn't return, I nosed around. Someone gave you false intel. Janine won't be released even after your marriage. You aren't going through with it, are you?"

"Not if I can help it." Annabelle glanced at Geo and smiled.

"Good, I'd hate to think—"

"Who's the traitor?"

"No names until I'm sure." Julianne took off her glove and mopped her forehead. "What's your plan?"

"Edwards killed Geo's father. We're looking for help to rescue Janine and make Edwards pay."

"We can't just waltz a mech team into Biltmoor," Julianne asked. "We're under strict orders."

"Remember the party house?"

Julianne nodded.

"Ever wonder why it's so heavily guarded?"

"It's in no-man's land."

"There's a bunker beneath the house. I'm guessing it's a special prisoner, and our traitor knows." Annabelle explained her theory about Appalachian President Hardcastle being there.

"You want to break him out? He's the enemy."

"I'm not so sure," Annabelle said. "He controls no territory. They'd execute him if they thought he was a threat. We had peace before Edwards took over. We want to bring Hardcastle to Biltmoor as leverage to remove Edwards."

"That's insane," Julianne said. "I don't know what you're in the middle of, but it's dangerous."

"Can you trust your team?"

"Yeah, though you just scared the hell out of them."

"I'm sorry, Julianne. I didn't know how else to reach you."

"Speaking of which, how did you—"

"I'll trade that for the traitors," Annabelle said. "I need your help springing Hardcastle."

"If you're right, the traitor will be watching."

"Move Hardcastle to the border by tomorrow morning. We'll take him from there."

"I have family," Julianne said.

"So do I. If I'm right about Battani and Edwards, it won't go well for my family on this side of the border."

"I can't make any promises."

"I don't know who else to ask." Annabelle held the device Tommy modified. "This will allow you to bypass the mech com-link and talk to me, up to ten miles."

"You're serious."

"Attach this over your helmet's com-link and switch it over. The com-link will hear breathing and you'll be able to hear them and us, but they can't hear you. Switch it off to talk to your team and remove it when you're not using it."

Julianne nodded. "I'll link up an hour after dawn. If you don't hear from me, don't chance it."

* * *

Geo and Annabelle trekked east across the mountains, riding workhorses Peterson had scrounged up, while avoiding Ranger patrols. Geo tried not to think of the futility of asking Carlos and his father for help.

Annabelle was dressed like a boy, with a cap covering her long blonde hair. They reached a rocky slope too steep for their horses. After dismounting, Geo led the horses. Below was the forbidden Medallion territory, controlled by Marcos Sanchez, Carlos' papa. At age twelve, Geo had accompanied Pa to meet Mr. Sanchez. Pa tried to negotiate a treaty between the cartel and mountain Anglos. It had been a tense meeting. They seemed to resolve nothing, yet on the way home Pa said they had an understanding. Geo couldn't make sense of those subtleties.

Through breaks in the trees, Geo saw square fields of corn and wheat bounded by rows of trees. Beyond them stood a fortified village with the telltale poppies of a bumper crop that would someday find its way to bored Civ girls.

At the base of the mountain, they reached an asphalt road that disappeared left and right around fields of diseased corn and wheat. A dirt road lay perpendicular to the asphalt, marked by a stone medallion engraved with the Sanchez coat of arms: a lion flanked by two eagles.

Geo tied his horse to a tree beside the road. "Wait here. Call on the wrist-com if you see mechs or Rangers. If I'm not back by sundown, head west and find Peterson."

Annabelle dismounted. "I'm coming. You need someone to watch your back."

"Too risky. You have no idea what they'll do to a mech."

"It's what they'll do to you that worries me. Mom wouldn't forgive me if anything happened to you."

Geo sighed. *She'll follow anyway.*

He made sure Annabelle's hair and figure weren't so obvious. He led her across the asphalt, past the medallion, and down the dirt road. Infrared was useless in heat that had sweat streaking down his neck. He dabbed some mosquito repellent and gave some to her.

Beneath a row of maples lining the road, Geo stayed close to the withered corn. Crows called out in the distance.

Annabelle said, "What—"

He put his finger to her lips and crouched down. The corn stalks showed signs of Civ herbicide that drones used to punish border villages.

"Pare! Hands up." The accented voice came from between rows of withered corn.

Geo raised his hands over his head and encouraged Annabelle

to do the same. Three boys in camouflage, all younger than 15, emerged from the corn holding assault rifles.

"I come to see Carlos Sanchez," Geo announced to the oldest, who had slicked black hair over a thin face.

"You stupid?" Slick asked. "No one comes here."

The middle boy with a cherub face pointed to the fields. "You bring mechs."

Gripping his rifle, the youngest boy, maybe 12, circled Annabelle. "We shoot them?"

"Go back where you came from," Slick said.

"I've come to see Carlos. Tell him it's Geo."

"Go, don't cause trouble," Slick said.

Annabelle backed up to Geo and whispered, "Give me the word."

"Geo?"

Turning, he saw the slender, muscular Carlos emerge from the withered corn. Slick stuck his rifle in Geo's face.

Carlos rattled something in Spanish and the boys scurried off. "Geo, my friend. What brings you so far?" Carlos hugged him. "And who's the beautiful girl?"

Geo cringed. "She's with me."

"Bold of you coming here. Trouble?"

"About like yours." Geo fanned his arm toward the withered field.

Carlos slung his rifle over his shoulder and started walking. "Drones and mechs came yesterday. They're getting bolder."

Annabelle followed. "They're under—"

Geo jabbed her. "You know Civvies, never satisfied with what they have. One day they'll grab all this."

Carlos laughed. "Isn't Edwards supposed to keep them out?" He pressed his ear and listened.

"He's using Rangers against his own people."

In the next field, grape vines looked healthy. The crop dusters must have run out of herbicide. Women in bright patterned dresses worked side by side with the men. Geo had never seen this among his neighbors; women feared going outside.

"So you seek refuge?" Carlos asked.

"Justice," Geo said. "Rangers killed Pa."

"Sorry to hear," Carlos said, "for your sake." He waved to field hands and they bowed, smiling.

They approached the village, a cluster of more than forty connected homes enclosing a garden. It reminded Geo of primitive fortified settlements. Screams like crows' calls pierced his ears. He tensed, until he saw no reaction from Carlos. He spotted boys and girls playing, running and yelling. Watching them was a wrinkled old man in a rocker on the porch outside the wall.

"Our parents' fight is not our concern," Geo said. "Pa didn't approve of pushing drugs on young girls."

"We give Civ girls an escape hatch," Carlos said.

Annabelle said, "There's no—"

Geo poked her harder. "You'll have to excuse her. She's a Civ."

"Thought so," Carlos said.

Geo gave her a stern look. "I want justice from Edwards."

Carlos laughed. "How do you propose getting that?"

"By taking the fight to him. I've got a handful willing to join me, but they have no fight training."

Carlos held up his hand and spoke into his wrist-com. Geo heard a low rumble and saw field hands and villagers scramble toward the buildings. Carlos moved between grape vines and pulled out binoculars. "Probably a false alarm, but after yesterday."

"Radar?" Using his own binoculars, Geo looked between trees and didn't see anything.

"Spotters in the hills. They alerted me before Papa ordered the boys to shoot you."

"Thanks."

The three boys moved toward the tree line.

Carlos crossed beneath pine trees. "You're crazy to take on Edwards. Don't expect Papa to help. We pay crop bounties, and Edwards leaves us alone."

"You've done well," Geo said. At least Carlos grew up knowing his mom and sisters. "Let's not lose. Do it like running mechs."

"Why don't you just move here?" Carlos said. "Then you won't have Edwards breathing down your neck."

"Do you really believe Edwards will leave you alone?" Geo glanced at the village. No one remained outside. "He wants to control everything, including your drugs."

"What about the lives your drugs destroy?" Annabelle asked. "I've seen girls turned suicidal."

"We don't give a crow's beak about Civ girls," Carlos said. "You don't think they'd wipe us out if they could? Our family had nothing before the war because of your silly regs. While everyone else up here is dirt poor, we raise families and have a normal life."

Carlos pointed to the western sky as two clunky drones dropped down over the mountains. The three boys fanned out into a withered wheat field. Two more drones descended over the mountain, chunky models struggling to stay airborne with mechs holding on. Geo checked his .50 cal and crouched into a shooting position. "What if we went into legitimate businesses together to help both our peoples?"

Annabelle glared at Geo. "Shouldn't we hide before they spot us? We can't fight three mechs."

"I want them flying this way," Carlos said. "And our spotter only saw two."

"Then they can't be Civs. Civ mechs fight in threes."

Carlos stared at Geo. "Where did you find her? Never mind." Carlos fiddled with his wrist-com. "Geo, you sound like your pa, talking against my family."

"Pa never spoke against your family," Geo said. "I'm not asking you to give up what you have, just leave the door open."

The first drone leveled off over the treetops, heading toward the village and healthy fields, an RPG flared into action. The explosion burst the drone into flames, sending its deadly herbicide into dead fields. The second drone-duster cleared the trees a moment later, and veered sharp left. Too late. The drone burst into flames. A fireball rose over the tree line and drifted north.

"Impressive, but those mechs won't be so easy," Geo said.

"Guys, they're heading this way." Annabelle crouched down and raked through her backpack.

The bulky drones strained under the weight of airlifting mechs over the treetops. They split up. Carlos grabbed his assault rifle and ran toward the one heading south.

The drone and mech were closing in. Geo ran to keep up.

Annabelle followed. "Are you guys nuts?"

Holding up his arm, Carlos pointed his wrist-com at the approaching drone and mech. The drone lifted over a row of pines with the mech dangling by its mechanical arm. The treetop burst beneath the mech. Shrapnel shredded the tail, nose, and wings of the drone, which plunged like a stone. Carlos ran into the field, his assault rifle over his shoulder and grenades in both hands. The tumbling mech fired wildly.

Geo aimed his rifle at the spot where the helmet connected with the neck plate. He missed as the mech spun. He fired again, this time between the legs, aiming for the latches.

The mech crashed. Carlos tossed one of his grenades and tumbled behind a row of dying wheat plants. Geo dived as explosions shredded nearby plants. Shrapnel deflected off the mech's black shielding.

Geo hurled his flat grenade like a discus. The mech planted its feet and spewed machine pellets. The first explosion stunned the mech. The second converted the mech's abdomen into a chemical soup of blood, bladder and intestine. The mech shuddered and toppled backward.

To make sure, Geo ran to the mech. He removed the helmet and stared into the face of a young Ranger recruit, sweating like a hog. Geo checked the boy's pulse. None.

Tree bursts exploded behind him. Geo had forgotten the second mech. Turning, he watched the plunging beast head toward him, shooting while tumbling. The mech spun too fast to aim. Geo planted a grenade and rolled away.

Carlos tossed grenades at the mech but came up short. Geo dived for cover. After the grenade blasts, the mech got to its feet and resumed shooting. Geo fired and retreated. The mech honed in on him, pushing its way through emaciated wheat crops. Annabelle fired into the side of the mech's faceplate. Turning, the mech fired and lumbered after her.

Geo triggered his two-phase grenade. The first blast knocked the feet from under the mech. It wasn't close enough to do any real damage. The mech fell backward onto the grenade shell. Shields muted the second blast. *You should have waited, Annabelle.*

Palming another grenade, Geo ran toward the mech. Annabelle reached the mech first and flipped latches to get the helmet off. The mech stirred and raised its guns. Geo rolled beneath the mech's feet and repeatedly fired his .50 cal up into the groin plate. Annabelle dove aside as the mech began shooting, first toward where she had been, then straight up, and finally down toward Geo as the groin plate shattered, opened, and filled with blood.

When the mech stopped shooting, Geo scrambled to his feet and ran to Annabelle. "You okay?"

"It's a boy," she said between shallow breaths.

Sweat streamed down her face as she clutched Geo's hands and then hugged him. "Thanks. You sure that was the last one?" She looked up at the tree line.

"Nothing else spotted," Carlos said.

Annabelle pulled away. "I told you they weren't Civ mechs. Civ only uses girls, and these are older generation suits. Though the drones look new."

Carlos whispered. "She's a mech, isn't she?"

Geo sighed. "Yeah, one who can't keep her mouth shut."

"Excuse me," Annabelle said. "You can thank me later."

"I had it covered."

"Looked like he was ready to blast you."

Geo's heart raced. "If you had waited, he would have been over my grenade."

"Next time, let me know."

"Listen to you two," Carlos said. "You married? Forget to invite me to the wedding?"

"Heavens no," Geo said. "She's a work-in-progress."

"Thanks," Annabelle said, "but a woman shouldn't have to keep her mouth shut."

"I agree," Carlos said. "So why does Geo keep shushing you?"

Annabelle glared at Geo and picked up her rifle.

"You gave yourself away," Geo said. "You wouldn't make it as a spy."

"Whatever you do," Carlos said, "don't let Papa know. No telling what he'd do to you."

"I take it you've caught a few?" Geo asked.

Carlos grinned. "No males. This is new."

"How do you capture them?" Annabelle asked.

"You don't want to know," Carlos said. "Sorry if any were your friends, but we can't let them report back. We have the suits but no way to override the biochips."

"Then let's work together to reprogram them," Geo said.

"Sounds interesting," Carlos said.

"This proves Edwards is making a move against you," Geo said. "It's time to put an end to Edwards' monopolies."

"I'm willing to listen, but I doubt Papa will."

THIRTY-SEVEN

The ride by gas-cycle to the hacienda was smoother than riding the old mare down the mountain, except Annabelle held on so tight Geo found it hard to breathe. He didn't loosen her grip. He was still coming to terms with almost losing her. His anger over her deceptions vanished in that moment when she took on a mech.

Magnolias lined the asphalt road from the village to the town, nestled on a hill in the middle of Medallion territory. On both sides of the road, patchworks of fields, separated by pines and maples, held corn, wheat, gardens, and cash crops for Civ.

Men and women worked in scattered groups in the fields, obviously free of the constant fear Geo's neighbors felt. Of course, they kept this by selling drugs and girls, and maintaining a militia. Well-fed field workers looked up and smiled. Children ran up to Carlos when they approached the huge mansion, which was far more expansive than when Geo last visited.

After dismounting, Carlos directed a plump young boy to gas the cycles. The boy wheeled one away as if handed his favorite toy.

Carlos headed up polished granite steps to a porch that spanned the long front of the mansion, the finest home in town. Mr. Sanchez appeared in the doorway.

"Why have you brought him?" The chiseled face with long black ponytail looked much older, yet still carried the formidable presence that held Geo's respect years ago. "Is Mr. Shaw with him?"

"Papa, Geo saved my life. I beg you to show him respect. Rangers killed his pa."

Mr. Sanchez bowed. "I am sorry for your loss. Excuse my insensitive remarks. What about the girl?"

"She's with Geo, Papa. They're my guests."

"Very well, make yourselves at home." Mr. Sanchez showed them into an expansive hall larger than all three of Pa's quarters. "Excuse us while I speak with my son." Carlos and his father left.

Geo walked the hall's perimeter, which was covered with impressive paintings depicting the mountains and Hispanic life: working in the fields, dancing, and family portraits.

"His father doesn't want us here," Annabelle said. "Let's go before we get Carlos into trouble."

"I came to ask for help. I'm not leaving until I try. They have the only trained militia that could stand up to Rangers."

"And a world with men and women working together with children of both sexes."

Geo nodded. He studied the fine details of a family festival. "It's up to us to put things right. No one else can."

"Geo! When did you decide to take on the world? This isn't real." Annabelle fanned her arms out. "He lives well while the peasants work their buns off."

"Yet even they live better than we do."

"Because they sell drugs."

Carlos returned. "Papa will see you."

"And Annabelle?"

"Remember what I said."

Carlos led them into an office bristling with shelves of music, paper books, and meticulously arranged collectibles. Mr. Sanchez stood behind a huge polished mahogany desk. A whiskey decanter sat on the table behind him, next to pictures of his large family.

"Please sit." Mr. Sanchez dropped his big frame into a high-backed plush chair. "I'm grateful to you for saving Carlos' life. He tells me you showed him how Rangers are working with Civ. I agree this poses a danger, so I have agreed to hear you, though I must place the welfare of our community above all else."

"Thank you for your time, Mr. Sanchez." Geo looked at Carlos and at his papa. "I was telling Annabelle how wonderful your community is. We'd like to learn from you."

"I'm a busy man, Geo. Get to the point."

Geo glanced at a picture of their family. "Edwards is working on a deal with the Civ governor to be finalized in a couple of days. We believe it won't be good for Mountain Anglos or Medallion. I propose to bring our people together, along with dissatisfied Rangers, and apply pressure to remove Edwards as Thane."

"How will this benefit us?" Mr. Sanchez asked.

Recalling Pa's negotiations, Geo realized he was in over his head. "We find someone who will consider our interests."

"Just like your pa. You would have us share our hard-earned lifestyle with you."

"Papa," Carlos broke in, "if we wait until the Anglos are gone, then we face Civ and Edwards alone."

"You must excuse my son," Mr. Sanchez said. "He believes he's ready to run Medallion."

Geo straightened up. "Sir, with all due respect, part of the deal involves Civ moving the border a few miles every year until they squeeze us into surrendering. This will push Edwards to move against the cartel with their newly acquired mechs."

"We can handle his mechs. You saw this today."

"These were boys with old equipment. With training and newer equipment, they will devastate your world. Between Rangers and Civ, they're already intercepting your shipments. Now they're hitting your crops."

"This is not our fight, Geo. We have enough problems. In my experience, Civs or Rangers don't matter. They'll probe because we're a thorn in their sides. When they do, we bloody them and they back off. It has been that way for twenty years. Rangers are a buffer between us and Civ. If we take them out, Civ mechs will move in."

"What if this deal is about easing border tension so Edwards can focus on us and you?" Geo asked. "He consolidates power and expands his monopolies while Civ gets rid of drugs and kidnappings."

"Your folk won't work with Medallion unless we give up lucrative businesses. Look at your farmers. They barely survive. We have as much to fear from them stealing as we do Rangers."

"What if we could change that?" Geo asked. "Eliminate Edwards' monopolies so we can build a new Appalachia together. If we win, you keep the businesses you have, get into legitimate ones with us, and keep the drugs away from our folk."

"Which I've done for twenty years."

"I thank you for that."

Shifting his bulk, Mr. Sanchez grinned. "You are passionate like your pa, but Rangers are too strong on their turf. It's best to let them come to us and then hurt them so they stay away."

"I know you and Pa didn't agree, but he was honorable and deserves justice. I can't get that without your help."

"Why would I fight for justice when your pa despised us?"

"He never said anything ungracious about you or your family, sir. He merely believed it was time that you switched to legitimate activities."

Mr. Sanchez laughed. "Perhaps I underestimated the young Mr. Shaw. I wish you well in your venture. Be mindful: if you lose, you will bring wrath upon yourself and those who join you. Today they pinprick and leave. If you wound them, they will come in force."

"What if we found President Hardcastle and got his support?"

Mr. Sanchez leaned forward. "You're dreaming. But out of curiosity, how would you do this?"

Geo sensed Annabelle wanted to speak, but he gave her a look that settled her back into her plush seat. "We're trying to free President Hardcastle and have him remove Edwards. Then he could lead or name someone who respected our people and yours, while protecting us from Civ."

"You won't get past the Rangers. Before you could get close to Edwards, he would have you arrested or killed."

"Unless we pin down the Rangers and get Hardcastle before the citizens. We believe enough Rangers will stand with us."

"While Edwards controls the Biltmoor Corporation," Mr. Sanchez said, "Rangers and the church will stand by him. You have to remove all three sources of power, and he won't give up without a fight to the death. Are you prepared for that?"

"After watching him kill Pa." Geo nodded.

"An eye for an eye?"

"No," Geo said. "If Edwards surrenders and goes to prison, and we're sure he can't regain power, I could live with that."

"You risk civil war," Mr. Sanchez said, "which would invite Civ mechs to take over. It would be better to neutralize the Rangers so they are intact and willing to fight for the new government. To do so, you will have to deal with Hanrahan. Assassinating him or Edwards will risk war."

"Civil war," Annabelle said. "That's what Governor Battani wants, any chance to ride in and claim glory."

"Civ girl, I take it," Mr. Sanchez said. "You're too bold for a Biltmoor girl."

She nodded.

"More focused than most Civ girls," Mr. Sanchez said. "You're a mech, aren't you?" He rose with his revolver.

Geo got to his feet. "I can explain."

Annabelle pushed Geo aside. "Go ahead and shoot me. Everyone else has tried. I've been betrayed by my own people. They sent me into slavery to Edwards along with my sister."

"Ah, his new bride," Mr. Sanchez said. "Sit down, Ms. Scott." He placed his gun on the desk and sat down.

"You realize if I'd wanted to disarm you, I could have." Annabelle dropped into her seat. "I come in peace with Geo, my brother. He was torn from us when we were too young to remember by the bastards who torn this country apart. I'll fight alongside Geo and die if necessary to free my sister, because those dreaded Civ mechs won't help. Every hour here is another hour Janine faces torture at the hands of that disgusting bastard."

"You've met him." Mr. Sanchez looked impressed.

"I have, and the thought of him touching my sister makes my skin crawl."

"Then I won't keep you. I can't put the lives of our people at risk. If I could help in any other way, I would." Mr. Sanchez displayed a subtle smile. "If you need refuge and can keep Rangers from suspecting you're here, you're welcome to return. I'm sure we can find you a young man who appreciates a strong woman."

Annabelle looked like she wasn't sure what to make of that.

"Carlos will show you out and give you provisions for your journey. I wish I could offer more." Mr. Sanchez turned his attention to an electronic pad on his desk.

Geo and Annabelle followed Carlos outside. The plump boy stood by the gas-cycles.

"That's it?" Annabelle said.

Carlos stopped on the steps. "I warned you Papa wouldn't approve. You came close to getting your guts ripped apart by a shotgun. Papa was testing you. He doesn't like or trust mechs.

"I wish I could come with you, Geo. I owe you one or two, but I have work here. Don't do anything foolish, my friend. I would hate to have to fend on my own in your mountains."

"Thanks for listening," Geo said. "If you change your mind, we'll be on the ridge overlooking Biltmoor in the morning. Send my best to your mom."

Carlos clasped Geo's hand. "Take a gas-cycle and leave it under a tree. I'll send the boy for it. Be careful." Then he took Annabelle's hand and kissed it. "My lady, I hope you will return so we can dine together."

"Let's go," Geo grabbed her hand. "We have a lot of ground to cover."

"He's so sweet," Annabelle said when she climbed onto the cycle behind him. "I'd like to return."

It didn't help that she held on tight as he rode away from the mansion.

THIRTY-EIGHT

Geo raced the gas-cycle toward the outskirts of Medallion lands. Annabelle sat behind him, firmly gripping his waist. Wilting crops lined the dirt road, harsh evidence that Edwards intended to starve out Mr. Sanchez with mechs and Civ drones. The tyrant was becoming bolder as the pending deal approached.

They reached the asphalt road at the Medallion perimeter. "I hope Julianne can come through for us," Geo said.

"Either way we have to rescue Janine, agreed?" Annabelle hopped off the back of the gas-cycle.

Geo dismounted and parked the cycle under a maple tree. He hurried across the asphalt road to where they had left the mares. He saw no sign of the scout who had tracked their movements.

Annabelle caught up and grabbed his arm. "Are you ignoring me?"

He pulled away and picked up his pace until he spotted the brown mares. *At least we won't be walking back.*

"You're upset because Carlos paid attention to me, aren't you?"

"Why tell him you're my sister? You've got him thinking—"

"You're jealous. He is rather cute and charming."

Geo untied his mare and climbed up. "And wealthy."

"I'm not looking for a man, though you have to admit he is interesting." Annabelle strapped her backpack onto her horse.

Geo hurried up the trail, ducking under low branches.

She mounted her mare. "Admit it, you're jealous."

"You don't know what you're getting into."

"You're so sweet to protect me."

"No more talking." Geo encouraged his mare up the trail, putting distance between him and Annabelle.

Within sight of the ridge overlooking Medallion lands, Geo spotted Rangers above him. His farmyard mare wasn't strong enough to outrun their stallions. They didn't shoot, no doubt knowing they had him in their sights.

Geo activated his wrist-com and waited for Annabelle to pick up. "Can you hear me?" he whispered.

"Did you say something?"

"No sudden movements. Rangers at one o'clock."

"One what?"

Geo shook his head. *A girl from Civ's digital world.* "Thirty degrees to the right, up the hill. We'll veer left and head south. Stay close, nice and steady. Stay off the com unless it vibrates. We don't need them tracking."

He swerved left and headed down an overgrown deer path below a thick cluster of bushes. Up the hill, someone barked orders. Shots rang out. Geo kicked his horse and headed for a rocky outcrop.

More orders, shots, and the snorting of horses being mounted. Geo's mare trotted along the narrow path. Geo ducked low branches that barely cleared his back.

At another split in the trail, Geo dismounted and pulled his mare off the path. When Annabelle caught up, he grabbed the reins of her horse. "Go ahead. Keep to the right until you see the valley below. Then follow the path down. I'll catch up."

"I'm staying," Annabelle said.

"Don't be stubborn. Get going." He smacked her horse's hind end, and the horse trotted off. Geo strapped a grenade at head level to a tall pine and dropped another on the path. Placing remotes in his mouth, he pulled his mare along the path.

Waiting in the brush, Geo assembled his crossbow and tightened the crank-spring. The lead Ranger on horseback reached the split in the path. Geo crouched down with his rifle beside him, the crossbow notched and remotes clenched between his teeth. A second Ranger joined the first and pointed along the path Annabelle had taken.

A third Ranger appeared behind them; lieutenant bars decorated his sleeve. "It's the girl. Catch her. There's a big reward."

Geo shot an arrow into the lieutenant's temple and prayed for forgiveness. The man reflexively fired into the trees as he fell off his horse.

"Listen to me," Geo called out. He notched another arrow and hoped he didn't have to kill again. "Edwards is not the legitimate thane. He misled you."

The first Ranger stared in Geo's direction. "Surrender or die." He urged his mount forward.

Geo aimed his rifle and triggered the grenade remote. The explosion blasted too late but knocked the first Ranger off his horse. Spooked, the horse charged past Geo. The fallen Ranger got to his feet and prepared to shoot. The second explosion ripped his legs from under him and shattered the pine tree's base.

The second Ranger's horse snorted and jumped with panic. The Ranger urged his mount forward and fired. Geo shot, missed. He prepared to release the second grenade when suddenly the pine toppled, crashing onto the rider. The stallion scraped the Ranger off his back and bolted past Geo.

The second Ranger got behind a tree, called for backup, and fired. Geo triggered the second remote. The first explosion brought the ghastly groan of an injured man. The second blast silenced him. Geo prayed for deliverance, while he ran to his mare. *Never take joy in killing,* Pa would say, and Geo didn't.

He galloped his mare until he caught up with Annabelle on the path down into the valley. When she started to speak, he took the lead, urging his mare along. If Rangers came this far looking for her, it would be worse once they got closer to town. Geo couldn't blame the cartel and mountaineers for not joining him, but he had no choice. Pa's spirit called to him to find justice in a world where there was no higher court than Thane Edwards.

THIRTY-NINE

Back at the factory, Annabelle watched Tommy reprogram wrist-coms while Geo went to make another appeal to O'Brien and the others. *This is all taking too long. When are we going after Janine?*

"This uses encryption that will take them time to decipher," Tommy explained. "You'll be able to talk to me."

Examining a unit, Annabelle saw no difference. "That's great, Tommy. How soon can you have these so we can leave?"

Tommy pouted. "You're not impressed. Most guys would take days to do this."

"You've done a wonderful job."

The boy beamed. Annabelle added, "I'm just worried about Janine."

"I hacked Biltmoor's security for you," Tommy said. "I'll watch in case they move her."

"You can do that?"

"Anything for you, Miss Annabelle. You're nice."

She shuddered at what lay behind that remark.

"Come back safe." Tommy didn't volunteer to join them.

Annabelle went looking for Geo. He wasn't in the lab with the others making grenades, nor in the tiny bedroom where she would love to curl up and catch up on sleep. She found him in the cafeteria, alone, brooding.

Maybe he's packing food for the trip. She approached him by the counter. *No food.*

"Geo, we have to go. Janine needs us."

"Not until Tommy and the others are done."

Annabelle placed her hand on his shoulder and forced him to face her. "I'm scared, too, Geo. If you can't help, I'll ask Carlos. I'm sure he would do it for me."

Geo walked away. "Stop doing that. If you want Carlos, go."

She grabbed his arm. "Listen to me."

He pulled away. "I said stop it. I don't want to fight. I want to be alone."

Maybe fighting was what they needed. Annabelle punched his arm and was surprised at how good it felt to make contact. "I'm not done talking with you."

Geo backed away. "I'm tired of running from Rangers, and watching folk get killed, and—"

Annabelle shoved his chest. He brushed her away and grabbed her arms. She wrenched free, pushed aside tables to make room, and assumed a fighting stance.

He held up his hands. "I can't do this, Annabelle."

"Sure you can."

She attacked. He blocked. She rotated and came at him from behind. He spun and blocked her. She came in low, kicked high, and spun left and right. Each time he stared into her and parried. She used every move she had learned in mech training, every move she had employed in the arena with brutes, but he stopped her each time.

She swept his legs. He jumped, dropped her to the stone floor, and pinned her arms, using his upper body strength to hold her down. She rotated and twisted to get him off. She stopped, smiled up at him, and flushed with unexpected heat. She sensed that though he had bested her, he still wanted to protect her.

Getting up, he moved away. "I can't do this anymore."

She grabbed his wrists. "Yes, you can, Geo. I need you."

Wrenching free, he went to the counter. "Don't make this harder. I—"

Annabelle caught his arm. "We had a deal. I've waited days for you to lead me to Janine."

Geo pulled away. "Just go."

She took his hands. "I'm not going anywhere without you."

He pushed her away. "Stop it!"

"Why? Talk to me."

Geo turned away. "I don't want to talk."

"Look at me."

"I can't. I—"

Frustrated, she flipped him onto the cave floor and straddled him. Before he could push her away, she leaned over and kissed him on the lips. She felt her body melt into his. He slipped his arms around her. She felt vulnerable and excited.

He rolled her onto her back and pulled up. "You're just doing this so I'll help you."

She stroked his cheek and tried to guide him closer. "I nearly died when I thought that mech had you." She wrapped her arms around him and pulled him toward her. "I know this is happening crazy fast, but I love you. This is real. Hold me."

She pulled herself up and kissed him on the lips. This time when she lay back, he followed, and rolled over with her on top. He brushed her hair back and kissed her. It gave her the same coming-home feeling she had sleeping next to him at night, lying next to him in the cave, and sitting behind him on the cycle—and more.

He rolled again and pulled her to her feet. "You know this complicates things."

"You're rejecting me?"

"No, Annabelle. I'm respecting you. Pa taught me never to take advantage of a girl."

"Didn't he also teach you not to embarrass a girl?"

"When we get through this, I'd like to court you proper."

"That sounds rather formal and unpleasant. Aren't we beyond that?"

"I'm serious," Geo said.

"I know. Being with you feels right, Geo."

* * *

Insane warmth permeated Geo's body and seized his mind. Mesmerizing turquoise eyes haunted his vision. His senses gathered her warm musk. Her sweet taste tickled his lips. Words from all the books he had read eluded him. Neither Byron, Shelly, nor Keats prepared him for Annabelle.

It took two alarms to wake him. He wanted to linger, gaze into her eyes, and imagine life with her, but it was late. He was ready to take on the world on her behalf, though the thought of facing Edwards terrified him.

Geo and Annabelle, along with Mickey and the twins, rode and hiked, then crawled through one cave and tunnel system after another to avoid Rangers. Four hours later, they reached the ridge. Below them lay the border to the right and the town of Biltmoor to the left. Geo had never seen so many Rangers in one day.

He knew if they caught him, they would put him through rigorous brainwashing, steroid enhancement, and physical training, but that was nothing compared to how Annabelle put herself at risk. No matter what he said or did, she insisted on riding into Biltmoor to rescue Janine.

Annabelle checked the modified mech com-link for the tenth time. Julianne was late. Geo held out hope that Carlos would sneak out for the challenge, but there was no sign of him. It was time to get moving.

When the com-link vibrated, Geo placed his ear next to Annabelle's.

"News not good," Julianne said. "Can't talk."

Annabelle said, "Where's—"

"Package at Palace." Julianne cut the link.

"At palace?" Geo said.

"Hardcastle must be part of the deal," Annabelle said. "Either he was freed to help Edwards or he's a prisoner."

"Hardcastle wouldn't help Edwards," Geo said.

"Can Tommy find out?"

Geo sent Tommy a text message and scanned the woods. Mickey crouched in a nearby tree, while the twins sat near the road below with a horse-drawn cart. *No Carlos.* "I guess your boyfriend isn't coming."

"Oh, I have a boyfriend? I've never had one before. Pray tell, how should I act?"

"Funny." Geo scanned the rooftops of Biltmoor and, in the distance, the Biltmoor Towers next to the crystalline Cathedral.

Annabelle rubbed his shoulders. "Don't worry about Carlos. Just concentrate on getting through this alive. Remember, if we get into a scrape, focus on your opponent, not me, or you'll get us both killed."

Somehow, Annabelle looked sexy even beneath male jeans and shirt. He tucked her hair under her cap and kissed her on the lips.

She pushed him away. "Not until after. Stay focused."

Geo joined Mickey by the trail and headed down toward the road. Annabelle followed.

"You want to turn back?" Mickey asked.

"You can," Geo said. Rounding an outcrop of rock, he spotted the Brache twins in their cart with two fattened pigs. "When we get past—"

"We've covered this," Annabelle said. "Stop stalling." She squeezed his hand, pulled a poncho around her, and climbed into the cart beside the pigs. She covered herself with straw.

Geo fastened his poncho and climbed in, wondering how the three of them would fit in this tiny cart. Annabelle wiggled behind a grumbling pig. When Mickey climbed in, Geo could barely move. He poked his remote scope above the straw and adjusted the connection to his goggles.

The cart rattled along the gravel road until they reached Thane's Highway 50. As they ambled along asphalt, cycle patrols and visitors for the celebration passed them.

For a moment, the cart stopped. Geo held his breath, with the smell of pig filling his sinuses. This was the first checkpoint at the outskirts of town. Soon, the cart moved on.

People crowded along the streets, visiting shops and making last-minute preparations before heading downtown for tomorrow's celebration. Security would be tight with thanes coming from nearby regions along with guests from Civ.

When the cart stopped again, Geo heard male voices challenge the twins.

"It's a gift for our beloved thane on this most blessed occasion," Dirk said.

The guard poked around and turned up his nose. He waved them on.

The cart stopped in an alley crowded with garbage Dumpsters. Mickey climbed out. Feeling stiff from their cramped quarters, Geo followed and helped Annabelle out. Then he turned to Mickey. "Take the pigs to market and leave town." Mickey and the twins left.

Annabelle removed her poncho and picked up her pack. "Find Willis. I'm going for Janine."

Geo removed his cloak and put both ponchos behind the Dumpster. "Can't you wait until we find Willis?"

"Janine has suffered long enough."

"Then let me go with you."

She patted his arm. "You're sweet to worry about me, but

rescuing damsels is what I do. Besides, you can't go where I'm going. Find Willis and figure out how to deal with Edwards tomorrow."

"It's too dangerous alone."

"Please don't fight me on this," Annabelle said.

"If you get caught—"

She kissed him on the lips and lingered. Then she pulled away and hurried down the alley.

"Be careful," Geo said as she disappeared around the corner.

FORTY

Geo straightened the dressy town-clothes Peterson had provided. He shouldered his backpack and headed onto the sidewalk, feeling naked without his rifle. Clusters of men hurried by. He scanned the faces of the few escorted women in floral dresses, imagining that any one of them could be his mom.

With no other plan than to find Willis, Geo made his way past Edwards Patriot Bank and Thane's Emporium to the Old Goat Bar & Grill. It was the only place in town that Geo could recall Pa mentioning. A large cracked window sported neon signs advertising beers not seen since the war. He stepped inside a dark, paneled room. A bearded bartender with thick eyebrows glanced at Geo and returned his gaze to a buxom blonde in a tight skirt. She was wiping down a table.

Geo dropped into a booth and nonchalantly arranged the salt, pepper, and sugar dispensers in a way he had seen Pa do.

"Either you're stupid or you carry elephant brass." A crusty voice came from behind.

Geo resisted the urge to look. "Elephants have incredible memories."

"Let's hope you have a thick hide."

"Not thick enough to conceal anything of interest."

"Then move your feet faster than your tongue."

Geo grabbed his pack and followed a bear of a man to the rear of the bar. The man turned down an unlit corridor and disappeared into blackness. Geo followed, felt sudden weightlessness, and suppressed a scream. He landed on a floating mattress in pitch darkness. Something above closed with a thud and a click. *No point yelling.* He groped for the edge of the floating cushion and heard guns cock.

Lights blinded him. When his eyes adjusted, he found himself surrounded by three grisly men with short-barrel rifles.

* * *

Annabelle crouched behind a Dumpster in the alley behind Undercover and waited. Spotting clients on the street out front made her ill. Several girls came out for their break: a quick smoke, a swig from a slender bottle, or something stronger before their next encounter. Haley lit up.

"Act natural," Annabelle whispered. "Don't look my way."

"What are you doing here?"

"I need to see Chrissie."

"You shouldn't be back here." Haley's hand shook. She snuffed out her cigarette and headed inside. "She's in her office. Be quick."

Shielding her face from cams, Annabelle hurried up a narrow stairway and knocked at the door. The door opened. She faced a revolver, and froze.

Julianne emerged from behind the door and pulled Annabelle into Chrissie's office. "I've looked everywhere for you."

"Why are you here? Where's Chrissie?"

"She'll be back." Julianne dropped the gun on a cluttered desk. "When I heard they moved Hardcastle, I nosed around. Dara arranged to have you kidnapped."

"Dara? Why? I thought she was killed."

"They never found a body." Julianne hugged Annabelle. "Damn, it's good to see you."

Annabelle savored the connection with a friend and sister warrior. "Dara's alive?"

"We have to be careful." Julianne pulled Annabelle onto the sofa next to her. "I thought you could use help rescuing Janine."

"Who else was working with her?" Annabelle removed her cap, letting her blonde hair dangle.

Julianne frowned. "Margarite."

Annabelle nodded. "Makes sense. They were best friends before Margarite was kidnapped. Did Dara make a deal to free her?"

"Possibly."

"What about a third?" Annabelle asked.

"It could have been just the two of them. If Dara operated alone at the base, there'd be less risk of slipping up."

Chrissie entered and locked the door. She closed her eyes and shook her head. "Annabelle, Bishop Kolinski is looking for any excuse to shut us down. You know what that means for my girls."

"It's good to see you, too." Annabelle hugged Chrissie. "I need help getting into the Towers."

Chrissie didn't look happy. "Edwards has dibs on new girls. When he throws parties for his inner circle, we have to pony up. Now and then a girl doesn't return."

"Meaning?" Annabelle asked.

"He doesn't return damaged merchandise."

"So he's having a party tonight?"

Chrissie laughed. "A bachelor party. You should get as far from here as you can."

"He's holding Janine in the Towers. I have to rescue her."

"He wants a lot of girls tonight. If you must go, let me outfit you."

* * *

The burly man Geo had followed spoke up. "What brings you to the Old Goat?"

"Information." The water mattress bobbed so hard that Geo couldn't get to his knees. "My pa was Bret Shaw, killed by Rangers."

"Words like that could get you killed around here." The big man kicked the mattress, stirring waves that knocked Geo down. "He smuggled weapons to traitors."

Geo felt seasick. "He was killed helping refugees."

"You the one got him killed over some silly Civ girl?"

"Can I get up?"

"I don't know. Can you?" The big man kicked again.

Feeling nauseous, Geo decided, *Time to go for broke.* "I don't suppose you have a daughter around nineteen?"

"What if I do?"

"Adopted 16 years ago…."

"That's when my wife got arrested," the man said.

"That silly Civ girl Pa and I were helping might be your daughter."

The big man's face hardened. "What are you talking about?"

"Are you Willis Montgomery?" Geo was ready to throw up if

the mattress didn't stop rocking.

The big man motioned for the others to lower their rifles. "I'm Willis." He put his foot on the mattress to slow the waves. "What's this about a daughter?"

"Her birth mom is Dorothy Montgomery. The girl is pledged to marry Edwards and doesn't want to."

"Now there's a story I don't hear every day." Willis held out his hand and helped Geo off the mattress. "Your pa was an honorable man. He talked about a son. I was starting to think you never existed."

Geo stood and tried to steady himself. "I do, and I aim to find justice for Pa's murder."

The big man gave a hearty laugh. "You don't say. How you figure to do that? Edwards owns this town and most of the region."

"He didn't own Pa, he doesn't own me, and he doesn't own Annabelle, yet," Geo said. "Pa said I'd find good men at the Old Goat. He mentioned your name and certificates."

Willis led Geo to a coarse oak table and bench where the other men sat. "Did he? Certificates. Hmmm. Do you have them?"

"No. I have no idea what they are or where they'd be."

"Someplace Thane Edwards wouldn't find them. Your Pa and Hardcastle owned shares in Biltmoor under shell companies to keep their names quiet after Edwards started killing people to consolidate his power." Willis sighed. "By the fates, I do owe your pa for rescuing me sixteen years ago, though you don't know what you're asking." He sat.

Geo remained standing. "You're right. I don't. I'm a country bumpkin, and the only one willing to help me is Annabelle. I owe it to Pa to make this right."

"Annabelle?"

"She's a good fighter."

Willis laughed. "At least she got something from her old man. You're starting to sound like your pa twenty years ago when we came this way."

"Will you help? I want to recover Pa's body and give him a proper burial. Then Edwards needs to pay."

"Have a seat before you wear out the floor." Willis patted the table. "Edwards nailed your pa to a cross at the edge of town as a warning."

"Then we have to get him."

"He's buried where Edwards won't find him. No man deserves what he got. If Annabelle is my daughter, no way in hell will Edwards lay a hand on her. Where is she?"

Geo closed his eyes. "She insisted on freeing her adopted sister from the Towers."

Willis got to his feet. "You let her go alone?"

"She said she'd be safer on her own."

Sighing, the big man shook his head. "Like my wife when I told her not to risk herself. So, I have a daughter, and you let her ride into the lion's den alone."

"Will you help?"

Willis' eyes lost focus. "She doesn't know what she's getting into."

"I think she does. She's a mech warrior and so is her sister."

Willis slumped into his seat. "A mech? You have no idea what Edwards will do to her."

"Then let's help her, and figure out how to stop him."

"You're talking treason," Willis said.

"Get me close enough to challenge him."

"You'll have to deal with Hanrahan and Kolinski. They owe their fortunes to Edwards."

"I have to do this," Geo said. "And if I make it through tomorrow, I'd like your consent to court Annabelle."

Willis stared at him. "Don't that beat all? What does she say?"

"That it's a silly custom."

"Let's get to the Towers before they catch her."

FORTY-ONE

Getting to the Towers turned out to be easier than Annabelle expected. She and a dozen other scantily dressed girls were packed into a paddy wagon. Their escorts eyed them like hungry men in a meat locker. Frisky Rangers surrounded the wagon when they arrived in the lobby of Tower One.

If I had my mech gear and weapons, I could crash through the front door or that plate-glass window. "Now what?" Annabelle asked.

Julianne nodded toward the corridor to Tower Two. "Follow me."

Rangers herded the other girls into the elevators as Annabelle followed Julianne toward two guards who blocked the connecting passageway. Behind them, stairs led downward. *That must be where Tommy had located Janine.*

Julianne sashayed up to the larger guard and pulled up her skimpy maroon top. "My bra's all tangled. Can you help?"

Both guards gawked at Julianne. Annabelle grabbed the smaller guard's chin and snapped his head; she heard the crunch of cartilage. Julianne swept the big guard's legs and jumped him, crushing his windpipe with her fist. Making sure the Rangers weren't watching, they dragged the guards into the stairwell.

Annabelle activated her wrist-com and texted: *Tommy?*

That was cool, he texted back. That meant he must have hacked into the Biltmoor cams. *Rangers checking lobby. They can't see stairwell cams, but I can. Sis in Tower Two, down two levels.*

Where can we leave the guards, she sent.

Broom closet, bottom of stairs.

Thanks. Annabelle grabbed a pair of hands and dragged one guard downstairs, his shoes scraping the concrete. Julianne followed with the big guard's body.

* * *

Geo felt awkward wearing the tight pants and dressy shirt Willis gave him. The outfit was even tighter after he stuffed pistols into his pockets. The face altering mask Willis applied to him itched in the heat.

Willis led Geo toward the Towers. On his wrist-com, Geo followed Annabelle's movements through texts from Tommy and wished he had a direct link. Geo was amazed she had managed to reach the Towers already, with so many Rangers and cops all over the place.

Willis stopped at every block, and waited for a wiry man in a cop's uniform to clear their crossing to the next alley. With so few civilians on the street, Geo felt conspicuous. The wiry man signaled, and they sprinted across another street, ran down the alley, and crouched by the next crossing. An armadillo rolled by.

"What happened when you left Civ?" Geo asked.

"They arrested me and used me for mech training until I refused to fight. Now my daughter's a mech." Willis shook his head. "After that they threw me into prison west of Knoxville."

They crossed the next street, ran down the alley, and waited. An armadillo stopped and let out two Rangers who blocked the intersection. Willis took Geo laterally a couple of blocks before they found a safe spot to cross. "My wife got me over the border where I was attacked by two squads of mechs I'd helped train. Your pa rescued me, but they arrested my wife. I never wanted to put our daughter through this."

"Then let's hope we get to her before Edwards does." Geo used his binoculars to spot the wiry man.

Rangers approached from the side.

* * *

Once again, Annabelle was thankful her mech training included study of the Tower plans. She and Julianne pushed the guards into the closet. Then Annabelle led the way down a wide concrete corridor to a huge room with industrial laundry equipment along the walls. In the center, tables overflowed with clothing and sheets.

It looked like a lot of laundry for an office building with a few suites on the top floors.

Annabelle sifted through a pile of white clothing, sniffing to make sure she got a clean service uniform. She stripped off her skimpy yellow outfit. "You sure got the guards' attention."

Julianne grabbed a white uniform. "Sam says when stripped of weapons, find new ones."

Annabelle pulled on a white linen top, tucked her hair under a maid's cap, and checked her image in the reflection of a stainless-steel dryer before moving toward the door. No telling when Rangers will realize Tommy has altered their cams.

They wrapped their discarded outfits in a sheet and tossed them into the garbage. Then Annabelle led the way down the concrete corridor to Tower Two. Hearing male voices, she ducked into an empty room, another laundry. Julianne followed. At a nod from Annabelle, Julianne checked the corridor while Annabelle slipped to the next door. It was good to work with another warrior who could practically read your mind.

Annabelle jimmied the door lock until it released, and went in. Julianne followed. They turned on a light to reveal a storage room filled with maintenance supplies. According to building plans, there was a three-foot gap behind these shelves.

They dragged the shelves away from the wall. Annabelle used them as a ladder, climbed to the ceiling, and found the mechanical release. When it gave, a section of wall fell back and musty air filled the storage room. Julianne pushed the wall in, revealing concrete stairs leading down.

They pulled the storage unit back into place and pushed the wall until it clicked shut. In the dark, they descended. Annabelle hoped she was right about where this came out or they would have to return to the storage room and find the latch in the dark. Then what?

Clammy heat prickled Annabelle's neck. Behind her, Julianne breathed hard. When she crashed against a concrete wall, Julianne collided with her.

"Sorry."

"Quiet."

Annabelle heard muffled male voices. In the darkness, her fingers found a latch. She waited. Ghostly echoes filled the nearby space.

Julianne grasped her arm. Annabelle put hers around her friend, grateful not to be alone.

When the voices stopped, Annabelle texted Tommy and got a reply: *Few cams. Rangers left storage room, headed left. Sis to right.*

Annabelle released the latch and ducked as the wall sprang out. Brushing Julianne aside, she stepped into a darkened space. Racks on both sides lined her way toward the other end, where light penetrated around a door. She found the light switch.

Julianne stood in the middle of an aisle surrounded by floor-to-ceiling shelves of munitions. Two more aisles, left and right, held a small arsenal. Annabelle checked the one to her right and found RPGs and heavy guns. They were too big to use in close quarters.

Julianne checked to the left, while Annabelle returned to the middle aisle. She stuffed a revolver into her belt, at her back. Her pocket sagged as she tucked a pistol into it.

"Got you." A husky male voice scratched at her ears.

Turning, Annabelle faced a gray-bearded Ranger.

He grabbed her wrist and yanked her toward him. "Why don't you show me what you've got?"

The Ranger touched her face. Annabelle removed her service cap, letting her blonde hair drop to her shoulders.

The brute dropped her wrists, and stepped back to take the full measure of her. "That's more like it. Come to papa."

"You're not my papa." Annabelle whipped out the gun from behind her back and waved to indicate he should move into the corner.

Julianne brought the butt of a revolver down on his head, hard. The man grunted and slumped to the concrete floor.

She dragged him down a side aisle. "I thought we were in a hurry."

Annabelle tucked her hair under the service cap. "Let's go." She pocketed her pistol.

They checked each other's disguises. Annabelle turned out the light, opened the door, and listened. The dimly lit hall smelled of dead fish, cellar dampness, and human sweat.

They moved into the concrete corridor, streaked in black mold. Annabelle eased the door shut with a click and motioned for Julianne to stay close.

This part of the tower contained holding cells from which she had sprung a kidnapped victim on her previous mission. She lost a sister mech in that raid. There were several clusters of cells. The one she wanted was ahead and to the left.

As they approached the guard post, Annabelle hesitated, hoping that there was only one guard. She cringed at entering a dead-end with no other way out.

Hearing shuffling feet and wheels on concrete, Annabelle pulled Julianne behind a pillar and took out a pistol and a hand-grenade. *Too noisy for such a confined space.*

A rail-thin girl in a service uniform passed them, pushing a cart with steaming bowls of rancid-smelling stew. Annabelle grabbed the girl. "Are you Union?" she whispered fiercely.

The girl froze, stared in astonishment, and forced a nod.

"Do you want to go home?"

The girl nodded, her eyes terror-stricken.

"Where is Janine Scott? Which cell?"

The frail girl drew a circle on her hand and held up five fingers. She pointed to her middle finger.

Annabelle folded the thin girl onto the lower tray of the cart. She draped cloth over the opening, and wheeled the squeaky cart toward the guard. She nodded for Julianne to wait and get behind the guard. Then Annabelle entered the guard's station.

The guard looked like a heavyweight wrestler on steroids. He glanced up from his screen and sneered. "Where's my kitty-cat."

So, you're using her. You pig. "She's wanted upstairs," Annabelle said, trying to make her voice sound haggard.

"Be quick."

The guard returned his attention to his screen. Annabelle entered a concrete enclosure surrounded by five rusted steel doors. After easing the girl from under the cart, Annabelle hurried to the middle cell. She peered through the bars.

Janine!

Pale, clothed in rags, her sister lay on a bed of straw.

Annabelle retrieved small tools from her uniform pocket and jimmied the lock. Julianne should have immobilized the guard by now. *What's she waiting for?* Annabelle eased the door open. The hinges squeaked.

Janine stood up. "Annabelle! You shouldn't be here. Edwards says he'll have you by tomorrow." She nearly fainted with the effort of standing.

Annabelle grabbed her sister's bony hand, pulled her from the cell, and motioned for the waif of a girl to take her place. "Only for a moment," Annabelle whispered. Once the serving girl was lying down, Annabelle closed the door and called out, "This one's dead."

The guard ambled into the enclosure. "No one dies on my watch."

Annabelle kicked the guard in the throat. He didn't go down. Janine planted her foot in his groin, sending him reeling backward. "That's for hurting these girls."

Julianne ran in. She kicked the guard in the back. He flopped forward onto his knees and grunted. Annabelle considered using her gun, but that would bring more guards and Rangers. She launched a kick to his belly; he grabbed her leg. Julianne jumped him from behind and got him in a chokehold.

Breaking free, Annabelle tumbled away. The guard threw Julianne over his shoulder and landed on top of her. She gasped. He pulled free and got to his feet. He wasn't one of the usual guards. They probably chose the best to watch Janine. Eyeing the three mech warriors, the brute backed up toward the guard station.

The cart materialized as if out of nowhere. The waif of a serving girl shoved it into the guard's legs. Grunting, he swung around and knocked the cart away. He grabbed the girl's arm, nearly tearing it from its socket when he flung her toward the others.

Annabelle jabbed a kick to the head that sent the guard crashing against a concrete pillar. He grabbed her leg, tugged her toward him, and managed to get behind. He got her neck in a vice. Julianne attacked him from the left. With his free hand, he swatted her away. Janine leapt up and rammed a hinge bolt into his neck. "Leave my sister alone."

Annabelle's service cap fell. The guard loosened his grip, perhaps in realization that this was the bride-to-be. *Thanks, sis.*

Julianne crouched and rammed her foot into the guard's knee. It popped. The man lost his balance and came crashing down with Annabelle still pinned. When they fell against the concrete wall, she rammed her elbow into his ribs.

The guard gurgled, blood spurting from his neck onto her white uniform. Annabelle punctuated this with rhythmic thrusts of her elbow. He refused to let go. Julianne tried to get inside, but they were in a corner between pillar and wall. The guard used his good leg and free arm to strike back. When Julianne pulled out her gun, he used Annabelle as a shield.

Fading from lack of oxygen, Annabelle rotated. She freed the pistol from her waistband and fired point blank into him. Her body muffled the sound. Searing pain from powder burns told her it was too close. His good leg twitched.

Still holding her neck, he went for the gun. She grabbed his free arm with her left and rotated the gun. The guard cried out in gurgling croaks. His grip weakened; he grabbed for the gun. Julianne lunged for one arm while Janine went for the other. Annabelle rotated the gun and shot up into the man's abdomen. He convulsed and went limp.

Pulling free, Annabelle slumped to the floor to catch her breath. She fished out the tool she had used to pick Janine's lock and handed it to her sister.

Janine picked locks, and Julianne helped four other Union girls out of their cells.

"You're the one Thane Edwards is looking for?" a frail brunette asked.

"I came for my sister. You can come with us if you make no noise."

Annabelle hugged Janine. "Can you ever forgive me for not coming sooner?"

Janine's smile came with sadness. "I was angry at first. But he kept questioning me. The more I heard about your arrangement, the more I was ready to sacrifice myself for you."

Annabelle held her sister tight. "You don't get to do that, Babe."

Annabelle locked the dead guard and cart in Janine's cell. She led the others down the concrete corridor to the storage room. She hadn't planned to rescue so many, yet she couldn't leave them.

FORTY-TWO

Willis led Geo to an alley behind Tower Plaza stores. By now, a general alarm had cops and Rangers scrambling around the broad plaza and nearby buildings. The two of them were surrounded, with no way to cross the plaza to the Towers or to retreat.

Geo scanned the plaza and the massive crystalline Cathedral with his binoculars. Willis pulled him down the deserted alley away from the boulevard that led to the plaza. They crouched behind a green Dumpster. Even here, Geo felt exposed. It wasn't like the mountains, where he knew how to act and how to get around.

Willis broke into the back door of Edwards' Fine Dress, a shop that faced the plaza. He scooted the broken glass behind a Dumpster, then pulled Geo inside and closed the door.

Geo checked his com-link. Annabelle had Janine, but they were trapped inside Tower Two. He was sick with the thought of Edwards marrying Annabelle. "She needs help."

"Come on." Willis found a stairway. "Let's see what we're dealing with."

Geo followed him up squeaky wooden steps to a second story filled with racks of clothes in protective plastic. Tommy texted that Annabelle was moving toward an exit but Rangers were everywhere. Geo texted: *Is there a tunnel?*

Willis opened an access door to the roof. "She shouldn't have gone. It was a trap."

They climbed a rusted ladder and squatted on the rooftop

behind the decorative façade. Geo started to get up so he could see the plaza.

"Careful," Willis said. "They'll scan for anyone trying to help her." Willis touched his earpiece. "We need a diversion by Tower One and an assist."

Geo placed his remote cam on a rod above the façade, and rotated. Six armadillos and at least fifty Rangers fanned out across the plaza. More moved along the side of the Tower complex and surrounding streets.

The next text sent Geo's heart into his throat. *She thinks com-link hacked, going silent.* Geo turned off his com-link and scanned Ranger movement below. "We have to do something."

"Patience. What did she say?"

"The link is hacked. She signed off."

Geo scanned Tower One, floor by floor, seeing honeycombs of cells with Biltmoor bees doing whatever Edwards asked.

"Edwards lives in the penthouse of Tower One." Willis scanned side streets. "Below are his private offices, board room, and quarters for personal aides." Willis spoke into his com and turned to Geo. "We'll have some excitement soon. Get ready to move."

Geo studied the penthouse. The sharp upward angle revealed only its ceiling. He scanned the floor below and switched to infrared.

"I'm telling you," Willis said, "Edwards and Governor Battani are up to something. Whatever they have planned won't be good for us or the people of this town."

"Other than both wanting this treaty, how can you be so sure they're working together?" Geo launched a bumblebee camera and guided it toward the upper Tower windows.

"Look at this place. Are you telling me Civ mechs couldn't take this in an instant?"

Geo looked at the crystalline Cathedral and the glass-encased towers. "War's over." Using his wrist-com, Geo guided the bumblebee to the windows of the floor below the penthouse, along the east, south and then west walls. He spotted Edwards, standing at the window of a conference room, his arm on the shoulder of a man. The man turned. It took a moment for the image to register. It was Cory Philips.

Geo showed Willis. "He's the one we were helping when Pa

was killed. I thought he was dead."

"He's a spy," Willis said. "He turned my wife in after helping me escape. I'd like to wring his neck."

To think I helped this sniveling worm. But if I hadn't, we wouldn't have gone to Biltmoor, and I wouldn't have met Annabelle.

"How can we help Annabelle with all these Rangers around?" Geo asked.

"I have an idea. Let's go." Willis headed down the ladder.

Geo recalled the bumblebee, retrieved his remote cam, and caught up by the back door. "Is there another way in or out of the Towers?"

"Not that I know of."

An armadillo sped through the alley. An explosion rattled windows alongside. Geo took control of the bumblebee and rotated for a view of the plaza. Near Tower One, an armadillo burned. Another explosion hit a second vehicle. Moments later, like iron filings to a magnet, Rangers flocked toward Tower One. Two more armadillos raced down the alley. The contingent of Rangers outside Tower Two dropped in half.

"It's not enough," Geo said. "We need to take out those Rangers."

"Listen to you, itching to go up against Appalachia's finest. Let's go." Willis crossed the alley away from the Towers.

Geo joined him. "You're going the wrong way."

"Don't you think I want to save my daughter? We can't help her here." Willis took off and zigzagged along several empty streets.

Stopping behind another green Dumpster, Geo pulled up the bumblebee, hovering over the plaza. An entire division of Rangers descended onto Tower One. They dragged several men into the street, shot one, and forced others to kneel.

Geo showed the image to Willis. "Anyone you know?"

Willis' face twisted. Geo thought he saw a tear in the big man's eye. "Buzz and two of his buddies. See? That's the problem with fighting the Rangers."

"I'm not giving up on Annabelle." Geo started back.

"Don't be a fool. That's suicide. We need to give the Rangers something else to worry about." Willis headed down an alley, away from downtown.

Explosions sent smoke into the air near the Towers, reddening the setting sun. Geo checked the bumblebee; he couldn't locate the source. He rejoined Willis. "Was that one of yours?"

"We're leading the Rangers toward Civ."

"What if Annabelle heads that way?"

"Hopefully, she'll change course."

Armadillos flew down a nearby boulevard toward the Towers. From the bumblebee above the plaza, Geo watched Rangers head west. "How about hijacking an armadillo and picking her up?"

"How would you get one without destroying it? Besides, they have tracking devices." Willis crossed to the next alley.

When they stopped, Geo looked at images of the plaza. *Still too many Rangers.* "We need another diversion, northeast."

Another explosion resonated closer to the border. Still, Rangers clung to the towers.

"What do you have in mind?" Willis asked.

"Set charges at the edge of town. Make it look like she's gone."

Willis nodded. "We should go, too, since they'll search house by house."

Escaping was the smart move, but Geo couldn't leave without Annabelle. They reconnected with the wiry man who led them block-by-block northeast until they reached the paved road encircling Biltmoor. An armadillo blocked the intersection, meaning twenty or so Rangers scouting the area.

Geo crouched down with binoculars. "You have any friends nearby?"

"Just Bud, the man who's been guiding us."

"Can you get me close to the armadillo?"

With Bud as a scout, Willis and Geo scooted alongside one aluminum warehouse and then another. Ranger patrols seemed to be keeping all the civilians indoors, leaving the streets quiet except for another round of explosions behind them.

Geo dropped down behind a closed coffee shop on the corner and faced the armadillo. He scanned for Rangers and saw only one behind the armored vehicle with his rifle resting on the hood. Geo assembled his crossbow. He cranked the spring and notched an arrow, then set it beside him. He checked his revolver, loaded, and scooted closer to the vehicle.

Armadillos had a weak spot where the exhaust pipe wrapped around the gas tank. Geo put a remote between his teeth and flung a grenade like a discus. It came up short.

The Ranger grabbed his gun and moved west along the road, followed by a younger man, probably a new recruit Geo hadn't seen. Geo waited until the men reached the crest of a hill and followed the road down the other side. He held his breath and listened, hating the hum of city electrics that masked human activities.

Geo threw a second grenade, which landed under the vehicle. Activating the second remote, he crawled beside a wooden shed next to the shop and waited.

The two Rangers returned, the older one giving instructions to the new recruit. Geo waited until they were near the armadillo before he let loose an arrow, right through the older Ranger's temple. Geo cranked the spring, notched a second arrow, and fired. He hit the young Ranger in the neck. Willis and Bud emerged from the other side of the coffee shop and dragged the Rangers toward the restaurant.

Spotting two Rangers approach from the other side, Geo prepared his crossbow and readied his revolver as a last resort. When the pair crossed the road, he shot an arrow. The first Ranger dropped. The second one got off two rounds before Geo hit him with another arrow.

Geo grabbed Willis' arm. "Leave the men. Let's go."

All three sprinted down the road. Rangers appeared on both sides of the perimeter road and began shooting. Geo and his companions ducked behind an aluminum warehouse. Two Rangers sprinted after them while others climbed into the armadillo. Geo released the remote, setting off an explosion, followed by the ghastly groan of metal against metal.

When the two Rangers chasing them turned to look, Geo fired two arrows, hitting one Ranger in the back of the head. His partner turned and fired. The second explosion burst the armadillo into flames. Geo fired his revolver several times, finally hitting the second Ranger. Other Rangers began shooting.

Geo returned to the cover of the warehouse; Willis and Bud were gone. A dozen Rangers spilled down the road without their vehicle. *That should slow them down.* Geo sprinted down the alley behind the warehouse and turned.

Winded, Willis joined him. "That was close. Rangers are coming down the other side. We've got their attention."

Geo followed Willis down the next street and turned to keep Rangers from getting a clean shot. He glanced at his bumblebee cam and saw Rangers leaving the Towers. *Yeah, they're heading our way. Bright move, Geo. What's your backup plan? Pa, I need advice.*

They crossed a boulevard. To their right, a caravan of armadillos headed their way. Geo dropped a grenade and ran while palming the remote. He didn't trust it between his teeth.

Willis darted into an alley. Geo stopped at the corner and activated the grenade. The first armadillo spun into the curve; Geo released the control. The explosion blasted the vehicle, which flew over the grenade and stopped. The second armadillo got the brunt of the second explosion and burst into flames. Rangers poured out of both, blocking the street.

Geo sprinted to catch up with Willis at the next turn. The sun had set. There was no one on the streets, though citizen eyes would be on alert.

Willis and Geo ran to the next street. Geo turned on his wrist-com and struggled to hit keys. The reply from Tommy stopped him in his tracks. *She escaped Towers. Signed off.*

Geo showed it to Willis.

The big man stopped. "Can you trust this?"

Geo nodded. "Let's not lead the Rangers to her. How can we lose them?"

"We should have left town," Willis said.

"Too late. After all this it'll be harder to get back tomorrow."

"Are you nuts?"

"I have to deal with Edwards," Geo said. Though he prayed he could come up with a better option.

"He has spies and cams everywhere. It will be practically impossible to get close to him. We'll be lucky to survive the night. Let's double back." They circled around and headed along a path parallel to the Rangers chasing them.

Geo dropped a grenade by the corner of a furniture warehouse, rounded the corner, and ran to catch up with Willis. They moved to the next street and stopped. Two armadillos crossed in pursuit. Geo counted off seconds for the vehicles to make it to the next street and detonated the grenade.

With the second explosion, Rangers in the street moved out. Geo followed Willis across the street and down another alley.

229

Street by street they worked their way to the Old Goat. By the time they got within two blocks, the streets were crawling with Rangers and cops.

"Must have linked Buzz to the bar," Willis said. "I'm out of safe houses."

He led them away from the bar, down an alley behind several stores. When they turned the corner, they bumped into local cops, two burly men busting the buttons of their uniforms. *One look in my pockets and we're done,* Geo thought. He reached for his revolver. The cops drew first.

"There a problem, officer?" Mickey stepped out of the shadows behind the cops.

Before the cops could turn to face Mickey, the Brache twins hit them over the head with bricks. They dragged the cops to the wall, behind Dumpsters.

Geo took the cops' guns and handed one to Willis. "I told you guys to leave town."

"Couldn't," Mickey said. "Border's tighter than—well, tight."

"Thanks for the assist." Geo bumped fists with all three.

Bud appeared at the end of the alley and waved them to approach.

Mickey followed Geo. "Where's Annabelle? Is she okay?"

"Not sure. I think she escaped from the Towers, but she turned off her wrist-com. We haven't heard from her since." *Where could a mech warrior hunted by Rangers hide?*

FORTY-THREE

The five of them crouched behind a Dumpster as gray armadillos raced by. Bud lingered across the street in the shadows, scouting escape routes.

"Every safe house is being watched," Willis said. "With the threat plastered over the Biltmoor Network, I wouldn't count on friendly neighbors. We should keep moving."

"And go where?" Geo asked.

Rangers patrolled both sides of the well-lit boulevard heading southeast. This was the working-class part of town. People wouldn't welcome rebels, or terrorists, or whatever Edwards had branded them. More important, where would Annabelle go? She and Janine were trained warriors, skilled at survival.

Then it hit him. She had somehow escaped from Undercover, even though she obviously didn't belong there. "Undercover" had two meanings.

Geo sent his bumblebee cam over the boulevard, which swarmed with Rangers and armadillos from downtown to the edge of town. A block away stood the distinct red and purple sign for Undercover. It was unlit. "Let's go."

He stopped across the street from Undercover, with its entrance on the corner. Two Rangers lingered in the intersection as another armadillo sped downtown.

Willis joined him. "I've contacted Bud. What's the target?"

The Brache twins plopped beside him. Geo pointed at Undercover. "How do we get past those Rangers?"

"You can't be serious," Willis said.

"I believe Annabelle can hide there."

Shaking his head, Willis picked up his com. "We get one shot at this."

It would be easier to approach the back door, but on a night like this, they would never open up for a fugitive stranger. "Wait around back," Geo told Willis. "If I'm not out in ten minutes, get out of there."

"If we get separated, let's meet three blocks east of the tavern," Willis said. "Keep the faith. Find Annabelle."

Across the intersection, Bud staggered out of the shadows in his cop uniform, holding up a bottle. "Nuptials for the newlyweds." He offered a drink to the Rangers.

"Move on, old man." A bulked-up Ranger walked toward him. "That's not until tomorrow. Shouldn't you be on duty?"

Holding a machine pistol, the Ranger's partner followed.

Geo gripped his revolver and waved the others to cross the street with him. He reached the brick siding of Undercover, tiptoed to the corner, and slipped through the swinging glass doors into darkness.

Geo knocked on the window, and kept to the side to stay out of full view of the intersection. One Ranger pushed Bud toward the curb, took his picture and sent him away.

A voice echoed in the enclosed dark foyer: the madam who had spoken to him before. "We're closed. Bishop's orders."

"I need refuge," Geo said, "or they'll kill me."

"Why should I stick my neck out?"

"Remember me from a few days ago? My pa paid a gold coin for me."

"We get lots of clients," the woman said.

"I was with a blonde who didn't work for you." Geo watched Rangers return to the intersection as another armadillo flew by.

"Then why would she be here?"

"I believe you helped her. She's in grave danger."

"If she is, how could you help?" the woman asked.

"I beg you. I have four friends who need shelter for the night."

"So I'm running a boarding house."

"Please." Geo strained to see her. "Rangers are everywhere."

"It's okay, Chrissie," Annabelle's voice said from behind him. "I'll vouch for him."

"Be quick and stay out of sight," Chrissie said.

Annabelle pulled Geo into the large maroon room that had paralyzed him days earlier. A single white light gave it a stark appearance, but he could still imagine the line of scantily clad girls beckoning him to choose.

"You okay?" He took her hands and looked her over. He didn't see anything obviously broken.

"Is that the best you can do?" She pulled him to her and hugged him so tight he couldn't breathe. "I thought we'd never escape. Then explosions drew Rangers away." She pulled away. "Was that you?"

"Sort of."

She led him by the hand through the lounge, as she had when they first met. "It was chaotic. Rangers abandoned one of their armored vehicles. I got the girls in and drove northeast. Then explosions drew Rangers that way. We ditched the vehicle and came here."

"How many girls?"

"Janine and four others," Annabelle said. "How did you find me?"

"I remembered how you came in and left, without anyone seeming to notice."

Annabelle laughed. "Chrissie helps these girls rather than return home. Bless her." She led him to the rear of the building.

"I found Willis. I think he's your dad."

She glared at him. "Don't tease."

"He's out back."

"I don't think I'm ready for this."

"Let me bring him in," Geo said. "He's with Mickey and the twins."

Annabelle nodded. "Be quick, lock up, and bring them downstairs." She disappeared down a narrow hallway.

* * *

Geo looked out a small window by the back door and saw Mickey with Willis. Geo opened the door and poked his head out. He waved them in, locked up, and waited a moment to be sure no one else was coming.

"Is she here?" Willis asked.

Geo nodded and led them down the hall to an open door and concrete steps leading down. At the bottom of the stairway, he saw four frightened girls huddled in the corner. Was one Janine? Annabelle descended the steps behind him with two other girls holding assault rifles. One was Julianne, without her mech gear.

Annabelle took Geo's arm. "It's okay," she told the girls holding guns. "This is Geo. Those three are Mickey, and Dirk and Harold; I can't tell which is which. I assume you're Willis."

He nodded.

"Geo, this is your sister, Janine." Annabelle held the hand of a slender brunette who somehow looked both fragile and tough.

Geo bowed and offered to shake the brunette's hand. She pulled away and studied him.

"This is Julianne," Annabelle said. "She helped me free Janine and the others."

Julianne shook Geo's hand. "Good to meet you without your gun pointed at me." She smiled mysteriously.

Annabelle turned to Willis, her revolver aimed at his feet. "We can talk in a moment, but you have to understand, the girls we rescued were traumatized. It would be best if you guys stayed on the other side of the basement."

Nodding, Geo motioned for Mickey and the others to settle in behind the stairs.

"We mean you no harm," Willis said. He followed the boys.

Janine nervously brushed back her brown hair and approached Geo. "So, you're my brother?"

Geo studied the girl/woman, hoping she would put her gun away. "So Annabelle tells me."

"Mom didn't tell me, either." Janine clicked the safety and slung the rifle over her shoulder. "It feels weird to learn I have a brother." She sized him up. "And that Annabelle was adopted." She turned to her sister. "I always suspected there was something you were keeping from me."

"I still love you, sweetie." Annabelle stroked Janine's hair and glanced toward Willis.

"I wish I'd been there to help rescue you." Geo wanted to hug his sister, but felt an awkward space between them. She did have Pa's dark eyes.

"That's sweet, Geo," Annabelle said. "But it wouldn't have helped. We needed your diversion. Now we need to get Janine and the others home."

"Not a chance." Janine faced her sister. "I'm a mech warrior, and I wouldn't miss standing by my brother for—well, for anything."

Annabelle shook her head and went to Willis. "You knew my mom?"

"Dorothy," Willis said. "Could this be my baby girl all grown up? I'm so sorry that you were left all alone when they arrested your mom."

"Even in mech service I couldn't track her down."

"Careful. If they catch you prying, they have plenty of ways to punish you."

"Like making me marry Edwards," Annabelle said.

Willis nodded. "Your mom loved you very much. I never wanted her to risk herself for me, but she was like that."

"Strong-willed?" Annabelle laughed. "I love Mom, the woman who raised me. She treated me like her own, but I always wondered what happened to my birth parents. They told me you died while escaping."

"Mr. Shaw rescued me. He used explosions to erase any evidence that I had survived. I can't believe you're really here."

While Annabelle and Willis shared stories and Julianne sat with the four girls they had rescued, Geo led Janine to another corner. He wanted to know so much about his sister, yet he wasn't sure how to begin. "It's not right they forced us apart."

"I know," Janine said, her eyes wide. "My mind's spinning. How do we get to know each other? Guys aren't welcome in the Union, and girls are treated horribly here."

"Not by everyone," Geo said.

Janine laughed and patted his arm as Annabelle did. "I wish more people were like you. I kind of wonder about guys. Don't tell Annabelle." Janine gave him a quick hug and pulled away, her face lined with pain.

"I'm sorry," Geo said.

"I'm a little crazy right now, but Mom says there's always another side to every problem."

"Like what?"

"We get to meet." She touched his hand, then withdrew.

Geo sensed her fear. *Well, no wonder. All her life they probably taught her to hate men. Now, she just escaped from a prison cell, where the jailers probably*—he stopped himself before the image could fully form. It was just too intense.

Geo looked away.

Janine placed her hand on his arm. "You didn't do this to me. While I was locked up, I wanted to nuke Appalachia. Now that I've met you, my *brother*," she blinked, as if she still couldn't quite believe it, "well, I just want to kill Edwards for trying to get his claws on Annabelle."

"Now you are talking crazy," Geo said. "I don't want you or Annabelle anywhere near this town come morning."

Annabelle approached them. "I can't go back home," she said, taking Geo's other hand. "My people betrayed me. And I can't stay here with Edwards in charge."

"So what are you saying?" Geo asked. "We can't take on the entire Ranger command. The cartel won't help us. The mountaineers won't, either. Besides, no one gets close to Edwards. Maybe if you and Janine had mech gear."

Julianne joined them. "With me, you have a full unit."

"We'll find the suits Edwards got from Civ," Annabelle said.

"Even so," Geo said, "there are too many Rangers. And if we win, no offense, but Appalachia would be defenseless against Civ mechs, unless that's your plan."

"Why would I want the people who betrayed me to take over?" Annabelle asked. "What if we don't take on the entire Ranger force?"

"How?"

"I don't know."

"You want me to challenge Edwards to a Patriot's Duel?" Geo asked, which is what he had been trying to find an alternative to.

"No, I guess not," Annabelle said. "The problem with that is you fight like an Outlander. Maybe if you learned to fight like a mech. Janine, Julianne. Let's give Geo a demo."

They moved everything from the center of the basement to make room. Annabelle and Janine sparred in what looked more like choreographed graceful dance than fighting, though Geo recognized the martial arts maneuvers. Janine struggled to keep up her end after her days in prison. Julianne took her place and the fighting grew more intense.

Geo watched with growing pride at how well Annabelle handled herself. She bent, arched, and twisted her body in amazing ways. Her looping jumps allowed her to kick, retreat, and prepare another attack.

When Julianne landed a blow to Annabelle's stomach, Geo rushed in. Big mistake. Julianne hammered him in the chest and shoulder, sending him reeling.

Annabelle shoved him from behind. "Okay, tough guy, show us how you protect the ladies."

He didn't want to hit girls…women. He dropped back when both women advanced.

"Defend yourself or fall," Annabelle said. "Pretend we're Edwards."

"Are you sure?" Janine asked from the sidelines. "He hasn't had the training."

"We'll give him a crash course."

Annabelle and Julianne charged like mad Rangers. Geo used the concrete wall to launch himself, catching Annabelle off guard. He grabbed her shoulders, twisted to cushion her fall, and landed with a thud next to Janine, who scooted away.

Willis got up to join Geo. "Hold on. The lad deserves a fair fight."

"He won't get one tomorrow," Annabelle said. "And I have no intention of marrying Edwards." Janine helped her up but didn't rejoin the fight.

Geo got to his feet and braced for another attack. "You need to take these girls and go home. This won't be the same as fighting with mech gear."

"You still don't think I can handle myself." Annabelle feigned an attack.

He deflected. "Don't be difficult. These girls need you, or they'll end up back where you found them."

"I'm going in with you." Annabelle rotated and landed a kick.

Geo caught her foot and spun her off balance. "If they play fair, it'll be hand-to-hand combat to the death. If they don't, none of it matters."

She sprung to her feet and looked to Julianne, who hesitated. "Then it's settled. I'm coming to ensure a fair fight. Show me how you'll fight." She punched him in the shoulder.

Geo blocked the next two blows and tried one of Annabelle's spin-kick maneuvers. She anticipated and blocked him.

"That's the idea." Annabelle rotated into a different move and caught him off guard.

"But you blocked it." Geo used moves he saw her and Janine

do, but Annabelle dodged each attempt.

"I've been doing this longer," Annabelle said. "Feel the energy flow through your body and mine as if we were one creature in a choreographed dance."

"I don't want to hurt you." Geo dodged a blow and launched one of his own.

She avoided the hit. "Worry about Edwards or Hanrahan hurting you."

"You think you can take them?" Geo faked a kick. When Annabelle went to block, he caught her off balance and tackled her to the concrete floor. "Sorry."

Annabelle rolled with him, got on top and went to pin him. "I don't know. He had mech training. He's a former wrestler, and much bigger. One good blow and you're out of action."

Geo grunted, pushed, and tickled her. He rolled on top and pinned her arms over her head.

"Not bad." Annabelle gazed up and grinned. "Do the unexpected."

He helped her up and saw all eyes riveted on him. The concrete room was so silent he heard his heart thumping. She kissed his lips and patted his shoulder.

Scowling, Janine approached. "You can't pull that stunt with Edwards. When I tried to escape, he kicked my ass. He has moves I'd never seen before."

"My pa died helping people," Geo said. "We have to avenge his death."

Janine patted his shoulder. "He wouldn't want you dying, and I'm just getting used to the idea of having a brother. I don't want to lose you."

Geo smiled. "Then we need more training."

* * *

After an hour of sparring and getting whipped by one or other mech warrior, Geo had had enough. Chrissie brought snacks of chips, salsa and cheese, along with water. "No alcohol on Sundays or Wednesday nights," she said.

Annabelle took Janine and Julianne aside. All three looked weary, though Janine had lost that frightened edge she had when Geo first saw her.

"If you're up to it, I want to hit the Towers and find Edwards' mech suits," Annabelle said. "Tommy thinks he's found them."

"I'm in," Janine said.

"Edwards called for another shipment of girls for the reception," Chrissie said.

Annabelle frowned. "I don't think we can work that twice."

"Unless we drive," Chrissie said.

"Too dangerous." Geo took Annabelle's hand and held her. "Promise you'll wait here."

"I'm not Penelope. I won't sit here waiting for word of what happens to you. I like Chrissie's idea. It gets us close. It shouldn't be hard getting into the Towers. Everyone will be focusing on the Cathedral. After we get the gear, we'll meet up with you."

"I don't want you downtown tomorrow."

Annabelle stroked his cheek. "Geo, focus on your part and let us do ours. How will you get close enough to challenge him?"

He hesitated. He wanted Annabelle at his side, the fighter, the determined woman, yet he didn't want her getting caught or hurt.

Willis joined them. "Hanrahan won't let anyone get close to Edwards. I'll guarantee they'll check for weapons, so we can't carry. Without weapons, we won't have any way to prevent Hanrahan from arresting us before we can act."

"So you're ready to give up," Geo said. "Is that it?" Closing his eyes, he took a deep breath. *If Pa were here...* "Willis, I have to do this. There has to be a way."

Willis grinned. "You ever play the Chinese game Go?"

Geo nodded, remembering the deceptively simple game that concealed layers of probability. "No matter how well I played, Pa surprised me."

"The fortunes of the game change in an instant. Find that moment."

Geo nodded. "If I get close enough, I will challenge Edwards."

"Are you certain?"

"Positive." Though Geo still wanted some other option so he could talk himself out of this.

"Okay," Willis said. "We might have a few things going for us. For starters, there will be throngs of people downtown. With a little disguise, it shouldn't be hard to get into the Cathedral."

"What if we can't find the mech gear?" Janine said. "How do we keep Rangers from arresting or killing Geo? Will anyone in town help us?"

"Not a chance," Willis said. "Edwards has them all in a panic."

"The Cathedral is a holy place, right?" Geo said, a plan forming even as he spoke. "Nobody will expect it. I'll hit him during the ceremony."

"Assuming he finds someone to marry," Annabelle said.

"Geo might be on to something," Willis said. He examined Geo's ring, the one from Pa, and looked pensive for a moment. "Edwards has an enormous ego. He has delusions of taking over Hardcastle's role as President over all of Appalachia. This deal of his with Battani is part of him gaining legitimacy as well as power."

"Meaning he'll be on his best behavior," Annabelle said.

"He'll go out of his way to show civility to prove he's worthy of being our president," Willis said, "instead of a thug. He'll have Civ dignitaries here as well as the thanes of the other two regions."

"So we might be able to use that against him," Geo said. "The Cathedral and the ceremony are the perfect time and place to challenge him."

Willis nodded. "But then you have to actually fight the bastard."

Geo felt ill.

Annabelle took him aside. "I'm exhausted. We should get some rest."

Chrissie came and showed them where to find blankets. "If you girls need anything, I'll be upstairs." She left.

"Someone should stand watch," Janine said.

"You've had a tough time of it," Julianne said. "I'll do it."

Geo pulled a thin mattress into a corner away from the guys and the Civ girls who huddled, watching them. Annabelle brought a blanket and lay next to him. "It's not as cozy as your poncho, but it'll do."

Janine squeezed onto the mattress next to her. *Doggone it. I wanted Annabelle all to myself tonight.* Seeing how cozy they looked, Geo faced the wall and thought about last night. Annabelle tucked herself next to him and draped her arm over his shoulders.

He couldn't sleep. Every time he started dozing, Edwards appeared, gloating over killing Pa. There was no higher authority in Appalachia than the thane, and no way to get justice except to challenge him, which would be suicide.

* * *

Geo dreamed he was getting his butt whooped by Annabelle for the umpteenth time. He woke to her shaking him. When he opened his eyes, she handed him his pack. He looked up. Chrissie and two girls he recognized from the lineup last week—a sweet little blonde and a lean redhead—stood there looking frightened.

Annabelle and Janine moved to the stairs, rifles aimed upward. Sitting with the four Civ girls was Vivian Kurdis. Geo recalled seeing her dead father and brother and ransacked home after Rangers killed Pa. He wanted to comfort her.

"We're being raided," Chrissie whispered. "Not by the Bishop's men." She went to the rear of the basement by Vivian and the four girls, and easily pushed aside a water heater. Beneath it was a hole in the floor.

Geo grabbed his pack. He checked his revolver and found it empty. He reloaded. Annabelle handed the redhead a gun and positioned her beneath the stairs.

"Everyone over here," Chrissie whispered. She guided the petite blonde toward a hole in the floor. "It's clear on the other side. Keep moving."

The blonde took a flashlight from Chrissie and climbed into the pit. Annabelle sent the redhead next.

Geo joined Vivian. She didn't look quite so innocent anymore. "I'm sorry."

"I don't want to talk about it." She helped the Civ girls down the hole one by one. "My pa trusted yours, and I'm glad you're here. Let's leave it at that." She dropped into the hole and followed the girls.

Janine and Chrissie went next, followed by Mickey and the twins.

Willis stared into the pit. "It doesn't look big enough. You first."

"I'm not leaving you," Geo said.

Willis sighed and lowered himself into the hole. He worked his way into the tunnel.

Julianne looked from Geo to Annabelle. "You guys go. I'll hold them off."

"No dice," Annabelle said. "Go. That's an order."

After Julianne disappeared, Geo turned to Annabelle.

"You don't know how to close it," she said. "Get moving."

"But—" Geo said.

Annabelle kissed him. "Go," she said, nudging him.

From above came gruff voices and sounds of a girl crying. Geo scrambled into the pit and crawled through. When he reached a dead end, he rotated and climbed out. The others were crowded into a concrete cell the size of his bedroom. The four girls sat bunched in the far corner with Vivian. Mickey and the guys sat in the corner near the tunnel. There wasn't room to lie down.

"We'll have to make do until morning," Chrissie said. "I don't understand why they would raid when we're closed."

Geo listened for sounds of Annabelle crawling through. Not hearing anything, he climbed down and shone his flashlight. Annabelle lay motionless about halfway back. She put her finger to her lips.

She resumed crawling. He climbed out to give her room and helped her up. Then Chrissie turned on a faucet that flooded the tunnel.

Geo held Annabelle, and felt her shaking. "What happened?"

"I thought they heard because when I moved the water heater, they charged into the basement. They were right on top of me."

He pulled Annabelle into a free corner, rested her head on his shoulder, and thought of the brief time they'd had. He wanted more.

"Go figure," the redhead said from the opposite corner. "Four days left on my sentence and now this."

"I'm sorry, Haley," Annabelle said.

"Don't be sorry. I'm sick of these bastards. Whatever you're planning, I'm in."

"Geo, Haley is a sister warrior. They brought her here for helping someone escape. Haley, this is my mom's son, Geo."

"How can I help?"

"It would be a huge relief if you'd look after the girls we rescued. With Janine and Julianne, I have a unit."

Nodding, Haley sat with Janine and Julianne. Geo sensed that the mech warriors had camaraderie like that among mountain folk.

FORTY-FOUR

At first light, Annabelle adjusted her brown wig and the uncomfortable nose and forehead patches intended to fool Biltmoor surveillance cams. Exhausted from the night's ordeal and the raid, she followed the others out of the cramped concrete cellar. She sensed Geo wanted to talk, but her mind was already in warrior mode, checking the few weapons she could carry.

Geo hugged her and slipped her a grenade disk with remote. "Stay safe," he whispered. He kissed her on the lips.

She slipped the disk next to a 9mm under her skirt, a gift from Chrissie, and then pushed it up until it settled into the small of her back. She climbed into the van, smiled at Janine in back with several of Chrissie's girls, and sat next to Julianne. "We'll have to hurry to find the gear and get to the plaza. You ready?"

Julianne nodded, adjusted her wig under her bonnet, and leaned her head against Annabelle for the trip downtown.

Outside, well-dressed Biltmoor residents trekked downtown by foot or on gas-cycles, clogging the streets. Annabelle rubbed her shoulder where Julianne had talked her into removing the tracking implant. "Yesterday was too close," Julianne had said. "They must be tracking us."

Adjusting the grenade, which dug into her hip, Annabelle watched the van glide past stores she had dodged in and out of only days before. Her wrist-com had Tommy's instructions. Edwards was storing the mech gear from Civ in the basement of Tower Two, above the holding cells. *Returning to the Towers is insane.*

243

Yet, she felt strong with Janine and Julianne by her side. She was determined to help Geo stop Edwards' reign of terror.

They reached the plaza, crowded with men in their Sunday best and a few women in brightly colored country dresses. The crowds forced Chrissie to park and let the girls walk the rest of the way. Bands of Rangers patrolled the plaza's perimeter, around the Towers and across the plaza near the gaudy Cathedral.

Annabelle took a deep breath. "Ready?"

Janine and Julianne opened their mouths to respond. Annabelle motioned to cut them off and pressed her finger to her lips.

Everyone climbed out of the van. The crowd swept Annabelle and the others toward the Cathedral. Surrounded by her mech team and Chrissie's girls, Annabelle pushed toward the edge of the mob, and headed for Tower Two. Rangers stood on rooftops around the square. *All these people are coming to see me get married. Let's see what happens when I don't show up.*

At the covered walkway around the Towers, the crowd thinned, and so did the Rangers. Two guards stood in the lobby.

Annabelle hurried through the revolving door. She located the bathroom around the corner, and the stairwell behind the bank of elevators. She held the push-bar for Janine and Julianne, and nodded that Chrissie's girls could leave.

A lean guard approached. "You can't be here."

Annabelle gripped a revolver in the folds of her skirt. "Silly us, we didn't use the bathroom before. With so many people...can we please use yours?" She curtseyed and leaned forward.

The guard sighed. "Very well. Be quick."

Annabelle nodded. While the guard returned to the lobby desk, she slid into the stairwell with Julianne. Janine hurried to the bathroom door, banged it, and joined Annabelle in the stairwell.

That went way too easily. The three of them descended the stairs to the utility floor and proceeded to the laundry room. It was vacant. Annabelle picked out three maids' outfits, more comfortable than the flowery skirts and blouses Chrissie had provided. Annabelle struggled to change into the stiff white uniform without revealing the grenade, revolver, or her 9mm to any hidden cams Tommy hadn't blinded. She pocketed a steel mirror someone had left on the counter, and tucked the vial of sodium powder Geo gave her into a pocket in the maid's uniform.

Annabelle checked her wrist-com for messages from Tommy.

All clear. She led her team down the concrete corridor until they reached a crosswalk. She turned left, and then right, toward the far northeast corner of the building. Plans showed a back exit by the stream; they could use it once they got the mech gear.

When they reached the storage room. Annabelle used a touch code Tommy provided and entered. Bright lights came on, blinding her for an instant. She gasped. Two warriors stood there—Dara and Margarite—in mech uniforms without helmets.

"You're alive!"

"Shut up," Dara said. "You *are* a dumb blonde, aren't you?"

Julianne grabbed Annabelle's revolver, disarmed Janine, and moved toward the others.

"Julianne?" Annabelle's heart sank. "I thought we were friends."

"I had to make sure you showed up for the ceremony."

Janine looked as frightened and angry as she had in her prison cell. At least she wasn't in on this. *And I still have my grenade and 9mm. Didn't find those, did you, traitors?*

Dara and Margarite trained their weapons on Annabelle and Janine. Julianne grabbed an old-model mech suit from the wall. "Sorry, Annabelle. This is for my family."

"No explanations," Dara said. "We're late."

"For what?" Annabelle asked.

"Move away from the door. We're throwing you and Edwards a wedding party you'll never forget."

Annabelle pushed her sister behind her and tried to move the grenade from the small of her back so she could somehow slide it out. "Why didn't you turn me in yesterday?"

Julianne stepped into the mechanical legs. "Battani wanted to know who was helping you. When Edwards asked too much ransom for the prisoners, the Governor okayed freeing them first."

"Does Sam know?" Annabelle shifted the grenade over one butt cheek and realized she could touch it through one of the folds in her outfit, just not without letting Dara and her gang see.

"She'll play her role when it's time," Dara said.

Julianne fastened the chest and back plates. "It's rather touching how you got the boy to believe you loved him so he'll fight Edwards, but we're not done with the thane yet."

FORTY-FIVE

The suit and tie Chrissie provided Geo fit snugly. Willis, Mickey and the twins looked like penguins. Geo thanked Madam Chrissie for the facial disguise; he couldn't be sure Tommy had confused all of the Biltmoor cams. The five guys rode downtown in a horse-drawn cart, surrounded by well-dressed men. Thanks to Chrissie, the cart was full of bottled water and apples for the guests coming downtown.

Geo felt naked without his rifle and backpack, despite starched shirt, stiff pants, and bowler hat.

There were no friendly faces in the river of men and the few escorted women filling the boulevard leading downtown. To clear a path amidst the throng of well-wishers in the plaza, Willis offered refreshments to men trying to push past.

Geo received texts that Tommy pulled from Biltmoor confidential files. They summarized the Governor's deal. Edwards would get Annabelle and other Civ girls, weapons to take out the Medallion Cartel, and logistical support to overrun all of Appalachia, so he could replace President Hardcastle. Civ would get the border moved two miles, elimination of the Cartel, and disarming of Appalachian citizens by Edwards to make raids into Civ more difficult.

Geo told Willis about the deal.

"Folk won't like this." Willis parked the wagon and kept handing out water and apples.

Two men in Sunday attire approached. Willis handed each a

bottle of water and asked, "Are you okay with Edwards taking your guns?"

"Bastard wouldn't touch them," the taller one said.

Rangers approached, so Geo took Mickey and the twins around the cart and blended into the stream of well-dressed men crossing the plaza toward the Cathedral.

* * *

I can't get the grenade without them shooting me. Annabelle recalled Sam: *When stripped of weapons, improvise.*

"Will you let me take a pill? My stomach's killing me."

Without waiting for a reply, Annabelle reached into a pocket of her utility uniform and withdrew the vial of sodium powder. She snapped off the lid with her thumb and moved the vial toward her lips. She swung her arm out in an arc, throwing powder into the faces of her three captors. She pushed Janine toward the door and ripped a slit in her uniform to grab the grenade. "Go find Geo."

"Run and we shoot Annabelle," Dara said.

"Grenades!" Annabelle yelled. Activating the remote with her thumb, she rotated and threw the grenade over Julianne's head. She prayed the warriors would glance at their feet, a natural reaction to the devastating grenade threat.

Annabelle lunged through the doorway after Janine, who was already sprinting down the hallway. Annabelle triggered the grenade explosion and reached up under her outfit to retrieve her 9mm from her thigh holster. The explosion was deafening. Crouching down, she fired two shots, missed. Part of Julianne's pretty face was gone. Her body dropped like a ragdoll. The grenade's shell smacked against the concrete ceiling. Margarite raised her gun. The second blast shattered the back of her head, splattering bloodied brains over Dara's face. Margarite's body thudded to the concrete floor. Dara the amazon cowered.

Annabelle fired two more shots and sprinted down the hallway, praying her sister could get away. There was no way Annabelle could outrun a mech or outfight one without another grenade.

Machine pellets pulverized concrete nearby. Annabelle dove down the main corridor, thankful that Janine was nowhere in sight. She darted into the laundry room and locked the door. She turned on the hot water spigot and let hot water run into a wheeled washbasin. Then she grabbed the hot water hose to one of the washing units while Dara blasted her way into the room.

Dara stood in the doorway. Annabelle sprayed her with hot water.

"Is that the best you can do?" Dara asked. "Who brings a hose to a mech fight? I can't believe I used to like you."

"Go to hell." Annabelle shoved the wheeled washbasin, half-full of hot water, toward Dara.

Dara laughed. "You're pathetic, Annabelle. Shit. What the—"

The mech helmet reverberated with explosions like a popcorn machine. The odor of burning flesh filled the air. Dara did an awkward dance, exaggerated by mech suit hydraulics. The combination of heat, Dara's sweat, Margarite's body fluids and the sodium powder were doing their trick, scorching the amazon's face.

Annabelle hit Dara with the basin, knocking the mech off her feet. Dara clanged to the concrete floor. Annabelle upended the washbasin of steamy water over Dara's helmet, adding hot water to the chemical reaction.

Hands shaking, Dara tugged at her helmet. "What is this shit?"

"Nothing. I'm just a dumb blonde who paid attention in chemistry."

"Help! I can't see!" Crying, Dara removed her mech gloves and released the helmet. It tumbled away, lined with a sticky mixture of sodium scum and flesh.

Aghast at the blistered remains of the amazon warrior, Annabelle ran for the door. Looking back, she saw the amazon raise her gun. Annabelle dove into the corridor and heard the spray of machine pellets against metal. Using the metal mirror, Annabelle held the 9mm and looked inside the laundry room. Blood covered the industrial dryers. Dara's head looked like she had turned her guns on herself.

Stunned, Annabelle staggered to her feet. She texted Tommy the news and went in to check on Dara. She couldn't believe the amazon was gone.

Annabelle picked up Dara's helmet and toweled it clean. *Got to tell Sam.* She eased the heavy helmet over her head and shoulders. Thankfully, the electronics still seemed to work.

"Dara? You okay?" The modulated voice sent chills up Annabelle's spine.

Pretending to be angry, she lowered her voice and hoped her modulator did the rest. "Just a hiccup. We're ready." She held the helmet with both hands and headed for the storage room and the mech suits.

"Good. I need you and Margarite up here to contain the disturbance until we get mech reinforcements." Annabelle didn't recognize the voice. "Send Julianne around back to close off any retreat. Spare Edwards. Shoot the rest, Union visitors as well."

Annabelle listened in disbelief. This amateur field chatter couldn't be from a trained mech. Maybe it was Governor Battani.

"Your idea to marry the girl to Edwards worked to get everyone together," the modulated voice said. "Tell me when you're in place. If the bride causes problems, she's expendable."

I'm expendable, you bitch? Marry me off to Edwards so you can kill me?

Bearing the helmet's weight with her hands, Annabelle wondered what Battani had promised to persuade her sister mechs to betray her.

FORTY-SIX

Wills pushed in front of Geo, and worked his way toward the edge of the crowd. A line of Rangers kept guests away from upscale stores that lined the plaza and were closed for the day. Geo moved with the crowd until they merged with guests coming down the boulevard from the other end of town. He had never seen so many people, a crush of humanity. *Must be ten thousand or more.*

Up ahead, Rangers formed a perimeter in front of the Cathedral, checking for weapons with metal detectors, X-rays, and sniffing dogs. "We'll return your weapons afterward," a Ranger yelled through a bullhorn.

Geo didn't want to face the checkpoint in case they checked his identity. He pulled Mickey and the twins to the side of the Cathedral, where the crystalline façade shifted to stone. "Do any of you have anything they might find?"

A Ranger eyed them with suspicion. Willis grabbed Geo's arm. "You can't linger or they'll haul you in." He led them beyond the perimeter of Rangers along the massive stone wall on the side of the Cathedral.

"How do we get in?" Geo asked.

"Follow me."

Geo received a text from Tommy. *Mission compromised. Julianne gone. Janine fleeing. Annabelle alone.* His fists tightened until his knuckles turned white. This was what he had feared. He took a deep breath and called her wrist-com. It broke protocol, but he needed to hear her voice. It went to voicemail. "I have to find Annabelle," he told Willis.

Willis held him. "You'll get arrested."

"She's alone. So is Janine."

"You want to abort?"

* * *

Annabelle removed the helmet, replaced the biochip with her own, and settled the helmet back on her head and shoulders. While balancing the weight of the helmet with her hands, she kept moving and called Sam. She wasn't sure what to expect or who to trust. After all, Sam wouldn't let her rescue her own sister.

"The prodigal sister returns," Sam's voice crackled in the helmet.

"You abandoned my sister," Annabelle said, entering the mech room to the horror she had witnessed moments before. "I don't have much time." She explained about the three warriors and the conversation with who she presumed to be the governor.

"Quite a tale," Sam said. "Since the Governor put us on alert that you were stirring up trouble along with some rebel force."

"Sam, for once, can you trust me? I've never betrayed you or the corps." Except for Mr. Shaw's files. "It's not like it looks. The governor arranged for Cory to escape so he could spy on Edwards. Cory played both sides."

"Is that so?"

"The governor created a crisis so you'd ride in and help her take over. Don't do it. You have nothing to gain and much to lose."

"Lose how?"

"If there is a rebel army, they have factories pumping out mech grenades. I don't want more sisters to die."

"Well, well," a grisly voice said. "Right on schedule."

Annabelle turned to confront the gruff, scar-faced General Hanrahan. Someone tugged her wrists and cuffed them behind her. The helmet's full weight dropped onto her head and shoulders. *I should have put on a suit before calling Sam. Too late.*

"Annabelle?" Sam said.

"Hanrahan's here. Can you help?" Annabelle's head throbbed from the weight. "What do you want?" she asked Hanrahan.

"Sorry about your friends," Hanrahan said. "Or should I say thanks, since that's three less spies to deal with."

Rangers chained her ankles. Someone lifted off the helmet. Her wrist-com vibrated within the folds of her uniform. *Geo, did you get the message?*

Rangers linked ankle irons to a waist chain and her wrist cuffs. Hanrahan shoved her toward the corridor. "It's time to meet your groom. He has a deal for you."

"I'm not marrying him. All he wants is a piece of furniture."

Hanrahan attached a leash to her waist and pulled her like a dog. "You're more valuable than an old desk, but suit yourself. You want to hear the deal?"

"No." She stumbled. Hands lifted her. "Put me down."

"Then walk," Hanrahan said.

"Okay." *Think, Annabelle.* What would Sam say? "How did you find me?"

Hanrahan tugged the leash. "We got the code for your implant."

"But Julianne—" *No, she must have planted them. That meant they could track Janine. Did they have her?*

"Here's the deal," Hanrahan said, "You do the wedding and honeymoon nice and peaceful, and act like a dutiful wife."

Nausea welled up in her throat. Annabelle pulled on the chains.

Hanrahan yanked her forward. "That means bearing our leader many sons. In exchange, our benevolent thane will permit Mommy Scott to live, and we'll bring your birth mom, too."

"You have her?"

"We have both. If you cooperate, we'll even let Geo and Janine go."

Maybe they're prisoners, too. Or maybe not. "Why am I so important to you?"

"Not me, sweetie. Thane Edwards. Call it a peace offering. It's good diplomacy, and he'll get some heirs in the bargain."

"You're disgusting."

"And you have a decision to make. Don't take too long."

FORTY-SEVEN

Hiding behind a pillar alongside the Cathedral, Geo called Annabelle again. If Edwards caught her, he would bring her here. So here was where Geo needed to be. "I have to do this," he told the others. "The only way to stop Edwards is for me to face him. You guys can leave if you want."

"I'm staying until Annabelle is safe," Willis said.

"We're in," Mickey said, and the twins nodded.

"Let's pay the bishop a visit." Willis used a key to unlock the door. Inside they found the gray-robed bishop kneeling before a large marble statue of Jesus on the cross.

Bishop Kolinski rose unsteadily. "You shouldn't be here."

"Jon." Willis approached the bishop. "You don't mind me calling you that, since that's how I knew you before Edwards named you bishop."

Kolinski's eyes darted about. "What do you want before I—"

"And defile your fancy Cathedral? We came to chat."

Geo offered his hand. "Bishop Kolinski, it's an honor—"

"Cut the crap." Kolinski staggered toward a chocolate-colored desk in the corner.

Willis blocked the bishop. "I wouldn't do that."

"Join us," Geo said. "Join those abused by Edwards."

The bishop halted. "You speak treason, son."

Geo held up his hand. "Give no support to Edwards, let him hang himself, and there could be a role for you in the new order. Think about it."

"You don't know what you're up against."

Geo thought of Annabelle. "Neither do you."

"Now that you've heard our proposal," Willis said, "we will take our leave. Remember, if you stand against us, there's no place for you. And if you're thinking of betraying us to Edwards, then he will learn that you've been spying on him."

The bishop glared but didn't move.

Willis led the four of them through a thick oak doorway down a long dark corridor with rooms on either side. They reached a passage. To the right, it led behind the altar; to the left it ran toward a cluster of darkened doorways.

Geo received a text from Tommy. *Edwards holding President Hardcastle beneath Tower Two. Can't reach Annabelle.*

Willis pointed to Rangers taking positions behind the altar. He led Geo and the others through a shadowed archway to a narrow door. He opened the door to a large utility closet and pulled them inside as a pair of Rangers patrolled nearby.

By flashlight beam, Willis located a canvas bag. He opened it and handed each of them a revolver and ammo. "If they catch you, expect torture. They'll want names of accomplices. Then they'll kill you. From here on, we're in this together."

For the first time, Mickey looked scared. The reality was far different from the fantasy.

Willis handed Geo a small bag with his grenades. "If you can conceal them, they might come in handy. I hate to do this in church, but you can't trust Kolinski, Hanrahan, or Edwards."

"I take it you know them well?"

"So did your pa, but we don't have time to discuss it. You need to sneak into the main hall and find seats." He attached a wheat-grain-sized microphone to Geo's collar and handed him the remote. "I've arranged for a screen to project video. You won't have much time, so be careful."

Willis took Geo's hand and seemed to play with the ring. "Make your pa proud. Now go, I have business to tend to."

* * *

Two young female attendants in white uniforms began clothing Annabelle in layers of a bridal outfit suited for a princess. Mom and Sarah entered, carrying between them an oversized bouquet of orchids.

Annabelle hugged Mom and Sarah, and motioned for the young

attendants to leave. "A moment with my family, please."

When her wrist-com vibrated within the folds of her wedding dress, she dared not answer. She was certain Edwards was having her watched and monitored. It had taken her too much effort to transfer the electronic contraption from its hiding place in her maid's outfit to the dress. She wasn't about to give it away.

The attendants left. Annabelle closed the door and took the flowers, which were far heavier than she had imagined. Sam always said, "When they take your weapons, find others." *Could this be?*

"You don't have to go through with this," Mom whispered. "I didn't protect you all these years only for you to end up like this."

"It's okay, Mom. I need you to hold me and help me get ready."

Pulling Mom into an embrace, Annabelle felt a grenade disk on the bottom of the flowerpot. She whispered, "Who gave you the flowers?"

"A friend said you needed cheering up."

Thank you, Willis, Dad. Hadn't he said that in the Chinese game Go, fortunes could change quickly? Sarah hugged her from behind, a love sandwich. Hiding within their embrace, Annabelle palmed two grenade remotes and pulled a grenade from the base of the flowerpot. She slipped it under her petticoat in front with the primary blast away from her body, just in case. She hoped she had enough support so it wouldn't drop. Its cold heavy weight against her belly was comforting, if potential suicide could be considered a comfort. She winced.

Slipping the second grenade into the small of her back was trickier. She needed the support of a belt to hold it in place. Sarah and Mom pulled away and added layers to the ridiculously fluffy and now puffy bridal outfit.

"It's not too late to chicken out." Mom nodded toward the door, her dark eyes intense.

Annabelle shook her head. Too many people had betrayed her. Too many she still loved would remain behind and suffer as Edwards' hostages if she escaped. She considered how to use the grenades. She had no intention of committing suicide. She just needed time to formulate a better plan.

Her wrist-com vibrated. Annabelle wanted to tear it out of her petticoat and smash it. *Sorry, Geo.* Instead, she tucked it deeper within bunches of lace around her waist. Yawning, she placed the grenade remotes in her mouth. Despite training, preparation, and awareness that she might die on any mission, the realization of what she was committing to, the line she was crossing, sank in.

Hanrahan appeared with six Rangers. *Ah, you don't trust me.*

"I love you Mom, Sarah."

Mom winked. "I love you, too, Belle."

Annabelle's heart tightened as she viewed the love in Sarah's face. The poor girl still expected things to turn out okay. That was maybe the hardest part of all this, shattering Sarah's innocence.

From the dressing room to the entrance of the church, escorted by Hanrahan and four Rangers, Annabelle wobbled on four-inch heels and shaky legs. The red carpet down the center aisle of the Cathedral gave the appearance of formality and significance, or was it like British uniforms at least partly to mask the blood.

Outside of the Cathedral, a semicircle of Rangers and a lone mech kept throngs of guests, most of them male, from mobbing her. She couldn't believe she was dessert served up for all these people. They yelled, "Blessed be Annabelle" and "Long live Annabelle."

Yeah, long enough to stand between Edwards and Hanrahan at the altar. Somehow, that had to factor into her options. In ten years, no one had gotten this close to Edwards.

The Ranger commander pulled her along, as if she could flee in ridiculous heels, a long white train, and a dress with more layers than the church had crystalline arches. The wrist-com vibrated quietly in her pocket. *Run, Geo, run.*

One thing Annabelle knew for sure. She would not permit Edwards to consummate the wedding nuptials with her tonight. Yet, if she didn't come up with a better plan, could she go through with sacrificing herself? Having met Geo, she wanted to live, to experience more of life than she could in Civ, to be with him.

Her mind buzzed. What if she activated the grenades, then sneezed, coughed or yawned? Releasing the clip would set off the explosions too soon. She had oriented the grenades so the primary blasts would be outward, but the kickback could be deadly. If lucky, she would die instantly. If not, the grenades would scramble her guts or sever her spine. She could end up writhing in pain at Edwards' feet.

Hanrahan pulled her into position at the rear of the Cathedral. The outdoor crowd shouted behind her. She could feel the weight of them pushing and shoving to catch a glimpse of her. Pulling away, Annabelle stared down the red-carpeted aisle of doom and activated voice-send on her wrist-com. *Might as well share with Tommy and whoever he could get this to.* "Sam, I wish you could see me dressed in this ridiculous outfit to attend my own funeral."

"Shut up," Hanrahan said in a harsh whisper. His com buzzed; he tapped his ear.

"No, I haven't seen the Governor," Hanrahan whispered. "If she's this unreliable, how can we trust her?"

Annabelle thought of the lone mech in the plaza. Was that really the governor, waiting to hear from Dara and friends? *How do you like standing alone?* She smiled, then shed that sentiment. A single mech could do a lot of damage.

The wedding march began. Hanrahan pulled Annabelle down the aisle.

The Biltmoor Cathedral's great domed crystalline hall loomed around them as if hung from the sky itself. Annabelle guessed it had seven thousand seats, and figured maybe ten thousand had crowded in to witness the ceremony. A few Rangers hovered by the entrance and up front with Edwards. Most stood outside, restraining the crowd.

Yelling and commotion erupted behind them, outside the Cathedral. Two of Annabelle's escorts split off and headed back. Annabelle picked up her pace. She didn't want to get trampled and lose her grenades or the element of surprise.

Hanrahan tugged. She wobbled forward. Hanging along one side of the altar, a huge white drop cloth with pale blue lettering read *Blessed Thane.* Such a cheesy sign was out of place in the elegant glass church. In the first row, Mom stood with Sarah and political friends. Next to them were the thanes from the other two Appalachian regions.

The closer Annabelle got to the altar, the slower her feet moved and the rougher Hanrahan manhandled her. She trembled at her backup plan. Maybe she could make use of having the grenades and being next to Edwards. *Kidnap him.* It was a thought.

Then she was standing before the congregation with Edwards to her right and Hanrahan to her left. A mech warrior with two grenades could be a potent threat. She could kidnap the bastard, but then what? *Think. You're running out of time.*

Clutching the remotes in her mouth, Annabelle considered activating one or both so all she had to do was release pressure on the clip to detonate. One grenade gouged the small of her back while the other pressed against her belly. She had no delusions of surviving the pair of twin blasts.

If she stood between Hanrahan and Edwards, she could make them pay for what they did to Janine, for making Annabelle kill her friend Julianne, for kidnapping her into slavery, and for countless other crimes. She steeled her nerve. They're probably wearing blast-proof vests. *Patience. Focus. Don't do anything rash. Find another path.*

Recalling Sydney Carton at the end of *Tale of Two Cities*, Annabelle thought it might be a better thing she was doing, but it wouldn't be a better rest she would find. *Forgive me, Geo. Forgive me, Lord. Is there any other alternative?*

She gazed out over the congregation.

Geo! Run. It's a trap.

Her wrist-com vibrated.

FORTY-EIGHT

Even though he knew Annabelle couldn't answer, Geo kept ringing. Willis joined him and sat to his right, looking worried. To his left, Mickey looked from Geo to Annabelle. Behind him, he smelled the twins' breath and could feel Zak's eyes boring into him.

His gaze returned to Annabelle in her fluffy white wedding gown that looked big enough to serve as a tent. His stomach churned. He swallowed hard and pushed the urge back down.

"Dearly beloved," Bishop Kolinski began, "we are gathered here today—"

"Yada, yada," Edwards broke in. "Fellow Appalachians, we're here today to celebrate my nuptials to this attractive creature, a new bond between us and the Union, and a new era of peace and prosperity. Let's get on with this so we can celebrate."

Flustered, Kolinski mumbled a quick version of his wedding spiel.

"Skip to the end," Edwards interrupted again.

"If anyone can show just cause—"

"Okay, move on." Edwards waved his hand.

Knees shaking too much to stand, Geo slumped in his seat and activated the miniature microphone attached to his collar. He lowered his voice. "I object! Edwards kidnapped Annabelle to coerce her to marry the legitimate thane of Biltmoor. Edwards is *not* that man."

Gasps from the congregation. Edwards glared at Hanrahan. "Do something."

The crowd jeered. Hanrahan spoke into his com and motioned for the handful of Rangers up front to hunt for the source of interruption. "Everyone remain seated," Hanrahan shouted.

More Rangers entered the Cathedral and walked the aisles. Annabelle bowed her head and faced Edwards.

"Edwards must go," came a ghostly chant from behind Geo. It was Zak, cupping his hands over his mouth and projecting his throaty voice. "Edwards must go."

Geo sank lower in his seat. This had sounded better when he'd rehearsed it in his mind. He cupped his hand over his mouth and proclaimed into the mike: "Appalachians! Have we traded one tyranny for another?"

"How dare you disrupt our joyous moment!" Edwards yelled, hunting for the source.

"Edwards made a secret deal with Governor Battani," Geo said. "He sold you out. Look at his splendor, while you suffer."

"Show yourself, you coward," Edwards said.

"I challenge Edwards to a Patriot's Duel," Geo said. "Don't let him hide behind his guns when he has taken yours. Disarming you is part of his deal with Battani. He gets mechs and other weapons to oppress you, and to fight the Medallion Cartel and the northern thanes." Geo set his wrist-com to projection and shone an image on the white cloth. It showed trucks brimming with weapons driving away.

This riled the crowd into chaotic shouting. Rangers pulled men and women out of several rows. Edwards whispered to Hanrahan. More Rangers entered.

"Return our guns," people chanted.

"I appeal to Rangers," Geo said. "Stand down. Don't defile this holy place. Remember your roots with the great patriot, General Scott. How many times did Hanrahan or Edwards order you to kill innocent men, women and children? Stand with us against his tyranny and there will be a place for you in a new Appalachia."

The crowd grew louder. Several of the younger Rangers backed away. Edwards wagged his finger at Hanrahan, who yelled into his com.

With Tommy's technical aid, Geo projected images of Hardcastle in chains, led by Hanrahan. "Edwards is holding our beloved President Hardcastle as a prisoner behind the altar. I say free him now." Geo thought it apt that people would assume

Edwards had held Hardcastle all these years.

"Free Hardcastle now," the crowd chanted.

Several younger Rangers looked questioningly at Edwards. Older veterans filled the aisles looking for the source of interruption. Several raised their weapons, hunting for targets. At the end of the row before Geo's, a Ranger nudged a seated man. "Stand up." It was Stu, back in uniform.

The man stood. So did Peterson and O'Brien toward the right and, with them, dozens of mountaineers. Zak moved to the left edge of his aisle, chanting, "Down with Edwards." A dozen men stood around him.

"This man is a terrorist," Edwards said, squinting into the audience. He moved backward, toward the altar. Rangers grabbed Zak. It took two to hold him.

Geo continued: "Edwards murdered in cold blood our true Patriot, General Brandon Scott, also known as Bret Shaw."

That brought gasps, and more parishioners rose up.

"Edwards treats your wives and daughters like property to take as he pleases. These are not the actions of the head of our church or a legitimate thane."

The crowd jeered. Rangers began hauling people from the ends of nearby rows. More Rangers entered the Cathedral, leaving the entrance unguarded. People poured in. So far, Willis was right; Edwards was showing restraint.

Geo projected onto the white cloth a naked Edwards abusing one of Chrissie's girls. Half of the congregation rose to their feet, shouting and heckling. Geo had to speak louder. "Bishop Kolinski, condemn Edwards for his crimes against God and his people. Condemn the imposter who steals tithes from the church to buy his monopolies."

Edwards got hold of a loudspeaker. "I see the terrorist. It's the traitor's son. Rangers, remove him by any means."

"Remember, thane," Annabelle said in a muffled voice, "if Geo dies, the deal is off."

Edwards turned to the bishop. "Proceed."

Geo stood and held up his hand. "I, George Shaw, son of Bret Shaw, now wear the Earl's ring and emblem. You knew my pa as General Scott during the war. He collaborated with President Hardcastle and Thane Burke before Edwards imprisoned our president and killed the legitimate thane. Again, I challenge the coward Edwards to the Patriot's Duel."

Hanrahan motioned for veteran Rangers to form up at the front of the Cathedral.

Willis activated his microphone. "Geo speaks the truth. I was there when Edwards had Hanrahan shoot Burke. Have your assassin bring us our President."

Edwards pulled out a revolver and fired into the crystalline dome, sending shards of glass showering onto the congregation.

FORTY-NINE

Willis pushed Geo down and covered them both with his jacket. Geo heard screams all around as the echo of the shot died down, and tinkling glass splattered all about. In order to see, Geo launched his bumblebee-cam. "Edwards has defiled our sacred Cathedral. He is not worthy to lead."

The shaky image from the flying cam showed people around him dabbing cuts and shaking off glass. Others clamored to flee. Rangers clogged the aisles. The center aisle was a chaos of bloodied Rangers lying on the ground beneath the shattered dome. Blood was everywhere.

So much for Edwards' concern for his image.

"Everyone sit down," Edwards yelled.

Geo turned his flying cam toward Annabelle, who stood defiantly between Edwards and Hanrahan. "Don't let Edwards intimidate you by desecrating our holy places," Geo said.

Edwards fired again, spraying plaster in all directions. "Clear the hall."

"Not so fast." The voice was from Carlos.

Using the bumblebee, Geo found his friend standing amidst a crowd toward the rear.

"We've bottled up your Rangers in the plaza."

Geo saw confusion in the younger Ranger ranks as they absorbed the news.

Edwards pointed his gun at Hanrahan. "Do something."

"Citizens of Appalachia," Carlos said. "I've known Geo all my

263

life as a friend and a man of his word. I believe his cause is just. If he says he can change things for the better, I believe him."

* * *

Annabelle bit back tears and clenched the remotes in her mouth. It was time to act. Hanrahan had fifty or more loyal Rangers gathering around him. Edwards stood alone, inching his way back toward the altar for safety. She reached under her puffy dress and began to move the grenade in front.

KaBOOM! The ground rumbled like an earthquake.

Jaw quivering, Annabelle's first thought was that she had triggered her grenades. She felt no pain. Ringing in her ears masked screaming; the husky Edwards cowered; Hanrahan barked orders. The Cathedral's massive rear stone and crystalline wall crumbled in what she recognized as a mech attack. *Who's firing?* When her hearing returned, a cacophony of cries flooded her ears.

Glass and stone sprayed the parishioners trying to reach the exits and Rangers trying to control the crowd. Crammed into tight groups, civilians scrambled for cover. A lone mech climbed up rubble that had been the wall and stood above the congregation.

The mech scanned the great hall and sprayed machine pellets in all directions. It was the haphazard shooting of an inexperienced fighter, not a mech warrior.

Annabelle grabbed Edwards and dropped behind a railing in front of the altar. His rancid breath made her want to gag.

The mech kept shooting. The thane of North Appalachia and his entourage scattered like tenpins. The mech mowed them down. The thane of Central Appalachia ran to the side of the church, shielded by his men. The mech blasted stone and glass pillars along the side before decimating the guests.

Rangers' shots were useless against the mech's black titanium plating. The crowd screamed and trampled each other, diving under seats and anything that provided even flimsy cover.

Annabelle squeezed out the front grenade and hefted the weight in her right hand. She moved closer to Edwards. He grabbed her waist and pulled her to him. "Come on. There's a back way out."

"We're not married yet." She reached behind him with her left arm, grabbed hold of his blast-proof vest and shoved the grenade up between the vest and his shirt. When he stood, his pants and belt would hold it in place. She activated the remote with her tongue. The grenade was live.

"What the—"

"Listen carefully," Annabelle said, making sure she didn't release the spring clip between her teeth. "I open my mouth, they can spoon you off the stage. And don't try to remove it."

His dark eyes filled with rage and terror. He grabbed her neck.

"I'll scream."

He released his grip.

"Good boy. Now call off your attack dogs. Agree to this Patriot's Duel."

* * *

Geo watched with disgust as Annabelle and Edwards disappeared behind a barrier. He couldn't rush to her while this rogue mech was shooting up the place. *Do your part,* Annabelle would say.

Geo removed a grenade from his satchel and used the bumblebee cam to gauge direction and distance. He rose up and flung the grenade like a discus toward the feet of the mech at the back of the Cathedral. He activated the clip and clasped it in his hand.

The mech turned toward him, looked down at the grenade, and stumbled backward out of the Cathedral. All around, Rangers fought with parishioners scrambling for cover.

Geo waited.

The mech fired on Rangers and parishioners at the back of the Cathedral, as if its only plan was destruction. The mech climbed back into the Cathedral, firing bursts all around. Hanrahan scrambled at the front of the great hall, yelling at Rangers to charge the mechanical monster.

The mech reached the top of the rubble and stopped. A grim female voice said, "I have with me the lost Union ownership certificates in Biltmoor. I demand—"

Geo released the clip. The first blast stunned the mech, freezing the mechanical suit in an awkward position. The second blasted her guts. The mech fired a few bursts and tumbled onto her back.

Rangers scrambled up the glass and stone rubble. They removed the helmet, cut off the head, and displayed the frozen shock in the face of the governor of Tenn-tucky.

FIFTY

Annabelle brushed aside the horror of seeing Battani's head held up like some medieval trophy and returned her attention to Edwards. "Now get up and agree to the duel."

"You are dead. You hear me."

"I train for that. Remember, you try to remove the grenade and I'll detonate it."

Edwards grumbled and got to his feet. He brushed off his suit and reached toward his back. Annabelle wrenched his arm away, making sure the grenade was tucked into place.

Hanrahan had maybe a hundred men lined up between Edwards and the seats, aiming toward the retreating parishioners. "What are your orders, sir?"

Edwards nodded for Hanrahan to proceed.

Two mechs climbed the rubble at the rear of the church. "Geo? Annabelle? Sorry we're late." It was Janine's voice.

Annabelle's breath caught. Chills sprinted up and down her spine. *Good girl.*

Standing on his seat, Geo waved. "These mechs are with us," he said. "Any Ranger who doesn't put down his weapon is fair game."

Many Rangers complied, including some of the loyal band up front with Hanrahan. Looking confused, citizens clung to whatever cover they had found.

Edwards pulled the Bishop from his hiding place beside the altar. "Finish the I-do part."

Annabelle was tempted to have Janine and her partner open fire on the Rangers. End this war once and for all. It was what her mech training called for, but she couldn't with all these civilians, and not with Geo, Mom and Sarah in the crossfire. "Not until after the duel."

"Big reward for whoever kills the Shaw boy and the mechs," Edwards said.

Janine took a gun from Battani's mech suit and aimed it at Edwards. "Not so fast. I'm a trained sharpshooter."

"Look at how the coward hides behind brute force," Geo said. "I'm one of you and I seek justice for General Scott. Edwards, will you accept?"

Chanting began from a few at first, over by Peterson and the mountaineers. "Patriot's Code." Then the entire congregation joined in, anything to stop the slaughter.

Unless Edwards complied, his authority would vanish. Yet he had a good seventy pounds on Geo and years of experience. He had been a professional wrestler and—

Annabelle glanced at her mom. Mom nodded: *do the right thing.*

Annabelle placed her arm around Edwards' waist. She led him onto the main floor, past Hanrahan, who just glared at her. She stepped over bodies of a Ranger and one of the northern thane's guards.

Edwards turned to Geo. "You don't know what you're doing. You're turning our country over to the Civs, boy. You hear me? You're letting them win. I'm all that separates us from oblivion."

Annabelle kept guiding Edwards to the back of the Cathedral. She carefully stepped over shards of glass and the bodies of Rangers who caught the wave of falling glass. As she passed, she glanced at Geo out of the corner of her eye, and saw confusion in his face. *Is that jealousy I see? Rage?*

The crowd chanted, "Patriot's Code."

Geo followed, along with his friends and Willis. *Thanks for the grenades, Dad.*

At the shattered entrance to the Cathedral, Edwards held up his hands for quiet. "If this young man feels the need to fight for his treasonous father, then let's do it."

The crowd's chants changed to "Geo, Geo, Geo."

Geo handed his satchel and suit jacket to Willis and hurried after Annabelle. It took all her concentration to keep moving over the rubble of stone and glass in heels, and stay ahead of him. *You need to concentrate on the duel, not me.*

By the time she reached the plaza, Annabelle was sweating buckets inside her enormous wedding gown. The grenade digging into her back didn't help. She shifted its position and almost dropped it. She looked up and saw Carlos' men in position on the rooftops around the plaza. One mech cleared the center of the plaza for the contest.

The mech Annabelle identified as Janine went to Geo. "I'm so proud of you, but you don't have to do this. I can finish him off."

"And bring civil war?" Geo asked. "The only way this works is if I fight the duel. I dishonored Pa by putting him at risk. I have to do this right."

"Then watch for him cheating."

"I'll be okay." Geo didn't sound very convincing.

Annabelle smiled. She was glad Janine could give comfort to Geo. Annabelle had to keep her eyes on Edwards and his cronies. She made sure the grenade was securely in place behind Edwards' back.

"You're not going to make me fight with this," he scowled.

"Why, of course I am." Annabelle patted his shoulder and smiled to show him the grenade remote.

Hanrahan rushed over to Edwards and handed him something.

Geo approached her. She backed away and clenched her teeth. *This isn't over yet.* "Go focus."

He stopped and stared. "Annabelle?"

"Go." She turned away.

Hanrahan leveled his revolver at Geo. Annabelle wiggled loose the grenade at her back and let it drop to the ground. Nearby commotion of the crowd masked the sound of metal against concrete. She grabbed Hanrahan's gun wrist and made sure with her toe that the grenade faced up. She armed the second grenade and pulled the general toward her. She started to back up.

Edwards pushed Hanrahan aside and leaned in to kiss Annabelle. His eyes narrowed and he pulled away.

"You didn't think you could force a marriage without consequences, did you?" she asked.

He clutched her neck in a preview of what she could expect. "When I kill your boyfriend, you'll pay for your rebelliousness."

So will you. Annabelle looked for Hanrahan, but he had moved away. She didn't see any way to pick up the grenade.

FIFTY-ONE

Geo watched Edwards with disgust. The thane seemed assured he could take what he wanted.

Nearby, two mechs stood back-to-back, scanning the crowd and rooftops. The remains of several hang-gliders hung from trees lining the plaza, evidence of how Carlos had brought his men. Rangers formed in groups, a disciplined lot of 100 around Hanrahan. More formed a perimeter behind him, taking aim at rooftops, while others like Stu scattered among the civilians.

Geo expected the plaza to erupt in a volcano of blood. Yet with the mechs there, Rangers hesitated to take the first shot. To his right, Geo saw Peterson, O'Brien, and the three compadres with others from the mountains. In the end, they had stuck their necks out for Geo. *I can't let them down.*

Across the way, Willis held onto a stately blonde woman with an intense-looking girl who bore a striking resemblance to Janine. *Mom? Sarah?* The woman seemed to want to rush in, but Willis held her back. Rangers took positions on the second floor of Edwards Fine Clothing across the plaza.

Janine must have noticed. "We stand here not to fight you, but to ensure a fair fight according to your code. Anyone who attempts to intervene will be dealt with."

That's telling them, sis. Geo stared across the concrete void to where Edwards conferred with Hanrahan. His mind scattered with all the reasons he shouldn't be here. *Live and stay free,* Pa would say.

Edwards tore off his wedding jacket and tossed it to a Ranger.

269

"Let's get this over with."

Geo assumed a defensive position and familiarized himself with the space he had to work with. The massive professional wrestler faced him and growled.

This wasn't such a good idea, Pa. Was I too eager?

Edwards bowed toward Geo and the crowd, ending with what looked like a signal. The blast of mech pellets rattled Geo as a bullet grazed his left shoulder. He looked up in time to see three windows of the clothing store blown away. An arm dangled out. *So much for a fair fight.*

Thane Edwards approached, a man of experience, size, and confidence who knew mech moves even Janine didn't. *Let your energy flow with your opponent,* Annabelle would say. Pa would say, *Save yourself for another day.* Geo tensed, held his position, and let energy flow between his limbs with a fluidity he hoped to put to good use. His mind clouded trying to recall every move he had seen or read about, anything to help him defeat this mass of beef on steroids.

Geo jumped aside, forcing his opponent to change direction. Edwards closed with determination and resolve.

Seeing a knife, Geo said, "A curse on the first to use weapons."

He spun and kicked his opponent's back, hitting something hard. Quick for a big man, Edwards swung the knife, missed, rotated and swung in a wide arc. Geo parried for a kick, ducked the knife, and spun behind his opponent. Edwards was too swift with a grin on his coarsely muscled face.

Blocking the knife blow, Geo hit Edwards smack on the jaw. It didn't remove the grin. Edwards swung. Geo ducked, tripped, and landed on his back. He rolled over on top of—a mech grenade. *What the hell!*

Edwards kicked Geo's arms so that he fell flat onto the grenade. *Is it active?*

* * *

Annabelle watched in horror as Edwards removed the grenade at his back in such a way that she couldn't trigger it without hurting Geo and bystanders. He dropped it, tripped Geo, and dove for cover along the edge of the cleared plaza.

Hanrahan turned and charged toward Annabelle while Geo was still lying on the grenade. Clenching her teeth to keep from triggering the grenade, she fell and rolled onto her back like a turtle. People scrambled out of her way. She pushed a second clip from between her teeth and prayed it was the right one.

The focused blast shot straight up into the general's groin, nearly splitting him in two. Annabelle didn't wait to see what happened next. She pushed off and rolled away from the blast area as everyone around her rushed to escape. The second-stage explosion rattled her teeth as its targeted blast fired straight up. She clutched the remaining clip between her teeth and got to her feet. Not even the scar remained of the fearsome General Hanrahan.

Weapons drawn, Rangers encircled her. She couldn't see Geo.

* * *

Janine fired over their heads. "Fair fight."

"Come on, Edwards," Geo said, moving away from the grenade he had been lying on. "Just you and me this time. Or, we can let the mechs declare victory and go home."

Edwards wiped his chin and moved back into the now wider clearing. It looked like fear in his eyes, as if he now had something to prove. He moved cautiously around the grenade. Geo kept the grenade between them as he sized up how he could best this animal. Edwards glared in Annabelle's direction, faked left and then came around to the right, staying just far enough away from the grenade that the first blast wouldn't hit him.

Geo faked a kick. Edwards swung his knife. To avoid the blade, Geo fell back, toward the grenade. He kicked the man's thigh before tumbling away. The man lunged, Geo backed away and rotated. Edwards blocked a kick and advanced. Geo rotated to avoid the knife; he was too close to the grenade. *Who has the trigger?*

Geo swung his leg up. Edwards swiped the knife, got leather. Geo backed up. Edwards swung; Geo rolled out toward the middle of the open concrete, toward the grenade. That seemed to be Edwards' plan. The big man charged, swinging the knife in broad motions, making it hard for Geo to attack. Edwards moved in, arms out as if anticipating a wrestling throw. On concrete that could prove fatal if Edwards landed on top.

Backing away, Geo kept a wary eye on the knife and another on the grenade. Edwards lunged; Geo spun away, a moment too late. Pain seared his left shoulder near where the bullet had grazed him. Through a slit in his shirt, a line of blood oozed, a flesh wound. It burned.

Geo tried moves he'd learned from Annabelle and Julianne: spins, kicks, and punches. Edwards blocked and went for another slice. Tiring, Geo was running out of moves. Edwards had experience and mech training. *What do I have? Annabelle pledged to marry this swine.*

Anger pumped Geo with adrenalin. He imagined Annabelle facing men like this in the arena. *Focus on your opponent,* she would say. *Focus.*

Edwards attacked, a vulgar grin on his thick, weathered face. He swung his knife in a wide arc. He knew mech moves, and was stronger, bigger, with bulging biceps, triceps, and quadriceps. Yet he relied on the knife. Why? *Focus.*

Instead of attacking Edwards, Geo faked a hand grab for the knife. Edwards jabbed. Geo kicked the arm putting the full thrust of his body into the wrist. Edwards dropped the knife. Geo kicked it toward the crowd and dove into the thane, knocking him onto his back. Edwards grabbed Geo around the chest in a bear hug.

Geo punched his opponent's ribs and rammed his knee into Edwards' groin. *Less reason to want Annabelle.* When his opponent groaned, Geo wedged his way free and got to his feet.

"Come on, Edwards. Man-to-man this time." *Pa, give me strength.*

Edwards got to his feet, and scanned the crowd, which cheered Geo's name. Rangers held back, covered by two mechs and Carlos' men on the rooftops.

Using his bulk to advantage, Edwards lunged at Geo and grabbed. Geo spun away and brought his full weight down with his arm against the back of Edward's neck. The thane sprawled onto concrete, scraping his forearms. He rolled, sprang to his feet, and charged like a bull.

Geo couldn't help feeling intimidated. *Focus.* Edwards was massive, yet he didn't vary his moves. Geo dodged. Edwards grabbed Geo's bloody sleeve. Geo tore it off and saw blood oozing down his left arm. "Keep the souvenir."

Edwards tossed the sleeve and moved in with the same wide stance. "Your old man was a sniveling worm, a coward. You'll beg for mercy before I kill you, or did you forget this is to the death?"

"Pa could have taken you any day."

Geo dodged. Edwards kicked, hitting thigh and sending Geo sailing onto the concrete. He rolled away and scrambled to his feet.

Edwards charged. "You'll be begging like a dog before this is over."

How can I take this thug? Focus.

Edwards grabbed. Geo leapt higher than he thought possible and brought his arm down across the back of Edward's neck. The big man groaned and fell face first onto the concrete.

Geo leapt on top before the man could get up, and got him in a chokehold. "Will you yield to face justice?"

"Never!" Edwards tore Geo's arm from around his throat and rolled over.

Pulling free, Geo rotated away before the big man could crush him under his massive weight. By the time Geo got to his feet, Edwards approached with his knife, or another, swinging his arm in wide slashing arcs. *Same pattern, no imagination.*

Edwards was upon him. Geo took a deep breath, dropped to the concrete, and pumped both legs into Edwards' planted right knee. The older man twisted in pain and swung the blade wide before going down. He landed on his left knee and howled. Geo caught the man's wrist.

"You son of a bitch." Edwards rolled to get on top of Geo.

Geo kicked Edwards' good knee out from under him. Then he wrestled with the knife, pushing against the muscular arm that had tried to crush the air from his lungs. Edwards couldn't thrust the knife; he was using that arm to hold himself up.

"Will you yield?" Geo jumped and dropped his weight onto Edwards' shoulders.

Edwards got onto hands and his good knee. "Go to hell."

Geo shoved the man toward his right arm, which clutched the knife, and kicked the left knee. Edwards plopped onto his belly. With his right arm free, he stabbed behind him. Geo grabbed the knife wrist with both hands and wrestled to dislodge the knife. Even on his belly Edwards was powerful. He sliced into Geo's right shoulder, and tried to get on top.

To avoid being crushed, Geo got to his feet. Edwards got up on hands and knee. Geo jumped and dropped his weight between the big man's shoulders. The knife thrust into Edwards' thick throat as his weight settled down. He started cussing; words gurgled out. Blood pooled around his face.

Geo begged the Lord's forgiveness. *For I have taken another life.* Yet, Edwards would not yield and would not have hesitated to take Geo's life. *Pa, I know this won't put things right, but he is gone.*

FIFTY-TWO

"The thane is dead," the crowd yelled, their voices thundering in Geo's ears. "Long live Thane Shaw. Long live Thane Shaw. Long live Thane Shaw."

Geo stood up. He didn't want to be thane. He only wanted justice for what Edwards did to Pa and his friends, to Annabelle and Janine, and to his home, and for making their world unlivable.

Willis took his hand and raised it, displaying the ring.

Rangers approached, including those who had rallied around Hanrahan. They knelt and placed their weapons on the concrete before Geo. "We pledge our lives to Thane Shaw."

Geo fought his way through the crowd toward Annabelle, her fluffy white gown with its long satin train blackened by her fall.

She held up her hand and pointed toward the grenade. "It's still live," she whispered through clenched teeth.

"That was yours?" He took her hand. "What was your plan? Blow yourself up?"

She pulled away. "Can you help me disarm it?"

"Everyone move away from the live grenade," Geo yelled. He took both of Annabelle's hands.

"Geo!"

He lifted her veil. "Let's remove the remote without releasing."

Closing her eyes, she leaned toward him. He reached into her mouth and clasped the top and bottom of the clip. "Open wide."

He removed the clip, placed it to his lips, and flipped the switch to deactivate it. He slipped the remote detonator into a pouch in his pocket. "Janine, can you bring me the grenade?"

Annabelle let out a deep breath and slumped into his arms. "I thought I'd lost you when Hanrahan..."

"It's over, Annabelle." Geo brushed hair away from her turquoise eyes and wiped a tear from her cheek. His own stomach did somersaults. "You were amazing." He pulled away and looked at her all dressed in white. "You look gorgeous, by the way."

"My dress is filthy, you mean."

Groups of Rangers, mountaineers, and shell-shocked townspeople gathered around. Geo knelt. She took his hand and pulled him to his feet. "What are you doing?"

"We've done what we came for."

"Not everything. Look around. They expect you to be thane."

"I don't want that," Geo said. "I want you."

Annabelle turned toward the gathering groups. "Citizens of Appalachia and guests, you came here today for a peaceful ceremony you believed was part of a new beginning. I was pledged against my will to marry Edwards, who imprisoned my sister so I wouldn't flee. Edwards and Hanrahan killed Geo's father and destroyed his home."

Geo whispered, "We should go."

Annabelle smiled and squeezed his hand. "Edwards and Battani conspired on a deal: Appalachia would tear itself apart in civil war while Civ took your lands and stopped refugees so your population would collapse. You see me as Civ, yet my people betrayed me. At heart, I am an American. Edwards and Hanrahan are dead. We have a choice. We can keep bickering and watch Appalachia get swallowed up, or we can show Civs there's a better way, of peace and cooperation.

"Geo didn't come here to be thane. He's hesitant to take that role. Though I've only known him a week, I believe he can do this with your help, not as Edwards did, but down a better path."

Willis approached with the distinguished-looking woman who resembled Janine. Her face creased with emotions Geo couldn't read.

He pulled Annabelle aside. "I know you mean well."

"By rights, you're thane. These people need guidance. You have a great opportunity here. Stop focusing on me. Look at them."

"Quite a speech." The husky male voice was familiar like Pa's, and yet not.

FIFTY-THREE

Geo glanced up to see a haggard, gray-haired President Hardcastle, and didn't know whether to kneel like Rangers and civilians or bow like Willis. Before he could decide, the President of Appalachia grabbed Geo's hand in a firm shake.

"I've waited ten years for someone to put Edwards down like the mangy dog he was. No, that's an insult to mangy dogs. When Edwards killed Thane Burke and attacked me, your pa wouldn't risk civil war. I've got to hand it to you, son. It took a lot of brass to take on Edwards. You have my debt of gratitude and my support. I hope you'll accept your role and fill it, as your pa would have. He'd be proud of you."

"Yes, sir." Geo faced the crowd, Rangers who fought against him, mountaineers who came to support him, Carlos who helped tip the balance, and weary townspeople nursing cuts. They all stood in clusters. He looked at Willis, who nodded, at the woman who held onto him for support and at the intense girl who resembled Janine.

"I'm young for this role," Geo said. "I know you've suffered. If I can make your lives better, then with the help of President Hardcastle and all of you, I'll dedicate myself to doing so in memory of my pa, General Scott."

The crowd's cheers were interrupted by shouts from the roof of the clothing store across the plaza. "Mechs and drones coming."

Rangers pulled away from the crowd. Some moved toward the southeast corner of the plaza. Others aimed their weapons at

Janine and her partner. Willis pulled the woman and the girl away. Geo turned to Annabelle.

"Don't look at me that way," she said. "Janine, get me Sam."

"Just a moment." Janine moved closer.

Rangers pointed their weapons at Annabelle. "We don't have a moment," she said.

Janine stood back-to-back with the other mech. "I've got her."

"Tell Sam the crisis is over. We don't need her support."

"She wants to hear directly from you. She asks if you're married."

"Put her on speaker."

"Okay," Janine said. "Don't get testy."

"Sam, can you hear me?" Annabelle asked.

After a moment of static, Sam's voice boomed on speaker. "Someone's been sending chaotic com-feeds. We're approaching the plaza. What's your situation?"

Annabelle headed for the plaza's southeast corner and motioned for Janine to follow. "I'm here with Mom, two mechs in gear, and Mom's son, Geo. The disturbance is over. Edwards, Hanrahan, Cory, and Battani are dead. People have asked Geo to be thane. I'm asking you to stand down. Please don't shatter the peace. Battani tried, and it was a disaster."

Geo joined Annabelle and the two mechs. Rangers formed up around him. Civilians hurried back toward the Cathedral. Carlos directed his men to consolidate their positions on the rooftops. Geo only had a couple of grenades and his revolver. It wasn't enough to withstand a mech attack.

"We have an opportunity to end the war," Sam said.

Geo lifted Annabelle's train to make it easier for her to walk.

"Sam, you're on speaker, talking to the citizens of Biltmoor," Annabelle said. "The war is over. Edwards and Battani kept it alive to hold on to power. These people want peace and a chance to start over."

Willis caught up with Geo. "Do you have a plan?"

"I think so." Geo hurried behind Annabelle, who wobbled on her high heels. Flanked by Rangers and mountaineers shouldering rifles, they were three-quarters of the way across the plaza to the boulevard heading southeast. Geo was proud to see the groups finally working together, a hopeful sign for a new Appalachia.

"Annabelle, you've completed your mission," Sam said. "Stand aside and let us finish. We need to secure these lands."

The first Civ mechs entered the square and fanned out on either side of the boulevard while drones swooped in from the north.

"Unnecessary and unwise," Annabelle said. "These people want peace and in peace you're welcome. But if mechs cause trouble, many will die."

Geo stared at her. *What are you thinking?*

"Is that a threat?" Sam asked.

"A reality." Annabelle said. "The plaza is rigged with grenades. I've seen enough bloodshed. These people represent no threat to the Union. Let's open a new era of cooperation."

With Civ mechs pouring into the plaza, a stalemate approached. Geo stepped forward and faced the Rangers. "We won't surrender to Civ threats, but I'm asking you to lower your weapons. Let's offer the olive branch to our American neighbors."

"Sam, I beg you to stand down," Annabelle said. "You were set up by Battani. Don't follow her lead."

The distinguished woman left the girl with Willis and marched forward with the air of authority, holding out her hands. "If you would shoot your own people, then you're nothing but cowards hiding behind mech gear. I'm Senator Coriander Scott of Tenntucky. If Commander Hernandez is among you, let her step forward."

Geo approached Annabelle. "Is that Mom?"

She nodded, took his hand, and led him forward.

A lone mech marched toward them, took off her helmet and mech gloves, and shook Mom's hand. It was Commander Samantha Hernandez. "I didn't recognize you in the crowd, Cora."

Annabelle hugged Mom and then introduced Geo to the commander. He hesitated, then he held out his hand. "Pleased to meet you."

"I doubt it," Sam said, "though thanks for saying so. Annabelle, I'm impressed that you freed your sister, found mech gear, and patched me in through some mysterious intermediary. You show promise despite failing to follow orders."

"I'm sorry, Commander. Janine means the world to me. Now, if you'll excuse me." Annabelle turned to Geo. "I'd like you to meet your mom."

"George?" The senator held his hand and looked up at him with dark, penetrating eyes. She threw her arms around him.

"It's...it's...really you."

"It's Geo. Mom." He couldn't feel his feet.

She hugged him so tight he could barely breathe. "I never imagined seeing you again and here you are a grown man, a fine man. I'm so proud of you. Your father would be, too." She pulled away and dried her eyes on a handkerchief. "Though you had me in knots over fighting that horrid Edwards."

Geo couldn't find words to fill the void that hung between them all these years, all the things he had wanted to say that no longer mattered.

"Sam, Geo showed restraint," Annabelle said. "Please restrict your troops to the plaza's southeast corner and lower weapons."

Sam approached. "Since I am stripping you of your lieutenant rank and giving you a field promotion to captain over these troops, I suggest you make your orders known. I need a word with the Senator."

Mom squeezed Annabelle's hand before heading off with Sam.

Annabelle stared at Sam and then at Geo. Janine removed her helmet and held it out. With Geo's help, Annabelle adjusted the biochip and steadied the helmet over her head. She looked ridiculous in a fluffy white dress and mech helmet, though he was too much in awe to say so. She gave orders and returned the helmet to Janine. "Geo, can you have the Rangers stand down?"

"I'm not sure. I don't know who's in charge."

Willis brought a Ranger with a single star on his lapel. The Ranger saluted. "General Grove at your service. What are your orders, sir?"

Geo scanned the plaza, clear of civilians except for armed mountaineers. With its crystalline facade gone, the Cathedral looked like a medieval ruin.

He looked to Annabelle and then to Willis. *What to do?*

"I'd like ten trusted men with me. The rest need to withdraw to the Cathedral."

FIFTY-FOUR

Annabelle turned to Janine. "You did great. Who's the mystery mech with you?"

"Haley," Janine said.

"Then who's watching the girls?"

"Vivian," Haley said. "She helped us relocate the girls and got them comfortable. She understood their suffering."

Three of Sam's mech warriors marched forward and removed their helmets.

Realizing how close she'd come to killing herself, Annabelle let out a deep breath and turned to the three mech lieutenants.

"Orders, Captain." Lieutenant Polanski nodded to acknowledge their friendship.

"Bring ten warriors out of gear. The rest of you stay in gear at the southeast corner and await my instructions."

The three mech lieutenants saluted and returned to their troops.

"Annabelle? What's going on?" Geo asked.

Annabelle patted his shoulder. "I know Polanski. She'll bring troops I can trust. I'm still nervous around Rangers." She turned to Janine. "Besides, I'd like Janine and Haley out of their sweaty gear." She removed Janine's mech glove and held her hand. "I was so worried they'd grab you when Hanrahan caught me."

"They almost did," Janine said. "I figured out they were tracking me and found the implant. I hid it and got away. I hated watching them drag you off in chains. I wanted to help, but I didn't know how until Haley showed up." She turned to Geo. "Thanks for staying alive." She reached out to touch him, but withdrew.

Haley removed her helmet. "I know you're mad that I didn't stay with the girls, but I had to help."

"I'm glad you did." Annabelle closed her eyes and hugged Janine despite the bulk of the mech suit and her wedding gown.

Sam returned with the senator. "Seems Battani arranged the wedding to get everyone together so she could kill two thanes and your mom, and claim a share of the Biltmoor Corporation. Sounds as if the documents supporting her claim were destroyed. So you two brought the peace our leaders couldn't."

"Maybe a start." Annabelle held Geo's and Janine's hands. "Commander, as much as I admire and respect you and I'm proud of being a warrior, I hope we can put this war behind us without destroying Appalachia."

Sam laughed. "You want to put mechs out of business."

"As you once said, America will always face dangers."

"Then best wishes to you. My mission is to guard the border and rescue kidnap victims. If we don't have border problems, I won't need to cross looking for trouble, will I?" Sam smiled at Geo. "Will she be doing all your negotiating?"

"No, though I like what I hear."

Mom took Geo's arm and squeezed. In her face, Annabelle saw all the love Mom had for Geo and yet Annabelle didn't feel the jealousy she had before. He was home.

"You have my blessing to improve relations," Sam said. "I'd like to take the bodies of Governor Battani, Cory Philips, and the dead warriors."

"You're welcome to them," Geo said. "We should bury Edwards and Hanrahan."

"Agreed." Sam turned to Mom. "Tenn-tucky needs a new governor. I don't suppose you'd consider the interim position."

The Senator smiled. "I thought you'd never ask."

"It could be a good start toward improving relations," Sam said.

"You mean you weren't coming here to shoot up the place?" Annabelle asked.

"No, Captain, I came to restore peace. I received enough of your garbled transmission to surmise what was going on. If Edwards had won, we were prepared to act. If Appalachia is prepared to rejoin the Union—"

"That's not what we want," Geo said.

"Hear me out," Sam said. "I offer what President Zell offered Edwards: self-government, no federal involvement, with your assurance of non-interference in our relations with other nations or with the rebels in Tex-SoCal and Northern Rockies."

"Then what?" Geo asked. "You move the border two miles each year?"

Sam sighed. "That was to push Edwards to negotiate. I offer improved relations. If we achieve peace, I'll be assigned out west. I could use good warriors."

Janine squeezed Annabelle's hand. "I can't return. Sister warriors betrayed me."

"I'm sorry," Sam said. "It wasn't your fault. You'll always have a home with us."

"I don't," Haley said. "You sent me to a cathouse for helping a boy. Mechs won't trust me. No one will hire me."

"For your efforts I'll find you something," Sam said.

"I want to help Geo rebuild."

So did Annabelle. "Being a mech has been a great honor, but it's a young woman's path. There are few old warriors. They burn out or die. I want to try something new, and the Union limits my options. I don't want to be a cop. I want to help people change their lives."

Sam frowned. "I promote you to captain, and you offer your services to the other side?"

"With all due respect, Sam. We're all Americans."

"Yes, we are," Mom said. "Leave it to the young to remind us."

"I guess I should feel encouraged," Sam said. "This change doesn't frighten you?"

"Scared out of my wits," Annabelle said. "Like strapping on grenades to take out Edwards and Hanrahan. But I believe we can make a better society here."

"Ah," Sam said. "Then before you reinvent the wheel, you might want to talk to the folk in Austin, see what's worked for them. I'll deny ever saying so."

"There may be hope for you yet," Mom said.

"I believe in second chances," Sam said. "We still have families on both sides of these borders."

"So, help us," Annabelle said. "Give us no-man's land to develop new towns friendly and amenable to couples and families. Let's see what happens."

"Us?" Geo asked. "Does that mean—"

"Let's not get ahead of ourselves."

"It would be an outlet for rebellious girls," Mom said.

Sam laughed. "That would require Union approval."

"The land is of little use now," Annabelle said. "And it has to be better than cutting down more forest."

"Good point," Sam said. "Let me see what I can swing."

* * *

Geo needed to talk with the people of South Appalachia— Rangers, townspeople, cartel, and mountaineers—about creating a new government of the people, by the people and truly for the people. But that would have to wait.

He looked at Annabelle. She had her promotion to captain at age nineteen, impressive, a family in Civ, and an offer to go with Sam. On impulse, Geo took Annabelle's hand and pulled her away from her conversation with Sam. He dropped to one knee. "You've brushed me aside twice—"

Her face flushed. "Not now, Geo. Stand up."

"Not until I finish. We've only known each other a week, but I feel I've known you my whole life. It's as if we've shared a lifetime already. Would you do me the honor of marrying me?"

"Geo, don't."

"Son, don't embarrass her," Mom said.

"Mom, you may have known her since she was three, but believe me, she doesn't embarrass this easily."

Annabelle pulled away. "Such impertinence—"

"I'm in love with you. You're dressed, and let me remind you, pledged to marry the thane."

"Don't you dare."

"We have a church, well, most of one, and I'm sure we can find the Bishop, else he won't get to stay."

"There are too many considerations," Annabelle said.

By then, ten Rangers and ten warriors had gathered around them. Looking anxious, Willis stood with the girl resembling Janine. *Must be Sarah.*

Annabelle glanced at all eyes on them. "You have me at a disadvantage."

"How?"

"I almost killed myself today to stop Edwards and Hanrahan. It made me realize how precious life is and how much I want to live.

I'm on an emotional high I don't trust."

"Why not?" Geo remained on one knee. "Tell me this wasn't just about getting me to fall for you so I'd help rescue Janine."

Tears filled Annabelle's eyes. She tugged him to his feet. "I would have done anything to rescue her."

"You're saying no."

"I hadn't counted on falling in love. It scares me."

Janine approached. "Annabelle, I love you so much, but sometimes you can't see what's right before you." She squeezed Annabelle's and Geo's hands. "Do what's in your heart. By marrying Geo, you'll give me more chances to get to know my brother."

Geo studied the pensive look on Janine's face and a similar look from Sarah. He returned his attention to Annabelle. "I want to spend the rest of our days together, to build a life with you, and to build a better life for the people of this region. I need you."

She shook her head. "Geo, I fear we're responding to the moment. And yet I've never been so certain of anything than that I love you. I was miserable when I thought I might lose you. You may have only known me a week, but I have known you my entire life. I'm not disappointed."

"Then you'll marry me?"

"What happened to that timid boy I met?"

"He learned from the best," Geo said. "I don't want to lose you."

"You won't, but I grew up thinking I'd marry a girl. This is so strange and new and—"

"Annabelle?"

"Isn't it customary to offer a ring?" Annabelle smiled. She had him.

Mom removed her engagement ring and handed it to Geo. "Your pa would want you to have this."

Geo looked from Mom to Annabelle and back before taking the ring, another token from Pa.

"Of course, Annabelle," Mom said, "we'll have to restore your true birth certificate so people won't accuse you of incest."

"Mom!" Annabelle said. "Does that mean we can finally rescue my birth mother?"

Mom nodded and hugged Annabelle. "She would be so proud of you. It's only fitting that she should get to see you now." She moved back and patted Geo's arm. "It's okay, son. Go ahead and ask her."

"Annabelle, I need your help and—"

"Make it personal, son."

"Annabelle." Geo took her hand and knelt. "From the moment I first saw you dressed like a businessman at that party."

She covered her face. "Will I never live that down?"

"What party?" Mom asked.

"Not important," Geo said. "Ever since then I've felt connected to you. That's why I helped you escape and why I let you come home with me."

"As I recall, you sent me away," Annabelle said.

"To go home where you'd be safe." His knee throbbed against the concrete. "I've welcomed you into my heart, and you're running out of excuses."

"You're not giving up, are you? I shouldn't be surprised given how Mom is." Annabelle raised his chin. "I'm not saying no. I'll stay and help, but let's take it slow and see how things work out."

"I want your help. I also want you as my life partner," Geo said.

Her eyes moistened. "Could I get an occasional Angus steak, sautéed in onions and mushrooms?"

"Absolutely."

"That's not healthy," Sam said.

"I can think of worse," Mom added.

Annabelle turned to Geo. "Of course, if you restore your birth name I won't have to change my name."

Geo laughed. "Does that mean?"

She slipped the ring on her finger. "I accept this if I can have time to breathe before we tie the knot. Right now you need to address the patient people of Biltmoor." She held up her hand for all to see.

The crowd cheered, "Long live Thane Shaw!"

Geo rose to his feet, surprised to see that groups of civilians had gathered as he focused on Annabelle. For that, he was thankful that she didn't say no.

"Long live his new bride!" someone shouted. Annabelle looked at him. He shrugged: *Let it go.*

"Give them some words of encouragement," Annabelle whispered.

"Before I do," Geo said. He turned to Sam. "Can you get

Annabelle's birth mother released?"

"I believe Battani already did. I suggest you check Edwards' prison."

Willis looked visibly shaken. "I'll find her." He grabbed General Grove and hurried off.

Sarah joined Mom and didn't take her inquisitive eyes off Geo. "So you're my brother."

Geo nodded. "Good to meet you, Sarah."

He felt a deep ache to get to know his family, but too many eyes were watching them. He looked at the mass of people intermingling, more than he had seen before and yet this was a small town by Union standards. Civilians nursing cuts and scrapes looked at him expectantly. He smiled at Sarah and took Annabelle's and Mom's hands. "You really believe I can do this without becoming someone's puppet?"

"I believe you can," Annabelle said.

"So do I," Haley said. "I want to help make this a place that would never do to girls what was done to me and Janine, Vivian and others."

"Wouldn't you find that in the Union?" Geo asked. Then it sank in. Except for Vivian, Civ had punished the others in cruel ways for resisting a different oppression. For Pa, Geo would do all he could to provide a place where that didn't happen.

"People of Appalachia and guests from the Union, I don't have all the answers. But that isn't the point. I welcome the chance to work with the Union to create something that will benefit both our peoples. At the same time, we must remain vigilant against tyranny that masquerades as benevolent government and that which professes to diminish government only to replace it with a different tyranny. Let us not repeat the mistakes that divided us."

There was more he needed to say, but his shell-shocked audience already had enough to deal with: the end of Edwards' reign of terror, the return of President Hardcastle, the promise of peace. Geo would now have to deal with the women in his life: Mom, Annabelle, and two biological sisters. Without her mech gear, Janine stood beside him. Sarah smiled up at him.

Annabelle squeezed his hand. *Maybe this isn't as scary as strapping on grenades.*

ACKNOWLEDGMENTS

I want to thank my wife, Sue, for putting up with my devotion to writing. I am grateful to the staff at the University of Wisconsin for prodding me when I needed it. I am also grateful to my writing groups for their input over the years: The Troubadours, The Barrington Writers Workshop, and the Algonquin Area Writers Group. I especially wish to thank my editor, Leah Carson, for her patience and diligence in making up for my editorial shortcomings and keeping me on the right track.

OTHER STORIES BY LANCE ERLICK

THE REBEL WITHIN (prequel)

After the Second American Civil War, the Federal Union pursues a world without men by rounding up the remaining males.

Annabelle is a tomboy who lost her parents at age three. Despite her rebellious acts against a conformist society, the state pushes her to become a cop intern at age 16 to catch escaped boys. Then she's forced to choose between joining the elite military unit that took her parents or being torn from her beloved sister and adoptive mom. Meanwhile, she meets a handsome boy who escaped prison, and helps him get away.

While facing a cop intern boss who hates her, a military commander who demands too much, and an amazon bully who won't leave her alone, Annabelle struggles with conscience. Will she risk everything by hunting for her imprisoned birth mother and helping escaped boys avoid the federal roundup? Can she stand up to the amazon? Will she survive the rigorous military qualifying program so she won't be sent away, while remaining true to herself and protecting her family?

Will she cross paths with that handsome boy again?

WATCHING YOU (short story)

At the intersection of global tracking, pervasive networks, mass storage, and the Patriot Act, we have the ability and some say the obligation to know everything about everyone. Can privacy survive? Can the individual endure?

Harold is a second-class citizen and a low-level worker in a government surveillance system charged with reviewing "criminal activity." He has private thoughts about a woman he's forbidden from approaching, and he will not be deterred.

ABOUT THE AUTHOR

Raised by a roaming aerospace engineer, Lance Erlick grew up in various parts of the United States and Europe. He took to stories as his anchor and was inspired by his father's engineering work on cutting-edge aerospace projects to look to the future. He writes speculative fiction, science fiction, dystopian and young adult and likes to explore the future implications of social and technological trends.

Find out more about the author and his work at LanceErlick.com.